# An Abundance of Wild Roses

# An Abundance of Wild Roses

### FERYAL ALI-GAUHAR

CANONGATE

First published in Great Britain, the USA and Canada in 2024
by Canongate Books Ltd, 14 High Street, Edinburgh EH1 1TE

canongate.co.uk

Distributed in the USA by Publishers Group West and in Canada by
Publishers Group Canada

1

*British Library Cataloguing-in-Publication Data*
A catalogue record for this book is available on
request from the British Library

ISBN 978 1 83885 816 2
Export ISBN 978 1 83885 817 9

Typeset in Van Dijck by Palimpsest Book Production Ltd,
Falkirk, Stirlingshire

Printed and bound by CPI Group (UK) Ltd, Croydon CR0 4YY

*For Khadijah Marsina Ebrahim*
*Cape Town, South Africa, 17 July 1928 –*
*Skardu, Pakistan, 21 July 2003*

The forest, letting me walk amongst its naked
limbs, had me on my knees, again in silence
shouting – yes, yes, my holy friend, let your
splendour devour me

*Shams-ud-din Muhammad Hafiz (1320–1389)*

# Hik

## 1.

*We could see them in the distance, the ibex and the mountain goat, their spirit-forms hovering above them like mist gliding on the surface of the Winter River. Hidden behind the grey bluff, the hunter lifted his rifle and cocked it, cracking the air with a lightning stab. It was quiet amongst the junipers at this time. Even the light from the sky was still, barely moving, settling softly on the branches of these ancient trees, pouring slowly over the rocks, warming them to the young boy's touch.*

*The boy was just seven, perhaps six. The tooth in the front of his mouth had come loose; he teased it with his tongue, curious to know if pain was always so sweet. Now, he could see the eyes of the ibex, that magnificent Spirit-Horse, the Tish-Hagur of Times before the Cut Path, and he could see that fear was present in her eyes, that the Spirit-Horse knew that the end was edging near, gliding like an eagle's shadow across the black surface of the cliff looming up before her.*

*He could see that she had a younger one beside her, kneeling down on its forelegs to suckle the milk from her teats. The rifle trembled in his father's hands, as if it knew that what was about to happen would set off an unending tale of devastation and despair. The boy looked up at the sky. There were no clouds, and the birds had frozen in mid-air, their wings motionless in the stillness of that quiet day. He knew as surely as he could see his own reflection in the eyes of the Spirit-Horse that this was the beginning of the end.*

*The boy opened his mouth to speak, to tell his father to let them* go, *to let the Spirit-Horse raise the young one, to let them roam the tallest peaks, to graze amongst the ancient junipers, the progeny of the Baltar Tree of the Boiber Valley, rich with fruit and goodness in Times before the Travelling Wheel. He found the words and tried to nudge them forth with his tongue, but they got caught in the path of the loosened tooth, ricocheted against the bloodied enamel and fell onto the ground, shattering soundlessly, slipping into the crevices in the earth where the Yatz, the Giants, had carved spaces for light to filter into Zameen Andar.*

*A bullet pierced the silence; the explosion shook the air, stirring the wings of the birds, moving the sky around them, causing them to awaken. One by one they dropped onto the grey schist of the mountainside. One by one they sacrificed their soft, warm bodies, full still with many songs, to the spirits who commanded their lives from the Chartoi, the Place where Four Streams met and cut the earth open with their waters.*

*One by one his father picked up the dead birds and slung them across his shoulder. They would eat well tonight, around the hearth of their small home in the Village of a Hundred Sorrows, Saudukh Das, high up in the Black Mountains where spirits live and sing and never die.*

# Chapter One

We are from dust, he said, turning towards his younger companion, his movement gentle, deliberate, a bird weaving a loop around a leafless branch.

Both men reached for a handhold on the steep slope of the Chartoi Nullah. Here four streams met, cutting open the frozen ground.

And only our bones remain separate from the soil that buries us. Otherwise, we are from dust, Hassan Ali. Never allow yourself to believe otherwise.

Noor Hussein paused, not sure that Hassan Ali had understood his words. He watched the younger man wedge his feet between the rocks jutting out from the vertical mass of moraine heaped high before them. Hassan was staring at a woman's form veiled in a crimson chaddar, slowly making her way up the precipitous slope. She was at a considerable distance, but it was clear that she was moving up the steep path, placing each foot carefully before the other. Noor had seen her too, and wondered why any woman would undertake such a risky journey. But now, there were perils that lay before them as they, too, climbed up to the tree line, lush with growth and beckoning them with their bounty, sprouting despite the hardness of the soil in years when the rain had forsaken them.

Beneath the mesh of random rocks and ancient debris of things long dead and forgotten, a glacier paced out its journey with unbounded patience. Across the slopes, snow spread wide, unblemished, undulating, a freshly washed sheepskin.

Black rocks crouched, hard granite cowering beneath soft snow, leading the two men to believe that all was well, that the path ahead was tame, the breeze gentle. The pattern of the weather had changed in recent years, rain coming when the crop had to be harvested; long, dry periods stretching across the cherished filament of summer, cracking the soil, parched, an old spinster's skin. The glacier, white where it had fractured with its gathered wealth, its pitted surface littered with mud and debris, melted ice bubbling beneath the rainbow curve, wedged between two black gulleys, bled quicker than before, flooding the fields just as they had been sown, the labour of a hundred men and women destroyed in the time it takes for a falling egg to break. Everything was different now: girls went to school, women tended shop, men sought comfort in bottles of cough syrup swallowed in one long, unbroken gulp.

Life was fragile in these parts. Boulders, lanced through the heart, perched on top of granite spires. Rutted, speckled moraine edged closer to the village; gushing streams dried up before winter; cows calved in autumn, their young not surviving the freezing cold. Spring was no longer heralded with the distant haze of blossoms; fruit died on the stem before it could ripen, empty husks withering like the shunned corpse of a fallen calf. Even the hearts of men and women were more brittle than ever, breaking with the first suggestion that the love they offered passed unnoticed, detritus thrown into a gurgling brook.

Much had changed since the Old Times, save for the uncertainty. It had always been a part of the lives of the people of Saudukh Das, like the fragrance of lucerne and the bleating of goats and the shadows cast by floating clouds upon the fields and mountains and small homes built of stone and the wood of the deodar tree.

Noor Hussein cautioned his younger cousin to slow down, to look carefully at where he placed his foot, to ensure that the soil beneath him was firm and could take his weight. A moment's miscalculation could be the difference between lying at the bottom of the mountain, bones smashed against rock, or lying before the hearth, a fire stoked by the worn hands of a woman who may not have loved the man but had served his every need.

This was a hard journey, taken twice a year, once in the summer when the cattle had to be shown the grazing land along the glacial streams flowing into the high nullahs. Then again when the animals would be brought back with the first frost of autumn, when the breeze brought with it the bite of the first snow, after the corn had been harvested, apples picked, apricots piled into sacks, walnuts cracked and peeled, their hard, bitter shells carefully collected and stored for kindling.

It was that time now, time to take stock of the year that was almost over, of the many births of baby boys and lambs and calves, of the several deaths: frail old men with gnarled knuckles, garbled memories and disintegrating teeth; fragile girls found with rope tied around their necks, broken reeds, silent vessels. It was that time, a hard time, a time to bid farewell to the calm of summer, to the gold of the fields and the silver of the sky, the burning rust of the trees. It was time to take stock of the sadness and the loss, the occasional glimmer of joy, the parting and return of loved ones, the growth of the orchards, the golden gift of a mare who foaled once in two years. It was time to prepare for the long nights ahead, the only sound the wind raging, firewood crackling in the hearth, the ghostly silence of smoke disappearing into the skylight like a song of lament at daybreak.

This was a land where many had come and struck the hard ground with harder resolve, scraping top soil from near the riverbank and carrying it on backs bent double to terraces which would become fields, pale shoots of barley pushing through the rocky soil.

Noor Hussein was the stronger of the two men. Both of them laboured to carry back the firewood they had piled up and hidden behind boulders marked in their memory as if on a map. This was to be their last trip, for the snow would hinder their movement, burdened as they would be with the weight of the firewood. Hassan Ali never accepted his youth as a reason for lagging behind his older cousin. Sure-footed and steady, he climbed that mountain path like a goat, while Noor, striding and stepping slowly, measured his progress with deep breaths exhaled through his mouth, emitting a low whistle, keeping rhythm for the two men.

Hassan had other things on his mind. He was the younger of the two, still unmarried, and had recently seen a girl of the most startling beauty. He dreamt of her during his waking hours, talked to her in his sleep, imagined her body next to his, her breath on his, her hair spread out on the pillow.

He had seen the girl in the village when she was on her way to school – she carried her books close to her chest as a mother would her child. The girl he loved was Sabiha, golden eyed and golden haired, the youngest daughter of the village headman. Sabiha would be the one to give him daughters to help with her chores, and bear him many sons to help him clear the field his grandfather had left his father, to lift the boulders which stood in the way of planting the crops they would harvest. Sabiha would comfort him in his illness, care for him in his old age, mourn for him if he was to die first. Sabiha, of the luminescent smile and glistening teeth, Sabiha of the full mouth and plump arms.

*Sabiha*
*Sabiha*
*Sabiha.*

Watch your step, Hassan! Noor shouted.

Hassan stopped. Before him lay the large trunk of a fallen tree, its branches crushed beneath its own weight. There was a dip in the ground where the snow had collected, forming a cushion for Noor to slide onto. Hassan followed his cousin and skidded into the depression, thudding to a stop. He stared at the tree's roots stretching in front of his face, plucking the air. Noor had already begun to swing his axe at the branches.

It's dead, must have collapsed with age, Noor said.

Hassan felt his way along the length of the fallen tree, wedging his feet beneath the trunk and moving towards the boulder that had struck the tree, ripping up its roots and felling it. He sat on the boulder and caught his breath. This tree should see them through the winter, or at least half of it, a good three months. Hassan took a deep breath and exhaled, relieved at this stroke of good fortune.

Something brushed against his leg. He looked down. A streak of red stained the snow. Hassan stood up. Beneath his foot a pool of frozen blood had congealed. The imprint of his boot was stamped on the surface of the scarlet ice.

Noor! he shouted. There's something here, look! Blood, fresh, frozen.

Noor halted, the axe poised in mid-air.

What is it? What have you found? An animal? Must have been caught beneath the tree when it fell.

I'm not sure, I can't see anything yet, Hassan said. If it's a trapped animal, we'll have to move the trunk. Are you up to that, old man?

Noor snorted and lunged forward, plunging the axe into the flesh of the tree. He walked towards Hassan, now on all fours, peering beneath the fallen tree. Hassan reached into a gap between the tree and the frozen earth and shouted.

7

*Ya Allah*, it's a man. A man. Buried beneath the tree. Hurry up, Noor. He may still be alive.

Noor moved Hassan aside and slid alongside the tree. Reaching in, he touched the cold flesh of the man's body. He pulled his arm back, recoiling. Getting up, he wiped the blood on his fingers against the bark of the dead tree.

He seems to be badly injured. Don't even know if he's still alive – he's probably frozen to death if he's not bled to death by now, Noor said, breathing hard. Icicles had formed on his thick moustache. The air smoked out of his lungs in slow, indifferent gusts.

No, no, I'm sure he's still alive – I felt him move. I swear. That's why I bent down to look, thinking it might have been an animal. But look, Noor, look – the blood is still fresh on your fingers – he can't be dead, can he? He wouldn't still be bleeding if he was dead, would he?

Noor bent down, placed both hands on the middle of the trunk and took a deep breath. Come, let's push this as far as we can. We have to get him out from under here. We can't possibly get him out any other way.

The two men leaned into the fallen tree and pushed. The muscles on Hassan's neck stiffened. The sweat on his forehead froze, gripping his head in a vice. Noor grunted. He took a deep breath. Uttering a low command, he made a final move and hunched his shoulder against the trunk, leveraging his feet against the boulder. Heaving, the two men rolled the tree away from the depression.

Sunk into the dead tree's grave, the bloodied body of a man lay inert, lifeless. One of his arms appeared to be severed from his shoulder. A pale strip of muscle showed through the lacerated flesh. The blood from the gash had spread onto the snow. The man's body was still, the skin of his face pallid, a sickly yellow, like a leaf that has not seen the sun for a long while.

There was snow in his hair and on his beard, and his eyes were closed. The breeze swept through the man's hair, blowing the snow away. Nothing else moved.

The cousins stared at the body in front of them. In the distance a bird dived between two trees and disappeared.

Noor fell to his knees and cradled the man's head in his arms. He put his ear to the man's nose and listened for the rise and fall of breath, any suggestion that he was still alive. Then he grabbed the man's hand and felt his wrist, seeking a pulse.

Hassan stood before the fallen man and prayed, mumbling words that he barely understood, chanting them, pausing to catch his breath, shutting his eyes to the possibility that they had found this man too late, that the breath and blood had already flowed out of him. *Ya Allah let him live let him live Ya Allah let the Periting of Chartoi have mercy on him this stranger this man just like us helpless alone in this harsh land, Ya Allah, Ya Allah*

He's alive! Noor shouted. Here, help me, we have to get him down as soon as we can. Otherwise he doesn't have much of a chance.

Hassan leapt towards Noor. Lifting the man's limp arm and resting it across his chest, Hassan helped Noor drag the body out of the depression.

The men stood for a while beneath the snow-capped peaks of the Black Mountains and considered their options. Leaping to the task, they untied the piles of wood lying hidden behind the large boulder shaped like a sleeping bear. It was not hard to remember this place, for directly above it, perhaps at a climb of two hundred paces, was the Doorway of Chartoi, named after the four glacial streams that met at this juncture in the massive outcrop of black rock, cascading down to meet the river. The doorway could be seen from most points in the village below, carved out of a cliff rising a thousand feet and more above the ground. It was the doorway leading to the Castle of Stone and Ice, abode of the Spirit-Beings who lived inside the black mountain, watching everything that unfolded in the world beneath, Zameen Par, watching two men struggle with a wounded man whose battle to live was an ordinary thing in these parts, but whose death would mark the village of Saudukh Das in ways no one could ever imagine.

# *Altó*

## 2

*From that place it was possible to see the two men carrying the stranger between them. It was a long journey, and for dwellers of Zameen Par, with no power save that of betrayal and belief, it was longer still, burdened as they were with a weight that was more than just the bones and the flesh and the skin that held the stranger's life unbroken. We, Spirit-Beings, Periting, knew it was a journey of immense significance. We watched the two men carry their burden, stepping carefully over rocks and skirting around boulders the shape of sleeping beasts. We watched till the two men disappeared from the Chartoi, until nightfall compelled us to shut the tall Doorway to our castle, shutting out the stillness that marked such a night.*

*We knew that these men would turn to the man they called the Sagacious One, the large man with the ungainly stride and bulbous mouth and large, square teeth, the one the others thought was wise. For us, he often spoke words of foolishness, a sum total of nonsense and fantasy married unwisely. It was his power that made those words heavier than the nuggets of gold panned from the waters of the Sherdarya, power that turned words of deceit into promises unintended. It was the Sagacious One who held in his hand the answer, cradling it the way he would the Spirit of the Yalmik Sky, a young bird he had captured from beneath the Great Oaks, stroking its fine, striped head, raising it to his fleshy lips and kissing it on the beak as if it was his own child. But who would enslave a child and keep it confined*

11

*in a cage, hard and cold and suffocating even as the winter wind blew through it, piercing the bird's feathered shell and chilling its spirit so that it was dead even before Aakhir, the Spirit of Death, had claimed it? Who would say with deepest conviction that the man loved the creature like his own child, a creature he had locked up, spilling seed into a cup for it to pick at with a beak muted for ever, the songs unsung and silent, crushed against its ribcage? Who would believe him when he said he had saved the creature from predators, all the while mocking its freedom, now shrivelled like a withered leaf in its wings? Who would say this was evidence of his love, this was the nurturing the creature longed for? Who would say that by mutilating the creature's spirit, by disdaining the feathers on its wasting shell, he was protecting it? Who would believe such a man except for hapless men who were not allowed to ask questions or to answer them, even though in their hearts they knew both the reason why and the reason why it was not the way it had been promised?*

*So it was that the Numberdar was drawn away from the soft embrace of his youngest wife to attend to a problem which was just the beginning of the tale that awaited its unfolding like the tail of a village dog; curled, concentric, confounding to those who could not unravel it, seeking to make sense of what they could not see but what lay before their eyes, a coiled snake shaped like a silver river stone resting against the sand of that vast desert between suffering and salvation.*

# Chapter Two

For the children it was something to do at that time of the day when all was done, when there was really nothing else to keep their minds from wandering towards useless games like chasing the stray dogs who quelled their desperate yearning for food by chewing on the leather soles of the shoes left outside the entrances of the small houses of Saudukh Das.

The time between dusk and dark hung over them like a dragonfly hovering over ripe peaches. Hunger rubbed its hands over the children's bellies and pressed down hard against the empty spaces. The children grimaced, sucking in their breath, passing the time between the memory of a meal long forgotten and the promise of the meal yet to come.

Noor and Hassan turned the corner in the lane. Between them, they carried a man tied onto a structure crafted from lengths of chopped wood, each twisted length tied to another with an orange nylon cord. The cord was wound around the man's limbs and girth and secured him to the wooden stretcher. His head dangled to the side, lifeless.

The children followed the two men steering their strange cargo through lanes bending between home and orchard, bordered by fields shorn of their harvest. They laughed and chattered until silenced by the forceful jostling of an adolescent boy burdened by a soldier's winter coat hanging off his thin shoulders. On his feet he wore oversized boots, and on his head an embroidered cap embellished with feathers and autumn leaves, a few bedraggled flowers drooping towards his large, protruding ears. His face was painted with an orange beard, the smell of rancid butter mixed with turmeric rising from his cheeks in nauseating gusts.

M-m-m-make the way! L-l-let pass! That order n-n-n-now, I tell you. Now long journey is begin! Long night come, dark with blood of wounded tree! H-h-h-hurry, let me p-p-p-pass.

The boy's stuttering voice was hoarse, grating against the sides of his mouth. In his hand he held a long staff, the top decorated with a tuft of goat's hair. A bell swinging from a string struck against the staff each time the boy dug it into the ground, pulling himself forward on his good leg, dragging the lame one behind. The children laughed at the young boy as they let him pass, pulling at his coat, some reaching for his cap, others just jeering and sticking out their tongues at this spectacle in the middle of a village where winter had stripped life bare.

That – that – that – my rope, shouted the boy, waving his staff at Noor and Hussein. He rushed towards them, limping like a cart with a broken axle, and pulled at one end of the rope. Give back me, I – I – tell you! Rope for me and you t-t-take rope, steal rope, Allah's curse b-b-be upon b-b-both of you three, the boy repeated, pulling at the nylon cord with his free hand.

The two men stopped. Noor rushed to the boy and yanked the cord out of his hand, cuffing him on the side of his head. He bent down towards the stretcher and checked if the wounded man was still securely tied to the wooden frame, then he turned to the boy and barked at him:

What is your problem? Can't you see that we are trying to get this man to the Numberdar's house? Can't you see he is seriously wounded? Allah knows why he didn't give you any brains, but at least you have eyes! Can't you see?

The boy lunged at the frame and tried to yank the cord again.

He stumbled, tripped over his staff and fell. His staff hit the ground and the bell tinkled, an unexpected trill like a bird's call piercing the evening's stillness.

Noor joined Hassan, and the two continued to drag the wooden contraption further up the lane, Hassan carrying the far end. The wounded man's feet jerked, swaying from side to side as Hassan stepped over the ruts and pits scarring the path. The lame boy lay at the bottom of the lane, yelling in his gravelly voice that the nylon rope belonged to him, that the English Madam had brought it for the women to hang their washing on, that the English Madam had asked him to protect it after the old man with the glass eyes and the teeth of a donkey had stolen it to rescue his goat that had fallen into a ravine, after the imam tried to hoist a dish antenna onto his roof, tying the thing with his orange rope, after the headmaster at the school tried to use it to secure the flag at the end of the long pole that stood in the cemented courtyard where boys and girls chanted the national anthem. The boy stopped blubbering and broke out into a hoarse rendition of the national anthem, singing it at the top of his voice, without pause:

*Pak sar Zameen shad baad Painda tabinda shad baad Mazi shaan e haal shad baad manzile murad aa aa galley se lag ja tu meri jan hai Paskintan hai Haseena ho Haseena tum ko aaya hai Paseena I love you Raja Zameen shad baad Aye mere watan merey pyarey watan shad baad tu mera jehan hai tu mera badaam hai shad baad gulshan hai hamara yeh pyara watan hai hum azaad hain abaad hain hum terey dilshaad hain hum sub barbaad hain*

By the time Moosa Madad lumbered out of the baiypash into the courtyard of his home, the boy had stopped singing. Moosa's steps were heavy; feet splayed wide, spread out like a web of streams feeding a river, held back by a pair of well-worn plastic slippers. He strode towards the metal gate barricading the house. A small cage sat on the wall beside the gate. Two birds, partridges, sat inside. They watched Moosa Madad open the latch on the gate. One of the birds fluttered; the other buried its head beneath the soft down of a folded wing. The evening air was chilly; the birds could feel it too.

Who is it? Give me a minute, will you? Have the mountains fallen?

Moosa stuck his large head out of the gate and peered into the dark lane. Shadows fell on the mottled surface of the incline leading to his house; a chill breeze stirred dead leaves in the orchard across the wall. One of the birds in the cage trilled, a soft sound like a low whistle. Like the boy's wailing, this sound, too, slipped beneath the dark veil of night.

Moosa stepped into the lane. Noor and Hassan stood in the shadows, their cargo propped up against the wall of the Numberdar's house.

What's this you have here, Noor? Moosa asked, shaking hands with the elder of the two men.

Salaam, Saheb. We found this man trapped beneath a tree that had fallen — we were going to chop the tree for firewood when we realised there was a man buried beneath it.

Noor bowed his head low as he spoke. Before him was Moosa Madad, tall, imposing, the headman of their small village, *Moosa Madad fifty-seven years old illiterate father of two sons both dead killed in the war several beautiful daughters all but one married the youngest the most beautiful Moosa Madad husband of three women the youngest even more beautiful than his youngest daughter Moosa Madad tall muscular hair and moustache dyed deep black large square teeth pushing through bulbous dark lips Moosa Madad to whom they would turn in times of trouble in Troubled Times Moosa Madad the Sagacious One*

A man? Wounded? Beneath a tree, you say? Where? Up there?

16

Moosa shook his head towards the mountain behind them, a massive outcrop with a flat cliff-face more than a thousand feet high looming into the night sky. Moosa did not wait for either of the two men to respond. He grunted, as if his questions had been answered without a word being spoken by any of the three men.

Right, then. Take him inside. Must be frozen. Poor chap. The first night of the season. Must have snowed somewhere.

A good, kind man, tough and decisive when necessary, Moosa Madad flaunted a large, taut girth, rounded out by reasonable prosperity, broadening his torso and reaffirming his position of power. Moosa Madad had enough to eat, even in these times of uncertain harvests and tenuous jobs. He was the Numberdar of Saudukh Das, the Number One man, a title given by the British during the Days of Empire, signifying the most important man in the community, the leader, the man with power vested in him to make decisions in the absence of the local administrator appointed by government.

Hassan Ali stepped forward and extended one hand towards the Numberdar, placing the other one across his heart. The young man was confident, the crest of his red hair ablaze in the sudden spread of moonlight filtering through the clouds.

Salaam, Saheb. I found him, Saheb. At first, I thought it was an animal caught beneath the tree, but then I crawled alongside the tree and saw a man with his arm all twisted and almost torn off at the shoulder. I think the tree fell on him and injured him badly, for he was bleeding a lot. Thank Allah he was still breathing.

Still breathing? Bleeding? Yes, yes, I see. Well, then, bring him in, I say.

Moosa stepped towards his house. The two men picked up the stretcher and followed the Numberdar.

Saheb, at first we thought he was finished, but then I listened to his breathing and his heartbeat, and we saw that the blood was fresh, and then we decided to bring him down, to you, so that you can decide what needs to be done, Noor said.

Yes, yes, it's the right thing to do. Get him into the house, come along, don't delay. Let's see what we can do for him. Know him at all? Someone from here, around here? Never seen this face before, Moosa said. He turned sideways to look at the wounded man's face, slumped to one side of the stretcher.

No, Saheb, he is definitely not from the village, perhaps from a village beyond the high pass, on the other side, beyond the river and the last police check-post. He is definitely not from here, Hassan said.

Right, so it's clear. He is a stranger. Anyhow. We have to look after him. More so than if he was our own. Hurry up, men. It's already late.

Noor and Hassan lifted the wood frame and carried the wounded man through the metal gate into the Numberdar's courtyard. At the bottom of the lane the boy in the soldier's coat watched the men disappear into the house. He brushed the dust off his coat and, leaning into his crooked staff, limped up the steep incline of the lane. A bird suddenly shot through the air, startling the young man. He shook his staff at the darting bird, shouting weird, unfamiliar words. The bird had already disappeared into the orchard.

The sky was low and hung heavy. Dense clouds shut out the silver light of the stars and the moon. Here and there small fires signalled an open hearth in the forest, a woodcutter spending the night amongst the trees, fearful of the Periting, blue and purple as they moved beneath the canopy of trees, some several metres tall, others the size of a goat. Lower down the slopes of the Black Mountains, grey smoke coiled out of the chimneys in every house. The fragrance of walnut oil spread itself along the walls and the wooden rafters of these homes and comforted those sheltered inside, grateful and safe from hunger and the biting cold of winter's arrival.

Inside the Numberdar's home a fire had been lit in the baiypash. Shadows played on the whitewashed walls of this space, the beating heart of the house. A pot of red beans from last year's harvest lay to the side of the hearth. A silver kettle whistled, steam rising from the spout, making the air moist, warm, like the embrace of a father back home after a long day of toil. Moosa's eldest wife, Khadijah, removed the kettle and placed it next to a cauldron of boiled rice. She was a withered woman, with fingers bony and long, bent and crooked like old wooden implements used to till the soil. Deep lines etched her face.

Khadijah removed the spectacles from the hooked bridge of her nose. With the sleeve of her frock she wiped the steam condensed on the thick lenses. Her eyes were dull, weary, worn out. She blinked as the steam hissed past her, leaving a film of moisture on the fine hair above her thin upper lip, the skin creased, sweat running in little rivulets from the crooked overhang of her nose. Khadijah peered into the pot of beans. A cluster of pearls and garnets strung together dangled from her bony neck and caught a clutch of safety-pins fastened to the bodice of her frock. Khadijah replaced the spectacles on her nose and unhooked the string from the pins, a task practised with regularity through the day, like breathing.

Moosa led the two men into the room. The wounded man's arm dangled like a lever, swinging from the edge of the rough wooden stretcher. Blood, dried and dark, was congealed on the cuff of his shirt. The two men lowered the wooden frame onto the floor. The wounded man's arm folded into itself like a jack-knife.

Khadijah rose. She covered her nose with the edge of her

shawl, biting down with the few teeth left in her mouth. Taking a step towards the men, she hesitated, then turned back and called to the woman sitting on her haunches near a heavy wooden door leading to a small room in the corner of the baiypash. Fatimah, Moosa Madad's second wife, looked up. Turning towards Fatimah, Khadijah thrust the sickle of her chin towards the three men standing at the alcove, untying the inert body from a wooden frame. Fatimah heaved herself up and walked towards the men, shooting an indifferent glance at the man lying on the floor. It was not someone she recognised. She turned towards the alcove where Moosa Madad would sleep occasionally on nights when he was not with his youngest wife. Fatimah drew the curtains aside. The men lowered the stranger onto the mattress within the alcove. Fatimah handed Moosa a quilt from a pile by the wall, avoiding his eyes. She retreated to the corner near the door, skirting like a cat around a heap of kindling stacked beside it. The metal blade of an axe propped up against the whitewashed wall glinted in the fire of the hearth.

The stranger moaned, a deep, low sound emerging from an empty well from where a fallen beast called. The two men dragged the wooden frame into the courtyard. Returning to the room, they watched as Moosa inspected the wound at the shoulder. Moosa turned to Fatimah and shouted instructions, all the while holding the man's arm.

Hurry, bring a bandage, a cloth or something, woman. We need to tie up this man's arm. Looks like it's about to drop off, it does. Hurry it up, now. No need to be sitting by that door all night long.

Fatimah heaved herself up again, and, holding up her chaddar, she ripped off a length four fingers wide. This she offered to Moosa Madad, avoiding his eyes as they bore holes into her flaccid form.

Here, come here, Noor, Moosa said, turning to the men behind him. Hold his arm while I tie the bandage around his shoulder. That should stop his bloody arm from falling off.

Noor did as he was told, Moosa did the best he could do with a length of torn cotton, and Hassan held his breath, watching the wounded man flinch as the Numberdar applied pressure to the place where his lifeless arm met the shoulder.

This task accomplished, Moosa stroked his moustache and asked the men to sit beside the hearth.

This is all we can do at the moment, my friends. I am no doctor, and these useless women are no nurses, but somehow we will get this man through the night and then take him to the District Headquarters Hospital in the morning. Let's hope he lives, my friends! You know how tenuous life is in these parts, eh? Here today, gone tomorrow.

Noor and Hassan shook their heads in agreement with the Numberdar and lowered themselves onto the floor before the hearth. It had been a long day, and they were grateful for the Numberdar's largesse, for taking this burden and making it his own. They were grateful for the safety of this warm house, for the fire crackling before them, for the fragrance of boiled rice and beans, bubbling in cauldrons black with use. Indeed, the man should get through the night, and tomorrow was another day.

Moosa Madad asked Khadijah to serve food to the men. Heaping the boiled rice and red beans onto an aluminium platter, Khadijah stuck two spoons into the side of the steaming mound and handed the platter to Moosa.

Eat, Moosa said. You must be hungry. Come. It will get cold.

Moosa grunted, asking his eldest wife for some tea. Raising himself off the floor with the agility of a young bull, he spread the quilt over the wounded man and removed the man's shoes, picking each foot up in his large hands as if they were sleeping birds. He lifted the man's injured arm and rested it on his chest. The man moaned. Moosa patted the man's chest. He felt the pocket on the man's shirtfront for a wallet, anything that would tell this stranger's story. There was nothing in any of the pockets except a few kernels of apricot seed, some raisins and a crumpled receipt for a roadside hotel, dated from a few days earlier. Moosa crossed the baiypash and dropped the pair of shoes near the bundle of firewood where Fatimah sat, staring at the floor. At his approach Fatimah turned her face away and pulled her veil across her face.

Moosa sat beside Noor and Hassan while they ate, the clatter of the spoons on the metal plates a reassuring sound in the stillness of the hushed night. From time to time, Moosa watched the wounded man. His breathing was ragged, uneven.

Found him under a tree, eh? Moosa asked.

Noor nodded. Hassan Ali chewed a mouthful of food, swallowed and reminded Moosa that he was the one who had found the man, pinned under the old tree.

Up in the Chartoi, eh? Moosa asked.

Yes, Saheb. We had gone to pick up the rest of the firewood we have been collecting before winter sets in, Noor said.

Well, my friend, winter has certainly arrived, and with a vengeance, I say. You may need more firewood than what you have collected.

There is more, Saheb, Hassan Ali said. We had to leave it there in order to bring the man down.

Yes, of course, I see. You did a good thing, young man. What is your name? I haven't seen you around before, have I?

He is my cousin, Saheb, Hassan Ali. He spends a lot of time up in the Chartoi, taking care of the goats and sheep and a few cows our fathers have raised.

Hassan Ali, eh? A good name, and taking care of the animals is a good thing for a strong, young man to do. Keeps you out of mischief, I am sure. Am I right? Moosa asked, smiling. His teeth gleamed in the light of the fire.

Khadijah handed her husband a cup of tea and placed a small tray with two brimming cups before the men. The room was quiet, except for the sound of the spoons against the platter and the slurping of hot tea. Moosa wiped his moustache with the back of his shirtsleeve. He gazed at Noor's face with small, dark eyes shaded by thick brows.

Do you think he will survive? Doesn't look good, you know. Afraid you may have found him too late. What do you think, Noor Hussein?

His arm is badly injured, Saheb. It seems to have been hit by the falling tree. You saw for yourself that it is nearly severed from his body. Let's hope that bandage you applied stops the bleeding, Saheb.

Moosa sucked his breath in and lowered his voice.

Too late now to hire a jeep to get him to the District Headquarter Hospital, you know. Roads not safe, as it is, you see. Not after that incident with the bus and the fire. All pilgrims, all burnt to death.

Stillness fell over the three men. No one spoke, the women in the corner did not move, the embers in the fire stopped glowing, and the smoke curling up to the skylight dissipated into the silent air. Until Hassan threw himself forward and spluttered out words which were better left unsaid, before memory brought more misery into the already gloomy room:

I was still a boy at that time, Saheb, but I remember being told that one survived, Saheb. The boy, the young boy, Saheb. He managed to get out from between the metal bars slatted across the windows. And he ran, Saheb, he ran as fast as he could, Saheb, as fast as a little child small enough to crawl out of a narrow space could run, the glass window having shattered with the heat of the fire that the mullah lit, Saheb,

23

dousing the bus with kerosene and sealing the door. The child ran, Saheb, all the way to the river, Saheb, he was barefoot, and the jagged stones must have cut his feet, Saheb, the little boy with tiny feet, Saheb, he ran as fast as he could . . .

Hassan Ali stopped. Noor looked up with reproach. He shook his head slowly, shutting his eyes and grimacing. Sucking in his breath, he shot recrimination at Hassan. Why must this young man always say the wrong thing? Was it not enough that they had burdened the Numberdar with a wounded man of unknown origin? Why must Hassan always bring things up that are better buried, even if not forgotten? Noor's fingers picked at the threads in the fringe of his chaddar.

Yes, yes, I know this, young man. I know this. How can I not know this? Eh? I, Moosa Madad, Numberdar of Saudukh Das, how could I not know of this cruelty, eh?

Of course, Saheb. Noor spoke with his eyes focused on the leaping flames in the hearth. Of course you would know, Saheb. We know that child was very dear to you, Saheb, and I apologise on behalf of my cousin, this young man, who was only a child himself at the time of that terrible incident. He has brought up something which most certainly has brought you grief.

Moosa looked up. His voice was now a whisper. He looked away at the door and spoke, to no one, to all of them, to anyone who had or had not known of what happened that day.

They shot him in his back, the cowards. They shot a child, a burning child, in the back. It is said that when he fell, he dropped onto the boulder he was trying to reach, possibly to shelter himself from the bullets, the fire, the hatred. Hassan Ali looked at Moosa Madad. He spoke to the Numberdar as if he was an old friend. The wounded man was forgotten for a moment, laid aside for the remembrance of a greater sorrow.

Yes, Saheb, I have seen that boulder, Saheb. It is the huge one right on the banks of the Sherdarya, the large black rock with the Yatz carved on it, the Yatz with flames rising from his head. You know that one, Saheb?

Moosa did not reply. He did not look at Hassan Ali. Breathing deep, Moosa spoke with words heavy and burdened.

He was my grandson, my eldest daughter's only son. Hussain Haider, we called him, after the Prophet's grandson. He was only five years old when this happened. Small enough to squeeze through the bars of the window, but too small to escape his persecutors.

Hassan stared at Moosa until Noor cleared his throat and apologised once again for this unnecessary intrusion on his cousin's part. Hassan was just a young lad then, and even now he did not understand what should be spoken of and what needed to be left alone. Moosa grunted and smiled a weak smile, saying only that some deaths carve a deep wound in the heart, that they never heal. But some deaths must always be remembered, like the sacrifice of his sons.

Now, if this man, this living corpse that you have dragged into my home, now, if he dies, and if we do not know whom to inform of his death, then who will remember him? Who will mourn him? Some widow, some mother, will wait for the rest of her life for his return; all the while, his bones will be nourishing the earth here, in Saudukh Das, the Plain of a Hundred Sorrows.

The men stopped talking. A flame in the hearth rose up and roared. The wood crackled, hissing, spitting moisture through the splintered limbs of a fractured tree. Shadows flickered across the wall where Fatimah sat. She stared at the fire in the bukhari. Flames consumed the wood, licking the smouldering, charred ends. Behind her sat the bundle of kindling used to light the fire. Outside, stacked beneath the wooden platform fitted into the side of the verandah, there was just enough wood to last a month or two, not more.

Who would bring more firewood to last them through the six months of winter?

In the alcove, the wounded man stirred. Noor got up; Hassan followed him. Moosa watched them as they peered into the dark space where a strange man lay, his shoulder bleeding, a long gash visible where his ear had been scraped away from the side of his head like a mud wall in a flood.

Moosa closed his eyes and turned away.

# Iskí

## 3

*Each of us has our own place, Taghralim had told us. Each of us has our own ways. It was known that there are the lesser and the greater amongst us. It was something that was not questioned, not by the spirited marmot, nor by the soaring falcon or brooding, bearded vulture. We knew that, even as we lived side by side, an otter swimming in the same water as a fish, an eagle soaring in the same sky as a flying squirrel, we must know that in the order of things that had been given us, there were those who were the hunters and those who were hunted. And even the hunted were, at times, the hunters.*

*Even so, we continued to live in the same manner, finding our nesting places, digging into the earth and between the rocks in order to keep our young from danger. But then they came, from Zameen Par, and began to walk in our pastures, stealing from our meadows what was not theirs. They came and cut down the forests so that the eagle-owl and snow-cock had no place left for them, so that the songs of the warbler and the wagtail were silenced. That was not long ago. We had not known such a creature, who would take away what was not meant to be theirs, who would waste what they had stolen, who would take pleasure in causing so much suffering. We had not known that for this creature from Zameen Par, we were all the hunted. But even so, we remembered the words of Yakh-Sherlim, the Mother of the Snow Leopard, and we waited. She had warned us that the destruction caused by the inhabitants of Zameen Par would return to haunt them, in the*

27

*fires which would rage, filling their lungs with smoke which would choke them; in the snow which would flood their fields, the ice which would freeze their hearts.*

*Yakh-Sherlim told us that we would face hunger and danger, for these creatures would invade our lands and take away our young, destroying our pastures, cutting down the forests, ripping up the Juniper of the Baltar Valley, burning what they could not use, scattering the remains of whatever grew on the land to the Blue Wind of Toofan. But we must bide our time, Yakh-Sherlim had said, and we must wait, for whatever is ours will come to us, and whatever was theirs will be lost for ever. That is the punishment meted out to thieves and trespassers tearing our world asunder. That is what the Mother of the Snow Leopard had told us, so we waited, watching. Biding our time.*

# Chapter Three

That morning, before the first snowfall of the season, before two men had brought down a stranger from the Chartoi, Moosa Madad's youngest wife, Mariam, had gathered the firewood scattered in the courtyard and, stacking it neatly against the low wall dividing the house from the orchard, she had seen a dead bird, its wings tipped with green and the top of its head scarlet. Mariam had also seen a woman making her way to the Doorway of Chartoi, her upper body draped in red, the pale, worn gold of her clothes evident against the black rock. The woman had not come back till the day was almost over; they said that she had stopped talking and just stared into the distance, waiting for something. Her eyes were glazed over and her mouth hung open like the narrow entrance to a cave. It was as if she had died and was just an empty husk, the grain chafed and beaten out of her.

Towards dusk, Lasnik, the young boy who couldn't speak any words which made sense, had limped all the way to the Numberdar's house to declare that it would not be long before calamity would fall. He said that he had seen that woman in a vision, a circle drawn around her, her head twisted to the back. Mariam felt her skin go cold when the boy reached for his own neck with his hands, gripping it, choking himself, speaking words flat and shapeless. The strange boy-man in the large overcoat stuttered and spluttered as he gesticulated, crafting his story out of the air: *She is bird like one you captured put inside cage she want to fly but she no wings what is bird with no*

*any wings what is man with no any coat what is woman with no any*
*hair what is boy with no any rope*

The blood left Mariam's face. Moosa held his youngest wife by the elbow and led her away from Lasnik to the room he had built for her at the edge of the orchard. He told Mariam that the woman who had dared to climb to the Doorway of Chartoi was Kulsoom, married to a wastrel who did nothing but sit around drinking bottles of cough syrup and cursing his wife and four daughters. But to climb up to the Chartoi and walk past the Castle of Stone and Ice was complete madness, worse than her husband's lunacy. That she had clad herself in a bright red chaddar suggested that she had lost her mind. All women were forbidden from approaching the Chartoi. And a woman wearing red was putting her life and her mind at risk. Everyone knew that. Everyone.

That woman – broken the tradition. Offending the Periting. Gone against all teachings of our elders. You know, she dared, dared to do wrong things. To sow, nurture, harvest, then eat aubergine she grew in her garden. She even spiced it with red chillies, you see. Red chillies and aubergine. The food of the Periting. She was mocking them, you see, the cursed woman. She must have eaten that chicken, the one that was killed on her wedding night, I'm telling you. Slaughtered on her wedding night, you know. Left out for the Periting on the Offering Rock. Now she cannot bear a male child. It is because she ate that chicken, that offering. That is the reason her wretched husband beats her, you see. Gets drunk on cough syrup. What else is he to do? Eh? What else is that fool to do?

Mariam looked up at her husband. She watched the spit edging his thick lips as the words tumbled out of them, no pause in his thoughts.

What madness is this? Eh? What to do? If something terrible happens?

Moosa sat down on the edge of the double bed he had bought when he married Mariam. He stared at his hands, then looked up and around the room. It was well-appointed, with a dressing table in one corner where Mariam kept a pot of face cream, a bottle of hair oil, an ointment for eczema, a comb, a small vase with a few sprigs of fresh wild flowers. It was a pleasant room, a modern room. No one else in Saudukh Das had furniture like this. Moosa sighed, pushed his hands down against his knees and got up. Mariam looked away, towards the window opening in the direction of the Doorway. A feather floated beyond the window; Mariam remembered the dead bird. She must bury it in the orchard, in a proper grave, deep enough to keep the creature's small body from being scavenged by the many starving dogs of Saudukh Das.

Kulsoom's journey to the Doorway would not augur well for Saudukh Das. This thought, and other disquieting flashes of undesirable things, harried Mariam as she fed the two partridges in her husband's courtyard. Already the girl, Sabiha, Moosa Madad's daughter with Fatimah, had been punished by her father, locked up in the storeroom until she revealed the name of the person who had sent her a love note, a letter in the form of a poem. Such a transgression had infuriated Moosa Madad, and even though he could not read the neatly scripted words, he knew from the scent of the sweet perfume that wafted up from the lined notepaper that his daughter was breaking rules, subverting order. Surely, the young girl would see that rebellion would only lead to remorse. Moosa had slapped Sabiha hard, marking the smooth rise of her cheeks with the shape of his thick fingers. The girl cried inconsolably; her mother vowed never to let Moosa hit his youngest daughter again, asking him to promise her this. But Moosa mocked Fatimah; he told her that she was clearly not good enough to give him any more sons, had given him this daughter, this wayward girl who would bring nothing but shame upon them. Moosa growled at mother and daughter, chastising both of them for daring to question his rules. How could they think that he would allow such deception to play itself out beneath his roof? How did they imagine that he would allow his daughter to form a liaison with some unknown man, who, for all he knew, was just passing time before he moved on? No one, not a single man in Saudukh Das would have dared to transgress the moral order by writing to the Numberdar's daughter, or to any self-respecting man's young girl. Only someone who dared to flout this unwritten code would have done something so reprehensible. A city man, one of these educated men with new-fangled ideas in their heads, many of them leaving behind a wife and a string of several whining kids. These men with their fancy education, wearing Western clothes with a silken rope around their necks like a noose, only such men could dare to affront the dignity of the Numberdar.

Moosa had thundered until the vein in the middle of his forehead had threatened to burst and Khadijah had run towards the baiypash to calm the raging waters of his fury.

Sabiha was taken to be locked up in the small, dank store-room with a low roof and a narrow window set high in the wall. Sacks of grain, half a goat's carcass strung up to dry, piles of walnuts and a mound of potatoes and dried turnips took up most of the space. Sabiha stumbled towards the far corner of the unlit room and crumpled onto the floor. Her hands trembled, breath catching in her throat as she realised the horror of what had come to pass. She clutched her head in both hands and sobbed. Her mother begged Moosa to let her at least bring a mattress and a quilt for the girl. Moosa bellowed; the walls shook. The cow in its shelter stopped chewing, birds stopped in mid-air, the water at the edge of the river slid back from the rocks and froze. Moosa thundered, he threatened not to let Sabiha out until she revealed the identity of the man who dared send a note covered in hand-drawn hearts, the red of their centres vulgar, scornful of the Numberdar's honour. Once the girl had done so, spitting out the name of that bastard, Moosa would take care of him in such a way that he would never be able to write another letter again. He would break every limb in the man's body, starting with his arms, splitting them into two, or three, then smashing his hands, pulverizing each finger, crushing them so that he would never be able to write another letter again. How dare he humiliate Moosa Madad? He would gouge out the man's eyes for daring to look at his daughter with desire and evil intent; he would smash his legs to pieces and watch him crawl for forgiveness; he would hurt him as much as the family's honour had been wounded. *How dare he how dare he how dare he?*

Moosa turned away from the storeroom. He walked to the door and stood beside it for a while before turning his head towards the pile of bedding amassed in the alcove where he occasionally slept. The baiypash seemed to be colder now that the morning's fire had died.

Give her a quilt. To keep her from freezing. We don't want her to die, you see. Not before she spits out the name of that bastard. The man who wrote to her.

Striding out of the baiypash Moosa slammed the door shut. In his pocket he carried the offensive poem – childish drawings of hearts and flowers scrawled on its borders, mocking symbols of an unforgivable travesty. Moosa walked across the orchard to the new room and opened the door. He thrust the piece of paper into his youngest wife Mariam's hands and grunted.

Read it. What does it say? A letter from the damned head-master? Asking for some additional fee? A fund? For a ridiculous picnic perhaps? Why do they go on a picnic, these people? Don't we feed them well enough at home? Eh?

Mariam stared at Moosa. She had seen her husband slap his daughter on her return from school, later than usual, her lovely face flushed and her golden hair uncovered, gleaming in the sunlight. Moosa had berated her for being late. The notebook Sabiha held against her chest had slipped out of her hands. A piece of paper folded many times over fell out and tumbled across the floor towards her father's feet. Sabiha scrambled for the note. Moosa grabbed it before his daughter could retrieve it. He held the note the wrong way up, then realised the hearts drawn onto the border were upside down. The coal of Moosa's eyes smouldered; his nostrils quivered. Head sinking with shame, Moosa shrank until his form cowered to half its size, a wizened dwarf, diminished.

After the shouting and the threats, after the young girl had been shoved into the storeroom, after the terrible wailing and pleading, the regrets and remonstrances, Mariam knew that what she held in her hands was the cause of deep grief and terrible misgivings. Her hands trembled as she passed an index finger over each word and read the missive in a low voice. Moosa strained to hear the words, inclining his head towards his wife's murmuring:

> Beloved Sabiha,
> Your eyes of gold
> Put the sun to shame
> For they shine with a light
> So pure and radiant
> That even my darkest nights
> Are illuminated by the memory
> Of your eyes of gold.
> Beloved Sabiha,

I wait for you like
A blind man waits for sight
I wait for you every day
And every dark, sunless night.

With each word of the love poem Moosa felt a dull steel rod boring a hole into his skull. *Ya Allah!* My daughter. My unblemished child, subjected to this crudeness. How can this be? How could he protect his youngest daughter from the predators who hid behind every rock? A young girl, her brothers cold in their graves, and he an old man now, how will he protect her, *Ya Allah*?

He snatched the letter out of Mariam's hands and shouted:

The bastard! Bloody defiler of his own sisters! Eyes of gold? Blind man? By the time I finish with him. By the time I get my hands on him, he will be bloody blind. The sodomising bastard. The damned defiler of his own mother.

Moosa had rushed out of the orchard, staggering in his plastic slippers, frightening the birds perched on the bare branches of silent trees, his girth swaying with each awkward but resolute stride. He continued to shout curses at no one and everyone. He strode across the courtyard and kicked open the door to the baiypash. Striding across the hearth, he threw open the door to the storeroom. His daughter stood near the high window. Her mother, Fatimah, held the girl in an embrace at once tender and fierce. She looked up and saw the rage in her husband's eyes. Contempt scurried across the ridge of his large mouth. Moosa planted his feet in front of mother and daughter and lunged at Fatimah, flinging her arms aside, pushing her against the wall. Fatimah fell and let out a cry.

Moosa! She is your daughter! Have mercy on her. She is just a child.

Moosa thrust the letter in Fatimah's face.

A child? Look. Look here, woman. This, this is what your beloved child has been up to. I told you. Even my late mother, may the Almighty bless her with an abode in Heaven. Even that blessed soul said sending this girl to school will only bring sorrow and disgrace. Don't you recall? What the imam at the mosque said? When this infernal school for girls opened? The girls will learn to read and write. They will use this learning to conduct affairs with men. This will only lead to great misery. To great shame. And so, it has! So, it has, Fatimah. Your daughter is no longer a child. You hear? She has turned into a bloody harlot. She goes to school only to bring shame upon this house. The house of Moosa Madad. The Numberdar of Saudukh Das. A bloody laughing stock, if anyone gets wind of this travesty. She goes to school. I pay bloody good money for her uniform. And her books. And her fees. And this is what she does? This?

Moosa turned to his daughter and shook the letter in Sabiha's face, threatening to stuff it down her throat. He pulled his arm back and struck the girl's cheek. Sabiha crumpled onto the floor. Fatimah threw herself between Moosa and the girl. Moosa pushed Fatimah towards the door.

Leave this room, woman! Leave this foolish girl to pay her penance. Do as I say, or pay the price. You hear me?

Moosa grabbed Fatimah's arm and led her out of the storeroom. He yanked the heavy door shut and bolted the latch. Stuffing the letter in his pocket, he wiped his hands across the front of his shirt, cleansing them of the defilement contained in the missive. He pushed past Fatimah and pulled open the door to the baiypash, cursing. Khadijah stood in the courtyard, her long face drawn into a dirge. Moosa stood before his eldest wife, clenched his teeth and instructed her:

Make sure the girl stays locked in that storeroom. She can be fed once. Or twice. If the girl needs to relieve herself, make sure you accompany her and her mother to the latrine. I am going to ask Mariam to keep an eye on those two. I want to make sure she tells me the name of that bastard who wrote this. This infernal piece of shit. Bloody blind man. Bloody golden eyes. I'll make sure, I'll make sure he never sees again. Never sees those bloody golden eyes. Or anything else for that matter.

For a moment, Moosa stood before his eldest wife, unsure where he was to go now, from this point of no return. His fingers twitched without purpose. Then he took out the offensive letter and crumpled it with his powerful hands. He flung it into the orchard and strode across the courtyard towards the gate.

Mariam had stayed at the door of her room in the orchard, regretting that she could read. She had made a choice to obey her husband, and in doing so she had betrayed his daughter, a girl just a few years younger than herself.

Now, this betrayal rushed through Mariam's gullet to her mouth. She ran out into the orchard and retched. Shutting her eyes, she passed a hand over her forehead. A thin film of sweat spread across her smooth brow. Mariam took a deep breath and opened her eyes. Before her lay a piece of paper crumpled into a ball. She picked it up and threw it into the tin cannister placed outside the latrine, half full of discarded bits of paper, balls of hair, an old toothbrush, an empty tube of cream. She would empty it out when she felt better, when the fear that caused her insides to churn passed, leaving her to stroke the roses embroidered on the edge of her pillowcase as if she was caressing a sleeping child.

# *Wálti*

## 4.

*There was nothing in this world, our world, which was not connected to everything that existed, that had ever been created, even before Nihibur had appeared on his horse and brought light and warmth to all of us. We knew that every act would beget another one. Like the arrows that sped towards us, there was a path which every act followed, there was a destination. But there was no end to the act, an endless circle looping around all those who lived within it. Let us say that if one of us is hunted, and that one falls, that would be the end of a child, or a mother, eyes glazed over with loss. That act would then lead to another one: the hunter dragging his prey away, the hunter skinning the creature, the hunter's wife curing the hide that had covered the flesh which the hunter's children would consume, growing to be like their fathers and mothers, and continuing that one act which led to the other, which made them the hunters and us the hunted. But who was to say then, that if all of this, all of this death and fear and conquest, was all the result of one act, then how was it that we were not all connected by that same rope which tied us together, all living creatures, our skins clothing our conquerors, our flesh feeding them? How was it then that those who hunted us did not see their own image in our eyes when they slashed our throats and pierced our hearts with the arrows they fashioned from the branches of the trees that gave them shade in summer and firewood in winter? How was it that they saw themselves as better than us when they were nothing but bits and pieces of us cut up and put together, their hats the wool of the goat, their shoes the skin of the ibex?*

# Chapter Four

It had been a difficult day for Moosa's youngest wife, as much as it had been a terrible one for his daughter. There was the dead bird in the morning, and in the evening Lasnik had blabbered about his grim vision, and now this stranger had been brought to the house with an arm that swept the earthen floor with fingers stiff and twisted with cold.

The sky darkened, and the birds in the orchard roosted for the night, seeking branches which still held on to the last of the season's leaves. Mariam heard the eldest wife call out to her. She stepped into the courtyard where the stack of firewood lay against the wall separating the house from the orchard, feeling her way through the narrow gap in the wall and stumbling against Lasnik hunched over a frame of chopped wood. Mariam pulled her veil around her body, sheltering herself from the sudden chill and this strange boy's piercing gaze.

Lasnik was still for a moment, his eyes glazed over and fixed upon something in the distance. He hummed under his breath, a sound like an old man's laboured wheezing. His fingers, clenching and unclenching themselves, moved of their own volition. His arms dangled from the precipice of his knees as he hunched over the pile of wood before him. He mumbled in a rhythmic chant, *Lasnik good boy rope good rope English Madam good Madman.*

Tearing herself away from the garbled mutterings of this boy-man, Mariam hurried to the baiypash. Her husband sat with the visitors she had seen from her window, crossing the courtyard with a strange burden suspended between them. She stopped in the doorway, breath stuck in her gullet. In front of her, on her husband's bed, lay a man under a quilt. She could see his ear hanging from a thin strip of flesh stretching from the side of his head to his shoulder like a weighted fishing line.

Moosa Madad looked up. He frowned.

What is it? Have you seen a Yatz, woman? What is it? Moosa asked.

Mariam dropped her gaze and stared at her feet.

That boy – outside – he says someone stole his rope . . .

What boy? Which boy, now?

I think he's that soldier's son, I could not see, it is dark outside. I wanted to get some firewood, but this boy was in my way, so I couldn't get the wood for the hearth, and he's saying strange things about the rope being stolen from him – but I . . . so I . . . couldn't get the wood for the fire . . . Saheb . . .

Mariam faltered. She stared at her feet, the toes dyed orange with henna. Noor and Hassan averted their gaze and shifted on their haunches, sipping tea that had already become cold. Mariam's beauty was legendary, and many men had dreamt of marrying her after she had been widowed, just a young girl then, young even now, not more than eighteen, certainly less than twenty years old. The Numberdar was old enough to be her father, but he was a wealthy man, with many goats and sheep and fertile fields terraced on the side of the mountain which received the sun in winter and rain in the summer. He was a man who had the power to make decisions that could make or undo the residents of Saudukh Das. Mariam had no choice but to marry him, for what was the future of a woman on her own, widowed with no one to look after her, a brother in the military serving in the wars of the Congo and Sudan, another in Karachi cooking at a seafood restaurant, and a third a government clerk, feeding a family of eight children? Her mother was long gone, dying six months after Mariam's birth, tired and worn from thirteen pregnancies, of which only six children survived. Her father was old, senile, barely able to swallow his own spittle. Mariam had no choice except to marry this man who now got up and moved her aside as one would a forlorn child. Moosa spoke with a rare tenderness.

You are talking about Lasnik, are you? He is just a simple boy. Allah's chosen creature, you know. Harmless. You do not know him yet. He wears his dead father's overcoat, has given himself his father's military rank: Lance Naik. Lasnik. No one even remembers what the boy's real name is, you see. Not even his own mother. He was born after his father was martyred. Killed at the front, like my sons, Akbar Ali and Asghar Ali, may the Almighty keep them safe in His protection. His poor mother raised this child on her own. Nothing to feed him. Other than the charity I would arrange, you see. He is a bit slow. A bit strange. A bit smelly, even. But there is no need to fear our Lasnik. He has a special connection with the other world. And he is the son of a shaheed.

Mariam choked. Something round and hard stuck in her throat. She swallowed. Shaheed, martyr. That was what they had said when they came to her father-in-law's house a year ago, carrying her husband's uniform, the white shalwar kameez she had washed and ironed and packed in his tin trunk, his soldier's identification card, his watch, the wallet with her photograph stuck behind the plastic pocket which also held a thin book of the *Ayat ul Kursi*. Mariam had held onto her composure until the soldiers who had accompanied her husband's body handed over his boots and the pair of slippers he would wear in the house before he had left to fight a war which had little purpose except to make mothers and widows mad with grief. The boots were handed over to her dead husband's father; the slippers, wrapped in a plastic bag, were handed over to Mariam.

Mariam had been pregnant at the time, she was sure. It was still the first three months, but she knew it as well as she knew the contours of her husband's embrace and the cold nights of his absence. She had bled heavily the night they brought news of his martyrdom. Her clothes and the mattress she had shared with him were soaked with her blood. Towards morning she had fainted, trying to cleanse herself and desperate to get rid of the soiled mattress. Zarina, the Lady Health Worker in the neighbourhood, had taken care of her, sponging her to cool down the raging fever, forcing spoons of tea down her throat. Mariam remembered all that now, and her throat constricted at the bitterness of memory.

Moosa Madad stepped into the courtyard and took down a lantern from a ledge in the verandah. Mariam watched him as he pumped the oil which lay at the bottom of its tin cylinder. He lit the wick and walked over to the place where Lasnik continued, with insignificant success, to untie the knotted rope holding the wood frame together. Taking a deep breath, Moosa Madad lowered himself beside the boy, setting the lantern down on the courtyard floor. He smiled, placed his hands on the rope and began to undo the knots, his large teeth gleaming in the golden glow of the lantern. Moosa's fingers were quick, dexterous. As he exhaled, vapour rose from his mouth and the faint smell of sweat drifted over the courtyard. Lasnik breathed in deep and shut his eyes, rocking back and forth on his haunches. Was this what a father smelt like?

See. I will help you. You can get your rope back quickly. Then you can go to the Lady Health Worker's house. Bring her here. You know her, don't you? That nice woman. She bound your foot. Zarina Bibi, remember? Her husband is a soldier, like your father. Remember him? Haveldar Ibrahim Ali? You know their house beyond the bridge. You must go and fetch her, son.

Lasnik opened his eyes and stared at the Numberdar. He watched the large man's fleshy lips move over perfect blocks of enamel, each one square, without flaw or fault. Moosa's teeth were whiter than the moon. Lasnik passed his tongue over his own teeth, yellow, his gums long and pink. He continued to stare at Moosa as the man tugged at the rope. With one last flourish Moosa undid the remaining knot and handed the rope to the boy.

Here. Take it. Your precious rope. Protect it with your life, young man. Your English Madam will be proud of you. Right?

Lasnik's mouth parted and he grinned. His gums shone where the light of the lantern fell on his face.

English Madam good Madam! Rope good rope! Lasnik boy good boy!

Lasnik grabbed the rope and coiled it into an untidy bundle, stuffing it inside his huge overcoat. Moosa rose and patted Lasnik on the shoulder.

Now hurry up. Go to Zarina's house. Bring her back with you. Tell her there is an urgent matter, you know. She needs to attend to it. Tell her to bring some bandages. And salve, for a bad injury, a deep wound. Do you understand me, Lasnik Saheb?

Lasnik nodded. He had been given a task by the Sagacious One, he had been trusted to do something important by the man who smelt of fathers. Grabbing his staff, he made his way to the gate. Night had fallen; the birds were now asleep in their roosts. It was a lonesome night, with just an occasional dog barking and the distant puttering of a motorbike making its way over the rutted roads of Saudukh Das.

At the gate, Lasnik looked at the birdcage and stopped. He turned around and limped up to the Numberdar. In a low voice, almost a whisper, Lasnik said:

> She
> Will
> Fall
> Into
> A
> Circle
> And
> Will
> Fly
> Never
> Again

Looping his hands into a clumsy circle, Lasnik peered through its aperture. Moosa sighed. He gestured to Mariam to go back to the room in the orchard. He took Lasnik by the elbow and led him towards the gate. Lasnik stepped into the alley and let out a shriek, a squawk like a chicken being slaughtered. Moosa could hear the boy stumbling through the alley, the purposeful *tak tak* of his wooden staff beating against the stones. He latched the gate and turned towards the orchard, the lantern swinging in his hand. Something stirred in the birdcage sitting on the low wall near the entrance. Moosa stopped and peered inside, holding the lantern at a distance, to cast its light inside the cage. One of the birds was dead, lying on its back, its head almost severed. The other sat mournfully beside it. The bloodied feathers of the dead partridge made a bed on the cold floor of the cage.

Moosa Madad rubbed his forearm across his mouth and swore. He opened the cage and reached in, removing the dead bird. Its small body was stiff, legs like the shoots of a young plant. Moosa Madad swore again and wrapped the dead bird in his shawl. Grabbing a shovel from the shed beside the wall, he dug a small grave in the orchard and buried the bird, heaping the moist earth over the small, still body. Moosa wiped his hands on his shawl and stood in the courtyard; he could hear his own heart beating. Moosa knew that things were not right in his village, this small hamlet where everything seemed to be turning upside down. Even as the mountains remained still, unmoving, there were things that were happening which did not bode well. He shook his head. It was easier to understand a storm, or the rain, or pestilence, but this thing that was happening now, this absence of rain when it was needed, this shaking of the earth when the fields had been cleared of falling rocks, this breaking of the streams which flooded his fields, the letter his daughter carried in her soft, unworked hands, the stranger in the baiypash, bleeding onto the floor of his home, the dead bird – all of this was upside down, none of it made sense.

Moosa stood beside the wall for a long while. He could not leave this place at the edge of the courtyard, returning to the two men in the baiypash, until he was ready to return to the business of adjudicating, supervising, restoring order to the disarray of his life. It would not do for a man of his stature to show the raw wound inside, that rotting pit, the faltering indecision, the overwhelming confusion that shrank him into something small, powerless. Moosa waited till the fear passed. There was no need to mention the dead partridge; after all, there was a graver issue that required his attention. Sometimes, if one did not mention something that was painful, the anguish of that sorrow would pass like water through a narrow chasm. It was better to wait for the sand to settle so that the bottom of the river could be seen for what it was, just a bed for the water it cradled, nothing more, nothing less. He would wait until the sun rose again. After all, the mountain cannot see what lies before it once the sun has set and all is dark, hidden in the shadow of the mountain itself.

Indeed, the morning usually brought news of birth and renewal. Moosa would wait for the morning. Surely, there would be a solution to the many problems that lay before him. Surely, the darkness would lift and the first of winter's storms would blow away the clouds that gathered now, across the silver sky sheltering his home, his village, the world he knew best, the best world of all.

# Čindi

## 5.

*In the Time before Redemption, all was dark. The colour of the river was black, like the colour of the sky, like the colour of the earth upon which our children searched for tender shoots of grass; black, like the fruit on the trees, black, like the stones on the ground, black, like the snakes that slithered between them, seeking warmth when there was none, when there was nothing, except the dark.*

*Our Mother Taghralim tells us it was her brother, Nihibur, who rode upon his horse, across the high mountains, black, across the sky, black, across the river, black. In his hands, stretched for a distance of a thousand keslik, he carried two things that took away the darkness: in one hand he cradled a ball of gold, in the other he held a crescent of silver. The ball of gold he threw up into the sky; it burst and brought forth fire and warmth. The crescent of silver he threw into the river. It slid across the black water, riding the silent crest, swelling, curving around the black rock that loomed out of the centre. And then the crescent broke and turned the water into a mirror in which the sky was no longer black. Shafts of silver rising from the river pierced the firmament. Then Nihibur rode his horse into the sky and broke a piece from it as round as a river stone. It is through that hole that the silver light appears to show us the way in the dark. In Zameen Par they call it Agon. When the clouds hide the moon, letting it rest, they call it Ghuanon, the time without light.*

*In that strange, haunting glow, that which is becomes that which is not. It is from that light that we must hide, for only darkness can shelter us from those who stalk us, taking our young away as the grass begins to ripen, just as the fruit of the Hilderish Tree yields its sweet pulp, just before the Sherdarya opens up its secrets and brings forth a bounty of otters and fish for us to feed upon.*

# Chapter Five

The air in the small storeroom was dank; it smelled of sodden earth and the wet skin of animals. In the far corner sat two black metal trunks marked on both sides of the handles and clasps with neat, white, stencilled lettering spelling the names of her dead brothers. A cover embroidered with roses cloaked the top of the trunks. Sabiha pushed the sacks of grain and potatoes and dried turnips against the wall, beneath a small square window letting light and air into the room. Climbing on top of the sacks she reached the window. Mesh wire blurred the view of the courtyard and the orchard beyond it. Sabiha made out the form of her father as he stood in the courtyard, his back towards the orchard. She knew it was him. She could smell his sweat and the faint scent of hair oil Mariam massaged into his scalp; slim, fair fingers stroking the man's curly hair, made coarse with black dye. Mariam, once a friend, now an enemy worse than disease and desolation. It was Mariam, her friend Mariam, her father's youngest wife, the beautiful widow, who had read the love poem, betraying her, bringing upon her such cruel punishment.

Sabiha stood at the window until her father trod towards the baiypash. She could hear him open the door. Then she couldn't hear anything. Nothing stirred; even the birds did not flutter. The moonless sky began to recede from her vision, leaving in silhouette the trees in the orchard, bare branches feeling the air for a coming storm.

★   ★   ★

Fire roared beneath the soot-blackened cauldron, fed on the wood left strewn in the courtyard once Lasnik's rope had been freed. Khadijah passed the knobbled back of her hand across her forehead. She sighed and stoked the fire. She began to prepare a broth of fermented rice and chicken for the stranger. From a corner of her eye, she glanced at him, this man who had become a guest without his acquiescence. He shifted fitfully in his sleep. She lifted the lid from the cauldron, and a cloud of scalding steam billowed out. Khadijah drew back, covering her face. Without warning, the wounded man convulsed with a spasmodic jerking of his body. The injured arm slipped from his chest and fell against the floor with the dull slap of a dead fish. Khadijah gasped, dropping the heavy lid. The man thrashed his head from side to side, exhaling short spurts of breath through clenched teeth. His mouth was twisted, stretched to one side, lips pale and cracked, bleeding where a gash cut through. Khadijah stifled a scream, and Fatimah rose from the floor, two women staring at the wounded stranger. From the corner of the baiypash, Noor and Hassan watched too. Then Noor moved towards the man, tapping his shoulder as Hassan leaned over and stared at the stranger's face.

What has happened? Has something happened here? Did he wake up? Did he — say anything?

Moosa stood in the doorway. Noor shook his head. Hassan addressed the Numberdar:

Saheb, his body began to shake, as if he was very cold. We thought he had woken up, but, Saheb, he seems to have lost consciousness again, Saheb.

Moosa looked past Hassan and lowered himself onto the floor beside the wounded man. Holding the lantern up, he peered intensely at the stranger's face, gazing at it as if trying to recollect where he might have seen him before. Then, his hand suspended in the air for a brief moment, he reached for the man's forehead and placed his palm on it. Noor moved forward and knelt down beside Moosa Madad, carefully placing his fingers on the stranger's pulse.

He is still alive, thank Allah, said Noor. Moosa smiled. He looked back at Khadijah and asked her how long it would take to prepare the broth.

It was an old chicken, Saheb, a stringy old thing. It will take a while to cook.

Well, hurry it up. As much as you can. This man probably hasn't eaten a thing for several days. And he appears to have a fever.

Moosa turned towards Noor.

I have asked for Zarina to be brought here, you see. That Lady Health Worker. She should be able to wash his wound, you know. And give him something for his fever. I sent that boy, Lasnik.

Noor nodded. Nudging Hassan with his elbow, Noor offered both his hands to the headman.

We thank you, Saheb, for taking this man into your care. We did not know what else to do with him. We are sorry if we have caused you unnecessary trouble, but we thought it was the best option, to bring this man here, Saheb, into your care.

You did the right thing, Noor Hussein. We shall look after him. In the morning we will have him taken to the hospital, you see. That girl, Haveldar Ibrahim Ali's wife, Zarina. She should be able to look after him for the moment. Now you go. You both need to rest, after your courageous deed of rescuing this stranger. May Allah shower his blessings upon you. For you have done a kindness that shall not go unrewarded.

Moosa Madad stepped forward, patted the men on their backs, shook their hands and walked with them to the courtyard where the disassembled bits of the wood frame lay dispersed on the floor. Noor walked around the pile, pushing the kindling into a stack. Hassan asked Noor if he could see the orange nylon rope anywhere. Moosa smiled to himself, shaking his head, and walked back to the small verandah. Taking down a length of twine hanging from the wall, he doubled it, and laid it out on the courtyard floor.

Your rope has gone back to where it belongs! Strung between those two poplar trees along the river bank, guarded by the watchful eye of Lasnik Saheb! The English Madam's Thanedar, her Inspector General of Police!

Noor and Hassan chuckled, glad of some respite from a taxing evening. The three men stacked the wood and tied the twine around the mound's girth.

We shall be happy if you would accept our offer of at least two loads of firewood for your family, Saheb, Noor said. We must return at daybreak tomorrow to bring the firewood we have collected. That tree, the one that had fallen on this man, we will chop it up and bring you at least two basket loads. It was an old tree, perfectly dry for kindling. It will see you through a part of the winter, and when you run out, we can bring more, so that you don't have to haul any this season, Saheb, you being alone, no one to help you, Saheb.

Moosa looked at Noor and pursed his thick lips into a line.

It is a good offer, young man. I am no longer as strong as I used to be, you know. Not after losing those two boys, my sons, fine young men they were, remember? They were about your age, Noor Hussein, born within a few months of each other. Strapping and handsome like their father. Thank Allah neither took any attributes from their mothers, eh?

Moosa laughed. The low rumble of his voice swept over the courtyard. In the storeroom, Sabiha rose from the floor and climbed on top of the sacks of grain. She could see her father standing in the lantern's gentle glow. She could hear him speak to the two men of his sons, her brothers, Akbar Ali, Asghar Ali, the ones who were not there and yet there all the time, their absence filling every corner of their home. Her father still searched for his lost sons, walking through dark nights like this one, guided by the light of his memory and the longing to hear their voices once more, to smell the fragrance of their skin. For so many years she had heard her father calling out to his sons in his sleep, yearning to see them in his dreams, longing to hear their voices, to touch their hair, Akbar, Asghar, fused together in death when the fire that engulfed them melted their flesh and joined them for ever, inseparable, just as they were in life.

Reaching behind a wooden platform in the verandah, Moosa dragged towards him a large basket woven from mulberry shoots, offering it to Noor. Hassan bent down and slid his arms through the leather straps attached to its sides. Noor and Moosa packed the firewood into the receptacle and then Hassan straightened his back, shifting the weight in the basket until his feet were steady.

We will bring back several loads of firewood for you, Saheb, Hassan said. He was willing to carry much heavier loads for Moosa Madad, Numberdar of Saudukh Das, the father of the girl he desired more than life itself.

Moosa Madad opened the latch and pulled the heavy metal gate open. He led the two men out of the gate and shut it slowly. Beside the gate, the surviving partridge sat amongst the clump of bloodied feathers on the floor of the cage.

Moosa stepped past and made his way back to the room where the elder two wives waited, tending to the broth and the wounded man. He would see to the matter of making the cage more secure in the morning. Now, it was late. In the morning, Moosa would organise the jeep that would take the wounded man to the nearest hospital at a distance of forty kilometres, a journey of almost three hours, if the road was clear. He would also have to inform the police. The man brought down from the Chartoi was unknown to him. What was this stranger doing in these parts, at that altitude, where only young men trek, leading the goats and sheep and cattle to feed them on the summer grass? Young boys really, becoming men during the time the animals they tended became fat and healthy, ready to face the long months of hunger after a brief season of abundance.

It was a time of uncertainty in the valley. Nothing was the way it used to be; nothing was what it seemed to be. Moosa could hear the wind picking up. Outside, the branches of the apricot trees rubbed against each other, frigid gusts of wind and the creaking of wood signalling the beginning of winter. Tomorrow he must move the surviving partridge inside. A storm was at the edge of the village, waiting.

# *Mishindi*

## 6.

*When the grey mass began to move, we knew it was time. It had been told to us before, and to Taghralim before us, to our mothers and to their mothers before them. It had been said that the darkness of the hearts of the people of Zameen Par would fall upon the vast fields of frozen water, deep with life's source held within its many folds. We knew that the time was near, when the grey mass would displace our ancestor, Yakh-Sherlim, the Queen of Queens, each black spot on her hide a mark of survival. The grey mass moved rapidly now, and moved the Snow Leopard further down, towards the habitations of the very people who feared her and who, in their fear, wished to destroy her.*

*We knew that the time was near when the hardness of the people's hearts would visit their own children, just as it had visited ours, hunting them, terrorising them, seeking them out in the forests and the nullahs and the slopes of the Black Mountains, hunting them down, taking their lives, as much as they revelled in destroying thousands of Years of Growth, the brutal skinning of the soil, the caging of the water in the dams they built, the extinction of the forests that were our homes. How much would they take from us? The land was not theirs, nor the air, nor the water. They had done nothing to keep the fields of frozen water from harm. Instead, these heedless people had left the marks of their shod feet upon the white mass now turned grey with debris and ire. They had dug into its flesh and pierced its skin, and now it came down upon them, burying them with its frozen burden, colder than their own hearts.*

# Chapter Six

In the swift arrival of the season's first snowfall there was a fury that mocked the calm of the serrated landscape soaring twenty-one thousand feet above the level of the sea. High up on the bluff, projecting from a spur, a tongue of black rock formed a ledge, wide enough to carry a fibreglass igloo, two soldiers, their guns, food rations, two metal drums of fuel and three mountain dogs, one of them grey-gold like the sky at the moment before dawn.

Perched beneath an overhang, just behind the igloo, hunched under a corrugated iron sheet, Haveldar Ibrahim Ali hacked the bones from the rib cage of a sheep's frozen carcass, a treat for the three Himalayan mastiffs he had been feeding on scraps, leftovers from the meals he shared with Sepoy Mohammad Zaki, a man who laughed a lot, sometimes for no reason that could be discerned by the unsuspecting. He laughed at the fact that Ibrahim Ali spent hours trying to melt the snow so that he could wash, or have a cup of tea, or boil bits of dried meat strung up in the dry air. Just wash your face with the snow, man! I hear real men do that! And why bother about making tea when the damn brew will freeze the minute you take it off the stove! And why waste time cooking those strings of black meat? God knows your teeth are strong enough to just chew the chunks raw, eh? And what's this business of letting the dogs have the juiciest bones when you know that I thrive on chomping them, like a wild beast, a snow leopard, a mountain wolf, my friend! It seems like you care more for these four-footed creatures than you do for your only companion, eh, Haveldar Ibrahim Ali? Your only friend here for miles and miles, onwards till the NJ9842, *thence north to the glaciers*!

In fact, there were many glaciers in the north, an unchartered territory, with rivers of ice cutting through mountain gorges, endless miles of packed snow. No line had been drawn through a forty-mile section leading to the Chinese border, and this had become the cause of countless, meaningless deaths on both sides of a non-existent boundary. It was as if the altitude of the battle ground was extraordinary enough to make men mad, to make them forget what they were fighting for, what they were willing to die for. And that was perhaps why Mohammad Zaki laughed at anything and nothing; it was a way to find relief in the desolation of the landscape, the futility of their mission.

The dogs had found their way to this post guarded by two men who had pledged their life to the protection of the country and its tenuous borders. Shepherd dogs, they had escaped an avalanche that had hit the village much below the post, burying everything in it: humans, livestock, stone houses, the few trees that remained and the small mosque with the loudspeaker that never worked, the muezzin's masterful voice carrying itself unaided across the slopes and the crests, calling the faithful to prayer. On some days it had been possible to hear the azaan even at the furthest post. Now, after the avalanche had buried the village, there was no sound, except the wind and the snow blowing towards the bluff. Days after the village had been obliterated, Ibrahim had heard the fierce sound of a wolf calling, howling. He had rushed out of the igloo and stood before three huge dogs, two of them sitting on their haunches, their tails wagging behind them, and the third walking steadily towards him. That one was the female, the leader of the pack. Ibrahim befriended them, and, assured of shelter and food, they stayed. By the evening, Ibrahim had names for the dogs. The males were Rustam and Sohrab, father and son, legendary heroes of Persian folk lore, and the female, the one with the amber eyes and grey-gold coat, he named Malika, for she was a queen amongst all creatures, her coat thick, her eyes luminous, tail curving like a golden crown, devotion fierce.

The sky had darkened earlier than usual, and then the snow had begun to fall, blurring the faint, jagged line of the furthest peaks. The men acknowledged the coming of winter in this already frozen land with submission. That is what they had been taught, to obey and accept. Like thousands of other men, they had been sent here to protect the border, a line known only by its coordinate on the curvature of the earth. It had not been considered necessary to name it, the men at the Office of the Geographer told disputing parties. After all, what lay within those forty miles other than wide, endless spans of snow and ice and emptiness? What was there to fight for, the American cartographer on C Street, thousands of miles away in Washington D.C., asked. There is nothing there, no resources, no settlements, no possibility of building military bases. The men did not question the wisdom of this exile, of the many deaths wrought not by battle but by struggle against the elements, a battle in itself. They were used to hardship. They had heard the songs that others hummed as they waited for the end to bear down upon them. They had seen flesh torn apart and bones stripped bare, heard the sound of another's head exploding when hit with shrapnel, flying through burning air. They had seen bodies mangled, twisted, burnt, disfigured beyond recognition. They had healed bleeding wounds, broken limbs, broken souls, broken men.

Ibrahim held the cleaver in his hand and brought it down where the thin, curved bones met the spine of a young lamb, small and delicate. The porters who brought the soldiers vital supplies had carried the flank of a frozen lamb all the way to this post. Ibrahim was told that the animal had been freshly slaughtered and hauled all this way so that the soldiers could have a feast of fresh meat instead of the tinned food that saw them through their service at these incredible heights.

Haveldar Ibrahim Ali was grateful for this small animal. One of the porters stayed behind, the one who had carried the lamb. He was small, like a young boy, but he told Ibrahim that he had six children, from two wives. The first had died delivering the third child, a girl. It was poverty, the porter had said, that killed his wife. He could not get her to hospital on time; there was not enough money to hire a jeep that could take them the four-hour distance from the village to the District Headquarters Hospital where she might have been saved. The girl, he said, didn't live either, dying in spite of the cocoon they had stitched for her from the hide of a slaughtered sheep. That winter, nothing could keep her breath from freezing inside her tiny lungs. She was blue when they buried her, a small child who had never been warm, who had never been held by her mother. He said that just before the baby girl died, he had held her for the first time, keeping her small, limp body close to his heart, desperately hoping that the heat of his body would warm her. She had not cried, not even whimpered; but he had wept, helpless, grieving for his lost wife and for the baby he would never know, who would never know the love of her father as he held her, his body racking, while, she, his little daughter, lay still.

That winter the porter had dug three graves, two of them tiny, cradling lives now cold like winter's dark soil. One was for his own baby girl, the other for a pure white baby lamb whose fur had yet to unfurl, tufts of soft white wool clenched like tiny fists holding onto life.

Ibrahim had listened to the story in silence. Both men stared into the fire of the Petromax stove. Ibrahim rose to make the porter a cup of tea. He offered him some dried apricots and almonds harvested from the trees in his small orchard in the village. There were also a few biscuits in a tin. The men chewed in silence; the flames of the fire puttered and hissed; silver ghosts spiralled upwards and disappeared. From his corner, Mohammad Zaki took out a harmonica and, blowing through its tiny windows, he made music, stopping to catch his breath, breaking into song:

*Changge howan yaar te har koi sarhda ai*
*Tayon saara sheher meray naal larhda ai . . .*
If you have a beautiful beloved everyone is jealous
No wonder the whole city quarrels with me . . .

Ibrahim smiled, pulling out his wallet and showing the porter a photograph of his wife, Zarina, and his children, two daughters and a son. He told him that Zarina was a Lady Health Worker, properly trained and certified, looking after the women and their babies in five villages. Ibrahim advised the porter to visit the local Lady Health Worker before his second wife got pregnant again. The porter nodded. He reached out to stroke the dog sitting closest to him, Malika. She placed her large head on the porter's feet and exhaled. Vapour rose out of her mouth and warmed the porter's leg. He smiled. Ibrahim Ali noticed that the porter's teeth were broken. He asked how that happened. The porter smiled again, and said that he had fallen into a crevasse once. He had held onto the safety rope with his teeth since his hands were carrying the supplies he could not afford to lose. If he had lost them, the contractor who sent him with the supplies would not have paid him. Then how would he have fed his children and his wife?

Mohammad Zaki laughed.

So, a toothless provider is better than one with many teeth but empty hands!

Ibrahim laid out the spare sleeping bag onto a wooden platform alongside his own bunk. Mohammad Zaki slapped the porter's back with a broad grin, his perfect teeth glinting in the light of the Petromax stove. He added a blanket to the sleeping bag and told the porter that since he didn't seem to have much fat on his scrawny body, and since there were no women around here to keep him warm at night, he might just need to wrap himself in another layer before snuggling into the sleeping bag. The porter laughed, the gap in his mouth cavernous, but his heart filled with the warmth of the friendship offered by the two soldiers living in this wretched place. Ibrahim offered him a cigarette; the men shared one amongst them, taking turns to suck the smoke into their lungs, blowing it out slowly, squeezing their eyes into slits as the pale grey swirls seared them. None of them spoke, each lost in his own thoughts, his own longing. Winter was here; it would be many days before another porter would struggle up the snow-crested incline, bringing a welcome cache of supplies and news of the world, breaking the tedium of exile.

# *Thalé*

## 7.

*When he was created, we made sure that he did not have an extra finger, or a toe that turned to the side like an eagle's beak. There was no need to mark him in that way, for our presence amongst them no longer needed to be known. Many had stopped believing, and laughed, the children foolish in their youthfulness. But we knew he had been born, silver skin encasing his human form peeling back as he slid through the narrow passage of birth, his crooked feet emerging first from the womb of his exhausted mother, thin legs attached to a shrivelled groin where his sex slept inside a fleshy sack. His head was larger than that of other children, obstructing the bloody passage from where he was to enter Zameen Par. We knew that he would never come to understand what it would mean to be a man; we knew that he was not one in all the ways in which those of Zameen Par understood it. He was more, and less. He was ours.*

*We stood around his blathering mother as she screamed and writhed in agony, legs splayed apart, shameless, desperate to expel the thing that had grown inside her for more than ten months. His father was fighting a war where men killed each other without knowing the reason why and women grieved dead husbands without knowing the length of their grief. She was not alone. The other woman, the one we have marked, the one who dared to cross our threshold, the one with whom we play like shadows darkening the spaces beneath the giant rocks alongside the Winter River, she was with her, holding her down with fingers worn to the bone. His mother thrashed; we had seen this amongst the fish in summer, struggling to escape the suffocating grip of the otter, and we had pitied her, for this was just the beginning of her suffering. Soon this boy, this creature who would never converse fluently in the language of his tribe, this boy who would never be a man, this creature would be the only one she could lean against when the wind from the Chartoi blew across the terraces they had planted with barley and corn and promises lying scattered across the dry, cracked soil of Saudukh Das, a village born of retribution, too close to our home, too far from redemption.*

# Chapter Seven

Night had fallen by the time Lasnik had limped down the rutted path leading down from the Numberdar's house to the little bridge straddling the banks of the rivulet dividing Saudukh Das into upper and lower halves. It was not easy to find one's way on a night as dark as this, but Lasnik had the instinct of a blind person for whom the map of things that made up the world was etched on the insides of their eyelids. Lasnik knew where to find Zarina. She was the person Lasnik liked best, after his mother, for it was Zarina who had not laughed at him when his soldier's overcoat had got stuck in the chain of his bicycle, throwing him off balance, his foot caught in the spokes of the cycle's wheels. She had cleaned and bandaged the gash where one of the spokes, broken and dislodged, had pierced his foot. Lasnik hobbled around on one leg for a few days until Zarina offered him a long staff, her husband's, a soldier just like his father, fighting a war in a place from where news of his welfare came rarely. Lasnik learnt to use the wooden staff as a cane and grew so used to it that even after his foot had healed, he walked with it still, a long stick decorated with the tuft of a goat's tail, feathers from moulting chickens and the last of summer's flowers.

Lasnik tapped the staff lightly against the door of the small house where Zarina lived with her mother-in-law and three children. The door was already ajar; Lasnik could see Zarina sitting before the hearth, tutoring her family. Her children were reading and writing by the lantern's light. Their grandmother, Api, watched a pot of boiling milk on the hearth. The air inside the room was warm and smelt of cumin and butter.

Zarina looked up. Lasnik watched the bird of her hand glide in the warm air as she beckoned him into the centre of the room. Beside her lay a canvas satchel with a leather tongue hanging over its lip. Pencils, erasers and a geometry box spilled out of the satchel's wide mouth. Lasnik stared at these and swallowed the memory of the first time he had seen a pencil topped with a soft pink hat. He had bitten both ends, anticipating something sweet and soothing. He bit his tongue now, looked away, lowering his gaze, rubbing out the memory.

Bending down to remove his heavy boots, Lasnik teetered over his own feet. He knew this awkward stumbling would cause much merriment for the clever children, always looking for something to laugh at. Lasnik gritted his teeth. He tried once more to undo the many bits of string looped through the eyeholes of the military boots several sizes too big for him. A long length of string was coiled around the boots and tied at his ankles. Zarina watched as he passed his tongue over his lips and then flicked it across his mouth, a lizard hunting for its dinner. Lasnik shifted from one foot to another, then shook one boot free. The boot thumped onto the floor and released the putrid stench of something rotten into the room. Zarina drew her veil over her face before getting up to open the window slightly. Carefully shaking off the second boot, balancing himself with the aid of his staff, Lasnik stepped with the agility of a goat over the books and pencils the children had spread out onto the floor and stood before Zarina. He looked down and stared at the holes in his socks, toes sticking out like small, hairless mice.

Come, sit with us, son. Come and have some freshly boiled milk, Zarina said. She patted a place next to the bukhari.

Api shook her head from side to side, the lone tooth in her mouth glinting in the light of the fire. Lasnik stared at the tooth suspended in the cavern of her mouth. The old woman coughed; the tooth quivered.

Alone tooth, Lasnik said, pointing at the old woman. L-like last tree at Chartoi. A-a-alone tooth, alone.

Zarina winced. She placed her hand on Lasnik's knee. The children smiled, looking up from their homework. Encouraged, he spoke again, his voice grating against the roof of his mouth.

L-l-like l-last soldier standing on ridge where f-father f-fight b-big b-battle. *Allah o Akbar, Allah o Akbar*, Lasnik shouted, brandishing his staff in the air, waving it at the children. Zarina's older daughter, Zainab, pubescent and rounded out like a pat of butter, reached for the bells and feathers on the end of the staff. Lasnik pulled the staff back. He averted his eyes. He could never look at Zainab without staring at the gentle slope of her bodice where her breasts budded. He tried to speak to her, without looking at her, but the words would not come.

Lasnik did not have proper words. Words meant less than the silences between them, like the spaces between seeds planted in the dark earth. It was where things were not that things were to be found, Lasnik would try to tell those who doubted him. But they did not understand. Lasnik had watched these men and women struggling to keep their fields from flooding, to keep their cattle from dying, to keep their sheep and daughters from going astray. He had seen them bury the daughters who had decided that death was better than marriage to a cousin for whom a goat and a woman were more or less the same thing. He knew that these wretched people thought they understood things about the land in which they lived, about the river and the water that cut through the hard rock, ribbed and unrelenting until it, too, turned to dust. He watched them when they suffered the loss of a child, he watched them when they stole the mulberries meant for the Periting, pretending to have nothing in their mouths even as the juice of the ripe red fruit streaked down their mouths in bloody drips.

Lasnik had seen all this and he knew, even though they thought he knew nothing. Only Moosa Madad knew that Lasnik understood these things. Moosa Madad with sparkling white teeth the size of small marble pillars holding open the entrance to a mosque, the gap between them just large enough to allow a small man to enter.

M-moosa M-madad! Lasnik spluttered. He call you, B-b-aji! Numberdumbar c-c-call you c-c-come quick.

Lasnik leaned towards Zarina, rasping into her ear, speaking in staccato bursts.

Thieves r-r-rope stealers, b-b-bring bleeding m-m-man, Numberdumbar house. You c-c-come hurry.

Zarina stared at Lasnik's open mouth.

Speak slowly, my son. Who has stolen your rope this time?

Thieves, rope stealers. N-n-numberdumbar Saheb house w-wounded man b-b-bleeding arm hanging l-l-like donkey t-t-tail.

Are you sure about this? It is late at night – the children have their exams in the morning, and I must prepare them. Are you sure the Numberdar has sent for me?

Lasnik nodded. Zarina got up. She removed a handbag suspended from a strap resting on a nail stuck in the wall. She spoke to the old woman and to her children. Then she asked Lasnik one more time if he was sure there was a wounded man in the Numberdar's house.

Lasnik nodded his head.

Arm h-hanging b-b-broken wing of b-b-bat. B-b-bring b-b-bandage, Baji!

Zarina rummaged through the bag. Opening a drawer in the cabinet, she took out a packet of cotton wool, a roll of gauze bandage and a bottle of Pyodine, and tucked these into the handbag. Reaching for her shawl, she slipped on her shoes at the door. Lasnik got up and shoved his feet back into his worn-out boots, the laces hanging like a few strands of hair on an old woman's head. He followed Zarina out, the bell on the staff tinkling, an odd sound in the deep silence of the night.

It was not often that Zarina left the house after the evening meal. Especially on a night when the clouds had begun to gather, blocking out the moonlight, making it difficult to negotiate one's way through the narrow lanes. On a night like this, not even the stray dogs in Saudukh Das wandered about the village, sniffing the ground for an improbable scrap of food. Jagged streaks of brilliant light had begun to slash through the heart of the clouds; thunder roared in the distance, a muted conversation becoming louder as rumbling Yatz walked through the valley. Cold wind stirred the bare branches of trees that waited to be cloaked in the first snow of the season.

The children begged Api to let them stay up till their mother came home. Ever since their father had gone to fight the war in the far mountains, Zarina's children feared that he may not return, for there were many homes in Saudukh Das where absences knew no end.

Zulekha, just six, her front teeth missing, had cried inconsolably at her mother's absence. Api, Zulekha lisped, has Mama gone away to the far mountains too?

The elder two children slid beneath their heavy quilts, pulling these over their heads to shield themselves from the sudden cold, from the nightly fear of loss. Api held Zulekha in her lap and stoked the fire in the bukhari. She wiped the little girl's tears and smiled at her, telling her that her mother was just around the corner, not far from their own house, attending to someone who was injured. She reassured the child that the Numberdar's house was just a short walk across the bridge and up the incline, that something must have kept Zarina there longer than usual, and that there was nothing to worry about. The Numberdar was a good man and would surely walk their mother home on a windy night such as this one. The old woman hugged Zulekha close to her shrivelled chest and traced the outline of the child's nose with a knotted finger. The girl looked so much like her son, Ibrahim, now hundreds of miles away from the comfort of his home. She held Zulekha in her lap and crooned a lullaby, the same simple song she would sing to Ibrahim when he was a child, small enough to crawl into her lap, curling up into the safety of her embrace, and falling asleep, his thumb and forefinger tugging at her ear as if it was a bell in a temple from long ago.

Every time a military vehicle came this way, Zarina would hold her breath, not wanting to stir the fear that lived deep in her heart. She would wait for the jeep to drive past, to some other house, with the news of another soldier's martyrdom. She could not bear the thought that Ibrahim would not return to her. His absence was the reason she filled her life with the business of healing the ill and infirm, always mindful of the fact that he could be hurt, and that she would not be there to heal him, to give him the will to live, for his country, his children, his mother, his wife who waited for him every day and every uncertain night. Ibrahim was the reason she had tended to the small bush of wild roses he had brought down from Sia-chen, carrying it in his duffel bag like a small child would cherish a kitten, wrapped in the woollen vest she had knitted for him. He had told her that she must keep the young plant warm in winter, otherwise it would perish.

Now, Zarina bent down and took the stranger's wrist in her hand; she saw that he was clad in a shalwar kameez, not the uniform of a soldier. She held her ear close to his chest and listened carefully to the faint beat of his heart. Then she placed his hand beneath the quilt and peered at the wound that had bled through his shirt. She turned to the Numberdar's wives and asked for a bowl of warm water, reached for her bag and spilt the contents onto the edge of the platform where the wounded man lay.

Zarina dipped the cotton wool in the warm water and gently removed the congealed blood and specks of dirt and fragments of brittle, dead leaves stuck in the deep gash almost separating the man's arm from his shoulder. Moosa stood near her, watching the man's chest rise and fall, his nostrils quivering like the gills of a fish fighting to find the river.

Zarina asked Moosa to get her a towel. As she rubbed the damp towel across the man's face, he emitted a strange sound, like the plaintive calling of a lost animal. Moosa bent down to peer into his face.

Do you know him, sister? Moosa asked Zarina. She shook her head. She did not know him. No one seems to know him, you see. We shall have to dig into his pockets in the morning. And check if he is carrying any identity. These days, you see, you never know who makes their way to this place. This village is near the new road they are building, near the dam they are building. We can't have a man here who has no business here, you see.

Moosa sucked on his tongue and whistled through the gap in his front teeth. Zarina nodded. She picked up her bag and turned to go, bidding farewell to Moosa and his wives. Stopping by the television perched in its cabinet, she placed the extra bandage and the bottle of Pyodine in a corner. For many days there had been no electricity. It had been a while since Moosa

70

Madad had been able to switch on the television to listen to the news. Its carved wooden cabinet was like a silent tomb, a suitable place to store precious medicines.

Moosa walked Zarina home, the rutted path lit up here and there by the moon peering through a cloud. He asked her about her husband, Ibrahim, when he was coming home, how were the children, how was their Api, still holding on to that one tooth hanging in her mouth? Zarina answered his questions and was grateful for his concern. It was not easy for a woman to look after a family without the presence of a man. At her doorway she thanked Moosa for bringing her home and watched him walk up the incline to his house on top of the hill. He was a good man, even if sometimes he seemed to be foolhardy. Taking in a stranger who looked like he may not last out the night was the kindness everyone in the village expected of Moosa Madad.

Zarina shook her head, chasing away a stray thought nagging her. Kindness, she worried, sometimes cut into the flesh and drew it back like the skin of a ripe fruit.

Along the banks of the river the night played out a drama of its own, the wind picking up and blowing sand into the frosty air, particles swirling, suspended for a moment before they whirled away in a ghostly dance. From the small window of her home Zarina could see the poplar trees and tamarisk bushes bowing before the fury of the wind, delicate tendrils plucking a solemn lament on that tumultuous night. She shivered, pulling her shawl around her. As Zarina shut the window, she saw the young bush of wild roses that Ibrahim had brought from the high mountains on his last visit home. Rain had started pelting its dark leaves. Soon, snow would cover it, burying it until spring when it would bloom, small golden buds, each the shape of a bird's head.

Zarina could not rest. Who was this man sleeping fitfully

71

in the Numberdar's house? She had not seen him in the village, or even in the next village at the end of the valley, where the glacier's nose nudged the moraine it carried from the top of the mountain to the edge of the river. She knew these villages well, walking the winding paths between them, attending to a birth or an illness, soothing distraught mothers, calming the fears of unwitting fathers. She had healed the cuts and scrapes of the young sons and daughters of these villages, bathed the bodies of the dead in preparation for burial. She had attended many weddings and many funerals. But she had never seen this man with his burnt skin and weathered face, his arm dangling from his shoulder, an ear scraped off the side of his head. Perhaps in the morning he would be able to speak. In the morning things would be evident, Zarina told herself. They always were.

# *Altámbi*

## 8.

*This she cannot heal, this that I hold in the cave of my belly, this thing that grows inside, sucking my blood and breath, taking away my life even as I cradle it, loving it before even knowing it. This she cannot heal; her hands are soft, unblemished, used to wrapping a wound, a cut, a laceration. This she cannot heal, she cannot reach, she cannot cut into my belly, much as I want to remove it; I protect it, hold it with grace, feel it grow, become, fill me. This she cannot heal, this wound within the wound.*

*I, Kulsoom, wife of Naushad the village drunk, mother to four unnecessary daughters, I have tasted the bitter skin of onion, I have eaten the soft flesh of purple brinjal, I have burnt my tongue on the fire of the red chilli. I have worn the crimson skin of my wedding, I have walked towards my death, holding this thing that grows within me, my life, my beginning, my end. I, Kulsoom, I have heard them calling to me. I hear nothing else but those voices, singing with the cadence of a celebration, filling my ears, the channels that run between my heart and my belly, filling them with a desire I have not known in that man's embrace. I, Kulsoom, know that only by giving life will I get life. That is all I hear now. All else is empty, silent, a riverbed long after the water forsook it.*

# Chapter Eight

Kulsoom rose earlier than usual. The girls were still asleep, their father snoring in the corner of the baiypash, his doting mother muttering in her sleep. She reached for the small mirror suspended from a nail in the wall. There was a mauve bruise on her cheekbone where Naushad had punched her with his fist, and a bleeding gash across the ridge of her brow. The eye below her brow had swollen shut.

Most of the time the beatings would take place when the children were at school. Once the girls came home, she worried about them watching the spectacle of the violence which played itself out with the regularity of a morning ritual. She tried her best to get the youngest two to run outside into the tiny courtyard or even into the lane, or to Zarina's house whenever she sensed Naushad's bile rising to his throat. That was her way of protecting them from the terrible things that would happen in that room, her mother-in-law sitting with the baby in her lap, watching with chilling indifference the punishment being meted out to a woman who dared to produce a string of four girls and no male to carry on her son's name.

Kulsoom put the mirror back onto its place on the wall. She opened a small drawer and dug out a tube of lipstick. Twisting the tube open, she rubbed what was left of the lipstick against her mouth. She looked in the mirror and stretched her mouth open. Her teeth were marked with specks of the red lipstick. She put the lipstick back into the drawer, pulled out a piece of paper, folded it several times and tucked it into her bodice. Kulsoom covered her head with her crimson shawl, drawing it across her face so that only her good eye was visible. She stared at her image in the mirror for a moment, then got up and walked out of the house, leaving the door open. The sun had risen on a new day, and she had a long journey ahead of her.

Morning rose from behind the Black Mountains. The porter prepared to leave, gathering the empty food sacks and folding them into a canvas duffel bag he strung across his back. Ibrahim pressed some money into his hands and told him to buy his children some sweets when he got to town. He must tell them the sweets were from their uncle, waiting at the end of the world to reunite with his own family. Ibrahim told the porter that his village was perched on the slope overlooking the river. That river had an island in the middle of it, like an eye looking back at the ever-present, yet ever-changing, sky. On that island there was a circle of massive stone pillars, the Place of Assembly for the Yatz. The Spirit-Birds of the Yalmik Sky flew to this place when something momentous was about to happen. The people in the village would keep their eyes on the sky at the slightest sound of murmuration. One would hear the air whirring with the sound of the bird's wings beating against it. When that happened, Ibrahim said, lowering his voice to a whisper, then it was clear that the Yatz were preparing to assemble. Those who were foolish enough to go to the island never returned. No one dared venture near that island, except, of course, someone as brave as you, Ibrahim said.

Zaki cut in with a roaring chortle, like a sudden rush of water in a glacial stream. Don't listen to him, friend! He's just making all this up. If there is going to be an assembly of any sort, it's going to be for my wedding, I'm telling you. And you're invited, along with your children and their mother and your mother and the neighbours and whoever else wants to join in the festivity. Cats, dogs, crows, goats! All are welcome! Don't listen to his nonsense about the Yatz-Matz, *yaar*! If there is a giant in this land, it is Haveldar Ibrahim Ali himself!

The porter grinned, his broken teeth scarred with the rust of cigarette smoke. Ibrahim shook his head and smiled. He said that he agreed with Zaki, not sure if these stories were really true. He was a believer in Allah and His Prophet, May Peace be Upon Him, but the people in his village insisted that all this was the way it was, the way it always had been. Let them believe what they will, Ibrahim chuckled. Allah knows that this land shows us many strange things others would never imagine, isn't it so, my friend?

Soon, Ibrahim said, my time at this post will be over. Another two weeks and my duty will change; another soldier will take my place and I will go home, leaving behind these beautiful creatures to watch over the others. I shall miss this one, Malika, especially.

Ibrahim stroked Malika's thick coat and then got up. My children are waiting for me, he said. And their mother too. And my mother, bless her. I had promised to get a new set of teeth for her. She said she will wait until the last one falls before putting a set of plastic teeth in her mouth. She says that every time she nursed one of the children, she lost one tooth.

Zaki guffawed.

According to that belief, my dear man, she had fed her milk to thirty-one children, with you being the last!

Ibrahim chuckled. The porter smiled back, deep lines in his face stretching across the bones beneath his skin and defining the contours of the map time had etched across it. Ibrahim gazed at the horizon for a long time, as if charting his journey back to his village.

The porter pulled his duffel bag close to his body, saluted Ibrahim and then began his journey back. Ibrahim stared at the small, receding figure until there was only the wavering form of something moving away, disappearing into the vast, frozen field of snow. Malika followed Ibrahim and stood beside him. For a long while Haveldar Ibrahim Ali stared at the horizon, watching as the wind blew snow over the porter's footsteps, erasing all trace of his brief but welcome visit. Nothing else moved here. There was only the wind, caressing the golden fur of the dog as she watched the horizon, waiting.

Sleep was a thin shell, fragile, a membrane slipping over the eyes of a bird.

Sabiha woke from a fitful sleep. In her dream she had seen a looming doorway carved into a cliff. She had been carried to this massive entrance by a flock of many-hued birds, some with their wings stretching from one end of the vast valley to the other, some with heads so large that they cast shadows on the clouds that floated beneath them. The doorway had opened; a gust of wind pushed her into the depths of the hollow. She stood before a colossal fortress. Another door opened, and before her stood several Periting, erect, taller than anyone Sabiha had ever seen, with mouths wider than a sickle and noses that started from the top of their foreheads and sped down to the philtrum like arrows. Their feet – large, toes spread like a winnowing fork – stretched out from the side of legs covered in long, green gowns. The Periting stood around the freshly severed head of a goat. Blood spurted onto the floor, forming a pool that glinted in the light of the crystal walls.

Sabiha gasped. Her breath caught in her gullet. A scream caught in her throat. She got up, shaking, staring at the cold floor of her prison. There was no goat's head here, no pool of viscous blood. Just the mounds of potatoes and turnips, the heap of walnuts next to the black metal trunks. Sabiha moved to the window and climbed onto the sacks. The courtyard, the orchard, all was covered with white. The moon shone bright now that the clouds had passed. Something near the gate caught her eye. She twisted her neck to get a better look and saw a cat slipping out of the birdcage. Sabiha held her breath. The cat leapt off the stone ledge and onto the wall and disappeared.

Sabiha stepped down from her perch on top of the sacks and kneeled on the cold floor. She prayed, shutting her eyes. She prayed for her father to forgive her, to release her from this prison, to let her breathe the air of the orchard. How long would her father keep her locked in this room, smelling of something sour, the bitter stench of onions, musty memories, strings of dried meat, decay?

A dead leaf, perhaps a small creature, stirred beneath the two tin trunks propped up on bricks. Sabiha read the names of her dead brothers stencilled onto the sides of the trunks: *Akbar Ali. Asghar Ali.* She drew in a deep breath and shut her eyes. She could see two graves clinging to the side of a mountain. Snow had fallen and slid off the graves and collected at the bottom of the slope that would flower in the summer. She knew her father had chosen this place for his sons because the snow would never bury the graves where two flags fluttered, green and white, crescent moon and star swaying gently in the wind. A raven called, black feathers beating against the white landscape. It was quiet there, on that mountain slope, only the susurrating flags, the soft hop of the birds as they pecked through the snow for seeds. There was nothing else there, except the markers signifying her brothers' remains. All around, the snow had obscured everything, softening the contours of the hushed valley.

★ ★ ★

Khadijah rushed out into the first snowfall of the year. She pulled open the door of the cage and grabbed the surviving partridge. The skin around its eyes was wrinkled; a purple membrane hid the light in its pupils. The bird was lifeless, still. Khadijah blew her breath on it, again and again, her thin form trembling in the cold. The bird curled its claws around her fingers. Khadijah wrapped the bird in her shawl and carried it back into the baiypash, still warm from the last of the embers glowing in the hearth.

Fatimah was asleep, propped against the door to the storeroom, the trench of her mouth wide open. Moosa slept near the wounded man, snoring like a defeated bull. Khadijah held the bird and blew on it, murmuring a prayer, willing it to live. Once the partridge began to breathe evenly, Khadijah placed it near the hearth. The bird blinked, shook its feathers, pushed out its chest and quivered in the heat of the burning embers. Khadijah sighed, grateful that the first snow had not frozen the bird to death. What would she have said to Moosa had the bird died? He always found fault with her, with anything she did. Nothing pleased him, except his youngest wife, Mariam. Everything that went wrong had something to do with the elder wives, the two women who had given him the sons he longed for, sons he had lost to war.

The boys had been born within months of each other, the elder one Khadijah's only son after several daughters, the younger boy born to Fatimah, her first child, followed by two daughters, the youngest Sabiha. The boys had been inseparable, sharing the love of the large, powerful man who was their father and provider and protector. Moosa named the elder boy Akbar, the Elder, and the younger one Asghar, the Younger, and took pride in the fact that they were both strong and sturdy like him, with keen dark eyes and thick hair standing on top of their prominent heads like a crop of wheat, robust and promising. The younger one, Asghar, Fatimah's son, had taken her fair skin, while the elder, Akbar, was swarthy, like his father. He put them in school when the government opened one in a distant village, carrying one on his shoulders while dragging the other one by the hand, alternating when either one of the boys got tired, keeping his eye fixed on that distant village and the dream he nurtured in his heart to give his sons the education he'd never had. When the boys were old enough to have a trade, he sent them to the military, for that was where young men found jobs that were guaranteed, even if the undertaking to become a soldier often meant that their lives were not.

The brothers were in the same battalion, fought in the same war, and were housed in the same barracks when it came under attack, the entire building catching fire after an explosion hit the vehicles parked outside, igniting their fuel tanks with the impact. Akbar and Asghar had helped the sepoys to get out of the blazing building, throwing blankets on burning men, running back into the barracks to make sure that their colleagues had got out safely. Both brothers had suffocated in the acrid black smoke, blinded by the searing heat of flames which devoured everything around them, twisting the metal frames of their beds as if they were the dry twigs of a mulberry tree.

When their bodies were brought home, wrapped in white cotton and placed in coffins draped with the flag of the country they had defended till death, Khadijah had fallen silent. Her hands had trembled as she stroked the coffin which held the charred remains of her only son. She was glad that the coffin was sealed and that she could not see his face. She wanted to remember him the way he had looked the day he had left, his brother beside him, never to return to the valley they had loved better than anything they had known.

Their bodies had been placed in caskets and transported to Saudukh Das on an unusually warm autumn day. Khadijah remembered it as if it had been a moment ago. She remembered the way the light fell from the sky in streaks of gold, softening the green of the fields, brightening the rust of the last remaining leaves. Khadijah had finished her chores and sat down to knit a sweater for Akbar. She had begun knitting the complicated pattern of the border when everything had changed. The ball of wool Khadijah cradled in her lap fell, rolling towards the door when Moosa entered. He was bent over like an old man, like a tree broken in a storm. His head was lowered, face clasped in his hands. Behind him stood several men in uniform. Khadijah did not hear what Moosa said, nor what the men had come to say. She heard nothing but the muted thud of her head hitting the earthen floor as she collapsed. When she came to, her husband was sitting in the alcove weeping. Fatimah sat beside her, her eyes dry, wide open, not registering this terrible thing that had happened. In her hands, Khadijah still held the knitting, her fingers curled around the needles. The soldiers were gone. Two steel trunks with the names of Moosa's sons sat on the floor. The ball of wool rested between the trunks, like a full stop, an end to the lives of Akbar Ali and Asghar Ali.

Khadijah shook her head free of the memory and, picking up the beige and brown bird blinking near the hearth, she held the partridge to her wasted chest, a living creature, a son without a name. Without warning, the wounded man gasped and let out a deep moan, flailing his arm in the air, knocking down the lantern that hung from a nail above him. The lantern fell, its glass globe cracking. Khadijah struggled to her feet and picked it up, approaching the man with caution. She peered at him. His eyes were stretched open now: blue, piercing eyes, fringed with thick, dark lashes. Khadijah took a step backwards and stumbled against the edge of the bukhari. Her hand struck the partridge, and the bird blinked, startled, shaking umbrage out of its feathers. Khadijah gathered her limbs, hobbled towards her husband and tried to wake him. Moosa Madad snored undisturbed, his moustache rising and falling in rhythm with his chest expanding and collapsing. Khadijah shook his shoulder. Moosa grunted and opened one bleary eye. But by that time the stranger had collapsed again, emitting a long, drawn-out moan that suspended itself across the length of the room like a fishing line cast in eddying waters.

# *Huntí*

## 9.

*What could we do that these men and women did not do to themselves? Our Mother Taghralim had spoken to us about the time it took for a human child to take shape inside the womb of the woman who bore it, bearing the discomfort of frail skin stretching across the dome of her belly, suffering the humiliation of her awkward gait, bloating up like the carcass of a dead cow. It would amuse us to think that so many years would be spent teaching that small human to do the simplest things like suckle, walk, dig the ground, plant seeds, hunt. After all, once that small human became a man or a woman, it would not take long for him or her to run a knife across the throats of our brothers and sisters, our children, slashing the artery that carried our life-force from the heart to our eyes and mouth so that we could see the one who did this terrible thing, so that we could cry out one last time, calling out to our brothers and sisters, calling out to the Yalmik Sky, asking that this injustice be noted, asking that its missing piece the shape of a fish's eye be retrieved so that we could once again claim our land, unseen, hidden from those who sought to take it away from us, taking our children, slaughtering them without mercy. So, when the dirty, drunken man they called Naushad beat his wife, a man whose name, we are told, means Joy, but who brings only sadness to his family, we waited, for we knew that we need not harm that woman for she was already marked for suffering. Nothing would change that, none of the medicines that her friend carried in that bag slung over her shoulder, would cure that woman of the fever that burned her and consumed her will to live. So, we just watched as these men and women struggled to heal the wound they had inflicted on themselves. It would not be long before justice would be ours. Then we would laugh, and they would think it was the breeze in spring, or the gurgling of the water at the Chartoi, or the call of migrating geese, but it would only be us, revelling in the retribution that we know is ours, even if these men and women presume that by naming a man Naushad, he shall actually be full of cheer, joyous, celebrating the births of a string of unwanted daughters. The Time of Reckoning was near now, as much as it was time for the marked one to return to us.*

# Chapter Nine

Light filtered through the smoke hole and brought the night to an end. From the sky, shafts of gold slipped down to the hearth, cold now, the last embers dying without plaint, one or two hissing as life slipped out of them, leaving grey ash where fire once roared. Naushad lay on the sleeping platform near the door while his mother lay at his feet, as if worshipping her son in her sleep, as she did in her waking hours. He was her world, especially after her husband had died, leaving her to fend for her only son and seven daughters.

Even in her husband's lifetime, Naushad's mother had clung to her son the way a newborn calf seeks the teats of the cow, or the warmth of its loins. It was as if she sought the attention of her son to make up for the fact that her husband barely even remembered her name, and hadn't cared to talk to her for a full seventeen years at the time that Naushad, her pride, her jewel, married Kulsoom, a woman who was plain, scrawny, with a broad nose plastered across pale cheeks. Only her bright eyes the colour of rust undid the irony of the fact that she was named Kulsoom, beautiful, for nothing about her, except those orange eyes, was anything less than ordinary.

The old man had cared for his only daughter-in-law with a gentle kindness, protecting her from Injeer Bibi's tirades, from her harsh opprobrium and constant litany of contempt. The old man had little need for words. He woke up early, worked the fields, fed the two cows and several goats, and made himself a cup of tea before attending to his toilet.

If he could avoid it, he would not say a word to Injeer Bibi, his wife of twenty-five years. She, as women do, would insist on having a conversation with the old man, even if he never responded, and waved his hands instead, batting flies in the air or dismissing a disquieting thought. And there were many such thoughts which would find their way out of Injeer Bibi's mouth: thoughts of forcing Kulsoom out of the home and finding a beautiful, wealthy girl for their only son. Thoughts such as finding a government job with medical coverage and a pension for their only son. Or thoughts as ludicrous as sending their son to the army so that he could become a karnal or a bargaidar or even a jurnal, not just a mere foot soldier.

It was clear to the old man that his wife could not see their son for what he was: indolent, surly, spoiled by the old woman whose life seemed to depend on Naushad's every movement. Dropping out of school early, the boy found it hard to get up in the morning, he found it impossible to do the hard work required in the fields, and he absolutely refused to take the animals to pasture up in the nullah during the summer. Injeer Bibi had numerous excuses for her son's wretched languor: he isn't feeling too well, poor lad, he is tired from staying up all night watching over his sisters, he has fallen and hurt his foot and can't climb up to the Chartoi. She would fuss over the useless oaf and feed him the good parts of the meat on the day of the feast, and she would ensure that his seven sisters attended to his every desire, even bringing a wet towel with which he would wipe his hands once he had partaken of a meal, burped and passed his sleeve across his grease-lined mouth. This the old man would watch, narrowing his eyes as if he was looking upon an oddity come to their village for the first time, a creature which mystified him, puzzled him, disturbed and repelled him as much as it beguiled his fawning wife, obsequious, servile, a worm crawling upon his back,

86

leaving a trail of silver slime as if to mark him and her son as hers, much as the red cow was branded with a dark line cutting down her back like a deep gulley.

Over the years, the old man found himself labouring long hours alone, preparing the small terraces where he would plant the season's crop, digging trenches for the water, securing buttressing walls, fertilising the soil, weeding his fields, harvesting the crop and then letting the seven girls thresh the wheat or the barley, spreading the grain in a circle about two to three feet deep, two girls driving the two cows, muzzles tied closely together, over the ripened harvest. He would close his eyes and listen to his eldest daughter shouting *'hai hai'* to the beasts, encouraging them to stamp the grain out of their husks, and he would say a prayer of thanks for the girls, for they had proved to be better than his son, ensuring that there was always a clean shirt for their father to wear, that there would be food even in lean times, that there was laughter in difficult times, tenderness in times of sickness and courage in times of fear.

Sitting beneath the shade of a walnut tree, the old man would watch his second daughter walk along with the cows, carrying a flat wooden bowl shoulder high, keeping pace with the two beasts, quickly bending to salvage any manure to keep the grain from being contaminated. The manure was stacked in a heap to nurture the soil for the next crop – nothing was wasted in this valley, not even the husk of the grain, for everything that grew had a use, if not for humans then for the animals who would serve them with labour while they were alive, and with meat and hide once they could no longer work.

When the wheat had been threshed, the old man would take a five-pronged fork fashioned from the wood of a willow tree and winnow the broken wheat by tossing it into the evening breeze. The husk and straw would blow away to one side while the wheat would fall into a pile, golden grain falling onto the beaten circle of the threshing floor. The girls would rest while their father winnowed the wheat, and then their turn to sieve would come, and they would carry onto the threshing floor their sieves made of thin strips of leather woven over a wooden frame. Together they prepared for the final stage of the harvest, ensuring that the family had enough to feed them through the winter, until the hunger months were upon them.

His daughters would pick any remaining bits of chaff or straw, finally pouring the precious grain into goatskin sacks. He would load these sacks into open-ribbed baskets and carry them to the store, knowing that his task would take half the time and effort if his son, the prince of their humble home, would have been more of a man and less of a sluggish parasite. Tired from the day's work, he would shout at his wife to at least get the boy to lay the straw out onto the roof so that it could be poured down a central hole in the shed for the animals to consume over the coming winter. But there was always an excuse: the boy is sensitive to dust and other things, he will become sick by inhaling the dry soil clinging to the stalks of straw. So, the old man would climb to the roof with sacks full of straw, spread it out in the dark, too exhausted to shovel it through the opening into the shed. He knew that he had no choice in the matter, that his family's survival depended on his labour and that of his seven daughters.

But what would happen once the girls married and left for their own homes? Who would help him then? Who would tend to him when his bones felt brittle and old and his eyes clouded over with the knowledge that daughters were borrowed for just a short while? That they did not belong to their parents, that they must leave, to tend to other men, other families, taking their soft voices and gentle ways along with them, weeping on dark nights when they remembered the homes from which they were torn away like the bark of a willow tree?

Morning spread itself across the sky wide and warm, like a gesture of welcome to a returning soldier. Zarina hurried the children through their breakfast and rushed them through the gate. Outside her neighbour's house, she nudged her elder daughter Zainab towards the door.

Tell Aunty Kulsoom that we have come for the pencil sharpener her girls borrowed.

Zarina prayed that Kulsoom's husband, Naushad, would be fast asleep, inebriated with the bottle of cough syrup he drank every night, drunk with the mulberry wine he brewed himself, the only thing he did other than curse and beat his wife and daughters. He was a harsh man, thrashing his wife almost every day, blaming her for not bearing him a son. Zarina had heard the woman's cries across the wall that separated their two homes, the dull thwack of his hand on Kulsoom's cheek, the sickening thud of her head hitting the stone wall or the hard floor. Kulsoom never spoke about this, and Zarina never mentioned that there were mornings when the light in Kulsoom's sunrise eyes would be so faint that it appeared as if she had already died.

Zainab knocked on the door. It opened with a shudder. Zainab stepped back, gasping. Naushad stood in the doorway, swaying on unsteady feet. His breath stank of dead fish, his hair stood up in wild clumps, his clothes were grubby and crumpled. A thread of saliva streaked down the side of his twisted mouth. He stared at Zainab, then saw Zarina. He barked:

What do you want here, woman? Haven't you caused enough trouble for us already?

He shuffled forward, his feet awkward, limp. Zarina took a step back, pulling Zainab close towards her, shielding the two younger children from the man who veered and weaved in the air like a snake in a state of hypnosis.

We have come for the sharpener your daughters borrowed from my son yesterday, Zarina said.

The man lunged at the air, aiming for nothing in particular. He spat, mumbling beneath his ratty whiskers, the ends dripping with that morning's tea.

Your son and my daughters? Eh? You want to make sure that I know that you have a son while I just have these cursed girls, eh? Is that what you have come here to say, you wretched woman?

Naushad took an unsteady step forward. He continued, his voice rising to a pitch.

Have you got nothing better to do than walk around these lanes like a woman with no morals? Does your husband know that is what you do when he is away, fighting on some battlefield while you walk around causing trouble in the homes of Saudukh Das? Eh? Does he know that or should I tell him, Miss Lady Heathen Witch? Suggesting to the wives of respectable men ways to cheat them, ways to cheat them out of a son by giving them those pills and injections on the sly, eh? Isn't that what you do? Isn't it? Eh? Isn't it?

The last words he slurred, then he slumped against the open door and slid halfway onto the floor. A shout rang out from inside the house.

Naushad! Hurry up! Your wife has lost her senses again. Hurry up, my son! Look, she is rolling her eyes now, the Periting have taken possession of the damned woman. Hurry up, Naushad! *Ya Allah!* What have we done to deserve a fate such as this?

Zarina peered into the dark room. Keeping her hands and feet on the floor, Kulsoom stretched her body towards the smoke-lined ceiling. Injeer Bibi, wizened and wiry, carrying a small child wrapped in a dirty blanket, slunk towards Kulsoom's arched body. Zarina ordered the children to hurry on to school without her. She turned towards the door. Naushad lay slumped onto the floor, exhausted from his raving, one of his arms flung outwards like the root of an old tree. She skirted around him and leapt towards the baiypash. Kulsoom's eyes were rolled into half-moons. She moaned; spit foamed at her open mouth. Injeer Bibi rocked the crying infant in her arms, mumbling prayers and incantations, her thin lips beating a rhythm against each other. Three small girls hid in the dark alcove of the baiypash. Eyes wide with fear, they stared at their mother from behind the pillars of the alcove, huddled close together in the freezing room.

A weak shaft of light from a small, dusty window fell on the floor near Kulsoom's arched body. Her belly was bare under a torn vest. The shirt she was wearing had ripped along the side and hung lopsided off her shoulders.

Zarina bent down. She peered into Kulsoom's face. Kulsoom clenched her teeth and grimaced. Zarina held Kulsoom by the waist and stroked her. She made soothing, calming noises. She had seen other women in this state. It was the first sign of possession after the initial days of complete silence.

Naushad hoisted himself off the floor, lurched towards Zarina, lunging. He fixed his gaze on her and started his rant again.

What are you doing? Can't you see it's all your fault? Eh? You must have sent this stupid woman to the Chartoi! Yes, you must have told this fool to go to that forbidden place, and now look! Just look what has happened to her! For the whole evening after she came back, she didn't speak a word, eh, not even to the children, these cursed girls who just stare at their mother like dumb cows! Dumb cows, eh, that's what all of you are!

Naushad loped across the room and lowered himself onto the floor where Zarina held Kulsoom around the waist. He stared at his wife for a while, then turned his watery gaze to Zarina and spat out spiteful words through clenched teeth, measuring each one with the precision of a chemist.

Get out.

Get out of my house.

I will not tolerate your presence here any longer.

You are the one to feed her the chicken slaughtered for the Periting when we got married.

You are the one to make her eat aubergine and chilli defying the orders of the Periting earning their wrath, ensuring that I shall never have a son, isn't it? You are the one, isn't it?

Isn't it?

Naushad leaned in towards Zarina and spat. He snarled, bobbing his head with every word: Get out. Get out. Get out of my house, you evil woman, shadow of the Shaitan, you Shaitus, you daughter of a demon. You have robbed me of a son, get out, get out, get out!

Naushad slumped over, sucking air through his open mouth. Zarina wiped Kulsoom's face with the end of her shawl. She did not have the strength to pick Kulsoom up and lay her down on the platform built into the alcove. She rose, looked at Naushad, then turned her head away. He was a snake slithering in the grass, a danger that would pass if one let it. Zarina walked to the alcove where the three girls cowered. Opening her bag, she took out a pack of lozenges, placed one in each girl's hand, and planted a kiss on their tear-stained cheeks. Then she turned to their grandmother and said:

Kulsoom needs to be taken care of — she only has three months to go before the birth. And it's not the Spirit-Beings, Api, it is your son who is driving her mad. If you and your son continue to treat her like this, she will most certainly die.

Then who will look after the girls, Api? You? Your son? Think about it, before you cause her more harm.

Zarina shut the mouth of her bag, adjusted her shawl and stepped out of the miserable room. It was the first time she had spoken to the old woman in that tone of voice. She had done it for her friend, Kulsoom, wife of a fool, a madman, mother of four daughters, desperate for a son, desperate enough to try anything which would save her marriage and save her life.

# Tóorimi

## 10.

*It was Sinopish who drove home the point that even the wisest amongst these men often sowed the seeds of his own destruction by desiring that which was not meant to be his. Sinopish told us about how these men disdained the wisdom of those different from them and feared us only because of their own cowardice. She told us the story about the Dome-headed Boy, the bald son of a powerful man who had prayed to the Creator to gift him a male child so that his name would not be lost like a leaf thrown into a swirling eddy. This child, we will call him Gunjah-Puttar, was sickly, his mother weakened from the many daughters she had brought into the world, each one of them like a stone around their father's neck, threatening to drown him in debt, for in Zameen Par, these people not only give their daughters away to total strangers so that she may slave for them, but ensure that each girl is well-provided for, taking with her grain and nuts and fruit and utensils and bedding and even cows and goats so that her husband can have fresh milk every morning and the warmth of her skin every night.*

*Gunjah-Puttar's mother wished for the child to be fattened on fresh milk and butter churned by his grandmother up in the furthest meadow where his grandfather pastured the goats and cows over the summer. So, one day, Gunjah-Puttar's mother wrapped a pancake inside a small cloth, tied the cloth to a stick, and gave it to her gangling, bald, awkward son, the Dome-headed Boy, telling him to climb up to the highest meadow and spend the summer with his grandparents who would fatten him up. Why, perhaps all that good air and good food will even sprout some hair on his bald head, his mother thought to herself, sad to see her only son go, walking inelegantly on his stick legs. His father, the fat man with the thick crop of hair like a blackberry bush growing on his square head, cringed to see his only son walk like an injured, wingless insect.*

*Along the way, over the bridge and across the nullah, just outside the village, Gunjah-Puttar met with a red fox; let's call him Laal Loomrhi. The fox expressed his desire to eat Gunjah-Puttar, but the little, scrawny boy pointed to his skeletal form, the skin loose and hanging off his bones. Eat me once my Api has fattened me up, Gunjah-Puttar said. I will be nice and fat once I have spent the summer up in the pasture, eating fresh butter and cheese, drinking fresh milk, frothing from the udders of my Daada's honey-coloured cow. If you eat me now, my skin and bones won't even fill a cavity in your tooth!*

*Laal Loomrhi gazed at Gunjah-Puttar's thin frame and sized up that this scrawny specimen would, at most, make up one or two morsels, certainly not enough to quell his ravenous appetite. So, patting the little bald boy on the back, he said he would be waiting for him at the end of summer. Laal Loomrhi went his way and Gunjah-Puttar went further up the incline towards the far pastures, relieved to have escaped with life and thin limb intact.*

*The same thing happened again, and again, and again, Gunjah-Puttar managing to ward off the hunger of a bear, a wolf and a leopard, using the same ploy, employing the wisdom his overfed father lacked, for he was a wise boy, even if he was a thin one with no hair on his head.*

*Once Gunjah-Puttar reached his grandfather's hut up in the highest pasture, his grandmother sang out to welcome him, beating a small drum dadang dadang dadang. Gunjah-Puttar danced and his Api sang, while his Daada looked on with disapproval, for this was his only grandson, but thin and bald, not worthy of carrying forward the great family name. Api churned butter and made cheese while Daada* milked the honey-coloured cow, but Gunjah-Puttar couldn't eat, for fear of growing fat and becoming a hearty meal for the red fox, the bear, the wolf and the leopard. Every day his Api would coax him to eat the golden pancakes fried in butter, and his Daada would ply him with milk that ran down Gunjah-Puttar's bony chin. Every day, Gunjah-Puttar refused, barely able to keep a mouthful of food or drink down his shrinking gullet.

The summer passed without incident, without Gunjah-Puttar becoming the handsome, healthy, strong boy his father dreamt of teaching all that had been taught to him by his father, and his father before him. Finally, on the night of his departure from the high pasture, Gunjah-Puttar whispered to his grandmother that he feared returning along that path for surely the red fox, the brown bear, the golden wolf and the spotted leopard would be waiting for him, waiting to devour him, thin bone by thin bone. Api understood what was eating her grandson. She took him in her comforting embrace and told him she would fit him into the drum and roll him down the hill. Why, surely, he was thin enough to fit into the drum?

The next morning, Gunjah-Puttar got ready for his return to the village. Slipping easily inside the drum, he shut his eyes and waited for his grandmother to roll him down the hill. But first his Api gave him some advice, telling him that if any of these beasts stopped him and asked if he had seen the little, bald boy, Gunjah-Puttar must say that he had seen the Dome-headed Boy take the other, longer path to the village, behind the ridge, over the spur and into the valley. And he must ask the fox or the bear or the wolf or the leopard to roll him down the hill. This way he would be able to get home before anyone could say dadang dadang dadang.

So Gunjah-Puttar, safely ensconced inside the drum, was given a gentle push. He rolled down the hill, through the pasture, past the cows and the sheep and the goats, past the streams and the bubbling brooks, past the rocks and the gulleys, until he was stopped, at various times, by the fox and the bear and the leopard and the wolf. Each time, *these creatures asked the same question. And each time Gunjah-Puttar spoke from within the drum and convinced them to search for the little, thin, bald boy, now fattened, surely, on ghee and butter and cheese, on the other side of the mountain.*

*It was the wolf, Sinopish said, a luminescent beam of pride glinting in her golden eyes, who finally discovered that Gunjah-Puttar was outwitting them. The wolf came out of her lair after the leopard had given the drum a push down the hill. She flung a stone at the drum, breaking its shell. Out fell Gunjah-Puttar, as skinny as he had been at the beginning of summer. The wolf caught the poor young child, but, taking a look at him, feeling the brittle bones through his papery skin, smelling the fear in his sweat, watching the few hairs on his head waver in the breeze, she released him and told him to walk the rest of the way home, since the drum had been smashed to pieces and the route was clear, now that the fox, the bear and the leopard were out looking for Gunjah-Puttar on the other side of the mountain.*

*Ever since then, Sinopish said, the children of men have befriended the children of the Spirit-Wolf. These humans trust the progeny of the Spirit-Wolf, for one of us saved him from death, one of us gave life back to him and, in doing so, gave him back to life.*

# Chapter 10

The sun was already climbing towards the Chartoi by the time Zarina got to the Numberdar's house. Noor and Hassan had arrived earlier. Both men always looked freshly bathed, their hair combed and glistening. Noor sported a moustache, carefully groomed and sitting above his mouth like a bow. Hassan was still young, the sparse growth of reddish brown hair along the sides of his face not yet a beard, the faint beginnings of whiskers a suggestion of what a fine young man he would become.

Lasnik hovered around the courtyard, eyes to the ground, clutching his oversized coat around the midriff. Zarina smiled at Lasnik as he circled the courtyard like a dog sniffing the scent of another. Hassan swept his gaze around the courtyard as if searching for something, his eyes stopping briefly at a barred window set high in the wall of a small room at the edge of the courtyard. A shadow moved behind the window. Hassan stepped closer to the window and stretched his neck upwards. The shadow disappeared. Hassan swore beneath his breath. He was sure he had seen a Peri, a Spirit-Being, behind that small window obscured with mesh wire. All he could see was the crown of light around the being's head and shoulders. The being had no features, just an arc of light spread around her like a halo. He pulled at Noor's sleeve and pointed at the window.

Did you see that? A woman with golden hair? Surely not a real woman, a Peri, perhaps?

Noor ignored him. Hassan was always imagining things, always seeing things that weren't really there.

Zarina stood before Noor and whispered:

Is he all right, that man you brought in last night? Has he lived through the night?

Noor looked up. Surely, had the man not lived through the night, the Numberdar would not be taking his sweet time to emerge from the room he shared with his youngest wife, Noor thought. He smiled at Zarina, shy in her presence, embarrassed at his impudence, even if the words had not been spoken.

He lives, sister. I am certain of it.

Noor returned his gaze to the floor of the courtyard where Lasnik had tramped concentric circles, punctuated by pock marks from the end of his staff as it pierced the earthen floor.

Zarina murmured to Noor about the Almighty protecting the wounded man, may he live to see his family, to return to his home. She stepped towards the baiypash as Moosa Madad emerged from the orchard, rubbing a towel across his face. Sleep slid from his crinkled eyes. He greeted Zarina with a nod and a smile and ushered her into the baiypash. Moosa shook hands with Noor and Hassan and patted Lasnik on the back, then invited his visitors to take a seat on the large wooden platform in the verandah. Lasnik hunkered down on his haunches in the middle of the circles he had stamped, keeping his staff upright, gazing with authority around the courtyard. The morning sun was gentle; it warmed Lasnik and lulled him to sleep.

Moosa hung the towel on a nail in the wall and arranged his bulk onto the wooden takht. The takht trembled, creaking beneath his weight. Moosa raised one leg and tucked it beneath his buttocks.

He is all right, it seems, Moosa said, to no one in particular. He turned to Noor.

We have to find out who he is, you know. He is unconscious, you see, or perhaps asleep. I did not want to disturb him last night, after you left. But we must wake him and ask him a few questions, you know — who is he, what was he doing up in the Chartoi, and where was he headed before he almost got killed by that falling tree?

Yes, of course, Saheb. We must ask him. Has his wound stopped bleeding? Noor asked. He looked out at the snow melting on the dark branches of the trees in the orchard, dripping down onto the mulch of the orchard's floor.

His wound? We shall have to check, you know. Zarina shall see to it. Then we can give him something to drink or eat. And then ask him these questions, eh? After all, how long can we harbour a total stranger in my house? Eh? What if he is a fugitive? A runaway? An absconder? Even a murderer? Eh? Have you considered that, young man? Perhaps he is a killer, you know?

Hassan jerked his head up from the floor and stared at Moosa Madad. He had not imagined anything like this. Blood rushed to his face. Flushed with excitement, Hassan burst forth with a volley of questions.

Saheb, is that possible? Could he have murdered someone and then run away? Saheb, do you think that is true? Could I have, I mean, could we have, Noor and I, could we have brought a murderer down into our village? Should we not report him to the police, Saheb?

Hassan did not pause for a breath and looked straight into Moosa Madad's eyes. Noor looked at Hassan, shook his head almost imperceptibly, then turned away. His young cousin was always exaggerating things, always making much more of something than it was worth. He would always think of the most absurd option, ridiculous ideas swarming in his foolish head, occupied with little else except keeping an eye on the goats and sheep and ensuring that they all got home at the end of the grazing season. Now again, Hassan was letting his imagination run wild, just because Moosa Madad made an absurd suggestion. But how could one contradict Moosa, the Numberdar of Saudukh Das? And yet, how could this stranger be a murderer? There was no weapon on him, and who could he have killed high up in the Chartoi when all the men and boys who go up there to pasture their herds or to chop firewood had returned to the village? No, Hassan was letting his imagination run away with him again.

Moosa fixed his gaze on Hassan and nodded wisely. His words carried a lot of weight in this valley, and few dared to contradict him. In Hassan he saw a reflection of himself, a younger version, a youthful Moosa who had the courage to tell it as it was, without hesitation. Moosa did not think this was such an absurd idea at all. He thought that times were bad, that anything could happen without warning and that it was necessary to be vigilant. As for informing the police, well, everyone knew that the police would end up suspecting the Numberdar of some wrongdoing, unless, of course, the gracious Numberdar made the wrongdoing right by greasing a palm or two. Moosa was sure of this, as he was of all the other pronouncements he made, sitting on his wooden throne, one thick leg tucked beneath his sizeable bottom.

After all, my young friends, he could even be a spy, you know. Someone sent by the enemy to spy on us. To check what is happening in the area, you know. To check out what is happening with that new road. The one being built by the China company.

Moosa spoke with sombre authority, nodding his head up and down, shifting his gaze from one man to another. He sucked on his teeth and emitted a low whistle.

You see, when a country progresses, it gains many enemies, you know. And these enemies, you see, these rivals, they send spies to check on the progress of projects which will make the country prosper, you know. Perhaps this man is one such spy, young men. I'm telling you, we may be harbouring a spy in our village.

Noor ventured to say something then thought better of it. How could he challenge the village headman? What would he say? That there was not much going on here to merit the presence of a spy? It was hardly as if the new road would cut through this small village which never featured in any news on the radio or even the local paper. And, certainly, there was nothing here, in this faraway land, except black rock, grey sand and a jade river.

But Noor did not offer his opinion. It was more prudent, at times like this, times of uncertainty, to keeps one's peace. Silence was often the safer course.

For a moment the three men were silent, considering the possibility that they may, in fact, be harbouring a criminal, a fugitive, a dangerous man who could hurt them in some un-expected way. Hassan, peering out at the courtyard, trying to get a look at the small window set high in the wall, broke the silence.

Saheb, what happened to the partridges? There were two in the cage last night and now there are none! What happened, Saheb? Did some cat get them? Hassan asked.

Moosa grimaced, then swallowed, pushing back something sour. The knotted lump riding on the ridge of his neck quivered as he cleared the phlegm in his throat. He rubbed his sleeve against his mouth and looked at the empty cage.

Yes, it must have been a cat, entered from the gap at the back, you know. Damn these creatures, always looking for a meal! But mercifully it got only one – the other one is safe, you know. Khadijah has taken it into the room to keep it warm. It almost froze to death in the season's first snow last night, I'm telling you.

Moosa shifted his weight forward and called to Khadijah to bring the surviving partridge out into the sun. He leaned back against a faded bolster and, reaching for a small mirror in a plastic frame, peered at his face and the white bristle sprouting on his chin. Moosa ran his hand over the bristle, cursing the hungry creatures who would eat anything that moved, finding their way into locked cages, damned murdering thieves.

Khadijah brought the partridge, wrapped in a shawl as worn as herself, and held it before Moosa like an offering. He took the bird in his hands and stroked it. Then he lifted it to his mouth and kissed it, calling the bird endearing names, my child, my heart, my joy, my precious prize, my dream, the light of my life. Hassan, eyes and mouth wide open, watched the Numberdar cosseting the bird. Noor, uncomfortable with a large man's display of affection for a small bird, stared at the verandah floor.

Bring our guests some tea, woman, Moosa commanded Khadijah. As Khadijah returned to the baiypash, Zarina appeared in the doorway, clutching her handbag, twisting the strap with restive fingers. She stood before the Numberdar and told him that the wounded man needed to be taken to the hospital as the bleeding had not stopped. It is not just his arm, she said, his ear has been prised away from the side of his head and is hanging there, the lobe suspended from a thin strip of skin. Zarina's voice quavered as she described the injury the men had already noted. Zarina had not seen anything quite so distressing; she had bitten her lips to keep from retching at the sight of the lacerated ear hanging from the side of the man's head like a question mark.

Please, Saheb, for the sake of this man's life, we must take him to the nearest hospital, before it is too late. The man may not survive if the bleeding does not stop, and I fear I cannot stitch his wound, nor stem the flow of blood, nor attach his ear back to the side of his face. Please, Saheb, it is my earnest prayer that you move him to the District Headquarter Hospital. Otherwise—

Zarina stopped. She turned her face away and covered her mouth with the edge of her shawl. Moosa opened his eyes wide. His mouth was pursed into a straight line, eyes narrow. He stopped stroking the partridge and did not speak. Noor cleared his throat, coughing into his clenched fist.

Saheb, with your permission, Saheb, I came to tell you that the road between here and town has been blocked with a massive landslide. The snowfall last night was heavy. It shall take several days to dig our way out of it, even if the whole village got to work today. No vehicles can get through until the road is cleared, Saheb.

What are you telling me, Noor? That we will have to keep this man here? That we will have to treat his wounds ourselves? Eh? Speak up, what is it you are trying to tell me, young man?

We shall have to keep him here, Saheb, until he is well enough to leave of his own accord. We don't have a choice, Saheb.

Moosa shook his head. He opened his mouth, then shut it, passing his hand over his face, suddenly tired.

How will we manage to treat his wound when the bleeding won't stop? Moosa asked, agitated. He shook the partridge, squeezing it hard.

So, what do you have to say, young man? How do you propose we treat this man? How do you propose we ensure that he doesn't die, eh? We don't even know who he is. If he dies, who do we tell? Where do we take him to be buried? Which graveyard, eh? Which one of the three imams will read his funeral prayers, eh? You know that they fight over the living *and* the dead, don't you? What do you say, Noor?

Noor trained his eyes upon one spot on the verandah floor. When he spoke, he chose his words carefully.

It is our duty to look after this man, Saheb, no matter who he is, for what if he is an innocent man, lost, looking for his way home, Saheb? We have to look after him, Saheb. I and my young cousin, Hassan Ali, we shall take full responsibility to ensure that he gets better and that we are able to take him to the DHQ hospital as soon as the road opens. I expect that it is a question of a few days before a narrow passage can be cleared from the debris of the landslide. If necessary, I will also join the men working on the road and help to clear a passage wide enough to let a jeep through.

Hassan dived through the opening in Noor's submission.

Yes, Saheb, we will promise to help you, Saheb, for we brought him here, Saheb, and I, I was the one who found him, isn't it, Brother Noor? I mean, we both brought him down, to your house, but I was the one who found him, and it is really my responsibility to see that he doesn't die on you, causing you any more trouble, Saheb. If you like – if it is all right with you, Saheb – I will keep coming here hour upon hour to keep an eye on him, to make sure that he drinks or eats, and says something, something to tell us who he is, where he is from, where he was going when that tree fell on him.

Hassan was flushed by the time he stopped his speech. His cheeks were aflame with excitement and the prospect of spending more time in Moosa Madad's house. Hassan was sure that the Peri he had seen in that small window was Sabiha, the girl he loved, the girl he would give his life for. He would do anything to save the life of that unknown, wounded man if it meant gaining the approval of the Numberdar of Saudukh Das.

Saheb, we must keep him here, and we are at your disposal at all times, Saheb. We will keep vigil, get more medicines, do whatever it takes to keep him alive until we can get help. Noor's measured words and tempered voice seemed to calm Moosa's fears, to restrain Hassan's youthful enthusiasm.

Of course, that is what we must do, keep him here, Moosa said. Have you ever heard of anyone throwing out someone who is sick or wounded, just because he did not belong here? What would Allah think of us if we did that? Would He forgive us? Could we forgive ourselves?

The Almighty presents to us opportunities to help our fellow brethren, Saheb, Noor said. Perhaps this is one such opportunity to please the Almighty by showing compassion and kindness. After all, Saheb, you are known in all the valleys for the justice with which you administer affairs for the people who come to you with their supplications. Perhaps this man is here for the very reason that your reputation for charity has spread far and wide, Saheb.

Noor smiled at his own exaggerated description of Moosa's largesse. The moment seemed to demand that the best, the most potent things be said, for rarely had the people of this tiny village faced such a perplexing situation.

Moosa also smiled. He looked up at Noor from beneath his shaggy eyebrows and narrowed his eyes, his mouth breaking into a wide grin.

Not exactly, young man! This man's being here, bleeding to death on the floor of my house, has little to do with my reputation, you know. It has everything to do with the fact that you and this eager young cousin of yours dragged him here on a wooden contraption tied with a piece of stolen rope! Moosa let out an explosive burst of air from his mouth, as if expelling all the thoughts of fear and failure now that he had the help of these two fine young men, so much like Akbar Ali and Asghar Ali, not as handsome, or accomplished, but fine men nevertheless.

Noor dropped his gaze and found that spot on the floor which commanded his attention when there was nothing sensible left to say. Hassan fidgeted with the label on the pocket of his kameez, wishing he had worn his new set of clothes, the one he had made for the last Eid, the pistachio green one. He was sure that if he could see Sabiha, then certainly, she could also see him. And here he was, wearing a shirt with a faded label he could barely read, having spent just a few years in school before his duty to tend to the livestock and the fields and the orchards took him away and made him forget the meaning of the shapes of the English letters embroidered onto his shirt pocket: DISCOQUEEN. He knew it was not his best shirt: a few faded stains and splotches showed here and there, defying his mother's devoted washing. What if Sabiha had seen him? What if she thought nothing of this shepherd with calloused hands and the faint smell of cow dung and goat droppings wafting up from his broken and mended shoes?

Moosa rose, his girth swaying, carrying the partridge with solemn dignity, as if it were a holy relic. He herded the torpid bird beneath a reed basket. Unwilling to make a pronouncement on how he would proceed with the new circumstances, Moosa looked up at the sky and peered at the sun casting a pale light over the courtyard. He stared at the sky as if the answer was writ in the heavens, along the horizon, in the nebulous space between the drifting clouds. Unable to see anything but a wide expanse of dull gold shot with streaks of sombre grey, he dropped his gaze and strode up to Lasnik, shook him by the shoulder and woke him from his morning nap.

Look after the bird, my son. From today, it is your responsibility to ensure that none of these vile creatures lurking around here in the middle of the night or day can attack this bird, you see. Do you understand? You will have to feed him, you know, provide him with clean water, and clean out the droppings from the cage. Do you understand, son?

Lasnik rose from the ground, leaning on his staff.

G-g-give me b-b-bird. I take home n-n-now. T-t-tie with rope. He n-n-no fly then. G-g-good rope g-g-good bird g-g-good Lasnik.

No, my son, no need to tie up the bird. It's the bloody murdering creatures which need to be tied up. And drowned in the river, you know.

Stepping towards Moosa, Lasnik undid the string that fastened his overcoat. The heavy coat flapped aside like a goat's flayed skin. Lasnik fumbled with his shirt, lifting up the many grimy folds to reveal the orange nylon rope he had wound around his middle.

R-r-rope for you. For to take w-w-wounded man to hospital. For you. To t-t-tie wounded man. Wounded man broken man. Lasnik p-p-pull, you – you – you push. To hospital t-t-together.

Moosa smiled. Patting Lasnik on his back, he led Noor and Hassan to the gate. Zarina watched the Numberdar of Saudukh Das taking charge of an unusual situation with his customary aplomb. She watched him ushering the men through the gate as if it was an ordinary day, not one with many unanswered questions muddying the waters of the jade river. Moosa turned back to the courtyard and nodded his head at Zarina, smiling despite the gravity of the situation. That was what she liked about him, that he was a true leader and took charge of whatever problems the villagers laid at his feet. He was a good man, despite his harshness towards his elder wives – but that was how it was in these parts: women were expendable and valued only for the services and the children they provided to their men. This was accepted as much as snowstorms in winter were expected; neither of these things were pleasant, but they were constant and unchanging, unquestioned.

Moosa beckoned Zarina towards the open gate, putting his hand on Lasnik's shoulder and gently turning the boy to face him.

Now remember your duties, young man! I expect you to fulfil your responsibilities with the same passion you show towards that precious rope of yours, you understand?

Whooping, ecstatic at his appointment as Bird-Keeper-at-the-Home-of-the-Numberdar, Lasnik raised his staff in the air and performed a dance in the middle of the courtyard, convulsing his body this way and that, pounding the ground with his good foot and his staff, bobbing his head up and down, grinning at his favourite aunt with teeth like the layered skin of a corncob.

Zarina watched this boy-man from the gate before stepping out into the lane and joining Noor and Hassan. Morning unfurled over the fields and the streams as it always did at this time of the year, in gentle waves, like the warm water of a spring seething from beneath the hardened ground.

# Turma-Hik

## 11.

The elders amongst us would gather around the Baltar Tree of the Boiber Valley and speak of the folly of the men and women of Zameen Par, arrogant in their belief that they could tame the wind and the water and the ways of our kind — we, who were here before them, we, the ones who will be here after them.

The elders would tell us about that time when we still had our streams and pastures, pure, protected from their need to devour everything that lived in the ground, on it, in the air, beneath it, in the water, above it. We had not known hunger then and had come to know that amongst the men and women of Zameen Par there was one who believed himself to be a Priest. It was this stupid man who had tasted the flesh of a young lamb fed on the clover of the eastern hills, where the setting globe of fire would warm the earth and coax the grass to clothe the ground so that the precious soil would stay warm, rooted to the place it was meant to be. This injudicious man, a leader of other senseless men, had become used to the tender flesh of young lambs, the progeny of Berugat, boasting the purest, softest, whitest fur amongst us. Each day as this man woke, his servants would send for the youngest of the children of Berugat until there were none left for Berugat to mourn. The elders told us that each time a child was taken away from Berugat, she would shed her fur in piles that collected in the gulleys and curves of the hillsides and appeared to be snow to the men and women of Zameen Par. Only we knew that the snow was her sorrow, the streams *flowing beneath the expanse of white actually her tears. Only we knew how she suffered, this patient beast Berugat, unable to stop her children from being slaughtered to satisfy the appetite of this man who professed to have abilities that other men and women did not.*

*It was when all her children had been devoured by this cruel and greedy man that Berugat wished upon him a fate worse than he could have ever imagined. It was during that night when the silver water of the river stopped flowing and instead ran backwards, flooding the valleys behind it, reaching up to the slopes and drowning the trees and the birds which sat upon them, that Berugat cried out for her lost children and cursed this man. She wished him a similar fate, that he should lose the thing that he loved most and that, in doing so, he should only know when it was too late.*

*The elders remember how Berugat wept, how the fur from her body crept up the slopes and formed glaciers, leaving her unprotected and naked, the wind eating into her wrinkled, withered body until there was nothing left except a pile of white ash from which rose a snake of smoke, rising, rising, to the silver sky, carrying a song of lament so long and so well remembered that the elders still sing it today. These men and women of Zameen Par think it is the wind howling, or perhaps it is a lost spirit, screaming to be united with its family, or perhaps it is Sinopish, the Spirit-Wolf calling out to its pack, but we know it is the dirge of Berugat, calling for her lost children.*

# Chapter Eleven

The gate shuddered as Moosa slammed the latch into place, bolting it. Across the courtyard, in the small, dank storeroom where the flanks of a slaughtered goat were strung from the low ceiling, Sabiha's eyes flew open. She gasped, unsure of where she was, the room still dark except for a patch of light falling from the window. A white mist curled out of her mouth. Unclenching her body from beneath the shielding warmth of a lumpy quilt, releasing her limbs into the frigid air, stumbling in the grey haze, her hands and feet unfeeling and icy, she crawled into the corner furthest from her brother's tin trunks and the piles of potatoes and turnips. Lowering her haunches onto the floor, she pulled down her shalwar and peed onto the floor, clenching her eyes shut at this degradation. Steam and a sour stench rose from the stream of urine between her feet. Sabiha shook her head in shame and disgust at what had come to pass. Like a cat, she shovelled stray bits of dried grass onto the source of her shame, looking away from the wet patch seeping slowly into the earthen floor of her prison, leaving a shadow shaped like a bird in flight.

Hoisting up her shalwar, she climbed onto the sacks beneath the window and perched on her knees, peering out. She could see the birdcage sitting on the cement platform near the gate. A fan of light fell upon the thin layer of ice floating inside a small bowl in a corner of the empty cage. Thirst scratched at her throat. Hunger gnawed at her gut, but she did not crave food. She stroked her neck the way that a hunter feels for the

112

carotid artery of his prey. She could hear her father's voice, soft, muted. He faced the orchard, his back to the window where Sabiha stood, watching him. Moosa called out to Mariam. Her father's youngest wife walked through the orchard like a deer, measured steps dancing on the raised path between the fruit trees. Sabiha gripped the bars of the window with both hands. The blood in her fingers froze. She watched her father as he put his hand on Mariam's back, helping her step over the low wall separating the orchard from the court-yard. Mariam stood next to Moosa for a brief moment, speaking in a soft murmur, her head lowered. Moosa nodded, then patted her shoulder, took her by the elbow and led her into the baiypash. Sabiha watched her father and his wife disappear from the line of sight. Sabiha turned to the cage; it was empty. The sliver of ice floating on the water in the tin cup was gone, melted in the morning sun.

Moosa Madad knelt beside the wounded man. He placed a finger beneath the man's nose and felt for breath. The stranger's face was ashen, his cheeks sucked inwards, lips dark, parted, cracked, dried blood congealed on the edge of his mouth. A thick, dark moustache curved over his mouth and merged with his beard, thick, dark, as was his hair, silver streaking it in patches like waves of moonlight on the river. He wore no cap, no scarf, no jacket, despite the cold weather. His shoes, made of artificial leather, scuffed, of an uncertain, liverish colour, had been removed the night he had been brought into the Numberdar's house. Moosa asked Khadijah where she had put the shoes. Khadijah nodded her head towards the corner of the room where Fatimah sat, staring at Mariam's delicate movements as she prepared their husband's breakfast.

Bring the shoes to me. I need to keep them ready, in case we can manage to take him to the hospital, you know.

Khadijah hobbled across the baiypash towards Fatimah. Leaning down, she whispered, her voice raspy.

Sister, he wants that man's shoes. Do you know where they are?

Fatimah stirred. She looked away from Khadijah, towards the dark corner where a heap of firewood lay stacked against the wall. She got up, her movements heavy, awkward, a cow struggling through a bog. Picking up a pair of battered shoes, she turned towards Moosa.

You seem to care more for this stranger and his shoes than for your own daughter, Fatimah said. She held the shoes in her hands as if they were clumps of sodden earth she had dug out from a field.

Moosa looked up and fixed his gaze upon his second wife's flaccid face.

This man, he is bleeding to death, you know. I have more important things on my mind than what I have to do about that wretched girl, your daughter.

Fatimah dropped the shoes at Moosa's feet. A musty, sour smell of something rancid rose from the ground.

You had better watch it, woman. Your insolence is not acceptable, you know. You'd better be careful, otherwise you will find yourself locked up in that storeroom just like your daughter. I don't have the patience for all this fuss, you know. There are bigger things on my mind, so don't bother me with stories about your daughter, all right? I know what I have to do with that girl, and don't you dare interfere in my decisions.

Mariam set down a tray of tea and a plate of pancakes before Moosa. He tore at the pancake with one hand, picked up the cup of tea with the other. He ate and drank as if it was just another day. Fatimah did not move. She watched Moosa as he broke off pieces of the pancake and crammed them into his large mouth, chewing, swallowing, slurping his tea in great gulps.

What about the girl? Your daughter – how long do you intend to keep her locked up in the store, without food or water?

Moosa lowered the cup from his mouth; a drop of tea hung from the edge of his moustache. He wiped his lips, burped, rubbed his sleeve across his mouth and swallowed the remains of the pancake.

Let her have a meal, then, if that is what you are saying, woman. But as for letting her out of that room – not over my dead body! Not until I find out who is this infernal bastard of a man who dares to write love poems to my daughter! Do you understand that, Fatimah? Do you even realise how serious this bloody nonsense is, graver than this business of this man lying here, without a name?

Fatimah looked at the stranger and then at her husband. She walked towards the door, stopping to look over her shoulder. She spoke clearly, her words unrushed.

She is your daughter, your own flesh and blood. She does not deserve this, Moosa. What is her fault if someone finds her beautiful? What is the fault of the moon if it is full and fair? Throwing stones at it will not hurt it. Locking up your daughter may hurt her today, but it shall hurt you for the rest of your days, Moosa, for she is your own flesh and blood, the last of your daughters. Had her brothers been alive today, you would have never done this under your roof.

Moosa jerked his head towards the door. He had never heard Fatimah talk like this. He tried to say something, but she was gone.

A gasp, then a deep moan of pain escaped the wounded man's mouth. His body jerked involuntarily. He spoke a few words, as if he was calling out to someone. A single word, a woman's name perhaps, a term of endearment. Moosa strode to the man's side and leaned over him. His pendulous belly swung over the man's broken shoulder. Bits of pancake flew out of his mouth as he asked the man, again and again:

What is it, what do you want, what are you saying, man? Speak to me! Who are you, where are you from, eh, what is your name?

The wounded man stared at Moosa, his mouth opening and closing like a fledgling bird seeking to be fed. Moosa shook the man from the shoulder. The man screamed, a long, drawn-out shriek, piercing Moosa's ears. Khadijah shuddered. She pressed her hands on the sides of her head, bent low over the hearth and rocked on the balls of her feet. Mariam's hands trembled as she gathered Moosa's empty plate and teacup, dropping both onto the stainless-steel tray. Snapping his head in Mariam's direction, Moosa raged:

Stop it, woman! Can you stop making so much noise? Can't you see I am trying to get some answers from this man here? Must you make that infernal clattering just as he was about to tell me his name? Must you?

Mariam held her arm to her face and sobbed. She ran out of the baiypash. Khadijah picked up the tray and watched Moosa. Dropping onto his haunches, Moosa looked away, exhaling, shaking his head. He clicked his tongue against his teeth. The wounded man shut his eyes. Silence settled in the room like ash in an unlit hearth.

In the new room, built in the summer by Moosa for his youngest wife, the air was always cold; cool in the summer but cold, icy, in winter. Wide windows looked out at the mountains on the far side. Curtains with a floral pattern against a yellow background fluttered, billowing in the breeze from the orchard. Mariam sat on the bed Moosa had bought when she had married

116

him, sobbing, her body racking. What had she done? How could she undo the damage that she had done to her friend, lovely Sabiha, just a year or two younger than herself? Could she have refused to read that ridiculous poem held out under her nose by Moosa Madad? Could she have made up something else, just in order to protect Sabiha? What had she done?

The breeze blew open a window and knocked down the glass Mariam had filled with the last of the wild flowers from Moosa's garden. Now she watched as the water dripped onto the brand-new carpet, red with a yellow zig-zag pattern cutting across it. The flowers had fallen onto the windowsill. Mariam got up and gathered the flowers. She stepped out of the room and dropped them into the tin can sitting outside the latrine. Then she wiped her face with the edge of her shawl and went back into the room, shutting the door behind her.

# Turma-Altó

## 12.

*Sometimes, Yakh-Sherlim said, the very thing which protects us is the thing which destroys us. Remember this, she said, and we had listened as she spoke about sadness so deep that her blood had become heavy and thick, making dark marks where there was once only the purest white fur, now spotted with circles that drew her fate around her like the eye of a target. This was not the way it was in Another Time, she said. We were not marked by these dark circles, we were one with the snow, for there was no sun, no disc of fire in the Yalmik Sky, nothing that could melt the boundless white expanse that stretched across the black mountains. And then, the fire descended from the emptiness above, and while it was good to receive its welcome warmth, it was the end of our world as we had known it, for now the snow melted, revealing the black rock upon which we had lived and hunted and slept. We could no longer hide amongst the black cliffs and the black crags, for we were white like the snow which was leaving us as quickly as the time it took to leap from the precipice to the saddle of that far mountain. That is when our blood began to turn black, and the circles you see now are just the marks of that blood, meant to protect us, make us less visible. But that did not last long, for as the fire from the Yalmik Sky burned across the world, so did the fire in the heart of men whose bellies were always empty, who always wanted more. There were more of them now, and fewer of us. As they moved towards our homes, we searched for new hiding places, moving higher and higher into the crags and the gulleys. They took away the hunt we preyed upon, taking these for their snivelling children, always hungry, always wanting more, leaving our own bellies empty. So, when we, crazed with hunger, took the sheep they imprisoned in their corrals, they came after us and flung their stone-tipped spears at us, piercing our skins where the circles had marked us, to protect us. Now, those circles were the very place where the force from their weapons wounded us, bleeding us.*

*It is not as if they wanted us for our flesh. They told each other they hunt us to protect the prisoners in their stone corrals. But it is not so, for what is the worth of a creature if it is robbed of its freedom? And do we not know that they keep these creatures imprisoned so that they can consume the flesh, use the hide and the feet and the head, devouring even the eyes, the tongue, the liver, the kidneys, the heart, every part of the creature that once lived in the wild, the progeny of Tish-Hagur and Mahabakara, the Great Spiral-Horned Goat? What is its life worth if the value of the creature is only in its parts once it is dead?*

*They say they do not kill us for our flesh, for it is forbidden to these men to eat beasts with paws or claws or hooves not cloven. We say to them, then let us give our paws to the creatures you corral, let them live, let them breathe air that is not contaminated with their own filth. But these men, they are deaf and also blind, for when they say they do not kill us for our flesh, they kill us anyway, ripping off our coats of fur to warm their hairless bodies, cutting off our paws to suspend from the doorways of their homes to ward off the evil that actually lives in their own hearts, crushing our bones to strengthen their own. So how are we to trust them when they say they will leave us alone, if only they are paid for every sheep that we take to quell our hunger? How will the ones who pay them know how many we have taken? We know that these men do not always speak the truth, they will say things just to appear brave, or rich, or poor. They will say things to fool others, liars themselves. They will tell the men to whom they sell our skins that this is the one who killed one hundred sheep in one night, and I, with my keen eye and steady arm, I lanced the beast right through the circle in the centre of its neck, drawn right at the place where its life-blood pulses from its heart, a circle which marks it for the death it deserves, this killer of a hundred sheep.*

*Yakh-Sherlim spoke with sadness. Her eyes were dark pools, the golden light held within dull, dying. We heard her and we turned away, for what else were we to do, now that the marks which were to protect us were the very same that marked us for ruin?*

# Chapter Twelve

When he was born, Lasnik did not cry. Instead, he looked at his mother and held his mouth open, spittle the colour of sour milk drooling out of his mouth, as if he had already drunk from her swollen breasts. His mother cleaned him, nursed him, comforted him when his belly swelled or his airways constricted with the smoke from her spluttering hearth. And now, even though he was older, she would watch over him while he bathed, for Lasnik would sometimes forget to remove his clothes before pouring water over himself. He would wash his face but forget to use the soap. At times Lasnik would spend an hour brushing his teeth; sometimes it seemed as if half a day had passed before he gargled his mouth and put away the worn toothbrush, hanging it amongst the other things he claimed for himself: a fused lightbulb, a clutch of chicken feathers, and an empty tin can with a picture of ripe tomatoes plastered on its side.

Lasnik had not even cried when news of his father's martyrdom reached his mother, Sakina, a sickly woman made sicker with grief and the incurable malady of widowhood. Now, Lasnik was a grown man, and he was not expected to cry, even when he felt like it, when things overwhelmed him, like the time when his baby goat died, or the many times his rope was stolen by men who thought they had better use for it. Lasnik was growing to be a man and his feelings were like those of other grown men. He, too, yearned for a woman's soft embrace, for a caress of her fingers against his cheeks.

He dreamt of what Zainab's breasts looked like when she was naked. He felt a swelling in his groin every time he made out the shape of a young girl's bottom. But no one considered that soon it would be time for Lasnik to settle down, marry, have a family. No one thought that Lasnik was capable of any of this. All that was known about him was the fact he had been claimed, even before his birth, by the Periting; he was the rope they had stretched from Zameen Upar to Zameen Par, bridging the Winter River, bringing news of tomorrow to that land of a hundred sorrows.

So, even if Lasnik was almost a grown man, and did not cry, no one thought much of his dreams and his desires. For who believed in Periting in this day and age? Who feared their powers, the mischief they wrought, driving men mad with longing, driving women to despair? Who could imagine that the man inside the boy, the boy inside the heavy woollen overcoat, would know, before all the able men and women in Saudukh Das, of the deaths about to occur in this small village at the edge of the Winter River, huddled beneath an endless, an endlessly indifferent sky?

The river in the first days of winter was calm, a snake fed on a fat animal. The women of Saudukh Das knew that soon the water would be icy, so cold that steam would rise from its surface in the early hours of the day. Today, the sun, promising warmth and renewal, crept through the thick layer of clouds that had laid themselves out over the mountains like a woollen cloak. Women and girls had gathered at the edge of the river, dumping bundles of washing onto the yellowing grass. The afternoon had beckoned to them with its golden light and fragrance of juniper. Now the women filled the air with the scent of their own longing and unspoken desire.

On the nearby slope stood two tall poplar trees, their trunks straight and firm, soaring into the sky. Between the two trees Lasnik had strung the orange nylon rope, stretched tight and buzzing in the gentle breeze like a string on an old wooden rubaab. Leaning against one of the trees, Lasnik looked out towards the river, his eyes hooded with deep thought and the wisdom of one who had been taught well by the English Madam, teaching the women to make porridge out of barley for the babies, telling the children to wash their hands before they ate, and asking the men to treat their women like equals and not like cattle.

This last bit of learning was hard for Lasnik to understand, for the cow tethered in the shed beside his one-roomed house was as precious as his mother. Of course, he loved the goat even more, for it was this creature that nudged him awake when he fell asleep while on duty guarding the rope. It was the goat who nuzzled him when he was cold and wet, caught in the rain or unable to get to the latrine in time. It was that magnificent animal with the tuft of white on her tail and a patch of black between her eyes who spoke to him of things no one else would, telling him of things that were yet to occur. The love Lasnik received from that animal was the same as the love his mother showered upon him. So obviously a woman and a cow or a goat were the same, so why should the English Madam insist that it was any other way?

Lasnik had followed the English Madam around like a duckling, shifting his weight from one foot to another with great care, rolling on steady ground, stiff and unbending on uneven patches, flailing his cane at anyone who dared to ask him to scram. The English Madam had noticed Lasnik early on. She had asked this strange boy his name in the few words she had learnt of his language. He had stared at her, gawping, a finger stuffed into the side of his mouth. The English Madam was a patient woman, one who loved all suffering people.

Arms outstretched, intending to embrace this wretch with the feathers and flowers and bits of coloured tinsel stuck in the fold of his cap, she stepped towards him. Lasnik stood rooted to the spot, and as soon as the English Madam put her arms around his shoulders, daring not to breathe in his stale odour, he yelped like a frightened pup and howled at the top of his grating voice. English Madam's arms lifted as if by some hydraulic magic. She stared with wide, uncomprehending eyes at this weeping boy, a strange combination of child and man, human and animal, clearly one who was in need of love and guidance.

She had laughed at herself later, in the privacy of her room at the government rest house set in a lush meadow dotted with yellow flowers, a small stream rushing past her window, stirring memories of the tidy stone and thatch cottage left behind years ago, chintz curtains fluttering in the blissful, tranquil air of the English countryside. Working with fervour and a missionary sincerity, she assisted ordinary people in ordinary villages living lives that were extraordinary. English Madam would smile at these simple people with beneficence, the lines running from the corner of her eyes and furrowed across her forehead telling a story of earnest compassion blended with consternation and even discomfiture each time she came across the things that indicated to her a kind of malaise that none of her modern ideas could heal or help. She had been mortified to learn of the number of women who died in the process of childbirth and distraught to see the many graves of infants who didn't live to see out a full year of their short lives. English Madam learnt to smile through the long hours of uncomfortable squatting on the rough floors of the poorer homes in the villages, patiently explaining to the women that they must provide good nutrition to their children so that they could grow to be healthy adults. She smiled when an unwashed and malnourished child chose to climb into her lap and play with the silver cross beating against the wrinkled, sunburnt skin between her pendulous breasts. She did not seem to mind that the child's fingers were grimy and sticky, its clothes filthy and torn, darned here and there with mismatched scraps of fabric, flies buzzing around a runny nose. English Madam would coo like a pigeon nesting in spring and comfort those children who wailed endlessly with pain or hunger while their mothers attended to the endless chores of raising large families and caring for a deaf father-in-law or a disagreeable mother-in-law. She would croon lullabies, *hush-a-bye-baby-on-a-tree-top*, and purse her lips, making gurgling sounds while tickling distended bellies, the cracks above her upper lip tiny rivulets fanning outwards, away from the dip between her nondescript, commoner's nose, and thin, bloodless lips. And when she turned to the window, watching the mothers gather the piles of washing or sunning a soiled blanket, the blonde hairs of her moustache would seem to glow in the afternoon sun like living things reaching for the warmth of the light.

English Madam knew that the key to a better life lay in making the village women understand that if they used modern technology that would leave much more time on their hands for them to embroider caps and handbags and even warm, furry bedroom slippers which could then be sold for a handsome amount, earning them a decent income, enabling them to buy soap and shampoo, picture books for their children, little plastic containers for tea and salt, and fresh vegetables and even fruit which did not grow in the orchards of Saudukh Das. She had hoped that the increase in income would help the women to improve their diet, their sense of hygiene, in short, their standard of living. And towards this end she had started with teaching the women to hang their washing on the orange nylon rope now strung between the two poplar trees at the edge of the river where the women had gathered to wash bundles of dirty clothing, quilt covers, shawls, sheets, and even the small squares of embroidered cotton within which they folded fading photographs of those who were long gone: girls married off to men in distant villages, boys working in towns they would never see, or men killed in faraway battle-fields the names of which were better unremembered.

And now, Lasnik watched over English Madam's rope, for it was a precious addition to the many schemes that would bring prosperity to the region, and it had been stolen on countless occasions, once by the old man who needed it to fish his goat out of the ditch into which it had fallen, another time by the village imam who needed to hoist his new dish antenna onto his roof in the middle of the night, a clandestine operation destined to go wrong when the circular dish the size of a large cauldron slipped from its knot and fell, clattering against the stone wall, causing even the dead to stir. Another time the Numberdar had stolen it to pull out the tractor he had borrowed which had slipped into the water channel and got stuck between the rocks directing the water from the Chartoi into the fields.

English Madam had been outraged at such irresponsible, uncivil behaviour. She had walked into the Assistant Commissioner's office to complain about the reprehensible acts of thievery, about the insensitivity of the men of Saudukh Das who could not see that the women needed the rope for their washing, for the general betterment of the community. The Assistant Commissioner, a local man from an adjoining valley, took a while to understand the issue, trying to make sense of the fuss being made over an ordinary piece of nylon cord. He had summoned Moosa Madad, the village headman, and asked him to offer his profound insight into a problem for which there seemed to be no immediate resolution.

It was Moosa Madad who had suggested to the Assistant Commissioner that someone be put in charge of the rope so that any vagrant walking past would not be tempted to steal it again. But who would give so much time to the safekeeping of a mere rope? Who would be able to put away their daily tasks of grazing the animals, collecting firewood, irrigating the fields, harvesting the crops, repairing the water channels and all the other work that was necessary to ensure that crops would grow and children would be fed and that life would go on? Was there such a person in all of Saudukh Das, indeed, in the long and expansive valley that stretched before them like a call echoed again and again in some deep ravine?

Once again it was Moosa Madad, a man with ideas and solutions to every problem, who had come up with the suggestion that Lasnik be given the task of guarding the rope, for whatever it was worth. If nothing else, it would make English Madam happy, which would mean she would stop pestering the Assistant Commissioner who had other things on his mind now that the roads were being widened for sixteen-wheelers bringing grain from the south and carting away potatoes from the north. They said that this road would open up trade with the neighbouring country, a giant flexing its muscles on the world's arena. Such trade would provide many opportunities for the young men in these valleys. They would find jobs in the many posts needed to build such a road, they would set up shop to serve the workers and the supervisors, they would earn a decent wage and feed their children and marry good women, bury their parents with the ceremony the old folk deserved. There would be so many choices for the young men of these valleys, forced now to join the army, every year seeing more flags erected on fresh graves of martyrs killed in wars, the intent of which eluded widows and orphans alike.

Such a solution would give the useless boy, the unfortunate son of a shaheed, something to do instead of getting into trouble time and time again. And so it was that the young Assistant Commissioner, with a smattering of what passed as English, and the Numberdar of Saudukh Das, with a smattering of what passed as good sense, jointly resolved a problem, and things fell back into place as if nothing had happened, despite the English Madam's earnest endeavour to do exactly the opposite, change the way things were done, had been done for centuries, and would probably be done in exactly the same way, despite the sharing of modern knowledge, despite the depth of affection and concern stored in her generous heart shaped like a vessel for the drinking of mulberry wine in times long forgotten.

Victorious in her defeat, English Madam had gone back to her small room at the ramshackle government rest house set in a wide meadow and cut through with a narrow, rushing stream. In the morning, shortly after the sun had risen on that fateful day, English Madam must have gone out to the stream to do her washing. A pile of her heavy, dark clothes, unimaginative and dreary, three pairs of socks, a pair of nylon stockings, snagged at the heels by parched and cracked skin, a garter, and a sagging brassiere, beige, cotton, unpadded, unembellished by roses and lace, were found heaped along the edge of the stream. There was no sign of English Madam herself, until late that night when news reached the Assistant Commissioner's office that the body of a foreign woman had been found where the rivulet met the Winter River. There were no signs of violence on her body, but her skin had turned blue from being in the water for many hours. How she could have slipped into the rivulet when she was so careful with everything she did, and why no one saw her falling, or why she did not cry out for help, or how she could have drowned in such shallow, temperate water – these were questions that were asked but not answered, the answers already known to every man and woman in the valley. English Madam had tried to change things in this place, she had tried to alter the order of the universe, and she had thus to be removed, defeated in her doubtful victory.

Zarina carried her bundle of washing carefully, stepping over the depressions carved into the black rock by water and wind, cups filled with snow, now melted in the triumphal glory of the morning sun. She knew that it would be more and more difficult for her to provide clean uniforms for the children as winter descended in the valley, bringing dark days and darker nights. Sometimes the clothing she left out to dry would freeze, and she would have to spread out the stiff trousers and shirts and shawls beside the bukhari, watching the water evaporate into a ghostly tail spiralling through the skylight.

Amongst the women at the edge of the river Zarina sought out the one who sat listless beside a pile of dirty clothing. It was Kulsoom, unheeding of the chatter and exchange of gossip that filled the air with thin voices and quick, unabashed laughter. She did not move when Zarina placed a gentle hand on her shoulder. Zarina lowered herself onto a grassy patch and sat beside Kulsoom, studying the odd bits of clothing mounded into a heap beside her. They were mostly girls' clothes, worn out, frayed, with missing buttons and patches where they had been darned and repaired. There was a faded pair of men's trousers, the pockets turned inside out, and a grimy vest with several holes in it. Kulsoom held a bar of soap in her hand, but she sat still, her rust-coloured eyes faded like the worn cuffs of a shirt. Zarina turned Kulsoom towards her, drew her close and looked into her eyes. She spoke to Kulsoom as one would address a child hesitating to cross a water channel:

Come, let me help you wash the clothes. You are very near your time. Allah knows you should not have to do all this heavy work now. Come, let us wash these clothes together.

Kulsoom dropped her gaze and stared at her belly: a taut, round dome protruding from beneath the frayed and darned sweater she wore, several sizes too small for her. The sweater had rolled up halfway over her midriff. She dug beneath the sweater and brought out a plastic wallet tucked into her vest. Opening the wallet, she pulled out various scraps of paper, some folded so many times and for so long that the creased edges had split the paper into small fragments. Kulsoom shoved the splintered scraps back into the wallet. Her fingers shook as she picked out a small rectangular piece of paper, marked with dark shadows and undefined shapes, splotches of ink bleeding into the surface. The paper slipped from her hands. Zarina picked it up and smoothed it out on her bent knee. Kulsoom looked over her shoulder at the huddled, chattering women behind her. She spoke in a whisper:

It is the result of the test you asked me to get from the DHQ hospital. I went last week, telling the girls' father I needed to pick up medicine for his mother and his bottle of cough syrup. Look at it. Tell me what you can see, sister.

Zarina held the piece of paper towards the sunlight. It was an image from an ultrasound. The clear white tracks of a baby's spine were visible. A foot was wedged at the grey curve of Kulsoom's womb. A thin sliver of white, bent at the knee, was the baby's leg. At six months, the hand of the unborn child was perfectly formed. The fingers were delicate, curled into a fist, the baby's arm drawn up over its head. A dark mass of amniotic fluid surrounded Kulsoom's unborn child. Zarina returned the paper to Kulsoom, uncertain of what she should say, what it was that Kulsoom wanted to hear.

It is a healthy baby, Kulsoom. You have another three

months to go before the birth, if the baby is going to come on time. Otherwise, like with your third daughter, the baby may just come earlier, and then you know how hard it is on you and the infant, small and weak and hardly able to suckle. You must look after yourself, dear sister, if you want to have a healthy baby.

Zarina reached out to touch Kulsoom's arm, drawing her closer. Kulsoom looked away. She sighed and then passed a hand over her forehead.

It is a girl, isn't it? Another girl. He said he would kill me if I brought him another girl, Kulsoom whispered. What will I do?

Zarina shook her head, clicking her tongue against the roof of her mouth.

You know how he is, your husband. He's just a bully. He's not even capable of standing straight without his dose of cough syrup, so how do you think he can harm you, dear sister?

Kulsoom turned to face Zarina. Her words were cold, distant.

He said he will kill me, dear sister. But he doesn't know that I am already dying, with each insult, each time he hits my head against the wall. How does one kill something that is already dead?

Zarina clutched Kulsoom's arm and pulled her up as she herself struggled to rise from the uneven ground, soaked with the night's rain and melted snow. Zarina gathered the bits and pieces of scattered clothing into a bundle, took Kulsoom's hand and led her to the edge of the river. She avoided looking at her friend's eyes. There was a hollowness inside them she had not seen before. It was like looking into the eyes of an animal tethered to a wooden stake before it was slaughtered. Zarina shook out the bundle of dirty clothes onto the bank of the river. She turned away from Kulsoom's hunched form and reached for the bar of soap, scrubbing the torn, tattered clothes.

Zarina did not look up at Kulsoom until all the clothes had been scrubbed, rinsed and wrung out, spread on the sun-warmed rocks alongside the cluster of trees where Lasnik and his goat kept watch over the orange nylon rope strung between two stately poplars like an idea whose time had come and gone without much consequence.

Clouds had gathered now; shafts of sunlight filtered through the soft haze as the day progressed towards dusk. The women at the river had gone home. By the time Zarina and Kulsoom finished spreading out the washing on the rocks and bushes and wooden fences tied together with scraps of fabric and bits of cord, Lasnik had fallen asleep. The goat with the tufted tail and black patch on her head nibbled at the dried flowers in his ragged woollen cap. Lasnik's staff stood against a poplar tree, a lone sentry at this place near the edge of the village, the river flowing between fertile fields on one side and, on the other, a barren stretch of land where nothing except stones and scree seemed to grow.

In the distance, where the river divided itself and surged at the contours of a granite island, enormous stone pillars forming a circle upon that island shimmered in the magical haze, silver stele shining in the gilded light of morning. A solitary clutch of brambles tumbled within the circle of pillars, repeating its journey like a dog chasing its own tail. Kulsoom stared at the tangle of thorny growth torn away from its roots, searching ceaselessly for something it had lost, something it could never find despite its unbroken turning, its unending quest.

# Turma-Iskí

## 13.

When the Spirit of Death, Aakhir, called us, we went to her willingly, for we knew that this was how it was meant to be. We had been told by Tish-Hagur, and by Yakh-Sherlim, as much as by our mother Taghralim, and by Sinopish, the mother of the golden-eyed wolf who stood watch over the hapless man, caught between wanting to live and wanting to die, both equally desirable for one such as him, neither in this world, nor in the next. We went willingly for we knew that our time here was not for ever, that we must make way for the younger ones, we must leave the pastures rich and fertile, we must nurture the seeds that grow beneath the shade of the Juniper and Walnut and Deodar trees, we must resist the red and black berries which grow in abundance, eating only enough to let us fly, or run, galloping on leopard's paws even if the horns on our heads were those of a goat. We had learnt that if we ate more than our needs, we would be sick, and the ones after us would be hungry, and no one would benefit from the orgy of greed which now visits our forests and the air where birds quiver in fear. We had watched how the forests had been destroyed, the trees hacked down, their skin peeled back to uncover the sap inside. We had watched as the fish had floundered in shallow waters, breathing mud into the delicate mesh of their lungs, defeated by the thick slime excreted into the water by those who live in Zameen Par, unheeding of the harm their every act of survival exacts on our world.

*When the Spirit of Death calls us, we raise our heads to the Yalmik Sky and seek out Nihibur, thanking him for bringing warmth from the disc held on his right hand and light from the sickle carried in his right. We know we are here only for a short time, the time it takes for a seed of barley to be buried in the rich black earth of our home. We know that, much like the seed of barley, we shall be reborn, in other forms, other shapes, with the webbed feet of the white-headed duck, with the pod of precious perfume found in the glands of the white-bellied musk deer, with the flared horns of the markhor, the grey fur of the woolly squirrel, soft and thick and comforting.*

# Chapter Thirteen

It doesn't look good, brother, Ibrahim said to his bunkmate, Zaki. They stood at the entrance of their igloo-shaped bunker. The sky was dark, a heavy, unmoving curtain. Clouds floated rapidly across the crescent moon, disappearing, then reappearing. Snow fell in sheets, covering the grey crags and softening the sharp spears of the pinnacles climbing out of the black rock, reducing visibility to a few feet. The danger of venturing too close to the edge of the furthest post in this battlefield kept the two men inside the bunker, perched on the narrow ledge protruding from the rock like a tongue. An overhang arced over half the length of the ledge. On sunny days, the snow blanketing the overhang softened, then froze at sunset, forming slender columns of ice suspended above the igloo, reflecting the last rays of the setting sun.

The two soldiers ate an early supper, not looking at each other, nor speaking. This was unusual for Zaki, always full of jokes, taking even the most serious of circumstances with a bucket of salt. Zaki bounced the heel of his foot against the frozen floor, his knee bobbing up and down. Ibrahim glanced at him, surprised at his mate's uneasy silence.

What is it, man? What troubles you? Ibrahim asked, afraid to give the question a shape.

Zaki looked up. His eyes were not brown and not green, something in between, and they always shone, like his gleaming teeth. But now they were dull pools of dread. He stared at

Ibrahim for a brief moment, then broke into a smile, pushing his enamel plate aside and making it clatter against his mug.

Nothing, my friend, nothing is wrong. What could be wrong, eh? At this ridiculous altitude, no one around for miles? What if the storm destroys our camp, this little shelter that has saved us from freezing to death, eh? What if we lose touch with base camp? How will we get down, a million miles away from this accursed, frozen hell?

Ibrahim turned away from Zaki. He had not heard his mate speak like this since arriving at this camp, some twenty-one thousand feet above sea level. It was disconcerting to hear this otherwise pleasant man ask questions that had lived in his own heart like a festering canker. Indeed, what would happen, what would happen if the storm took away the fragile skin they had called home for six weeks?

A pile of thick waterproof sheets sat on the floor of the igloo. The men would secure these around the bunker before the storm. Zaki got up and carried two empty cardboard cartons from the corner to his bed. With a knife, he cut open the flaps and straightened the cartons out into flat sheets. These he draped over his bed, leaving the flaps hanging over the edges. Ibrahim snorted, easing the disquiet that had settled onto the men.

What are you trying to do, my friend? Make a parcel out of your bed, hoping that I will pack you in it and send you down the slope to your village on the other side of the River Jhelum?

It's going to be a cold night, partner. I may as well add an extra layer of protection from the frostbite which is going to eat away at my toes, Zaki replied. He bent down to tuck the cardboard flaps beneath four metal jerry cans filled with fuel.

I'll help you secure the waterproof sheets around the igloo once I'm done with this, he said. You know, my wife-to-be will have a hard time figuring out what happened to me if she sees me without toes, or even without—

Zaki pointed to his groin, and grinned.

How am I going to tell her that she married half a man, eh, Haveldar Saheb? Or should I make her wait until all the things that rotted and fell off in this godforsaken hellhole grow back, eh?

Ibrahim shook his head, gathered the scraps left over from the meal and pushed aside his gloves and a box of cigarettes to the corner of the makeshift table holding the Petromax stove. He left the igloo, leaving Zaki to fuss around his sleeping arangements for the long night ahead. Outside, the dogs waited to be fed. Ibrahim led them into their shelter, a broad crevice in the wall of the mountain where the drums of kerosene oil and rations were stored. A corrugated metal sheet covered the supplies and protected the dogs from the cold. Ibrahim spread the scraps onto flattened sheets of cardboard that had once carried tinned food. The dogs sniffed the scraps but didn't eat, tilting their heads to one side, their eyes burning coal. Ibrahim did not stop to cajole the dogs, encouraging them to eat. There wasn't enough time; things had to be taken care of. He would worry about the dogs' curious behaviour later, when everything that needed to be done to guard against calamity had been accomplished.

He turned to leave. Malika, the grey-gold female, followed him, whimpering, pawing at the cardboard covering on the floor. What did this mean – was the dog in pain, had she hurt herself? Malika turned towards the other two dogs and rubbed her snout against their muzzles, her eyes bright and tail still. She stared at Ibrahim and bobbed her head up and down, whining. Ibrahim bent down and looked into her eyes. She gazed at him, unblinking. Spirals of white breath rose from her mouth, thawing the frost on Ibrahim's moustache. He could see himself reflected in the translucent pool of her eyes, a tiny image of himself receding far, far away, disappearing from the cocoon of her pupils.

Malika's eyes clouded over. She blinked. Ibrahim rose. Both of them knew something was coming. And when it came, it would take with it everything that stood in its path, the verdant expanse of forest where creatures made their homes, the golden marmot and the stone marten, the snow leopard and the lynx, the red fox with a white cross straddling its long back, sturdy on its large, black paws, always hungry, always watchful. Whatever was coming would take away the wolf and the musk deer, the ibex and markhor, leaving the golden eagle to fly higher than the silver dome of the sky, the rainbow-hued monal its only companion in that domain of permanent silence. Whatever was coming would darken the jade water of the rivers below the forest, it would sweep away the rich soil of the fields, tearing at the roots of the spruce and the pine, the birch and the willow, stripping the life out of ancient junipers. Nothing could stand in the path of this force, nothing would live through the fury of this thing that now waited silent, patient.

Ibrahim covered the crevice with the corrugated metal sheet and stood outside, several paces from the bunker where he could make out the light from the Petromax stove. Before him, the saddle stretching between two massive mountains curved and dipped like a woman's body. He thought of Zarina and saw her against the gold of the corn fields, her mouth parted, one front tooth overlapping the other the way a bird's wing folds over another. Malika nuzzled him, her snout warm against his freezing hand. He looked at her, then at the shadow behind them. Together they would brave whatever it was that was descending from the top of the mountain, its jagged, white peak obscured by the procession of swiftly moving clouds.

Ibrahim knew the gathering storm meant heavy snow on the further peaks, burdening the massive glaciers with more weight than they wished to carry. He knew the glacier on the slope above them was inching towards them, gathering speed as it broke apart from its own body. He could hear that fractured mass moving, a low rumble against the scree and slate. He must help Zaki with the waterproof covering for the igloo, before it was too late.

Ibrahim moved towards the igloo, keeping his head low, sheltering himself from the frigid wind passing beneath the overhang, a low moan rising around him. Malika whined, then barked. Ibrahim stopped. The dog ran towards the crevice, throwing up soft snow swirling in the quickening gusts of wind. She pawed the metal sheet protecting the entrance to the narrow fissure. Ibrahim shook his head and ran towards her. The wind picked up, slapping the hard surface of the ground. Freezing air punched him in the ribs. He bent double against the force of a mounting gale, struggling to see through the frenzied spray of snow pelting his bare face. His foot struck against a protrusion. He stumbled, falling headlong and plummeting down the frozen tongue of the ledge, nothing to break the momentum of his dangerous slide. In the rapid whir of his descent, he saw a black spur curling out of the snow like a hook. Ibrahim hurled his leg out towards the protrusion and his boot struck the spur. The impact swung Ibrahim around. He grabbed the spur with both hands and held on. Snow was falling rapidly now; flurries spat at and stung his face. Ibrahim clenched his eyes tight, took a deep breath and opened his eyes. He could make out the edge of the outlier. He was less than a few paces away from the curved rim of the black tongue; below him, the fall was over a thousand feet.

Turning towards the bluff, Ibrahim scrambled away from the lip of the scarp. He made his way to the fissure carved into the bluff, shielding his eyes from the pelting snow. He could hear Malika barking, her paws pounding against the metal sheet. What they had been waiting for had come. He must let the dogs out. Ibrahim grabbed the metal sheet covering the crevice, holding it against the force of the gale, trying to shift it away from the entrance to the cave. A violent blast of wind snatched the sheet out of his reach, and Ibrahim watched as it crashed against the black rock and slid onto the ledge. The clatter of metal against rock was thunderous, like sharp bursts of lightning. The ledge shuddered with the movement of the glacier; a low rumble, then a deep roar shook the scarp as piles of hardened ice collapsed onto the ledge. Ibrahim fell forward, hitting his head against the frozen ground. Malika and the two other dogs ran towards him, barking against the howl of the gale. Malika pulled at Ibrahim's white parka, dragging him to one side as the gale picked up the metal sheet which catapulted through the air and landed just beside him, its ridged edges slicing the hardened ice like a cleaver.

Ibrahim steadied himself as the wind pushed him against the cliff. Bending, he held on to the fur around Malika's neck. He looked in the direction of the saddle. He could make out the forms of Rustam and Sohrab running through the deep snow towards the saddle, where a faint glow of blue light spread itself over the slope like a river.

The dogs were gone. Ibrahim stood with Malika by his side, struggling against the wind and the pelting snow. He called out to Zaki. The wind muffled his voice and hurled it against the bluff. He called again, shouting his bunkmate's name over and over. He waited for a response. But there was nothing.

Ibrahim pushed his way through the storm. For every step he took, he slid back two steps. It was as if he was treading the air, moving backwards, the frigid, thrashing wind forbidding him from moving forward, mocking him, screaming spirits of hunted and felled creatures taunting him for his desperate flailing, his inevitable failing in this unforgiving, spectral place. Malika followed him, then ran past him, agile, gliding in the tumult of the frenzied air. Ibrahim was screaming now, repeating his partner's name, keeping fear at bay, wanting to believe that his friend had got out before it was too late. How would he manage on his own at this forward post, the last one in a series of high-altitude bases where men watched other men across an unseen, unmarked line, waiting to see who perished first?

Ibrahim squinted his eyes against the shrapnel of frozen rain. He peered through the sheets of falling snow, staring in the direction of the bunker he shared with Zaki. Where a small igloo-shaped bunker had stood just a moment ago, there was now a massive pile of ice and debris, snow, ice, moraine, detritus collected by the glacier over thousands of years.

Ibrahim couldn't see beyond the back of his hand sheltering his eyes from the sharp pellets of ice shooting through the furore of the storm. He heard Malika barking. The sound carried through the blizzard, through the howling of the wind, above the moaning of the grey mass moving still towards him, relentless in its pursuit of restitution. Malika continued to bark. She called out to her master, to the man who had come upon the three dogs, lost, hungry, seeking shelter and safety. She barked and called him, then she howled. Ibrahim stood still and listened to Malika raising her call above the wrath of this catastrophe, her body motionless, powerful, challenging the wind, defying death.

Ibrahim Ali stepped towards the bluff where the dog waited. He had nothing to lose. Here, in this place of absence, there was nothing to lose.

The dog stood alert, ears cocked, tail still, eyes fixed on Ibrahim struggling to reach her at the top of the mound of ice and debris deposited by the glacier. Ibrahim peered through the white haze, seeking her. Ghosts swept past, moving silently through swirling flurries that fell fast, unceasing. He called out again, shouting his partner's name into the heart of the snowstorm that blinded him beyond the shape of his flexed hand shielding his face from the harsh wind. Behind him, a huge chunk of ice the size of a small hut blocked the entrance to the fissure where he had stacked the fuel and food supplies.

A snowdrift, swirling like a living thing, growing, pulsing, threatened to push Ibrahim and Malika towards the edge of the rim. Leaning forward, lowering his form against the fury of the gale, he moved towards the snowdrift, stepping onto the pulverised mound of broken ice and scree. If he couldn't find Zaki, if he couldn't find a way to dig into the huge mass of ice and the jagged shards of broken rock, he had to find a place to protect himself and Malika. If he didn't move fast enough, both he and the dog would be blown off the ledge, plunging into a crevasse and disappearing, buried by tons of snow. No, he could not accept defeat in the face of this unholy havoc. He must continue his search for Zaki, he must make it inside the igloo, to get Zaki out, to find the wireless device left on the table beside his cigarettes and the Petromax. He had to find his mate, he had to save himself. And the dog, Malika, who had stayed with him instead of making her way to safety beyond the saddle. Malika, Spirit-Wolf, keeper of safe lairs, leader of packs known to gather together to face an enemy, never leaving behind the injured or the frail, marking her place with the scent of her skin.

Malika barked. She stepped down, onto the slope towards Ibrahim, her paws slipping on the ice, claws tearing into the flesh of this beast. Ibrahim stretched himself towards her and grabbed her collar, heaving himself up. Swaying from his exertions, unsteady, unsure, he tried to plant his feet on a narrow plateau below the pinnacle of the mound, orienting himself on the tiny ledge that hung above the tongue that had been their home for six tedious weeks. Around him was an unthinkable calamity. The avalanche had swallowed everything. High up in the grey sky, thunder rumbled; a streak of lightning shot through the gathered mass of clouds. Bits of broken rock struck the metal sheet and ricocheted off the corrugated surface. Ibrahim ducked. The wind screeched; eerie sounds pierced his ears. Malika howled; the muscles in her forelegs bulged, straining against the merciless wind. She turned her head towards the unheeding firmament and bayed. A deep, full call, asking the others to gather, to collect here, at this place where the world was ending, where the man who had fed them and kept them warm was in grave danger.

Ibrahim dug his feet into the skin of the mound, wedging them between treacherous obelisks of fractured ice, securing a foothold between the piles of fallen rocks and broken shale. Gulping the frigid air, he clasped a rocky spur and dragged his body up the icy slope, heaving, struggling against the wind. There was nothing to hold on to except jagged chunks of ice and shale. Malika stepped towards him, keeping her hind legs pinned to the spur, stretching her forelegs towards Ibrahim and holding her neck out. Her nose touched his hand, and Ibrahim reached for the dog and grabbed her collar, stretching the other hand towards the sharp ridge projecting out of the moraine. He hauled himself up, gritting his teeth against the weight of the wind pushing against him, freezing his face till he could no longer feel it. He fought to keep his balance on the slippery ice and sharp rocks piled up against the edge of the cliff where the bunker had been tethered just moments ago. Ibrahim held one hand out in front of his face, shielding himself from the rushing sleet. Malika was pulling him, dragging him over the mound of broken boulders and compacted snow. He shut his eyes against the force of the gale and lost his balance, his hand slipping from Malika's collar. He catapulted backwards, hitting his hand and the side of his head against the sharp rim of a metal pole protruding from the pile of debris. Pain stabbed him. Ibrahim called out to Malika, and she was by his side, licking his wound, urging him to get back on his feet, whimpering. Ibrahim reached out and put his arm around her torso. The dog stood erect, ears cocked, every muscle in her powerful body tensed. Ibrahim took a deep breath and raised himself up, grabbing onto Malika's thick coat. He sucked in the icy air. Vaporous puffs rolled out of his mouth; his throat constricted and he struggled to breathe. Even with so much wind there didn't seem to be enough air to fill his lungs. Ibrahim felt faint. Dark shadows slid before his eyes, his body now weightless, drifting. Beyond the wavering shadows he could see a man astride a horse, floating in the sky. In the man's hands were a shield and a sword. Ibrahim shut his eyes again, his head spinning from pain. He sank to the ground, nauseous, his breath shallow, spectres of things unknown circling him. He could feel his heart stop, then a faint beat pounded against his chest. He was alive: that he knew because his wound throbbed like a living thing. But where was he? Who was this man and horse floating high above him, balancing a shield and a sword, a disc and a sickle, in his hands?

The wind raged, unremitting. It continued to churn up the scree and sleet. Ibrahim forced his eyes open even though his lids had turned to lead. Everything slid past him and receded, further and further away. He kept his eyes on the metal pole that had held down the tethering rope for the bunker. It wavered in the thick haze. Silvery bands of moonlight streaked across the snowdrift. Everything was moving, the ground slipping away from beneath him. He floated, his body weightless.

His hand slipped from Malika's collar. Blood coursed through his limbs towards his chest and abdomen, his body's instinct to keep vital organs alive. Ibrahim's neck and shoulders tightened; his hands ached as the capillaries beneath the frozen skin began to constrict. His lids grew heavier, drooped, then closed. He hit the frozen ground with a dull thud. Malika whimpered. She nudged him with her nose, licking his face, warming his skin, breathing on him, shielding him. Then she howled, her cry rising above the ridgetop, soaring towards the dome of the sky. She called to Nihibur himself as he waited, poised atop his horse, waiting to decide if this man, this hapless mortal, inhabitant of Zameen Par, should live or perish in that frozen land where nothing was meant to live except the moving mass of ice and snow making its way down the precipitous slope that lay before it, an unmarked path, marked now with seething fear.

*We knew this man had suffered. We know that all men suffer in war. That all women who see the bodies of their sons and fathers and the fathers of their sons, that all these women go mad with grief. We know that the sons of lost fathers, of men who never come home, who were buried before their time, these sons search for their fathers in the scent of the sweat of other men. They seek them in the folds of the skin around the jowls of other men, in the knotted knuckles of the hands of other men. We knew this man suffered dark thoughts when he remembered what he had seen, what he had lost. We could hear his screams when he struggled with the knowing and wanting not to know, we could see what he saw etched deep into the inside of his eyelids. We heard him when he called out to the man whose skull was shattered and to the man whose legs had failed him, falling beside the capsized iron beast leading the others before the fire had burst through the earth and with its violent force thrown the beast into the air. We heard him as he called out: Fazaldad! Rahim Jan! Daud Khan! He called out, again*

145

and again. *It was burning, the fire was burning, and flames leapt high, cinders of shredded uniforms and charred flesh flew in the air around him. Lift him up gently, don't move his neck, get out of the truck, where is Daud, where is Daud?* He looked for the men in the back of the metal beast. The fire seared his skin. He shielded himself from the heat, holding up his arm. *We could see that his hand was on fire, his hair was on fire, he was burning, they were burning — who will get out alive who will make it home who will hear the sound of running water who will taste buttermilk churned by the worn hands of his mother who will hold his newborn child? We saw him as he looked into the cavity where the men had been seated just a moment ago.* The man he called Daud had told him the news he had just received about the birth of his first son. He had embraced him, patting him on the shoulder, and then there was the shock of the blast. Daud's shoulder tore away from his body. *This man catapulted into the dark, thick smoke surrounding the burning vehicle.* For some reason he landed on his feet. The rest of the men were scorched to death or ripped like pieces of ripe watermelon tumbling from the fruit-seller's overflowing cart in the bazaar.

*The iron beast glowed in the blue core of the fire the stench of incinerated flesh and smouldering tyres choked him men were strewn over the burning plain limbs caught in the branches of leafless trees he could see a part of a leg the boot still dangling black laces trembling in the wind their metal tips glowing with the orange of the raging fire.*

Ibrahim moved forward the heat beat him back he called out something shone he rushed towards it towards the truck he could make out the rear-view mirror and heard it splinter in the heat Ibrahim shouted into the silence he could see the men around him then he began to slide away from that place where all was burnt twisted black *but why was it so cold now why was the ground frozen after the fire of hell raged here taking so many with it why can't I feel my hands my feet what is this that blinds me now the searing pain the burning fluid that bleeds into my eyes where is Daud where is Fazaldad where is Gul Rahman where are the men where are the men* Ibrahim spun violently upwards

146

*through a dark vortex and found the light and the warmth of the sun carried by a man astride a horse the crescent moon held in his hand a golden-haired wolf beside him looking at Ibrahim with eyes the colour of his daughter's laughter when he lifted her up into the silver sky stretching across the forests and the rivers and the fields of barley keeping all creatures safe from harm keeping all creatures warm for only through the giving of life does one get the reward of life itself.*

Night passed. The broken glacier settled its ruptured mass on the slope where two men and three dogs had met and made a home. It was as if nothing had happened, for all was covered by the white deception of fresh snow. The wind had died down, and a faint light glowed across the vast cup of snow-laden peaks.

Malika rose. She nudged Ibrahim, pawing at the snow which had drifted around him, burying him till only his nose and moustache and the end of his woollen cap were visible. Ibrahim sank deeper into the snow, descending into a sleep deeper than that he had known in his mother's womb, resting in the hollow that invited him with its soft comfort, promising him renewal, respite, promising him a return to all that he had known, all that he had loved and yearned for in this white wilderness where the only warmth he could feel was from the breath of the creature who watched him, her eyes golden, fur golden, heart of gold.

Malika blew her breath over Ibrahim. The snow shrouding his face and hair melted and ran in rivulets down the side of his jaw. Droplets of thawed ice slid from his brows onto his eyes. Ibrahim's eyelids quivered; Malika whimpered, bobbing her head up and down, speaking to the man who lay motionless before her. The light from the sky was lavender now and bathed both beast and human in its generous warmth. Malika looked back at the crest of the mountain. Nihibur stood on the far ridge, Sinopish and Yakh-Sherlim beside him. In one hand Nihibur held a piece of crystal the shape of a fish's eye. In the other was a sword made of black granite. Malika howled. Her call reached Sinopish, the Wolf-Mother. Yakh-Sherlim heard it, too, and leapt from the snowy bank onto a rocky ledge. She stood, this spotted Mother of Snow Leopards, poised upon a spur, her paws spread over the black surface. Sinopish joined her, her magnificent tail sweeping the snow behind her. Both of them called to Nihibur. He stepped forward, leading his black horse standing at a height of one and a half keslik, taller than a Baltar Tree of the Boiber Forest, its lustrous mane longer than the tail of a dying star. Malika watched them as they came closer, but still distant, far away from the place where Ibrahim walked the narrow bridge between life and death. Nihibur joined the Spirit-Beings on the craggy outcrop. Malika howled, calling again and again. Nihibur held the crystal high into the lilac expanse. Colours flashed from the crystal, a radiance that matched the light of the sun, but was more. The colours spun in the Yalmik Sky and tinged the clouds with vermilion, rust, purple and gold. Malika howled again, stretching her head higher, reaching into the ether with her nose pointed at the sun. Nihibur raised the sword. Sinopish and Yakh-Sherlim stepped back, their tails swishing, ears flattened against the sides of their massive heads. Nihibur held the sword above his head. Malika raised her head again and howled till the breath swelled through her pounding chest, calling again and again, asking for Nihibur's mercy.

The sword glinted in the sunlight; Nihibur brought it down in one quick movement and shattered the crystal into a million fragments. Colours rushed down the steep slope of the mountain and bled into the snow until there was nothing but a vast whorl of white haze settling upon Ibrahim. Malika stood still, listening to the whirl of the haze as it enveloped Ibrahim, covering him with another skin, this one purple like the sky above him.

# Turma-Wálti

## 14.

*In that place from where we could see the small village, men and women played out their lives in the inelegant fashion peculiar to humans. From our place at the highest point in the valley, it was possible to smell the fear and the uncertainty which grew in between the neat rows of grain planted in the tiny terraces meant to feed ever-growing families, ever-needy, hungry, empty bellies constantly extracting sustenance from the land, the air, the water. Our Castle of Stone and Ice cut into the Black Mountain was carved out of rock before the fruit and the berries and the seeds could be stolen from us, robbing our children of the food upon which they survived. Inside this place, this huge cavern with no end and no beginning, we have hoarded what we could forage before we became the food the men and women of Zameen Par hunted. There is a place where we have strung up the small carcasses of the children of Berugat to remind the young ones that they could have been those unfortunate creatures whose mother could not protect them, to warn our young of the treachery of those who take a child from amongst us, feed it on corn and fodder and keep it warm in the stinking pens they build to confine it, only to fatten that small, helpless creature and pack it in the Rolling Chamber which carries it far away from those it thought had loved it. And what happens when that small creature, a child, really, is released from the vault of the Rolling Chamber? It is sold, herded, prodded, stuffed back into another Rolling Chamber that takes it further and further away from all that the small creature*

149

*has known. And once it has reached its destination, it is slaughtered mercilessly, its tiny hooves, polished black obsidian, bound and held down, its head pulled back, neck laid bare, a sharp steel knife slicing through its life-force, taking what was not given, for why give something so that it can die before its time, by the very hand that tended it?*

*These skeletal remains of Berugat's children are like small cages where the hearts of each young one throbbed. Now they are empty, for that man, that Priest of All Fools, would enjoy especially the heart, roasted over the burning branches of the Baltar Tree of the Boiber Valley. They say, those who took on the guise of maidens standing in attendance at the Court of Folly, that the Priest would hold the hearts of Berugat's children in both hands and bite into the raw flesh with teeth the length of white mulberries and the colour of rotting apricots. Each time he bit into the heart of her child, Berugat would scream in agony, wailing, pouring out her grief in her tears which formed the four streams the humans call Chartoi. The only thing we could do for her was to fetch the carcasses of her children after the Priest had had his fill. These we would wash in Berugat's tears, bleaching them white with her sorrow, and then string them up for all to see, for all to remember. There would be a time, we would assure the inconsolable Berugat, when the Priest would eat the heart of his own child. And then who would weep for her, that unblemished, pure creature who did not know of the fate that awaited her?*

# Chapter Fourteen

A plate of food – walnut oil congealed between two wheat pancakes; a cup of tea, cold, a thin skin floating on top – sat, untouched, by the door. It was all that Fatimah could do for her daughter, other than begging Moosa to let the girl out so that she could use the latrine in the orchard. Fatimah could smell the pungent odour of urine wafting from beneath the door to the storeroom. She had covered her nose with her veil and had wept at the disgrace her daughter was subjected to by her own father. Could this be the reason the girl was starving herself, so that she could avoid the indignity of squatting in a corner to relieve herself?

Bitter, stabbing thoughts had kept Fatimah awake for most of the night. The nagging fear of what Moosa was capable of doing to his daughter, to her, and the persistent odour of something stale and sour bore a hole into her forehead until she had to hold it with both hands and press against her temples to squeeze the last bit of strength out of her harried mind. She hated Mariam for what she had done, she hated her for her beauty, her youth, her smooth, fair hands, for the affection Moosa showed her, for the new room with its polished furniture and pretty curtains, for the new bathroom with the coloured tiles and matching mirror, plastic holders for Mariam's toothbrush, Mariam's toothpaste, a narrow shelf for Mariam's comb. Everything was Mariam's now; Moosa was hers too. He was no longer a loving husband or caring father. He was a fawning lamb suckling at his mother's teats, primping himself for his young wife, shaving his speckled stubble, dyeing his silver hair, standing with legs apart in the open area beside the latrine with the modern convenience of a water tank which flushed excrement and discontent into a cesspit dug at the bottom of the orchard. Moosa was proud of his new toilet, as much as he was proud of his new wife, as much as he had begun to loathe the elder ones, and now, his youngest daughter, Sabiha.

Moosa ordered Khadijah to accompany mother and daughter to the orchard. A procession of three women, two older ones, one still a girl, funnelled out of the baiypash, while Moosa stood guard at the door, watching them with searching eyes, his mouth pulled into a straight line across his leaden face like a road leading nowhere.

The orchard trilled with birdsong. Fatimah and Khadijah waited outside the latrine in silence, looking away from each other, unable to meet each other's gaze. Khadijah, weary, sat on the doorstep of Mariam's room, sighing, mumbling a prayer. Fatimah muttered something about Mariam, about the luxury Moosa had provided her: a separate room, a toilet right next to it. Just then, the door to the room opened; Mariam stood before the two older women, hunched over, holding one hand to her mouth. Khadijah moved aside, pressing her bones into a corner of the doorway. Mariam lurched towards the latrine, stumbling. Fatimah, arms reaching for Mariam, stepped towards her at the very moment that Sabiha pushed open the latrine door. Fatimah moved out of Sabiha's way, her heavy body slow. Sabiha stepped aside. Her foot knocked against the tin can sitting beside the latrine. The tin swayed over the uneven ground, tipped over, rolled away and halted in a shallow depression. A few withered flowers and a wad of crumpled paper spilled out of the tin. The ball of paper parked itself between Fatimah's feet. Mariam choked, smothering a cry in her throat.

She ran into the latrine and retched. Sabiha stared at the small ball of crumpled paper. She bent and picked it up. Looking past her mother, Sabiha walked through the orchard, amongst the singing birds and falling leaves. She did not turn back.

Time stretched across the orchard, strung between the branches of indifferent trees. Moosa drummed his fingers against the wooden takht in the verandah, waiting for the women to reappear. He saw his daughter emerging from between the trees, gaze lowered and steps faltering, as if she was fleeing, or reluctant, or both. Fatimah and Khadijah followed her. It was like a funeral procession. Turning away, Moosa strode into the house. There was a grave issue to attend to; his daughter's punishment would go on as before. It would not be long before she would reveal the name of the man who wrote that impudent poem to her. It would not be long before the man who lay bleeding on the baiypash floor revealed his own name. Then Moosa would be able to make decisions, to offer solutions to the two problems that had appeared like unwanted guests in the middle of a freezing night in winter.

Betrayal is perhaps the most difficult of acts to forgive. The slaying of trust, the crushing abuse of faith. In considering which was more terrible, her father's cruelty or Mariam's treachery, Sabiha wept herself to sleep, bitterness constricting her throat and making her breathing hard. She slept fitfully, dreaming, waking, talking to herself: *Nasser Nasser come and talk to him Nasser come and tell him that you meant no harm Nasser Nasser see what they have done to me Nasser.*

Time passed, looping itself around and round, like a fable, the telling of which had no beginning nor end. Sabiha heard the courtyard door opening with a loud clang. Shaking, unsteady, weak from hunger, she climbed on top of the sacks

153

and leaned in at the window. It was that strange young man in the overcoat, Lasnik, limping, a length of rope trailing behind him. He loped across the courtyard, calling out to her father in his grating voice. Sabiha heard her father's voice as he met Lasnik outside the entrance of the baiypash.

What is it now, young man? What have you come to complain about this time? The day hasn't even begun, most people are still asleep, and you've already got yourself into trouble, I see.

Lasnik held up the rope with one hand and pulled up the leg of his trousers with the other. Sabiha watched her father step closer to Lasnik. He ignored the rope and looked down at the gash on Lasnik's knee, a cut like a wide mouth, bleeding down his crooked leg.

Now what have you gone and done, young man? How did you come about with another injury, eh? It's not as if we don't have enough on our hands, you know. So, what's happened to your knee? Did you fall into a ditch, eh?

B-b-big Yatz big teeth t-t-try to eat g-g-goat. Lasnik k-k-kick Big Yatz. B-b-big Yatz eat Lasnik l-l-leg.

Raising his heavy brows, Moosa shook his head and turned towards the baiypash. Lasnik followed Moosa, dragging the rope behind him, a long orange tail sweeping the floor.

Sabiha gazed out of the window until her eyes grew tired of looking at the empty courtyard. She turned her head towards the orchard. She could see the new room with the toilet beside it, a blue sink installed in the corner of a verandah, a mirror in a blue plastic frame suspended above it, a sprig of plastic flowers stuck in the holder for the toothpaste and brushes. Nothing stirred, no shadows moved past the window facing the courtyard. Sabiha raised her hand to the light and opened her clenched fist. A small wad of paper sat inside her palm. She unfolded the crushed paper and smoothed it out

154

against the narrow windowsill. Holding her breath, she placed one shaking finger on the creased folds of the paper and traced the outlines of the crudely drawn hearts edging the love poem. For a moment the blood coursed through her veins, then slowed again, pulsing against her temples like someone knocking on a door.

Sabiha turned back to the corner where the apricots and walnuts lay scattered. A beam of light from the morning sun fell on the floor as she moved away, startling a rat feeding on the food her mother had pushed past the heavy wooden door. Sabiha gasped as the rat scampered across her bare feet. She fell in a swoon against the black tin trunks set one on top of the other. Her head hit the floor with a thud. The light from the window faded, and the little room sank into darkness.

Where on God's earth have you been, at this time of day when even the village dogs are still sleeping? Naushad spat the words at Kulsoom. Wiping his mouth against his sleeve, he burped, the strong stench of garlic pulsing across the musty room. He got up and rubbed his greasy hands against the edge of his shawl. His mother, half asleep, woke up, the folds of her face compressed into gulleys and grooves, mirroring the furrows and crevices of the valley outside.

Who is it, son? Who has come?

The mother of these wretched girls. Where does she go, this wayward woman? She must have been *consulting* and *insulting* with that wayward friend of hers, Zarina LHW! Heh! These English Consultants and Insultants! They think they know everything, and then our stupid women try to be like them, consulting and insulting each other! Stupid cows!

Naushad spat the words out, then brushed his sleeve against his mouth.

Just wait till that woman's husband gets back from wherever

it is that the military has sent him. Just wait till I tell him of the scandalous things his wife has been up to! That whore is never home! Always wandering around the village, making a nuisance of herself amongst respectable families, making herself available to those not so respectable. They call her a Lady Health Worker, Mother. I call her a Bloody Wretched Home Wrecker, for that's what she is, always teaching this one to answer back, to defy me, to keep producing a wretched string of wretched girls.

Naushad paused. He wobbled on his feet like a man whose joints had fused at the knees. He burped against the back of his hand, a gesture of civility at odds with his unkempt appearance, then rubbed his chest.

Where have you put that medicine for my stomach, woman? That milky liquid for the burning in my stomach, eh? Where have you put it? Or have you drunk it up, or drained it into the nullah, just to spite me?

Kulsoom stood at the door. She did not look at her husband as he swiped at the air, staggering towards her on limbs hesitant to be put to use.

Now, move out of my way, I have to go and relieve myself. God knows what you put in the food last night. My belly has been churning up bad air and I've been bloated like the belly of a dead goat. I need that medicine to get this wretched gas out of my wretched guts, woman. If I don't get rid of this gas, I may as well offer myself up to the Soniwal who can fashion a raft out of me and float their way to the middle of that wretched, cursed Island of Sele-herun! God knows what they look for over there – there's nothing but a bloody circle of bloody stone pillars carried by some infernal giant who had nothing else to do but rub himself against the pillars when the urge possessed him! Bloody, blood-sucking Yatz, preying on sinful women, fornicating with them in their dreams and

156

making the women scream out in pleasure in the middle of the night, shameless whores.

Naushad stopped blabbering, bent over, parted the cheeks of his bottom and expelled a rush of fetid air stinking of sulphur and something putrescent. He stood up, stared at Kulsoom and grinned. Kulsoom did not speak. She did not protest when he pushed her against the door and walked out of the room, stumbling. Kulsoom stood at the door and stared at the line of scuffed, worn-out shoes, a pair each for the elder three girls. She removed her own shoes and walked into the baiypash without raising her eyes. Kulsoom said nothing. She had nothing to say.

Lifting the man's arm gently, Zarina wrapped a bandage around the laceration, holding her breath as she avoided looking at the deep, raw wound. She was careful not to cause the man more pain than he already suffered. Moosa stood beside her as she wove the bandage around the man's shoulder, twisting it, then knotting the ends. She removed the bloody gauze she had unpacked from the wound and wrapped it in a piece of cotton, laying it aside. At the entrance of the room, Lasnik struggled to remove his boots while holding up the leg of his trouser so that Zarina could see the gash on his knee. She asked him to sit near the hearth where the sun streamed down from the skylight. Lasnik dropped the orange rope beside the wounded man and limped to the hearth. Moosa picked up the rope, walked to the storeroom, skirted around the heaped form of Fatimah stirring on the floor before the small door, yanked it open and threw the rope into a corner.

What is it, Moosa Madad? What did you want with your daughter at this early hour? Fatimah asked, raising herself off the floor.

It's not your business, you understand? This is my house, my storeroom, and that girl is my daughter, you understand?

Whatever I do around here is my business, you understand? Whatever anyone does around here, in this entire valley, is my business. What are you doing, asleep at this hour? Look at Zarina, she came here at first light of day, just to attend to the wounded man. And look at you, snoring away as if you had sold most of this year's crop and had plenty to eat as well.

Fatimah passed her hand over her face and clasped her mouth to keep the words her heart spoke from tumbling out. She stepped towards the door leading to the courtyard, one ponderous foot before the other. She did not stop when Moosa shouted at her:

Where do you think you are going, woman? Is this the time to step out of the house?

Without turning around, Fatimah shot her words at the ceiling. When they bounced back to the floor, bursting into Moosa's ears like missiles, she tossed her head and pushed open the door. Moosa looked away, not sure if he was ashamed or embarrassed or just confused. He was, after all, just a human being, not capable of perfection all the time. So what if he had asked Fatimah where she intended to go? How was he to know that this was the time she crossed the orchard to relieve herself, perching on the English-style commode he had installed for his youngest wife, in case she became heavy with the sons he longed for?

It was the last of her words that bit into him and made him wince, shame spreading itself across his forehead like a cold sweat. He would never forget those words, not as long as he lived, not as long as Fatimah lived. Spat out with such scorn, they would scar him as much as the dishonour brought upon his household by his errant daughter. What had his wife said to him just now? That he may be the Numberdar of Saudukh Das, but he could not control who shat when and on top of whose head.

Moosa clasped his head and sighed. These women were getting out of hand. Something would have to be done. Something to put them in their place. Curse that bloody school for girls. Curse the day he agreed with Fatimah to send their youngest daughter to school. Curse that man for writing that perverse poem to his daughter. Curse Lasnik for always getting into trouble. And curse this bloody man for bleeding onto the floor of his home, staining it for ever and more

Here. Come, sit here.

Zarina asked Lasnik to stretch out his leg so that she could examine his wound. Moosa grumbled about this unnecessary consumption of bandages, cotton wool, antiseptic solution, using up scarce medical supplies now that the roads were blocked by the landslide. After all, the wounded man's injuries were bad enough, and now this boy fetches up with his tall story about a Yatz with teeth the size of a cow's horns.

Cow's horns! Imagine! If that was so, how big was the Yatz, young man?

Lasnik extended his arms out as far as he could without slapping his hand against Moosa's firm, protuberant belly, resembling a heavy iron cauldron. He said something about the head of the Yatz being bigger than the boulder upon which the women laid out their clothes to dry. It was a huge Yatz, and he was hungry and wanted to eat Lasnik's goat.

What am I supposed to do with this creature, you know, this man-child who causes enough trouble for the whole village to want to throw him into the river? Eh? If only he wasn't a special one, a chosen one, you know. But what good have his prophecies been? And who can figure out what he says in any case? It's just garbled nonsense to me, you know. The boy can't see sense, so how on earth can he see the future? Eh?

Moosa paused, watching Zarina clean Lasnik's knee with a

bit of cotton gauze, swabbing the bleeding lesion with a dab of spirit from a small plastic bottle she dug out of her handbag. The torn flesh cut open by Lasnik's fall smarted, and he emitted a strange, high-pitched screech like a chicken whose neck was being severed by a slaughtering knife. Zarina grimaced, worried that her supplies were dwindling, that there was no way to get more until the road opened. Moosa continued with his rant about the inconvenience caused by Lasnik.

This fellow gets into trouble all the time, you know. Now he's gone and injured his knee, you see. He says he stumbled against a Yatz trying to crawl out of a hole in the ground. That he picked up a boulder to throw at the Yatz but the boulder slipped out of his hand by virtue of magic, you see. And then he fell over the boulder in his effort to hold the Yatz down in the hole. And that the Yatz bit him on the knee with its pointed teeth the size of a cow's horns. Hah! Allah knows how much of this is true, you know, and Allah knows how much patience one has to exercise to deal with all the calamities around here. As if we didn't have enough on our hands already, you know.

Moosa got up, waving his hand to dismiss Lasnik's story told again and again by his own mouth. Then he stretched his arms wide, as if testing his capacity to cope with a perplexing situation, brought both hands together and clasped them, clutching his own fingers, finding strength in this simple gesture of resolve.

Nobody has ever seen a Yatz except for this young man, you know. I don't know if he is making all this up or if he truly does see these things, Zarina Bibi. What do you make of his stories? I, for one, just don't seem to have the patience for this nonsense any more, you see.

Moosa slammed his fist into the palm of his hand, making a powerful point.

Saheb, if the boy had a father, things might have been different for him. You know how it is to lose a loved one,

Saheb. It is not just patience we need, but compassion. And I know you have plenty of it, otherwise why would you keep a total stranger in your house until he was well enough to leave of his own accord?

Zarina asked Moosa for some warm water with which to wash the cotton gauze, soaked now with blood, bits of soil and grass sticking to it. Moosa nodded and padded out of the baiypash like a dog that had been scolded and thrown a bone at the same time.

In the courtyard the sun filtered through a hazy sky onto the beaten floor. In the corner, beneath the awning covering the verandah, the sun cast shadows like waves of water in a shallow pool. It was a fine morning, thought Moosa. It was the kind of day which made one feel light, capable of surmounting the greatest of difficulties. Moosa strode towards the water drum, passing Fatimah as she turned away from the small, barred window. A shadow hovered behind the mesh, then disappeared. Moosa stopped just a few paces away from the drum. Looking away from Fatimah, he growled:

We need some warm water inside. And get some tea for Zarina. The boy will have some too. And then get Mariam to make me some tea. I wouldn't drink that piss you make even if my life depended on it.

Fatimah opened her mouth to speak, then changed her mind. She stood near the window and lowered her gaze, clasping her hands beneath her shawl. She didn't move. Moosa shouted:

Hurry up, woman. And stop loitering around that window. Don't think I can't see you talking to your daughter. I am not letting her out until she tells me the name of the scoundrel who wrote that scandalous love letter to her.

Fatimah heaved a sigh, drew her shawl around her bosom, and, walking like a cow tethered to a plough, lifted the lid of the drum. She scooped out a pail of water and held it out to her husband. Moosa ignored her and strode across the courtyard. He pushed the gate shut, latched it, muttering to himself about the carelessness of these women who couldn't do the simplest tasks such as shutting the gate, leaving it wide open for strangers and wild animals to barge in, any time of day and night. As Moosa walked back past her, Fatimah addressed him:

The girl, I shall talk to her. About revealing the wretched man's name. But I can't talk to my daughter through that window where I can't even see her – it's so dark inside, and I can't stretch my neck up like some sort of Jinn. You must let me talk to her face to face. Otherwise, we may never know what you want to know. I don't know what you are trying to do, Moosa Madad. How can you be so cruel? Isn't it better just to cut her heart out and throw it to the Periting? She is your own daughter, your own blood!

Moosa strode towards Fatimah and snatched the pail of water from her hand. The water splashed onto the courtyard, a wet patch the shape of a pigeon's claw seeping into the pressed soil. Moosa held one finger up to Fatimah and wagged it, blowing air out from the gap in his teeth, his voice deep, rumbling, dark clouds before the rain.

Listen to me, woman. Yes, she is my blood, but make sure that her blood remains pure, you hear? She isn't going to consort with anyone I don't approve of, you understand? In fact, she isn't going to make that decision of her own accord, you see? I will make that decision, and if you don't stop bleating like a bloody lamb, I will make that decision right now! I will ensure that she never goes back to that bloody school where she has learnt to read and write these bloody love letters. And I will get her married off to the first person who asks for her hand! The first person I consider suitable for her. I will make that decision, you understand that? Do you understand that, Fatimah?

Swinging the pail by his side, Moosa plodded to the baiypash. In the verandah he turned and shouted at Fatimah:

As for cutting out her heart and feeding it to the Periting, well, I'll have you know, woman, that I shall do exactly that and eat it myself! And yours too, you hear?

At the door Moosa swung around again and shot words he had chosen between the crossing of the courtyard and the point of command, standing at the threshold of his house, the house of Moosa Madad, the Numberdar of Saudukh Das.

If you're not going to desist from your crafty ways, woman, I have one such person inside this house who I will be only too glad to make my son-in-law, you understand?

Fatimah stared at this fat man with the pail of water sloshing in his hand. What was he saying? That he would marry off their daughter to the half-wit Lasnik? Had Moosa lost his mind?

Moosa waited for Fatimah to speak. When no words came, he grimaced, then grinned, confused by his own declaration. If this was the way to salvage his honour, to undo the insult his second wife had heaped upon him, doubting his authority, mocking it, then so be it. One bad thought begets another one – how dare this woman who had been merely plump when he married her but was now like a bundle of unwashed laundry, how dare she challenge his authority?

Yes, woman, that's right. If I wish to marry her off to this idiot who thinks a Yatz has bitten him, who smells of shit and dung, who hasn't cleaned his mouth since the government subsidised wheat in the valley, I shall do exactly that. And nothing can stop me, you understand? I make the decisions around here – get that into your thick head, you understand? And don't go near that blasted window, I'm telling you!

Fatimah shut her eyes and took a deep breath. A cold breeze

blew across the courtyard, lifting a few dead leaves that rose and floated into the open water drum, skimming the surface of the water like herons fishing. She wiped her face with the edge of her shawl and replaced the lid on the drum. The clattering of metal against metal startled a lone bird in the orchard. It was a white-winged tern, unusual in these parts. It flew up and beyond the walls of the orchard, a light, whirring creature fleeing from something it could hear but not see.

From her doorway, Mariam watched her husband's second wife leaning against the water drum like a tired animal, exhausted from a long trek, too tired to drink though the water was clear and cool. In the orchard the sunlight played with the shadows, the wind teased the few remaining leaves. On the cement platform near the gate, the surviving partridge dug its head beneath its wings and fell asleep.

# Turma-Číndi

## 15.

*We know when winter is upon us, without seeing the first snow, without hearing the distant roar of the moving glaciers. We know it from the way the light falls, the way it softens the shadows of the juniper tree, from the silencing of the torrents of Chartoi, from the fact that the many birds filling the air of our homes with their songs do not sing any more. We see, from our home here at the Chartoi, that the men and women of the village below also sense the coming of winter. We see them scurrying like rodents in a cornfield after the crop has been harvested. They are busy carrying sacks of grain into their little storage rooms, they are busy gathering the stalks of corn to feed the cows and goats tethered in their stinking stalls. We see them at the Chartoi cutting limbs from our brothers and sisters, the Deodar and the Chilghoza Pine. We see the women sweep their arms against the floors of their flat roofs, collecting the sweet flesh of apricots and mulberries, now dried, like the blood in their veins would be if they, too, were left out in the cold, witnessing the grand spectacle that shall wrap us all in its magnificent embrace. We know that they are ill-equipped, these inhabitants of Zameen Par, to cope with the freezing of life-blood and life-breath in their purple veins. We know they are not meant to be in places where the majestic Spirit-Leopard roams, the most splendid descendant of our Mother, Taghralim. We know that all of Taghralim's children, the lynx and wolf and red fox with its black stripes forming a cross at the base of its life-bone, fear these people scurrying to and fro like purposeful ants, carrying loads which shall one day burden them no end.*

# Chapter Fifteen

It takes several hours for a living thing to freeze to death. When the avalanche broke upon the ledge where Ibrahim and Malika stood, gripped by the roar of the moving spectre of ice and rocks, there was no question of getting out alive. The weight of the mass that hurtled down upon the camp was enough to demolish the sturdiest structure, twisting steel and metal into forms that did not resemble anything the material had been fashioned into before the glacier broke upon it. And even if by some quirk of fate, a person or an animal escaped the bone-crushing collapse of an entire mountainside, the ice and snow accompanying the storm would most certainly freeze them to death.

Through the narrow lair of oblivion, Ibrahim listened to the glacier moving above them. The ledge was below an overhang, and the boulders grating against the rock roared like a living thing, a suffering thing, bellowing in pain. Malika barked, one beast calling the other. Ibrahim stirred in the bed of snow where he had sunk, unable to keep his eyes open, the silvery light of the early morning sky spreading over him like the water of a spring. His hand throbbed where the metal pole had stabbed it. A crust of frozen blood cradled his hand, much as the snow had taken the shape of his slumped body. Ibrahim's temperature had fallen below normal; the lack of insulating fat on his sinewy form allowed the cold to penetrate to his heart. Beat by unsteady beat, the rhythm of his pulse slowed down. Ibrahim slipped into a stupor from which return was unlikely.

Malika stood near Ibrahim, her ears cocked, taking in the sounds of the beast moving above them. She watched the man as his body began to shiver, sinking into hypothermia, the trembling uncontrolled as his body tried to generate enough heat to keep him alive. Ibrahim groaned; Malika nudged him, licking his face, melting the ice crusted along his eyes. The rumbling stopped; there was an occasional sound of rock scraping against rock. A low hum settled around him, like the engine of a jeep making its way steadily on a tarmac road. Ibrahim tried to open his eyes, but his lids were weighed down by cold metal.

*He was with his fellow soldiers from the Northern Light Infantry, riding in the truck that was to take them to the base where they would learn to breathe slowly, taking in the air as if it was rationed, like food and water in times of scarcity, the Withering Time. Mohammad Zaki was next to him, smiling, laughing, telling jokes. Ibrahim felt Zaki's fingers on his arm, teasing him about the time Ibrahim had to pee standing up at the back of the truck, spraying the dusty road behind them with his urine. You couldn't wait till the truck stopped, could you, eh, my friend? You had to do it standing up, like the white people do? Mohammad Zaki laughed and clapped Ibrahim on the back. The truck lurched forward. Ibrahim felt nauseous, his stomach contracting, muscles squeezing his gut. He needed air, he told Zaki. It was hard to breathe in that space with so many men piled on top of each other like corpses left to perish.*

Malika watched as Ibrahim sank further into the shallow pit of snow where he had lain through the night, since losing his balance and stumbling, staggering, then falling headlong into the trench surrounded by the debris brought down by the avalanche. His body had stopped shivering, and his injured hand had taken the shape of a dead bird's claw. It was a miracle that Ibrahim was still alive, the breath leaving him in shallow spurts, stirring the snowflakes crusted upon his moustache.

Malika had lain over him the whole night, except for a moment when she seemed to call to another, unseen, beast, beyond the saddle where her companions were last seen.

Now Malika stepped back into the pit. Lowering her head, she sniffed Ibrahim's face, rubbing her nose against his frozen cheeks. Malika blinked, then pawed the snow around Ibrahim's head. She placed her forelegs along his shoulders, her hind legs on both sides of his buried pelvis. Gently she lowered herself onto his chest, offering him the warmth of her body, sheltering him from imminent death. Ibrahim could not feel the dog's body against his. His blood vessels had constricted in their effort to conserve his body's own heat, the capillaries and veins moving fluids to his centre, filling his kidneys. He desperately wanted to empty his bladder but could not move. The blood in his vessels had begun to thicken. He heard things that were not there, saw things only he could see. He saw his wife waiting at the gate with their youngest daughter in her arms. He saw his mother smiling with her single tooth suspended in the cavern of her mouth like a sleeping bat. He saw Nihibur astride his horse, watching. Behind him stood a wolf with golden eyes, tail erect, ears alert. Ibrahim called to that creature: *Malika Malika take me to where the wild roses grow Malika Malika place a wild rose on my grave Malika Malika don't let me die Malika don't leave me here to die Malika.*

Malika whined. She watched Ibrahim's eyes flit from side to side beneath his lids, red and blue rivers running beneath the fragile skin. She laid her head down next to his, snuggling her snout in the nape of his neck, against his carotid artery, throbbing like a small, gurgling brook. She could hear his heart beating, then stopping, beating again, stopping for a pause longer this time, then another, faint beat. And then, nothing.

★   ★   ★

The rumbling started before he could dig himself out of the tunnel of sleep that he had slipped into as soon as he wormed his way into his arctic sleeping bag, insulated against the sub-zero temperatures with corrugated cardboard sheets cut out of empty cartons. He was not sure if what he heard was thunder or the movement of a glacier. He could hear the wolves barking above the faint roar of something moving, grating against the earth. The sound was deep and distressing, and the wolves heard it before they saw the massive slide of rock and ice cascade towards the camp. The female, the leader of the pack, started barking and ran towards the door, the other two wolves following. But the door was locked from the outside. He unzipped himself from the chute of his sleeping bag and rushed against the door. The door wouldn't budge. From the narrow slit in the bunker he could see the huge cloud of displaced snow blanketing the beast which moved towards the camp: boulders, jagged rocks, scree, moraine, slabs of ice which had broken off the glacier as it moved at a speed which would crush anything in its path. The only way to get out of the bunker was to stick his arm through the slit the width of an envelope. His heart was pounding as he saw his arm shrink to the size of a young calf's tail. He slid the shrunken arm through the slit to the outside. He saw his arm grow longer and longer until he could put his bare hand on the metal latch to open the door. At once his fingers stuck to the metal, and he pulled his hand away to release them, ripping his skin where it had touched the latch. The wolves were already out by the time he felt the pain in his hand. He could feel the vibrations of the moving mass as it slid towards the camp. The sound was deafening now.

Mohammad Zaki, Mohammad Zaki, come out! Where are you, Mohammad Zaki? Hurry up, before it's too late.

He would not answer. It was comfortable now, beneath the debris and the detritus, and sleep was overtaking him like water released from a dam. He could hear the wolf, and the gale, and his mate calling out to him. But he didn't care; he would just settle further into the warmth of his cocoon, his heart comforted by the fact that the girl he loved

169

*would wait for him, her shining eyes fixed in the direction of his arrival, her heart beating in unison with his, even if he was far away, far, far away, even if the beast had descended, even if all was buried now. Lost for ever.*

The sun's warmth slowly slipped over the rocks and the fields, melting the frost of the night before. Running up the steep incline, Hassan banged with his fist on the metal gate of Moosa Madad's house. He was gasping for air when Moosa opened the door, alarmed and annoyed at the same time, the buttons of his shirt undone, a blue and yellow striped towel thrown over one shoulder, his feet splayed awkwardly in a pair of slippers several sizes too small. Standing at the door, Hassan spluttered between gulps of air:

Saheb, I have come to tell you, I have to tell you that two villages upriver have gone under the lake, the lake that was formed by the broken mountain, Saheb, falling rocks, the landslide, Saheb. Many have drowned. Many people. Cattle and sheep have been seen floating down the river, floating, Saheb. Dead. Drowned, Saheb, in the flood. The government had promised that they would send help, supplies, men to stop the flooding. But nobody has come, Saheb, nobody, not a single person, so people are helping each other, they are pulling the elderly and the young to safety. But some of them have slipped into the freezing water and disappeared from sight, Saheb. Some of them nobody could save . . .

Breathless, Hassan paused and wiped the flecks of spit from his mouth.

Noor has gone to help them, Saheb. I also wish to go, but I thought I would let you know what is happening as you may not be able to get the news on the television, Saheb, the electricity playing tricks, as usual, as you know, Saheb.

Moosa lowered himself onto the takht and chewed the ends

of his moustache, his eyes focused on a line of ants carrying the legs and wings of a dead insect. The wings were diaphanous in the mid-morning light slanting at an angle through the dappled shade of the orchard. Moosa watched the ants carry the wings, many times larger than themselves, all of them moving forward in unison, under the command of an unseen hand. He could see the veins running through the insect's folded wings, delicate, fragile, like the capillaries of a withered leaf.

Moosa nodded his head slowly. It was true; this was a fact that half the mountain had cracked down the middle and had fallen into the river, damming it for a length of twenty-one kilometres. This much Moosa had heard before the power disappeared and the television screen went blank, a prickly silence creeping across it like a tremor. Now, even if the road leading out of the village was cleared, it would not be possible to take the wounded man to the District Headquarters Hospital, for surely, the newly formed lake would have submerged the highest motorway in the world. Now it was time to be decisive, to take charge, to pronounce the way forward.

Moosa rubbed the palm of one hand with the thumb of the other and turned to Hassan.

You know, young man, it is as if this fellow, this half-dead corpse you and your cousin hauled into my house, it is as if he was meant to stay here, to be healed by none other than us. If that was what the Almighty willed, then that is how it shall be.

Moosa brushed his chin with gusto, then, squeezing his eyes into narrow slits, he ran his index finger over his bulbous lips, tapping his teeth, deep in thought. His head shook only slightly, as if his mind was stirring up the words which would carry the weight of his decision with dignity and authority. He exhaled slowly, a low, reverberating sound emerging from his belly like a living thing crawling out of a cave. Even if there was not much to say, even less to do, Moosa Madad, the responsible Numberdar of Saudukh Das, had to say something, anything, something which would preserve his position as the ultimate arbitrator of the cards his people had been dealt. Even if he had no solutions to offer, no wise words of counsel to pronounce, even if there was nothing that could be done, Moosa had to make a decision, and he had to make sure that it was known far and wide, between the right bank of the Winter River and the outer limits of the cliffs at Chartoi. The Almighty had presented them with a situation in which they, alone, would have to manage, and he, Moosa Madad, would be the one to steer this raft, a flimsy craft made of inflated goatskins strung between four water-soaked beams, through the fulminating water of a river in flood.

If this is not a sign of Dark Times, then what is, young man, do you see?

Hassan hung his head, worried. He had expected this magnificent man to say something more encouraging, a little less unsettling.

Moosa sighed and got up.

Zarina is doing the best she can, under the circumstances, you know. She was here early this morning, woke me up, she did. Diligent woman, she is, you know. Bandaged that silly boy's wound, she did, even though it is quite obvious we are running out of bandages and medicine, you see. How will we get the necessary supplies with the roads blocked? And how will we ever get this man to the DHQ hospital? Have you ever heard of this before, young man? An entire mountain cracking down its middle and collapsing into the river?

Hassan shook his head. He rubbed the faint reddish down on the sides of his face with one hand. With the other he searched in his empty pocket for something. There seemed to be nothing

172

there to allay his bewilderment. There seemed to be nothing but disquiet in the large head of the man he had worshipped almost as much as he adored his beautiful daughter.

Moosa looked his visitor up and down, taking in his strong, stocky physique, the flaming red hair, the soft haze of a beard on his chin. Moosa drew in a long breath and pronounced, measuring his words like a boatman rowing in calm waters, cutting the still water with clean slices of his oars, one, then the other, turn by turn:

We have no choice but to keep him here, young man. Let us hope he lives through this, you know. At least then we shall find out who you have brought into my house!

Hassan winced. He recalled having the same conversation with the Numberdar earlier, the same suspicion about the stranger's identity, the same trepidation of some calamitious thing about to befall them. It was as if the Great Man had nothing new to say, nothing to calm his apprehensions. Uncomfortable with an unfamiliar situation, Hassan began blabbering, as he often did; filling in a silence with nonsense seemed to relieve the agitation which churned up his stomach and made it twist and gyrate like a trapped otter.

Saheb, I can try to get over the road block and get some medicines and bandages from the small clinic in the rural health centre down past the next village. I would be able to climb that pile of rocks, climb over that broken mountain and get back before day's end, Saheb.

Hassan was desperate to make things better, to make amends for what seemed to have been a grievous mistake. Had he not found the injured man pinned under the tree, none of this would be happening. Moosa Madad had never appeared so perplexed, despite the posturing of composure. What if the man died on their watch? Who would they inform? Where would they bury him? What name would they write on his grave? Indeed, which graveyard would he be consigned to? Here, different communities had been assigned different patches of earth in which to bury their dead. Who was this man? Shia? Sunni? Something else?

Moosa looked askance at Hassan, measuring him, assessing this young man's ability to discharge the task he had volunteered to carry out.

You would do that, young man? Moosa asked. You would be able to climb over that broken mountain and get the medicines Zarina needs and find your way back before nightfall?

Hassan nodded. His eyes gleamed with the challenge he had set himself. He would go immediately, he would set this right, he would ensure that Moosa Madad, father of the girl he loved, had nothing to worry about. Hassan would do what Moosa's own sons would have done, carrying their father's burden, making it easier for him to ensure that the people of Saudukh Das received the benefit of his wisdom and his munificence. Hassan rose from the takht, shook Moosa's hand, placed one hand on his heart, then sprinted out of the courtyard, into the lane, running, the gravel on the ground flying in the air, the red in his hair like flames leaping up from a burning grate.

Relieved of last night's meal, Naushad returned to the baiypash where his mother had fallen asleep again. The girls stirred beneath their patched-up quilts. Kulsoom cleared the hearth of last night's ash. He mumbled something about goat stew, passed wind, a long, drawn-out sound, a clogged drain releasing air, and crawled back under his quilt, drawing it over his head. His mother snored, her mouth ajar like an unhealed abscess. Kulsoom watched mother and son. She rose. Pushing open the door to the small storeroom, she entered it and stood before a battered tin trunk.

Kulsoom raised the lid of the trunk, shrinking from its

174

creaking hinges. In the dim light slanting through the ventilator, she rummaged through the few bits and pieces of fabric, an old shawl, her husband's faded waistcoat from their wedding day. At the bottom of the trunk, she found what she was looking for and tugged at the satiny material, drawing it out. Setting the lid down, Kulsoom shook out what had been her wedding apparel. Silver fish flew into the dank air of the storeroom. A smell of something neglected rose from the clothes. The shirt was embroidered around the neck and front with gold tinsel, blackened now with time, like the scab of an old wound.

Kulsoom undressed in the storeroom, letting her shalwar drop onto the floor. She removed her shirt and left it on the tin trunk. Her belly bulged, the skin around her unborn child taut, scars running along the sides like rivers with no beginning and no end. Kulsoom shivered. She slid her legs into the shalwar and slipped the kameez over her head, pulling it down over her jutting belly. The clothes were tight, constricting, a red corset cosseting her middle. Kulsoom draped the shawl around herself and returned to the baiypash. Her hands trembled as she kissed each of her children, careful not to wake them. Averting her eyes from the alcove where her husband and his mother slept, Kulsoom walked across the room and opened the door.

At the gate, Kulsoom gazed in the direction of the Doorway of Chartoi, barely visible at this hour in the hazy light of early winter. Mist masked the leafless trees below the entrance of the Castle of Stone and Ice, veiling the confluence of the four streams. It was the water that produced the mist now shrouding the streams which met at the Chartoi. Kulsoom looked ahead at the path winding up to the edge of the village. She was not looking at the trees, nor the streams, now silent, indolent, after the rush of snowmelt in the summer. She looked past all this, past the eclipsing mist, past the memories, the markers of many journeys across that familiar landscape, changing with every breeze, every sudden season, every tremor of ice melting and dripping, drop by crystal drop, into the streams cascading down the steep slopes, running in subterranean aquifers through the dark, loamy earth like veins.

For all the heaviness in her heart, for all the sadness she saw around her, in the naked trees, the empty fields shorn of their bounty, the still water of summer's bubbling brook, the silence of the birds, the desolation of the orchards, the absence of sunlight to warm the rocks by the river, quiet now, languid, unhurried, it was a land she was accustomed to, like the fragrance of the beams of deodar that formed the stepped ceiling of her home, or the soft gold of fresh butter churned from the milk of the remaining cow. Now there was only one, the other having been sold by Naushad when she could no longer bear young, when her milk had dried up, her udders flaccid and useless. Naushad had taken the cow to the next town and sold her at a less than reasonable price. Before he returned to Saudukh Das, he had spent most of the money on himself, purchasing a pair of shining Rexine shoes the colour of a goat's liver, a yellow cardigan, a new woollen hat, a watch, the time on which he had barely learnt to tell, and a kilo of beef. For his daughters he had remembered to buy some sweets from the bakery, for his mother a shawl. For Kulsoom there was nothing.

When he had stepped into the baiypash where his family awaited his return, he gave out the sweets and the shawl, handed the meat to Kulsoom, barking at her about getting a meal ready quickly for he was hungry from his exertions. As Kulsoom took the packet of meat dripping blood onto the floor, he told her that he would consider bringing a gift when she bore him a son. Kulsoom had not spoken much after Naushad returned, his feet awkward in his new pair of shoes, tight and pointed at the toes, laces tied into untidy knots. Naushad refused to remove the shoes even when he sat beside the hearth, waiting expectantly for the stewed beef, running his fingers along the smooth edge of one shoe.

Kulsoom wondered if the shoes were leather, cowhide. She stirred the evening's meal, braising the pieces of vermilion meat, still bleeding, still smelling of the animal's breath and the fear folded into its flesh. She could only think of the cow that had been sold. The cow was gone. It would be slaughtered, cut down like all things that had nothing else to offer except the meat on their bones, a terrifying death waiting for her after a distressing trek, far away from all that she had known, far away from home.

Kulsoom began her journey, knowing deep inside the pit of her stomach that the thing which makes one worthy is the very thing that destroys one. She knew, like the mist which obscures the stream, that which emerges from one's own belly is the source of one's obliteration.

# Turma-Mishíindi

## 16.

*It was a sad thing, Sinopish said, to see the young child of a powerful man suffer needlessly, perhaps paying the price for his father's foolishness. Sinopish, Spirit-Wolf, spoke after a long silence. She was not given to much conversation, especially not when our Mother Tish-Hagur spoke, or when Berugat lamented her lost children, or when Bhura Reechlo regaled us with his stories about the time he befriended a strange creature called Banda Andar, the progeny of the species which most closely resembled the inhabitants of Zameen Par.*

*Amongst us, Sinopish was the closest to the Creator. She was the one who could outrun the ibex and the markhor, the fox and marmot, the one who could keep pace with the hawk and the eagle, the one who ensured that not a single one of her tribe was left behind when the mountain collapsed from sorrow, tired of watching the devastation wreaked upon the valleys and the forests by men who claimed to be made in Nihibur's image.*

*But that was not the case, we all knew that; for there was no image of Nihibur: he was without form, without face. Only the elders had seen him, when other gods had not crowded the skies, making us doubt the existence of the First Creator.*

# Chapter Sixteen

Beneath her, the body she covered with the warmth of her own, stirred. He mumbled something, a name, several names: *Rahman Shah! Sher Gul! Mohammad Ali!* His eyes were shut. Breath froze around his mouth as he exhaled. Malika whimpered. She raised herself up on all fours, keeping her torso suspended above Ibrahim Ali's body, sheltering him from the snow flurries descending on the scene of devastation, obscuring whatever remained unburied. Day had risen from beyond the saddle where her two companions had disappeared. The two dogs had run as fast as they could through the deep drifts of powdery snow, running from the terrible thing that was about to destroy this last outpost at the edge of the world, the distant roar of the avalanche alerting them to the disaster that was about to strike. Before Ibrahim Ali could hear it, all three dogs had heeded the ominous rumble of tons of hardened ice and broken boulders pushing onto the overhang and crushing everything in its path. The two males had bolted. Malika had stayed, wanting to fight this spectre alongside the man she had chosen to protect.

Now she scrutinised Ibrahim's inert face and whined. Breath rose in white spirals from her mouth. She pawed the snow around him, clearing it from around his head with her nose. Suddenly, Ibrahim threw up his arms and grabbed Malika by the neck, clutching fast with his hands. The dog howled. Silent peaks stabbing the sky echoed her call. Ibrahim tried to raise himself up, heaving his body upwards, hands clasped around

Malika's neck. Malika stood still, head erect, paws wedged into the snow, tail raised. Ibrahim struggled to keep his hands around her neck, the pain from his wounded palm piercing him. His hands slipped, and he fell backwards into the pit. Malika sprang to Ibrahim's side. She barked, then lowered her nose and wedged it beneath his neck, raising his head. Ibrahim opened his eyes and looked up at Malika, gasping, his lungs empty. The dog didn't move. Slowly, the man lifted his head, then grabbed her neck one more time and hauled himself up.

Ibrahim clutched the fur around her neck and Malika stepped back. Ibrahim pushed himself up, leveraging his feet against something hard. He pushed against this thing again and again, slipping, hitting his head on the packed snow, breathing in short bursts. Malika whimpered, calling to him. Ibrahim reached for her with one hand, and with the other he pushed against the hard surface of the glacial snow-pile. Patches of blood from his hand streaked the snow. Ibrahim shuffled on his knees across the pit and fell against its sloping edge, exhausted. He was now face down in the snow, unmoving. Malika stepped forward and grabbed the collar of his jacket in her mouth. She pulled, growling, paws slipping on the hard ice. She slid and fell, got up, returned to Ibrahim, seizing his arm at the shoulder, grasping his padded jacket in her mouth. Malika tugged, straining to pull Ibrahim up the slope of the pit. Ibrahim raised his head, pushing against the edge of the pit with one hand. He screamed with pain as the blood in his veins began to course again, awakening the sensation he had lost during the frozen night. He screamed again and again, shouting for Mohammad Zaki, shouting into that wilderness where no one could hear him: *Ta Ali Mushkil Kusha*, Oh, Ali, ease my burden, freezing on his blue lips as he prayed for one last chance at life.

★  ★  ★

At the end of the path leading to the furthest fields, Kulsoom turned towards the mountain and quickened her pace. The path was a difficult one. It was still early; there was hardly anyone about. A solitary bird sang on a naked branch. Kulsoom stopped and listened. Then she put one foot before the other and moved away, far away, from the call of the bird, from the remembered fragrance of her sleeping daughters, the warm, cherished scent of belonging.

She walked briskly over the rough track leading to the Chartoi. Soon the track ended, and a narrow trail wound its way further up the sharp incline. The trail was not wide enough for more than one person to tread it. At times, it dipped sharply towards the river, swerving towards the mountain just before it slid to the water below. The path wove its steadfast way across the moraine, the accrual of glaciers moving across the Black Mountains, rocks and scree and soil and trees, things that once stood proud, now heaped into mounds the size of mountains, only the porous grain of its skin giving away its perfidious nature. The path, twisting, curving, sliding over slippery slopes, led away from what was familiar, from the place where one believed one was safe. Such a path does not let the traveller linger, for there is nowhere they can rest, considering the journey, reconsidering the purpose, turning back.

The sound of the man's voice crackling like crushed leaves bore through the haze enveloping Ibrahim's mind. The staccato bursts of sound charged him with energy he could not have imagined he possessed after struggling to stay alive in sub-zero temperatures, glacial ice and debris piled around him to a man's full height and more. He was a different man after sinking into deep despair, courting death, staring at his own finality with eyes clenched shut. Now, he had light bursting from his eyes; there was warmth ushering from his mouth, his hands, his breath. There was a strength that he had not known before, that could not have come from the strenuous exercise expected of soldiers, the fatigue parades, the obstacle courses, the certainty that if one did not strike first and strike hard, one would perish. How was this unexpected vigour rousing his ravaged body? At first, he thought he was imagining things, that this voice was in his head, that he may actually be losing his grip on reality, hallucinating, his mind shutting down. Then Malika had started barking, then whining. She leapt into the pit from where she had dragged Ibrahim out with the strength of a pack of wolves and started to dig frantically, throwing up snow and scree with her paws. Each time the man's voice crackled, Malika barked.

*Hello. Hel—hello. Three for three-three. Three for three-three. Message over. Message over.*

Ibrahim followed Malika back into the pit and dug at the packed snow with nothing but his bare hands, the wound no longer painful, his mind focused on a task which required all his concentration. He was a crazed man, his movements frenzied, desperate. Clouds of white breath rushed out of his mouth. He panted and whimpered along with Malika, incredulous that he had spent the night so close to the one thing that could save them, him, Mohammad Zaki, Malika. The wound on his hand started bleeding, leaving flecks of red on the snow, but Ibrahim continued digging, unmindful of the pain. Suddenly he felt the surface of something hard and smooth, curved like a half-moon. He heard the crackling again:

*Hel—hello. Three for three-three. Three for three-three. Message over.*

Ibrahim shouted: It's the wireless! Malika, it's the wireless set! This must be the igloo, the bunker I share with Mohammad Zaki! Ya Allah! I spent the whole night on top of the igloo. Poor Zaki, he must be trapped inside. We are saved, Malika!

We will find our friend and tell the Company Commander to send help. They must have seen the avalanche hit our post, that's why they are calling us, Malika. They have seen what happened here, and surely, they will send help.

Ibrahim pounded on the smooth surface of the igloo, calling out to his colleague:

Answer me, Zaki! Can you hear me, my friend? We are near you, we will get you out. Just hold on, my friend. Help is on its way.

Malika dug herself into a depression in the roof of the igloo. Ibrahim could see her hind legs and tail. He called out to her; she continued digging. Again, the crackling voice; again, Ibrahim's frenzied calling to his partner:

Are you injured, my friend? Answer me, Zaki. Can you hear me, my friend? We are near you, we will get you out soon. Just hold on. Help is near. Don't leave us, my friend. We are near you.

Suddenly Malika disappeared. Ibrahim called out to her and rushed to the narrow opening where he had seen her last. He could not see her; she must have dropped into a crevice or an empty space, possibly into the igloo if there was an opening. Ibrahim kept calling. There was no sound, no barking, not even the crackling of the man's voice over the wireless. Ibrahim shouted for Malika, for Mohammad Zaki. He couldn't hear anything except the sound of his own heart pounding against his ribs. Ibrahim swept away the loosened snow and gazed at the top of the igloo he shared with his colleague. He had to find a way in. He had to find the wireless set. Where was Malika? Where was Malika?

Ibrahim stepped forward towards the curved dome of the igloo. Placing his foot onto the curvature, he slipped on the frozen surface, lost his balance, and hit his head against the packed ice. Ibrahim looked up at the sky as the blue receded, clouds turning to grey specks, the peaks around him circling like kites looking for prey. Then the blue firmament turned to black, and he saw no more.

Kulsoom stepped onto the narrow trail curving up to the Chartoi like the silver blade of a sickle. She continued to climb. The trail carved its way through the dead roots of trees chopped down for kindling. Here and there stunted trees, bent and broken like defeated men, clutched the soil; here and there shrubs grew out of the gravel, a wild flower shook its head in the passing breeze, rising, falling, rising again. As the incline grew steeper, the trees started to disappear, and there was nothing beside the rocks and sand, the colours merging into each other: dun blending with sepia, brown with khaki, grey with taupe. Here no grass grew, there were no birds, and the beasts that had pastured in the summer had long been herded back to their byres in the village, the dogged stamp of their hooves blown away by the wind. The river below was a thin artery snaking its way through the valley, its surface still, deep waters perilous. Along its banks weeping willows bowed, tall, lean poplars stood erect, slender arms reaching for the sky. Towering, majestic chinar trees guarded the river, protecting the water vital for man and beast and the fields carefully tended on the terraces, gold against purple lucerne. Every bit of the land had been scoured for plants and leaves, dried stalks and dead roots unearthed with the blade of a sickle, for anything that could feed all the creatures that lived here, anything that could sustain life from that which clung to the barren rock of this forsaken place.

The heat of her body seared him; he choked, swallowing something bitter.

Ibrahim Ali was not certain how long he had lain on the edge of the pit, sheltered by Malika's warm body. It was the distant sound of crackling, like lightning before a storm, that had penetrated the haze of sleep and woken him. Ibrahim hoisted himself up on his elbows, pushing against the snow and debris. He fell, rose again, fell again. He pulled up his knees beneath his hips and thrust himself forward. Malika pulled, her teeth clutching Ibrahim's jacket. Ibrahim stumbled to his feet, plummeted forward, then staggered backward, plunging onto the ground. He heard the crackling again, a sharp stab of static in the frozen air.

Ibrahim looked up; the sky was clearing now, clouds that had obscured the moon were drifting away. Patches of blue sky appeared; sunlight swept wide over the expanse of shimmering snow. He turned to face the pit that had threatened to bury him during the terrible night. He heard the crackling again, a hissing sound now, then a scratching, a spitting of electric current. Ibrahim held his breath. He reached out for Malika and pulled her close, straining to listen to the series of sounds that rose from the bottom of the pit. Ibrahim looked up again. There was nothing in the sky that suggested a storm. The avalanche had appeared out of nowhere, shaking the earth as it tore over the steep slopes of the mountains, obliterating everything in its way. Now, there was nothing here, no signs that anyone had ever lived here, just a metal pole sticking out of a pile of broken boulders and chunks of ice that melted drip by drip, burning holes into the soft, powdery snow.

Ibrahim scrambled to his feet. He stood still. There was no sound other than his own breathing and the dull thud of his heart pounding in his ears. He heard Malika pawing the snow, saw her staring at the bottom of the pit, whimpering, coaxing the thing that seemed to have survived the devastation. Ibrahim heard something again, a sputter, something rustling. He leaned forward, placed one hand on Malika's neck and lowered himself into the pit. His legs slid along the slope, and he landed on the bottom with a thud. Kneeling down, he placed his palms against the curved rim of something hard. Ibrahim lowered his head, turning it to one side, his ear touching the snow. He held his breath. There was nothing: no sound, only silence.

Ibrahim stood up. Dark flecks appeared before his eyes and his body swayed. Ibrahim put his hands out to the edge of the pit and steadied himself, dizzy from the sudden movement. He shut his eyes and took several deep breaths. He swallowed, looking up at Malika standing at the edge of the pit, staring at him, her golden eyes fixed on his. She stepped forward. Something rustled, a sharp crackle, then a muffled voice, broken, the words pulsing through the ice where they had lain, buried:

*Three for three-three . . . Hello . . . Three for three-three. Message over. Three for three-three. Message over. Hello. Repeat. Three for three-three. Message over.*

Kulsoom slowed down and rested against a boulder taller and wider than her crumbling home. Her chest hurt as she drew deep breaths of air. She felt the place below her breasts where Naushad had punched her, slamming his fist into her abdomen, cursing her for bearing him only daughters, hitting her as hard as he could, ramming his knuckles against her womb. A low moan escaped her lips. Kulsoom pressed a hand against her mouth and shut her eyes. Her head reeled from the height. She was afraid of slipping from her foothold on the precipice. Pressing herself against the boulder, she looked down. She could see the corn tethered in sheaves of gold. The narrow water channels, running along the terraces, glinted like mirrors in the sunlight. Water foamed as it fell from step to stony step, gathering force as it moved downward, forming waterfalls at the edge of every field. Kulsoom traced the grey line of walls; she could see the homes and their flat roofs gilded with apricots spread out to dry. She could see the sheep as they huddled in their pens, the cows as they were led out to pasture in the fields now shorn of harvest. There were not many people walking through the lanes of the village at this time. A dog loped through an alley, his nose sniffing the ground for food. She could see birds in the branches of the orchards, she could hear their song, and she wondered if she was losing her mind, for how was it possible to sense all this from where she now stood, at the edge of Chartoi, so high up, so far from her home where her daughters waited for their mother to return, so far away that she was just a speck now, a dot of scarlet clinging to the walls of the Castle of Stone and Ice as if the rock itself was life?

Grey-blue in parts, silver in others, ragged holes cut into the firmament, the sky sheltering the windswept landscape stretched without end. Snow-lathered mountains disappeared into the billowing clouds. Here and there the black ridge of a saddle shorn of snow rose like a bridge of slatted, dark wood.

Ibrahim stared at his hands: the skin on his fingers was ripped, shredded, peeled back from raw flesh. Blisters rose and burst on the ridge of his palms, the fluid freezing as soon as it was released from the capsules of dead skin. The gash in the centre of his palm was bleeding. His heart pumped hard, throbbing along the clenched curve of his jaw as he dug into the mound of snow piled above the domed roof of the igloo. Scrambling across jagged chunks of ice, his hands grasped the rough edges of broken rock. He lifted these, flung them aside, sucking air in short, shallow gasps.

Ibrahim squeezed his eyes shut and wiped the sweat forming a crust on his brow. With a deep breath, he opened his eyes and peered out at the scene of wreckage. The sun was spreading its clear light across the hushed landscape, silver turning to gold. Fresh snow concealed the crevasses, burying broken boulders, sealing the ruptures that had torn the earth apart just a few hours before. Nothing was as it had been. There was nothing here to suggest that two men and three dogs had lived on this ledge at the end of the world. Only the furthest tip of the rocky outcrop was visible. The overhang was heavy with the lip of the broken glacier weighing down upon it, the sun's warmth melting the frozen mass in crystal drops, icicles forming like a set of fangs in the mouth of a serpent. Before Ibrahim lay a mountain of debris and massive chunks of ice, the toothed wedges of a broken glacier, glistening in the sunlight with an unreal brilliance.

A sheet of corrugated metal lay across the skylight of the igloo, hurled there by wind, dislodging the cupola protecting the skylight. The metal sheet sat across the opening in the roof of the igloo, an aperture wide enough to let a man climb into or out of the fibreglass shelter in an emergency. Ibrahim put his hands along the edge of the sheet and pushed. In an instant his skin glued itself to the surface of the freezing metal. He pressed his eyes shut, gritted his teeth, clamped down hard, lower jaw protruding, lips stretched and cracking. He snorted, an animal sound bursting from his lungs. The sheet moved, grating against the igloo. Gusts of smoky air escaped through Ibrahim's clenched teeth. His breath came in short spurts. Ibrahim heaved. The metal sheet toppled backwards and crashed against a large rock. A rush of snow cascaded down the smooth slope of the rock, revealing graffiti painted on the black surface in bold strokes of red.

Mohammad Zaki's name, his regiment, a heart with an arrow piercing it, the letter F inscribed in the middle, F for the woman who waited for him, even if he may be just half a man by the time they got him down from this terrible place.

Mohammad Zaki, I am here, I am near you, Ibrahim yelled. The skin had torn away from the palms of his hands, pain surging through his arms into his chest. He plunged his hands into the snow, numbing the raw flesh. *Mohammad Zaki, I am here, I am near you.*

Ibrahim looked up at the sky. The sun was still edging over the saw-toothed ridge in front of him. From the position of the sun, it appeared to be noon now. If Mohammad Zaki had been buried inside the igloo, was he still alive? How would he have managed to breathe? Was there an air bubble inside the igloo? Had Mohammad Zaki grabbed the oxygen cylinder just before the avalanche struck? Was he injured? Was he alive?

Ibrahim stilled his heart. He slowed down his breathing and listened for Mohammad Zaki's voice, for signs that his mate was still alive, that he was within reach. *Mohammad Zaki I am here, I am near you.* He knew he had to rescue this man who had made the silence of their exile bearable.

*Hello. Three for three-three. Message over. Aap sab khairiat se hain? All okay at the post?*

Like a gunshot, something fractured the air. Ibrahim raised himself up, pushing his body as if it was a weight separate from himself. He heard the crackling sound again. Ibrahim struggled to his knees, placed his hands on the frozen surface before him and crawled into the narrow shaft. A few steps in, he backed out, his head reeling. He tried to stand up, sucking air into his lungs. He lost his footing, stumbled, fell against the debris piled up against the igloo. Ibrahim raised himself on his elbows. He could see Malika burrow into the narrow passageway. She whimpered, then moaned, a deep, muffled sound, like a cow lowing in a distant field. Ibrahim flung both arms forward and heaved himself up. A film of sweat had frozen across his forehead. His fingers burned and the raw flesh of his palm throbbed. Ibrahim crawled towards the tunnel and shouted:

Mohammad Zaki, I am here, my friend! I am near you. Don't give up, my friend. *Himmat na haar, merey dost. Mein terey paas hoon.* I am near you.

He couldn't hear Malika any more. Ibrahim pressed down on his hands and peered into the tunnel. Her tail was visible – stiff, held level with the roof of the tunnel. Ibrahim called to her, urging her to return. She whimpered, then started backing out of the tunnel. Ibrahim rose, unsteady, nauseous. He held his breath as Malika moved her hind legs backwards. Ibrahim coaxed her, calling her name softly, *Malika, Malika, come good girl, come Malika.* Ibrahim saw her hindquarters emerge from the tunnel. She turned around to face Ibrahim. In her mouth she clutched a square apparatus, black and heavy, a receiver cradled at its side. Malika had found the wireless set.

Ibrahim stared at the set for a brief moment, a moment when his life was strung between one breath and the next. Malika dropped the set at his feet. Ibrahim picked it up and held it, feeling its weight in his hands. The sheath of ice around the wireless was streaked with his blood, freezing into a pattern, marking the instrument with fine capillaries spreading out like a map of red rivers. Ibrahim folded his hands around the set, shut his eyes and drew a deep breath. The apparatus vibrated and hissed, alive and pulsating. Ibrahim brushed away the thin layer of frozen sleet and cleared his throat.

Three-three for three, send help. Message over. Repeat. Send help. We have been hit with a slide. One man is missing. I am looking for him. I need help. Send help. Message over.

Ibrahim stared at the wireless. He could hear his heart pounding in his ears. There was a hiss of static, a crackle, then nothing. Ibrahim held the mouthpiece up to his lips. The wireless came to life; a man's voice broke through the iced casing, leapt at Ibrahim, rushing at him like a fox running through a forest.

*Three for three-three, message received. Rescue team is being dispatched immediately. Are you injured? Message over.*

Ibrahim filled his lungs with freezing air. His hand shook. He spoke slowly, clearly.

Three-three for three, I am all right. Sepoy Mohammad Zaki is buried beneath the slide. Send help. Message over.

*Three for three-three, message received. Heli to be dispatched with rescue team. Message over.*

Ibrahim stared at the wireless. His legs gave way, and he slumped, collapsing onto the snow. All around him was hushed. The quiet land glinted in gilded sunlight. Malika stood beside him, her breath warm against his neck. There was no other sound now, just the distant settling of a snowdrift leaning against a sheer black cliff, unmoving, unmoved by the drama playing out in its shadow.

Ibrahim held the wireless close to his chest, raised himself once again, breathing slowly. Malika nudged him, licking the frost on his face. Ibrahim reached out to her, grabbed her neck, and steadied himself. He was on his knees now, looking straight ahead at the vast expanse of snow and ice spread out before him, here and there a dark protrusion of rock wounding the undulating wave of this frozen wilderness. Ibrahim slowed his breathing, his heart resting against his ribcage, a bird safe within its nest. Then he bent forward, touched his head to the ground. Prostrate against the silent snow, he said a prayer of gratitude:

*Subhaana thil-jabarooti, walmalakooti, walkibriyaa'i, wal'adhamati.*
Glory is to You, Master of power, of dominion, of majesty and greatness.
Glory is to Allah, The Almighty. Subhanallah.

# Turma-Thalé

## 17.

*Many years ago, Taghralim said, there was a man whose mother was a Peri, and his father an ordinary human, one so handsome that the Peri had been mesmerised and forgotten that she was only meant to seduce him, not marry him. But she did that, and the children she bore this man were considered to have special powers, touching on the divine. But when these children grew up, they disregarded the rules their mother had taught them, and proceeded to destroy all that lay before them, tearing up the earth, cutting down the trees, killing the beasts, spilling their blood and polluting the rivers. All of them did that, except for one son, one more handsome than his father, more gifted than his mother, a man who carried the best of Spirit and Human in his veins.*

*It was this man, Taghralim told us, who could push the mountains apart to let the water of trapped rivers flow. It was he, she said, who could hold the sky when the clouds descended and threatened to spread darkness such as was known before Nihibur brought the disc of fire. It was this man, this beautiful man, this gentle child of Peri and Human, who could talk to the creatures all others disregarded. And it was this man whom we must protect, whom we must stand guard over, sending one from amongst us to guide him in times of grave trouble. For even if he did not know his powers, we had been told about them, and we knew that in the small world where other humans went about their daily tasks as if they were travelling a path of great significance, we knew that he was the only one who knew which road to take, treacherous as it may have seemed when he chose it.*

# Chapter Seventeen

There is no precise temperature at which a human body perishes by freezing. What is clear is that in comparison to women, men were more prone to such terrible deaths, that those with lean bodies would succumb to freezing temperatures before those whose bodies were protected by a buffering layer of fat. The chances of a person being found alive if buried beneath the snow diminished after the first fifteen minutes of the occurrence. After this, only a pocket of air, a team of rescuers digging through tons of snow, or a miracle, could save a person's life. It was a question of time, or a question of fate.

In the time that it would take for the helicopter to take off from the base, to travel the miles across the wide glaciers spanning the impossible peaks, Mohammad Zaki could lose his battle to stay alive, buried beneath a ton of snow and the detritus of the avalanche. In the time that a rescue team could have been dispatched, in the time that help could be at hand, in the time that several men could dig out the lost soldier from the bowels of the igloo, in that time, it may be too late to save his life. It was already more than a day since the avalanche had struck. What were the chances of finding him alive?

Ibrahim said a prayer, asking for the Almighty to help him in this final effort to reach his colleague. He had to find him before he left this wilderness, now that the helicopter was on its way, sure to land as soon it could negotiate the snow which still fell, relentless, intent on obscuring whatever was left of a rocky crag or a protruding spur. He had to find Mohammad Zaki, even if it was to return his body to his family so that they may no longer stay up nights worrying for his wellbeing, praying for his safe return. There was no choice in the matter. That he may still be alive, this would be a miracle that Ibrahim prayed for, shutting his eyes, kneeling before the silent peaks watching him, watching a lone man and a dog struggling to survive the wrath of the Black Mountains.

Tucking the wireless into his jacket, bolstered by the feel of its hard melamine casing against his chest, Ibrahim crawled back into the tunnel and dug through the snow, softened by the afternoon sun. He reached a wall of broken rock and packed ice, flanking a narrow aperture wedged by a tumble of concrete blocks piled on top of each other, blocking the path of the avalanche. Ibrahim stopped. There was no way he could move the blocks aside or dig through the jagged slivers of ice and scree. Breathless, he backed out of the tunnel and sucked air into his lungs. Malika barked, jumped at him, animated, nipping at his sleeve, pulling him towards the tunnel. Then she leapt into the narrow passage and disappeared.

Regulating his breath, counting one-two, one-two as he inhaled and exhaled, calming his heart with the knowledge that soon he would find a way to reach Mohammad Zaki, that Malika would lead him to his friend, his companion, the person with whom he had shared this narrow place on the ledge for six unbroken weeks, laughing at his jokes, sharing the silence, grateful for his presence, Ibrahim bent down and peered into the tunnel. He could see Malika pawing at the wall, dislodging the slabs of ice and broken rock. She whimpered, nuzzling the serrated chunks of ice from time to time. She pawed at the wall again, throwing down jagged wedges of black rock, barking when she broke through the barrier, the scree and ice tumbling around her and opening a small space through which she crawled, whining, her tail wagging. She howled from the other side of the barrier; her call sounded hollow, as if she was inside a well. Malika continued to bark, then she whimpered. Ibrahim heard her yelping the way a mother dog does when coaxing her pups to follow her, nudging them with her nose, leading them to safety.

Ibrahim threw himself into the shaft feet first, sliding towards the wall. His legs hit the wall, dislodging a large chunk of ice blocking the tunnel, rupturing a hole in the barrier of concrete blocks and debris. Thrusting his hand through the opening, he could feel cold air stirring in what appeared to be an empty space. Frenzied, he pried loose broken bits of rock and ice, clearing a space large enough to squeeze himself through, dropping into a small chamber, a subterranean cavity, dark, silent, frozen. Ibrahim called out to Mohammad Zaki. Malika answered. She found Ibrahim, licked his hand, whimpered, urging him to follow her. Ibrahim called out to Zaki again. There was no answer. A chill current swirled around him. There was air in this narrow passage; there must be an opening to the outside somewhere. Ibrahim had no idea if the igloo had turned on its side, if he was walking on the curved roof of the shelter. Everything had turned upside down in that one calamitous moment. Extending his hand into the frigid belly of the chamber, listening to the dog panting somewhere near him, Ibrahim moved towards Malika. His head struck something hard. Ibrahim reached up with his hands. He could feel the manufacturer's logo embossed onto the fibreglass door fixed to the mouth of the igloo. The force of falling debris must have dislodged the door and pushed it far into the igloo. Ibrahim called out again: Mohammad Zaki, answer me, tell me where you are, my friend. *Kahan hai, merey dost? Jawaab de.* Zaki, where are you, answer me.

Ibrahim spoke the words without pause, without stopping to catch his breath. There was oxygen in this tomb-like space.

Ibrahim stood still for a moment, trying to orient himself. The door leaned inward. Ibrahim felt alongside the fibreglass surface, moving forward, shuffling on the floor. Where the door ended, his hands touched the freezing surface of curved metal. He stroked the surface of this thing, feeling the raised bands around the circumference of what was most probably a large drum, used to store kerosene. What was this drum doing here? Had it rolled down from the narrow shelf further up the slope? The lid was still in place. He knew there were at least twenty litres of kerosene inside the drum. But had any of it spilt out when the drum rolled down into the innards of the igloo? Would it be safe to light a match? Did he even have a matchbox on him? Ibrahim patted the pocket inside his jacket and felt the familiar rattling of matches inside their case. He remembered lighting the Petromax stove when the porter had come, carrying a flank of lamb. Ibrahim had put the matchbox back in his pocket, ready to light the stove to melt the snow for their ablutions the next morning. Zaki had laughed at the two of them as they had waited for the snow to melt, scooping up handfuls of the powdery flurries and rubbing them against his thick auburn beard. Smiling at the memory, invigorated, Ibrahim took a deep breath, drew out the matchbox and lit a match. As soon as a flame sparked from the matchstick, a gust of air blew it out. Ibrahim lit another. Again, a short-lived flame, wavering in the cold air, illuminating the chamber for a split second, then snuffed out. Ibrahim took a deep breath, inhaling the reassuring fragrance of burning sulphur. Now the darkness was no longer formidable. He breathed icy air into his lungs, grateful for each breath, for the tiny flame which had lit up this cavern even for a fleeting moment.

Kulsoom turned away from the valley and stepped onto a protrusion, a grey tongue suspended over the fields and lanes and water channels and homes of people she knew. An outcrop rose over the track, blocking her path. Her legs shook as she bent beneath the bluff, skirting the edge of the cliff. There was just enough space for her to wedge her feet, first one, then the other, clinging to the loose soil slipping beneath her weight. Kulsoom grabbed a tuft of wild grass and pulled herself towards the cliff. Her heart pounded with the effort to keep herself from plummeting over the edge of the trail. She clung to the outcrop, inching around it, facing away from the river, lightheaded, trying not to breathe, vertiginous, her body shaking with terror. Kulsoom pressed herself against the jagged surface of the bluff and moved slowly to the far side of the ridge. She could feel the gravel and soil of the moraine slide as she negotiated her way towards the path. She did not look behind her, below her. Through frightened eyes she watched her feet as they slid slowly down the rocky outlier towards its edge. Then she searched for the track that had brought her here, far from her home and everything that she had known.

Before her was nothing but the craggy, steep incline of the mountain. The path had disappeared. The Doorway of Chartoi loomed above her, just a few yards up the incline. Below her, the stone circle of Hele-Sehrun stood moored on the island in the middle of the river. The eye in its middle watched a woman dressed in clothes from another time, red like the juice of a mulberry, making her way across the hushed wilderness of this lonely place.

Kulsoom sought a foothold on the slope below the rock. There was no place for her to thrust her feet in order to steady herself. Teetering above the ground, her feet slipping from the rock, Kulsoom shut her eyes and leaned towards the outcrop, grasping at its contours, desperate to find something, anything, to hold, something, anything that would hold her. She wept, her body racking, ears bleeding where Naushad had struck her, ribs hurting where Naushad had punched her, just below the heart and above the place where her unborn child lay.

Sliding his feet alongside the drum, Ibrahim felt something obstructing his movement. He flexed his knees, lowering himself, keeping his arms extended for any objects that may impede his movement. He heard Malika panting, shifting her weight on the floor. She was whimpering, insistent. Malika rubbed against his knees as Ibrahim bent down and felt the rough surface of a concrete block, then another, and another, all prostrate against the floor. He called out again. Zaki, answer me, are you injured, my brother?

There was only a low murmur of air blowing through a fissure. Then a groaning, a deep sound, coming from somewhere beneath him. Ibrahim inhaled long and deep. He stretched his hands out and reached further into the darkness. His fingers touched the corrugated surface of a cardboard sheet, then the hard metal of a jerry can. Ibrahim shouted: Mohammad Zaki, I am near you, brother, I am here, near you. I know you are here. I have reached your bed. Here's the tent you made out of cardboard boxes. I know you are here, my friend.

Ibrahim fumbled amongst the layers of corrugated cardboard covering Mohammad Zaki's improvised bed of wooden planks balanced on concrete blocks, wedged between a fibreglass door, a heavy drum full of fuel and a compacted snowdrift. The space had been sealed off from the avalanche by the door, the drum and the blocks dislodged from the protective wall at the edge of the igloo. Malika barked and clutched Ibrahim's sleeve in her mouth, pulling him towards the bed. Ibrahim got down and crawled into the space between the planks and the floor. He ripped through the cardboard sheets, flinging them aside, calling out to his partner, intent on finding him alive.

Malika nudged her way beneath the planks, yelping. Ibrahim

reached in with his arm. The space between the bed and the floor was slightly more than eighteen inches. Malika barked. She kept barking, yipping, whining, sharp sounds piercing that compressed space. Ibrahim propped himself up on one elbow, reached for the matchbox, lit a match, cupping the nascent flame in the palm of his hand. Wedging his head into the gap, Ibrahim held the match as if he was offering a rose to his beloved. Before him, jammed against the edge of the igloo, lay Mohammad Zaki wrapped in his alpine sleeping bag, the cardboard sheets forming a tent over him, insulating him from the freezing cold.

I knew it. I knew you would come, my friend, Zaki murmured, a weak smile and the lit match warming his frozen face.

The flame, fed by the oxygen in the chamber, rapidly consumed the matchstick and died, plunging everything into darkness.

Mohammad Zaki, you're alive! I have found you! Glory be to the Almighty. I knew I would find you. Are you injured?

Ibrahim reached under the pallet, touching Zaki's shoulder.

It's broken, my friend. I think my arm is broken. But the rest of me is all right, other than being nearly frozen. Even the urine I passed is frozen inside this sleeping bag.

Ibrahim smiled. Zaki was always passing remarks of an unsavoury kind. In this dark chamber, at a point where both of them had nearly lost their lives, Ibrahim was grateful for Zaki's lightheartedness. Surely, His will had got him through this terrible time. Surely, His will would get them both through this terrible time.

Ibrahim pulled himself off the floor. There was only one match left. He would keep it for later, once he had managed to get his colleague out from under the upturned pallet. He had to find a way to push the pallet up to drag Mohammad

Zaki out from the cramped space where he lay, knocked back by the force that had pushed him into that corner.

What took you so long, my friend? Zaki asked.

Ibrahim smiled and shook his head. He forgot the lesions on his hands, the torn blisters, the nails ripped up from raw beds, the throbbing wound in the middle of his palm. Nothing mattered now but getting Mohammad Zaki out. Alive.

There are many paths before us, choices that take us to yet more crossroads, and at each bend, at each fork, we make another choice, peeling back the many skins which wrap an ear of corn. Sometimes the choices we make can yield a rich harvest; sometimes they can leave us with a barren field, the soil withholding, crumbling at the lightest touch. Sometimes the choice we make appears not to be a choice at all. Instead, it is the only path, the only means to end the suffering brought on by an earlier choice, which, frequently, was not a choice at all, buried in the skin of another's resolve.

Kulsoom stepped up towards the Doorway of the Castle of Stone and Ice. In just a short while she would present herself to the Periting, for they were the ones who had cursed her with the fate that marked her life like a bleeding wound. Perhaps they would hear her lament, perhaps they would release her from this prison.

Malika stood alone on the edge of the pit, scanning the sky for signs of the helicopter. She had heard the blades of the rotor whirring while inside the buried igloo. She had heard the blades chopping the air before Ibrahim had spun around, neck snapping upwards, alert to a distant hum. Malika had leapt up to the opening in the wall and scrambled up the passage, into the sunlight. She barked at the chopper as it disappeared behind the ridge. Bounding into the tunnel, she scrambled her way back into the dark chamber. Ibrahim was dragging Mohammad Zaki's sleeping bag through the narrow opening, his colleague swathed inside the thick chute of padded material, an emergency light in his hand that pointed the way out of the tunnel. Ibrahim was exhausted from trying to carry the weight of a man stiff with cold. Had Zaki broken his legs? Was he paralysed? There was no other way to get him out of this chamber. Ibrahim hoisted Zaki into the tunnel and pushed the sleeping bag upwards, Zaki moaning, shouting in pain. Malika grabbed the sleeping bag near Zaki's head and pulled, walking backwards through the tunnel. Together, Ibrahim and Malika brought out the injured soldier into the dying sunlight.

There was no sight nor sound of the helicopter. Malika tore through the snow and turned towards the saddle where Rustam and Sohrab, her companions, had fled the night of the avalanche. Malika ran fast, her paws wide and sturdy, pushing against the ice and the snow, jumping over the black rocks, climbing higher and higher until she had reached the corrie, carved out of the mountain when the glacier had been born. She stood still in the middle of the bowl-shaped depression, her ears cocked and tail held parallel to the ground. She could hear the faint purring of the helicopter, receding into the hazy vastness, leaving behind the massif of peaks huddled beneath the Yalmik Sky.

★

*Inside the prison of Damascus, near the shrine of Bibi Sakina*
*In the quiet of night, I can hear a voice softly calling out*
*Mother, blood drips from my ear, Mother, blood drips*
*My neck hurts where they have tied me, Mother, my neck hurts*
*I can't breathe when they drag you with the rope that tethers me*
*It tethers me, it tethers Kulsoom, then Ruqaiyya, then Kubra*
*It tethers Farwa, then Fizza, and little Zainab, just four years old*

*Mother, blood drips from my ears, Mother*
*How will I survive this prison in Damascus, Mother?*

★

Malika stood in the heart of the white-out whipped up by the helicopter. She watched as the craft hovered, lowering its belly between the frozen white surface of the ledge and the broken teeth of the glacier teetering above the overhang. The Alouette circled the area twice before coming in to hover at the edge of the tongue, pointing its nose towards the cliff, nudging the snowdrift piled up against the mountain while keeping its tail clear. The main rotors whirred just below the jagged icicles piercing the air.

A man stood inside the open rear door, signalling with both hands. Ibrahim peered through the white haze and saw the crew chief kneeling down, grabbing Mohammad Zaki's sleeping bag from one end. Ibrahim hoisted the other end into the craft. The crew chief was shouting above the roar of the motor, urging Ibrahim to get into the craft. The wind was picking up; it was dangerous for the helicopter to be hovering so close to the overhang, the treacherous icicles hanging like daggers. Ibrahim turned around to look for Malika, to rush her into the helicopter. But she was gone.

★

*Mother, the shadow of death accompanies me, the shadow*
*Blood from my ears merges with tears from my eyes, Mother*
*My wounds have blossomed like red flowers, red flowers*
*My throat is parched, Mother, the passing wind frightens me*
*I will never drink water again, not after Asghar died pleading*
*for water*
*I see his face when I gaze at the water running below, Mother,*
*I see his face*

*Mother, I sense my release from prison is near, it is near*
*In the quiet of the night, I hear a voice softly calling to me*

★

The crew chief shut the door, sending Ibrahim into the rear of the helicopter. Ibrahim shouted through the noise, urging the pilot to wait, Malika must come with them. There wasn't enough time — the sun was already setting, the wind was picking up, it was getting dark. The crew chief told Ibrahim that the risk to their safety mounted with every passing minute. Ibrahim pleaded with the men: the dog had saved his life; he could not leave without her. Ibrahim watched the pilot signal to the co-pilot to prepare to move away from the ledge. He moved towards the door and looked out. He could make out Malika's form emerge from the igloo. In her mouth, she held something. The helicopter shifted away from the ledge, its nose turning slowly away from the snow-drift, preparing to fly into the open sky. Ibrahim rushed to the door, opened it. Malika leapt from the ledge and landed with elegance beside Mohammad Zaki stretched out in his sleeping bag. She dropped something near Zaki's head. Ibrahim leaned forward and picked it up. It was the amulet Zaki wore around his neck, the one his mother had tied around him when he joined the military, a prayer for safety tucked into its silver casing.

The crew chief shut the door and held both thumbs up at the pilot. The Alouette shifted away from the cliff, veering away from the tongue, clearing the overhang, and negotiated its way into the open space beyond the white mountain, leaving behind the destruction of the avalanche. Ibrahim looked out at the ledge. He caught a glimpse of the blue igloo shrouded in white. He sank to his knees and held Malika close to him, looking into the golden orbs of her luminescent eyes, the colour of the setting sun, now sinking beyond the jagged peaks of the frozen land.

# Turma-Altámbi

## 18.

### Lasnik's Song

*I will bind the sliver of silver broken from the Yalmik Sky*
*I will bind the sole of my broken foot*
*I will bind Ding the Yatz of Yellow Teeth*
*I will bind the boulder that bounces back*
*I will bind the insects flying and crawling*
*I will bind giants and wild animals*
*I will bind the colt of a mare*
*I will bind the offspring of an ass*
*I will bind the lamb of a sheep*
*I will bind the kid of a goat*
*I will bind the bullet of a gun*
*I will bind the markhors of the Mountain*
*I will bind the Snake-Eaters*
*I will bind the Snake-Man*
*I will bind the tears of his daughters*
*I will bind the lies of demons*
*I will bind, I will bind*
*I, Lasnik, Son of Lasnik Rahim Jan*
*I will bind, I will bind, I will bind*
*Till ravens fall from the Yalmik Sky*
*Till fish fly across the Moon*
*Till circles follow the circle within*

# Chapter Eighteen

She was an absent sort of woman, Sakina, her eyes empty of gladness and her hands usually hanging limp by her side like dead mallards strung along a hunter's bird-hanger. At the edge of the little wooden shack she had stocked with women's things, an assortment of ladies' cotton and nylon socks, undergarments discreetly packed in cardboard boxes and wrapped in newspaper, red and orange plastic combs, talcum powder, hair-removing creams, skin-lightening cream, buttons and laces, fat containers of multicoloured toffees for the children, Sakina sat, holding a stick with the tuft of a cow's limp tail tied to its end. This she used as a fly-whisk with which she fanned the heap of sweet dumplings that lay piled on a newspaper transparent with grease. Flies and children were attracted to these regardless of the rancid fat in which they had been fried. Her son, Lasnik, her only child, the light of her lifeless eyes, the source of her only joy, the parting gift of her martyred husband, relished the dumplings, licking off the sugar before chewing the greasy dough and swallowing each bite in one, spasmodic gulp.

Moosa Madad barrelled down the lane towards the broken-down house with the crooked walls and lopsided door, home to Sakina the war widow and her peculiar son. Lasnik followed close behind Moosa, straining to keep up with the Numberdar's giant strides, his bandaged knee slowing him down. He had spent the day waiting outside the Numberdar's house, hoping to get his rope back. But Moosa had ignored him, preoccupied as he was with the many problems that he faced as the sole Keeper of the Peace and Normalcy in Saudukh Das. And now, as dusk fell over the valley and the breeze brought with it winter's first chill, Lasnik turned to follow Moosa as he lumbered down the path, ignoring Lasnik as one would a stray dog longing for a home, or a bone, or just the vague possibility of some affection.

Moosa Madad greeted Sakina and sat beside her shop, in front of the stone platform upon which the wooden shack teetered. Sakina continued to fan the dumplings, taking little notice of the large man sitting before her. Moosa was winded from the long walk down the rough path leading across the bridge. He took a while to catch his breath, then spoke:

Sister, I have come to ask you for help, you see. I need you to do something for me, sister.

Sakina looked up briefly, her eyes blank. She continued to wave the fly-whisk over the sugary treats and over her son's face. Lasnik sat beside her, staring at the sweets, a thin thread of spittle streaking down from his open mouth. Moosa spoke again.

It's about that boy, Hassan Ali. You know his mother well, don't you? They say she is from your village, isn't she? I need you to ask her something, you see.

Moosa waited for Sakina to put down the cow's tail and pay him the attention he was used to getting from most people in the village. But Sakina continued to mind the flies settling over the sweets, as if Moosa was an apparition, and his voice just the sound of the wind blowing through the leafless trees. Moosa shook his head and passed his hand over his bristly cheeks, the undyed silver stubble of his beard glinting in the last rays of the setting sun. He took a deep breath and raised his voice.

I came to talk to you about an important matter, sister. I need you to talk to Hassan Ali's mother and ask her if he has been betrothed to someone, a girl in their family, someone of their choosing. Will you do this for me, sister?

Sakina stopped moving the whisk over the dumplings. She set the stick down, picked up one of the sweets and offered it to Moosa, then picked up another one and gave it to her son. Lasnik stuffed the whole dumpling into his mouth and chewed, ravenous, having missed his mid-morning meal while waiting for Moosa to deliver him his rope. Moosa held the sticky sweet in his hand and grimaced. His temples throbbed with the exertion of rushing to this little run-down shop and with the patience needed to converse with a woman who appeared to be as dim-witted as her son.

I shall ask her, Saheb. Should I tell her you wish to enquire about Hassan because you are anxious about the future of your beautiful daughter?

Moosa stared at Sakina. Her words cut through him like an arrow lancing the throat of an ibex. How could she know what worried him? How could she know of his deepest concern, the distress eating his heart every minute, the knowledge that his daughter had betrayed him, betrayed the trust he had placed in her?

Yes, well, I think Hassan Ali is a fine young man, you know. But before I begin something, I need to know if any arrangements have been made for him, you see, Moosa said. He looked away from Sakina and mashed the dumpling in the palm of his hand, crushing it as if it was the very thing which had caused him to seek the assistance of a strange, pale-faced woman no sharper than a pebble at the bottom of the river.

I will do as you say, Saheb, Sakina said. Even if I believe that when plucking the fruit of the King Mulberry, it is wise to use a gentle touch, for the fruit is delicate, and what use is it if the juices burst out of its skin before one has tasted its sweetness?

Moosa didn't know what to make of the woman's words. All he knew was the fact that his stomach twisted, his heart pounded, that the greasy, sticky dumpling lay crushed in his hand, a discomfiting reminder that he, Moosa Madad, the most powerful man in Saudukh Das, was being treated with such condescension by a woman whose wits were clearly as dull as the gaze in her eyes.

Dusk was deep upon them now. It was a steep climb up to his house. Moosa was already burdened with the bulk of his weight, but now there was the other burden he carried: the burning recognition that he had taken on something that was bigger than most of the problems brought to him by the villagers seeking his wisdom. Moosa was alone; there was an agonising defeat evident in the way he walked towards his house that night, plodding over the rocks and gravel, his head lowered in a posture of resignation, vexation thudding against his chest like the annoying clatter of a door shuddering in a storm.

Something, a rat, a bird, stirred in the field to his right and scampered away into the darkness. Moosa shook his head and leaned forward, hunching his back as he placed one heavy foot before the other, climbing a path that was no longer familiar, the long shadow of his bent form making it difficult to see the ruts and sharp rocks. A dog barked in the distance; someone puttered past on a motorbike. Then there was silence, just the gentle gurgling of the stream running down from the Chartoi.

Darkness would fall soon; the path was unlit. He must hurry home before the wind picked up, turning the night to ice.

In autumn, when the light from the sky mellowed and a chill wind blew from the place beyond the Chartoi, it was said that the spirits were gathering for the feast at year's end. This was when the russet and crimson leaves of the poplar trees had already fallen, forming a bed for small creatures hiding from danger and the cold, leaving slender, naked branches reaching for the warmth of the winter sun.

Fatimah watched the evening as it fell, cloaking the mountains in grey light. She waited in the verandah, watching the gate through which her husband would return. It was cold now; the chill burrowed into her thin shirt. She watched as two birds in the orchard flitted from one branch to another, then darted away in the wintry air.

It was quiet without her husband's deep voice, without her daughter's laughter. Fatimah sighed, passed her hands over her face as at the end of a prayer. Stepping into the baiypash, she took a deep breath. She strode across the hearth and lifted the latch on the door of the storeroom, pushing it open. A gasp of musty air rose from within. Fatimah peered inside the shadowy room. She could make out the form of her daughter sitting with her back against the sacks of grain propped up in the corner. A shaft of hazy, pale light fell through the window onto the floor. A mouldy smell like something forgotten marked the place like a tomb.

Fatimah sank on her haunches and placed a hand on her daughter's shoulder. She pleaded with her to tell her father the name of the man who had written to her. This was the only way to get her freedom back, by telling Moosa who wrote the poem. It was the only way for the girl to resume her studies, to get back to her normal life, to go back to school, to meet with her friends, to sit with her mother around the hearth at day's end.

Tell him, my child, tell him what he wants to know, then it will be over. How long do you think you can stay in this room, this prison? How long are you going to starve yourself? It has been two days now, and you haven't eaten a thing. Why are you protecting him, if you have nothing to do with him,

Sabiha? Why don't you tell your father his name and be done with it?

Sabiha looked at her mother, grief shrouding her eyes. She turned away. She was pale; the blush of her cheeks had disappeared in just two days. Her golden hair fell across her face in untidy clusters, like sheaves of wheat scattered by an autumn storm. Fatimah pushed Sabiha's hair away from her clear, golden eyes and spoke again, pressing her bosom against her daughter's.

Sabiha, you know how stubborn your father is. For Allah's sake, have mercy upon yourself, just tell him the name of that wretched man and all will be over. Do you want to live out your life locked up in this suffocating room? Do you?

Sabiha looked up and locked her gaze with her mother's. She dropped her gaze and whispered:

And what will he do if I tell him what he wants to know, Mother? What will he do, Mother? Do you think he will just let me out of this room and let me go back to school? Do you think that, Mother? Do you think he will leave that man alone?

I don't know, my child. I don't know what your father plans. All I know is that I cannot see you suffer like this any more. Allah knows how much longer he will keep you here. I am just afraid for you, Sabiha. I am just so afraid that your father will make a decision that he, we all, will regret.

The gate in the courtyard opened. Fatimah heard Moosa walking through the courtyard. Rising quickly, she kissed Sabiha's forehead and rushed out of the room, picking up the plate of uneaten food from the corner near the door. She was struggling to put the latch back in its place when Moosa strode across the room and struck Fatimah on the side of the head. She fell against the door and slid to the floor, her heavy body collapsing onto the stack of firewood. The plate with the shredded remains of a pancake and the cup of cold tea fell on the floor and shattered.

Moosa raged: What are you trying to do, Fatimah? Why are you trying to get into that room? Are you trying to let that girl go? Eh? You want her to run away with that bastard who wrote that shitty poem to her? Eh? Answer me, Fatimah.

Fatimah shrank into the corner, her head throbbing, a small cut burning against the rough bark of firewood, now spread out onto the floor like the lines on a giant's palm. Moosa kicked the twisted branches of wood aside and stood towering above her.

Do you think you can let her out just like that? Without my permission? Without her telling me the name of that bastard who dared to write to her? Do you think you can just do things of your own will around here, eh?

Heaving herself off the floor, Fatimah took a deep breath and pulled her shawl over her head. The cut on the crown of her head throbbed. She winced, looked at Moosa and spoke words that were sharp, edged with bitterness:

She will never tell you his name, Moosa! Even if you keep her locked up in that prison for the rest of her life. She told me that herself. Ask her, ask your daughter. She'll tell you the same thing. Then what will you do, Moosa? Tell me, will you keep her in there for ever? What would be the point, Moosa? What if she never opens her mouth, then what? Have you thought about that, Moosa? What if your daughter refuses to tell you that man's name? Then what will you do? Bury her inside that room? What will you tell people who notice her absence? What will you tell them, Moosa? That your daughter disappeared into thin air, just like that? That the Periting took her? That a Yatz fell in love with her and carried her off? Tell me, Moosa. What will you say when they ask you about your daughter?

211

Moosa moved forwards and smacked Fatimah across her face. Fatimah stifled a cry.

You are a cruel man, Moosa. A hard-hearted man! You are kinder to the stranger and gentler with that half-wit half-man half-boy. You will regret what you are doing to your daughter. This will not end well, Moosa.

Fatimah covered her face with her shawl and fell against the wall, her body shuddering.

I will decide how this nonsense ends, Fatimah. I, Moosa Madad, the Numberdar of Saudukh Das, will decide what is best for that wayward girl you have produced. I will ensure she never gets up to mischief again. I have already asked for arrangements to be made. Inshallah, with the will of Allah, this will end soon, whether she tells me the name of that bastard or not. It is not for nothing that I am the one who decides things around here. You understand that, Fatimah? I have already decided.

Moosa leaned in towards Fatimah, growling like a leopard, taunting her to protect herself from his attack. Fatimah's heart quivered with dread, not for what this man could do to her, but at the meaning of his words.

What arrangements have you made for our daughter, Moosa? What are you saying? I must know. I am her mother. Tell me, Moosa, I beseech you.

I told you, I have decided. She will marry the man I choose for her. She will marry a decent man, one who knows how to respect the honour of a family, my family. I have made up my mind. Now, get away from that door, if you know what's good for you, what's good for that good-for-nothing daughter of yours!

Moosa turned to Khadijah. She sat with her head in her hands, staring into the fire in the hearth, moving her lips, mouthing unheard words.

You, Khadijah! Tell me, has he woken up yet? Has he spoken anything? Has he eaten anything? Is there anything to eat in this damned house?

Khadijah did not look at Moosa and continued muttering something only she could hear and understand. She got up and shuffled to a cabinet where plates and cups and cutlery sat, indifferent to the grief and grievances of the master and mistresses of the house.

Moosa snapped his head back towards Fatimah and barked at her:

Don't you dare go into that room again, unless it is to give her some food. If I find you trying to open that door, you will pay dearly, Fatimah. I have enough to deal with already, without you making it more difficult for me. Now get out of my sight.

Moosa moved across the room to where the wounded man lay. He stood for a while, studying the man's face, trying to remember where he had seen it, if he had seen it before. The man's skin was ashen, his lips a chalky line between a hooked nose and a chin which disappeared into a thick, unkempt beard. The man barely breathed. Moosa clucked his tongue and sank down to the floor. Peering into the man's face, he listened for sounds of breathing. Moosa shook his head. It did not seem that this stranger would last through the night. Moosa would have to make every effort to keep him alive. It was important to get the man's name, the name of his village, the name of a son, a brother, anyone who could be informed in case he died, or lived. Moosa must know the identity of this man whose blood had soaked into the floor of his home. Just as Moosa needed to know the identity of the man who mocked him with the impudence the literate display towards the unlettered like him.

From the corner of the room Fatimah watched her husband

213

as he lifted the wounded man's wrist and felt for a pulse. She wished the man would die, for perhaps with his death Moosa would relent and reconsider the punishment he was meting out to his own flesh and blood. Perhaps then Moosa would understand the value of life, the value of his daughter's life, Sabiha, beautiful Sabiha, the girl at whose feet the world lay, Sabiha, lovely Sabiha, waiting to open the door which led to freedom, Sabiha, pitiful Sabiha, languishing in a prison carved of black rock inside her father's heart.

Moosa turned towards the hearth, muttering something about the tragedy of not having sons, about the presence of so many useless women in his home, the cause of all trouble, always, fitna, the cause of trial and tribulation. Khadijah, suffering stamped onto her face like a certificate of eternal sacrifice, handed him a plateful of rice and potatoes, steaming, fragrant, an offering of comfort in that harsh night.

Has she eaten? Moosa asked Khadijah, drawing the plate closer to himself. Startled, not used to being spoken to by Moosa, by anyone, Khadijah murmured something about the food being left uneaten, the tea spilt onto the floor when Fatimah dropped the cup.

Fatimah? What does that wretched woman have to do with it? Eh? Moosa growled, shovelling the food into the cavern of his mouth.

The girl, Sabiha, she did not eat anything at all, Saheb, Khadijah managed to say, unsure of the response her husband expected.

For Allah's sake, foolish woman! I'm not talking about that wretched girl, you know. I'm asking you if Mariam has eaten! She is in the family way and hasn't been able to eat, you see. She has that sickness you women get in the early days of this condition, you know. She throws up anything she manages to put into her belly, poor thing.

Your daughter hasn't eaten for three days, Moosa, Fatimah said, rising from the floor where she had slumped moments ago.

I've told you, Fatimah, wretched, stubborn woman that you are, I've told you again and again, I don't want to hear about that girl, you hear? I let you give her a meal – if the miserable girl doesn't eat, what am I supposed to do about it, eh? The least you could have done is to have checked on Mariam, you know, instead of just loitering around the window of that storeroom! Now go and ask Mariam if she would be able to swallow some of this rice. It's not the usual rice we grow, is it? Did you boil the rice the Chinese sent during the last disaster? This sticky mess?

Moosa shook a spoonful of rice at Khadijah. A few grains flew upwards and pattered one by one onto the mat spread before him, like hailstones when the rain comes too late. Khadijah flinched, shielding her face from a slap. But Moosa harboured no ire towards his eldest wife, this woman with skin faded and frayed around the angular frame of her gaunt body like an awning weathered by the sun and the wind. He watched Fatimah get up and fill a plate with the food, slapping on spoonful after spoonful. Moosa grunted, shook his head, chewed and swallowed, took a sip of water, his hunger dissipated and anger somewhat assuaged. Again, he addressed Khadijah.

Is there nothing else cooked today? Are we to have only rice and potatoes today? She needs something nourishing, you know! She is going to be the mother of my son, inshallah.

Spine unfurling like a recumbent centipede rising, Khadijah rose and hobbled to the other end of the hearth where a pot lay to the side. Lifting the lid, she fished out the scrawny leg of a chicken, boiled for the broth made the night the wounded man had been brought into the baiypash. Khadijah carried the leg to Moosa and held it before him, seeking his approval.

This, the chicken leg, we can add this to the plate, Saheb, Khadijah said, bent over, holding the leg of the chicken as if it was the handle of a water-pump.

Moosa wiped his mouth with the edge of his shirt and nodded his approval, sucking his teeth, poking around his mouth for stray bits of food. He burped, blew the stale air out of his gut and inhaled long and deep. Fatimah waited at the door. Dropping the scraggly bone onto the heap of rice, Khadijah looked up at Fatimah, meeting her eyes for the first time since Moosa had struck her, announcing his decision to alter the life of the young girl locked up in the storeroom, making the arrangements between one meal and the next. Fatimah whispered something to Khadijah, then pushed the door open and stepped outside.

It had been a long time since Khadijah had felt the warmth of a living thing in her arms. She stood inside the storeroom, hunched over, cradling a plate of food for Sabiha under her shawl. Sabiha lay on a lumpy quilt, her hands and hair covering her face. Khadijah placed the plate on the floor, then put her twig-like fingers on Sabiha's shoulder and tried to raise her. She was no longer the strong woman she had been when she had come to this house, bearing child after child, burying child after child, surviving daughters married off to men who never brought them back. But this evening, this dark and desolate evening, when the sky had begun to descend, pressing against the roof of their home, Khadijah felt an unknown strength surging through her wasted body. She raised Sabiha off the floor and stood beside her, smoothing down the girl's golden hair, stroking her sallow cheeks, making soothing noises with her tongue. She held Sabiha as the girl wept, unable to stop the tears. She held the girl in her embrace, letting her weep her sorrow away. Once the tears were gone, there would be nothing but silence inside that empty place where hope had been nurtured, where dreams had been seeded, buried deep in the warmth of the bountiful soil.

Then, perhaps then, the girl would eat.

# Turma-Huntí

## 19.

*Heed us. The wind whispered these words as it pierced the heart of the young boy. Sweet white flecks of sugar stuck to his nose and cheeks. Heed us, listen carefully to each word. Listen to the silence when we stop speaking, when the wind stops blowing, when your heart stops beating. The truth will lie in between. As for the Priest, who was as big a fool as his belly could grow, for him we would wait. We would let him believe in his power, the foolish decisions he made for the simple folk who came to him with difficulties. Decisions such as the one to cut off the head of the goat that had got stuck inside the clay receptacle holding the grain stored for the months when hunger mounted. We had watched the blood of the goat as it spread on the earthen floor of that wretched peasant's house, the heat of it rising like steam. We had seen it seep into the beaten soil. And we had vowed vengeance, for was it not wiser to break the clay receptacle to free the head of the goat, our Father, the living embodiment of all that was sacred? To do what he did, earning our ire, our undying rancour, this was beyond that foolish man, for all he thought about was his honour, about how the witless people of his village looked up to him, about how he needed to effect a quick resolution to all the problems laid at his feet. It would not do to nod his head east to west and turn these people away, for in that repudiation there was no honour. So, this stupid man's life was spent spinning one tale after another, fooling the people who came to him seeking justice. He spoke lies, he spun tales, he punished the innocent and blessed the guilty with honour. And now that honour was vested inside the body of his daughter. Honour like grains of corn hoarded inside a clay receptacle. Honour which lay inside the girl's young, unclaimed body.*

# Chapter Nineteen

Saheb! Saheb, Lasnik c-c-come! For to do d-d-duty! To make h-h-happy b-b-bird!

Lasnik banged on the door to Moosa Madad's house. It was still early; there was no one about. Lasnik shouted once again.

Saheb! Lasnik here. Lasnik c-c-come. Open door n-n-now, Saheb. To give b-b-bird b-b-b-breakfast.

Moosa forced his eyes open. He had barely slept during the night, keeping an eye open for any changes in the wounded man's condition. He had waited in vain for Hassan to return with the promised medical supplies, then locked the gate around nine o'clock, trying to catch the news on the television, signal weak, power intermittent.

Moosa cursed Lasnik under his breath, thrust his feet into his slippers, threw his shawl around his shoulders and strode out of the baiypash, digging into his pocket for the keys to the gate. Lasnik stood erect, his staff upright. He was smiling, face washed and hair combed back. Moosa ushered him into the courtyard. He asked Lasnik to wait in the verandah while he went in and brought out the partridge in its cage. Mumbling instructions to Lasnik in broken phrases *put cage in sun, near gate, fill dishes with water and barley, in small sack, beneath takht, in verandah, over there, near door*, he turned towards the orchard and proceeded to make his way to the latrine.

Lasnik set the cage down on the platform near the gate. He limped across the courtyard towards the verandah. Hobbling back to the cage, one fist clenched tight around tiny grains of barley, Lasnik froze. Something hissed his name, something urgent cutting through the soft light of morning.

Lasnik! Lassss-nik!

Lasnik turned towards the orchard. There was no one there.

Lasnik, listen to me. Here, at the window.

Lasnik turned slowly. He looked up and stared at the small window set high in the wall. A shadow wavered behind it.

Please, help me, little brother.

Lasnik shuffled up to the window. A Peri stood in the shadows; golden light filtered through her hair, a crown of fire.

I need you to get me a pencil, okay? Or a pen. Something I can write with. But no one must see you doing this, no one. You must promise me this. It's a question of life or death.

Lasnik stared at the window and watched as the apparition faded into the darkness.

A rustle of something spilling onto the courtyard floor tore his attention away from the window. A fist of barley seeds spilt out of his hand like rain. Urine streamed down his legs, pattering onto to the beaten floor of the courtyard. Lasnik froze, his mouth hung open and the palms of his hands faced the sky in an aspect of a silent plea.

Have you filled up the tins with barley and water, young man?

Lasnik did not hear Moosa. He stared at the pool of urine seeping into the earthen floor, darkening it, spreading like a black cloud across a stormy sky.

What is wrong with you, can't you hear me? Hasn't your mother cleaned your ears since last Eid? Allah knows what you stuff inside them, bits of grass and feathers, to keep your brain from falling out, eh?

Moosa shook Lasnik's shoulders. He looked down at the stream spreading between the boy's legs. Moosa shook his head, clucking his tongue. This was the last thing he needed, after the drama of the night before, after the hard decision he had made to settle things around here, after he had waited up half the night, wondering if Hassan would make it back, wondering if the wounded man would live for another day. Moosa exhaled, annoyed, impatient with this man-boy who couldn't seem to do anything right.

Get some water, wash the soiled spot, go home, change your trousers, I will follow. Tell your mother, I will come. I have business with her.

This was not a good beginning to the day, Moosa thought. Allah knows what lies in store for us. May the Almighty have mercy upon us. These are hard times, made harder still by things which seem to fall apart in front of one's eyes, crumbling like the stone walls of water channels swollen in the monsoon.

That day the road stretched on and on for ever as Lasnik trudged along, dragging his bad foot behind him, burdened by soggy trousers, indignity clinging to him, stinking and sodden. He was crying now. In the distance Lasnik could hear a cloud of laughter, the scatter of children's conspiracies on their way to school. Lasnik was trapped. The children would be coming towards the bridge. They must not see him. Sticking his tongue between his lips, Lasnik limped across the bridge and disappeared into a narrow lane.

The cascade of chattering grew more distinct. Lasnik hobbled out of the path of the oncoming flood of children, leaving the faint stench of urine to hover over the bridge. Around the corner, a discordant commotion, an unpleasant breaking of the morning's still air, froze his heart. Lasnik stopped. Before him sat a small, shabby hovel with a crooked gate leaning to one side. Naushad, unwashed, frenzied, threw open the door to his house and hurled out a school bag, then another, and then another. The bags landed near Lasnik's feet, their contents spilling out onto the ground. Naushad bellowed:

That evil, wayward woman. That whorish mother of these useless creatures. Where the devil has she disappeared to, leaving me and my old mother to look after these snivelling girls? How am I supposed to dress them for school? Is my old mother supposed to prepare their breakfast, and mine too?

Naushad saw Lasnik standing at the gate, still and pale, like a young eucalyptus tree wavering in the morning breeze. Sucking his pitted yellow teeth, Naushad called:

Eh? You, boy! Here, you take all this stuff and go and sell it at the junk-dealer's dump across the barber shop in the main bazaar, all right? It's near that bakery which sells stale stuff and makes all the people sick, understand? You hear me, boy?

Naushad slithered towards Lasnik and stood an inch away from him, breath smelling of dead fish, eyes hazy, hair unkempt, his body weaving, rippling.

Lance Naik Lasnik? Eh? Self-styled soldier of the Pakistan Army, are you, my dear? Eh? Hurry now, pick these up, take them to the junk-dealer and bring me my money. I have run out of cough syrup, I need my cough syrup, you hear?

Naushad kicked the school bags towards Lasnik, lost his balance and teetered over. He got up, breathless, coughing and wheezing, holding his heart and massaging it vigorously, as if trying to bring a dead bird back to life. Naushad spluttered the words at Lasnik, that the girls had no use for these stupid books and all that rubbish they learnt in the wretched school; after all, a girl's place was in the home.

Naushad veered here and there, wavering, depleted. He bent down and dragged the satchels towards himself. Shuffling towards the gate on unsteady feet, suddenly very tired, he dropped the satchels at Lasnik's feet and croaked:

Go my son, go, my Little Lame Soldier, go to the junk dealer, Lieutenant Lance Naik Limping Loitering Useless Louse, hurry on to the bazaar and bring me some money for all this junk. I need my cough syrup, do you understand?

Naushad slapped Lasnik on the back and pushed him towards the bridge. He slammed the door shut. Lasnik stayed rooted beside the gate, staring at the school bags flung onto the ground like offal from a quartered sheep. He put his hand inside and drew out the books, laying them aside. Then he fished for the pencils. He found three, one in each bag. He put one pencil in each of the side pockets of his overcoat, and stuck the shortest one into the flap of his woollen cap.

Lasnik walked past the bridge and turned towards the small house with the shop at its corner. He was no longer afraid of what he had seen in the Numberdar's house, for he knew Periting would often speak to him, giving him missives to carry, telling him things no one else knew, for he was Lasnik, blessed by the spirits, given special powers to understand their language, to know that the sparrow's nest in his belly was full of secrets buried deep. He knew things others could not even imagine. He knew that tiny little sheep, round and white, were actually born in the pod of a red chilli. He knew that the white radish which grew out of the ground was actually his grandfather's beard, that the dadang drum had within it a small, bald boy who told him these secrets.

Lasnik stood in the small garden seeded with turnips and tomatoes, cauliflower and cabbage. He fetched a tin of water from the drum and rolled down his soggy trousers. He must wash himself and change before returning to the Numberdar's house. The partridge would be hungry, and the Peri with the Crown of Fire was waiting for a pencil.

Lasnik dug his hands into the pockets of the overcoat. He drew his hands out and stared at a wad of lint, a mottled feather, a clutch of hair, a safety pin, a walnut, and a half-eaten dried apricot.

The pencils were gone.

The sun was at its zenith when Kulsoom's body was found, lying beside a jumble of trampled tumbleweed in the middle of the island. Massive granite blocks bordering the stone circle of Hele-Sehrun guarded the twisted body of a woman whose neck was clearly broken, hair splayed like the scattered nest of an eagle. The gold-panners found her, spotting her from the raft they used to cross the river. They had seen a body spread out against the rocky ground and had imagined it to be an animal that may have lost its footing on the steep slope above Hele-Sehrun. This body had something grotesque about it, in the aspect of its contours, the limbs twisted, head bent to an impossible angle. Disregarding their fear of the island and the ancient stone circle, the gold-panners paddled the raft close enough to see that it was not an animal at all, but a woman, her head battered against the rocks when she must have fallen.

Word of this grotesque death was brought to the Numberdar's house by four men carrying a wooden raft between them, the woman's body stretched across the inflated goatskins used to keep the vessel afloat. The men banged on the door loud enough to cause Moosa Madad's youngest wife to rush out of her room startled and bare-footed, her shawl slipping from her head. Moosa staggered out as fast as his thick legs could carry him, alarmed by the insistent and violent beating of his metal gate. Mariam, distressed and confused, stood at the wall separating the orchard from the courtyard, heaving, one hand clasped around her mouth. Straddling the low wall like a hulking bull, Moosa yanked open the gate and shouted at the men waiting in the lane to be patient and to calm down. Why were they making such a clamour, loud enough to wake up the dead?

Slung between the four beams of the small raft which carried the gold-panners on their journeys across the Winter River, Kulsoom's body was brought into Moosa Madad's house with a degree of difficulty. The four men had to turn the raft to an oblique angle in order to get it through the gate leading to Moosa's courtyard. As they dipped the raft, her body slumped to the lower side, her head sliding into a corner, wedged between the goatskins and the wooden frame. Her belly, swollen, rounded, rose from the middle of the raft, half the moon shimmering above the black mountains. Her limbs flailed across the bloated goatskins, bouncing and slapping against the beams, as if they, and not her, were still alive, jerking like a lizard's severed tail. Her hair was wet from the water of the river rising between the wooden beams, strands falling across her face, bits of dirt and sand stuck to her cheeks, to her twisted hands. One foot jutted out from beneath the tattered shawl thrown over the lower half of her body, the chipped nail polish on the toes seeming to bleed.

Moosa stood beside the raft, unable to speak. His face was immobile except for the rhythmic pulsing of his jaw as he clenched it. Moosa's hands hung loose, fingers twitching uselessly. The gold-panners lowered the raft onto the courtyard floor. Kulsoom's body slid back to the middle, her legs slithering back to settle upon the goatskins, feet splayed outward. The gold-panners spoke in low voices, avoiding Moosa's bewildered gaze. They did not know who the woman was, but believed that the Numberdar would be able to identify her. Saudukh Das was the village closest to Hele-Sehrun; perhaps she was from this village, then. If she was from this very village, then they had brought her body to the right place.

Would the Numberdar of Saudukh Das confirm if they were right in bringing this woman's body to his house?

Moosa stared at Kulsoom's face for a long time, unable to shake his gaze from the gash cutting across her forehead, almost cleaving her skull above her brow. The dried blood around the gash was caked; the wound was choked with sand, gravel and bits of grass, like a furrow in a freshly ploughed field. He opened his mouth but no words came. A chill wind blew across the courtyard, stirring dead leaves into a whirl. Moosa wiped the droplets of sweat trickling down the side of his face with his arm. He could not look at the broken body lying across the goatskins and shifted his gaze to the orchard. Mariam had slumped against a tree. She held on to its trunk as if the tree were a beloved returning after an absence. Moosa winced; Mariam's head was bare; a rush of dark curls cascaded onto her shoulders. She was so lovely, so young, this girl, this woman, his wife, soon to be the mother of his son.

Moosa called out to Fatimah and waited, uneasy, shifting his weight on his feet, unable to speak any words of sense to the four men standing patiently before him. What could he say? Perhaps he was wrong, perhaps they were wrong, perhaps this was not a woman from his community, perhaps the men had made a mistake and brought her here for no good reason.

Fatimah trudged into the courtyard and stood behind Moosa, unsure of why her husband had called her out to the courtyard, the very place he had forbade her from frequenting. Fatimah lowered her head and greeted the men standing beside the wooden frame. Who were they? Why were they here at this hour? What is it that rises from the middle of that frame?

Moosa stepped aside and asked Fatimah to see if she recognised the body. Fatimah took a step forward and stopped, covering her mouth with her hand, smothering a cry. She screamed, clasping her mouth with both hands, sobbing.

Kulsoom, it is Kulsoom. That awful man's wife, Naushad's wife. It is Kulsoom, poor Kulsoom, unfortunate Kulsoom. It is Kulsoom.

Tears flowed down Fatimah's cheeks. She beat her bosom with her fists, inconsolable. Moosa laid a hand on her shoulder and turned her attention toward the orchard where Mariam sat hunched against the tree, holding her head in her hands and rocking back and forth on the balls of her feet.

Go and attend to Mariam. She is deeply distressed by all this. Go now, look after her. She should not fall sick, you know, not in this condition. Let her rest. Put her to bed. She has tossed and turned all night, that poor girl. Go now. I will take care of this business here.

Moosa told the men that the woman was, indeed, from his village, that he would take care of the burial, that her husband would be informed, that the men had done a good deed by retrieving her body and placing it in his care. The men asked Moosa if it would be possible to arrange for the woman's body to be lifted and placed elsewhere so that they could take their raft and return to the river. Moosa nodded. He pointed to the wooden platform in the verandah.

The men lifted Kulsoom's body and placed it on the platform. Picking up the raft from its four corners, tipping it on its side, the men bid farewell to Moosa and left his home. The sky was clear, the water was calm, there were a few hours of daylight left. Perhaps there may be some bounty yet that the sands of the river could yield.

# *Altar*

## 20.

*We heard him, we watched him, we could smell him even from our place in Zameen Upar, that man-boy with the silver skin and hooded eyes; he was ours, he was the rope that bound his people to us, he was the one who would bring the circle to a close, he will bind the bellies of pregnant women, he will bind the mouths of foul men, he will bind the tears of weeping children, he will bind men for fighting and for killing, he will bind the way of the Tallest Yatz, he will bind the Stones of Hele-Sehrun, he will bind the stars of the sky, he will bind the waters of the Winter River, he will bind the bleeding otters, he will bind the pieces of the Broken Land, he will bind the fissures of the Black Mountains, he will bind the barren plain, he will bind the torn flesh of the white fox, he will bind the severed neck of the slaughtered goat, he will bind the falling feathers of the snow-cock, he will bind the desolate sighs of Yakh Sherlim, he will bind the golden eyes of Sinopish, he will bind the drooping tail of Tish-Hagur, he will bind seven hundred fairies, he will bind the springs of glacier, he will bind the outlets of springs, he will bind Sumading, the Greatest Yatz of Zameen Andar, he will bind all creation, he will bind Soni of Zameen Upar, he will bind seven hundred daughters of Peris, he will bind the booming of drums, he will bind all this for in the moment that he has lived, the moment has also lived, and all things that are bound are boundless.*

# Chapter Twenty

So, it came to pass that in that neat, well-appointed house, built block by block with his own hands, Moosa Madad faced yet another challenge, burdened as he already was with the inexorable presence of an unknown man, barely breathing, lying in the alcove where he would sleep on nights when his youngest wife would pass her monthly blood. Moosa was already broken with the knowledge that his beloved daughter was torturing him with her recalcitrance. He sighed; the bristles of his moustache quivered, the harrowed whiskers of a river otter lamenting a lost fish. He held his head in his hands for a moment, then asked Khadijah to find a sheet with which to cover Kulsoom's body, lying in the verandah, one eye gazing at infinity, the other swollen shut with a cut slicing across its lid. Khadijah wrung her hands, shaking her head from side to side in refusal, her eyes haunted with the spectre of death and burial, heart tormented by the familiar, final act when the breath inhaled is released as the miasma of the soul. Moosa shouted at her, berating her, asking her if he was expected to do everything around here, even cover the damned woman's corpse so that the flies don't settle on the bloody wound cutting across her face? Khadijah continued to wring her hands, frenzied into motion, staring at something in the middle distance, speaking incomprehensible words, taking quick, small steps, hurrying from one corner of the baiypash to the other, darting like a frightened, blind mole, searching for a sheet which did not have florid whirls of colour or a splash of flowers sprayed across it.

Moosa watched her hypnotic dance with glazed eyes, following the bent figure around the room as if a thread led from him to her spectral, skeletal form, hovering from corner to corner like vapour after the rain. He was tired, not having slept much during the night, listening for the sound of a knock on the gate in case Hassan had returned with the medical supplies, as promised. Now, head heavy with the weight of so many burdens, Moosa left the baiypash and slid into his bed in the little room he shared with Mariam, a habit in which he found comfort, especially after a vexing day, or after a good midday meal. Moosa was tired, staying awake half of every night since the wounded man had been brought in, anxious, wondering if sheltering a stranger was wise, given this time of great uncertainty. Just the other day there had been news of a jailbreak; four prisoners convicted of murdering several foreign mountaineers and their local cook had attempted to escape. One had been shot outside the prison, one injured and apprehended. Two had escaped and disappeared into the ravines and gulleys of the Black Mountains. Was he harbouring one of them in his house? What if the police found out? How would he explain the man's presence? Why had he not reported him to the police? Of course, Moosa remembered, the road to the nearest police station had been blocked off by the landslide. How could he have informed the police when he couldn't even take the man to hospital and was now weighed down with his care? And what of this woman, lying lifeless in his verandah? How had she died? Had she jumped from the cliff, as so many women had done before? Or had she fallen, slipping from the precipice? Or perhaps she was pushed. By her husband? By the Periting? Why would she want to take her own life when she had four little girls to raise? Why did these women do something which was sinful in the eyes of the Almighty, for only He could give life and take life, *for whoever throws himself down from a mountain and kills himself will be in the Fire of Hell, throwing himself down therein for ever and ever, whoever takes poison and kills himself, his poison will be in his hand and he will be sipping it in the Fire of Hell for ever and ever, whoever kills himself with a piece of iron, that piece of iron will be in his hand and he will be stabbing himself in the stomach with it in the Fire of Hell, for ever and ever.*

Moosa's eyes flitted with every persistent thought. He wanted to rest, to forget about his problems for just a brief moment of respite. He wanted to be free of responsibility, he wanted to smell the musk of his wife's skin and stroke the silk of her body. He was of no use to anyone in this state, unable to keep his eyes open, unable to think clearly. He would rest for a while, just a brief while, and think about what needed to be done. The dead woman's husband, No-Show-Naushad, had to be informed; the imam at the mosque needed to be informed, a grave needed to be dug, the village men would have to accompany the funeral procession, and the mourners would need to be fed. All this would fall to him, a man with no sons, just two sulking women, another one with child, and a daughter stubborn, mulish, making his fraught life even more difficult. He would rest for a while, clear his head, then make important decisions, assign tasks to willing hands, who so ever chanced to turn up at his gate that morning. Hassan had not returned, Noor's cell phone was out of reach – he must still be at the site of the landslide, a day's walk back to the village. And where was that dull-witted half-man half-boy, Lasnik? He had never returned after pissing on the courtyard floor. Probably too ashamed to come back, mortified at the clumsy mishap of wetting his pants and soiling the courtyard floor. How could one rely on a witless creature like him to look after a living thing, his prized partridge, when he couldn't even keep from pissing in his own pants?

Sighing, Moosa clasped Mariam around her waist, smelling her hair, a billowing raincloud spread out on the pillow. He held Mariam close to his own bulk, feeling the softness of her flesh, stroking her porcelain cheek. At least there was something that gave him pleasure in this household of women who did nothing but annoy him. Nuzzling his moustache against Mariam's slender neck, distracted by her nubile presence, Moosa closed his eyes, golden shafts of the afternoon sun warming his grizzled cheek and lighting the insides of his eyelids with a rich glow, orange like the pumpkins he had harvested that autumn. Insistent thoughts drifted in and out of his head like spiralling mist, obscuring his sight, muddling his vision. Sleep descended upon him, a dark curtain, but pestilent thoughts cut through like brilliant shafts of sunlight:

*what was the point of this violent death would it make the lives of her daughters any better what did it cost to bury someone these days would Naushad have the money that man could barely feed his daughters let alone bury his wife and what about the soap and the incense sticks and the length of white cotton to drape around the corpse how much would all this cost how much did it cost to bury my sons Akbar Ali and Asghar Ali how deep is that hole where I have lost myself looking for them Asghar Ali Akbar Ali my sons pieces of my heart the light of my eyes how much I miss them where are you now when your father needs you especially when problems descend with the weight of water shapeless yet oppressive Ya Ali Mushkil kusha Oh Ali Ease my Burden.*

A rude clattering at the gate woke Moosa just as he sank deep into the well of dreamless sleep. It must be Lasnik. That boy had a knack of turning up at the most inopportune moments. Loath to leave his warm bed and reluctant to disentangle himself from the embrace of his sleeping wife, Moosa thrust his feet into his slippers and trundled out.

Walking through the orchard, he could see Khadijah sunk

233

on her haunches, moaning, clutching a blue sheet in her claw-like hands, her head pressed against the takht where Kulsoom's body lay, partially concealed by the tattered shawl left behind by the gold-panners. Kulsoom's feet were exposed, bare, already yellow, bands of grey sand edging her ankles. Moosa stopped. Striding into the verandah, he snatched the sheet out of Khadijah's hands. Fumbling, unsure of how to unfold it, he spread it over Kulsoom's shattered body. Swearing, muttering execration, Moosa covered Kulsoom's bloodied head and yellowing feet and bounded out into the courtyard.

Lasnik stood beneath the window of the storeroom, staring at the shadowy figure inside, blurred by the wire mesh. The Peri with the crown of fire held the tiny pencil he had salvaged from the fold in his cap and managed to push through a hole in the wire mesh while Moosa struggled to cover Kulsoom's body stiffening on the takht in the verandah.

Lasnik stared at the Peri as she smiled at him, a soft bow shaping her pink mouth like a small river boat. His own mouth hung open. He had no words to speak to her. There were no words to speak to such a being, a Peri more beautiful than any he had imagined in his deepest sleep, comelier than Zainab with the budding breasts, lovelier than the baby goat born last winter.

Startled by the weight of a heavy hand on his shoulder, Lasnik shrieked. He spluttered senseless words, shut his eyes, terrified. Lasnik did not dare to turn around to face the Yatz who would most certainly be watching over the Peri, beautiful as she was, silver like the light of the moon on the river. Lasnik opened his eyes and stared at the window. There was nothing there.

Moosa was saying something to him, words muffled in a thick fog, words he did not understand.

Where have you been, boy? I've been waiting, you see, there

are things to be done. And you, you're just standing there, as if you've seen a spirit, a Periting, young man! Now listen to me, carefully, you understand?

Moosa grabbed Lasnik's shoulders and turned the boy towards himself. Clutching Lasnik's chin in his hand, Moosa wagged a finger in his face as he explained the tasks that needed to be done. Something terrible had happened. Lasnik needed to rush to Naushad's house and bring him here, telling him that the Numberdar had to see him immediately about an urgent matter. Lasnik stared at Moosa's mouth. He watched Moosa's pink tongue as it shoved the words out of the vermilion cave of his mouth. He stared at the large white teeth and the fleshy lips rubbing against them, opening and shutting like an unlatched gate. Lasnik blinked when Moosa mentioned Naushad. Lasnik tried to protest, horrified that he would have to return to the snake-man's house, terrified of what the snake-man would do once he discovered that Lasnik had failed to lug the school bags to the junk-dealer, that Lasnik had stolen the pencils from the very same bags, that one of those pencils was now in the possession of a Peri, the one he had stuck in the fold of his cap, the others disappearing through the holes in his coat's pockets. The pencils were all gone now: how would he face the snake-man?

N-n-n-no go N-n-n-naushad house, S-s-s-saheb. N-n-n-no go, Lasnik stammered, his lower lip quivering and tears slipping towards the edge of his strange, hooded eyes.

You must do as I tell you, young man, do you understand? You must go to Naushad, tell him to come here immediately. It is a matter of grave importance. Then go to Zarina's house, tell her I need her immediately and bring her here. Now go!

Moosa turned Lasnik towards the gate and more or less shoved him out into the lane. Lasnik stood his ground, refusing to leave. He stood in the lane like a pillar, stiff, unyielding, both fists clenched into balls. Moosa raised his voice, spitting cruel words at him:

Do you want me to tell everyone in the village that Lasnik pisses in his pants, eh? Tell me that, young man? And look at you now, wearing your mother's shalwar, a woman's shalwar. Are you not man enough to wear a man's pants, eh? Tell me, come on now, do you want me to tell the whole village that Lasnik wears his mother's trousers, eh, do you?

Lasnik dropped his gaze and stared at the faded pink shalwar, the only thing that was clean, his other pair of trousers still wet and laid to dry on the big rock by the river. To get to the river, Lasnik would have had to walk past the homes of young children who would surely have mocked him and laughed at the dark stain on the crotch of his dirty pants. Too ashamed to tell his mother of his accident in the courtyard of the Numberdar's house, Lasnik had taken her shalwar from the washing line English Madam had strung up for Sakina in the small plot outside their house. Removing his urine-soaked trousers, dropping them onto the floor of the goat's tiny stall, he had pulled on the pink shalwar and rushed back to Moosa Madad's house, anxious to fulfil the task the Peri had ordered him to carry out. She had said it was a matter of life and death. Lasnik's eyes dimmed at the memory of the Peri's beautiful face. He squeezed his eyes shut. Tears splattered onto the cobblestones outside Moosa's gate.

Moosa stepped close to Lasnik and patted his back, embarrassed by the distress he had caused this man-boy. Lowering his voice, he told him to go, quickly.

Look here, my son. It is already quite late. I cannot leave the house with just these women here, and that other woman, that, that, corpse, lying in my verandah. I can't get any signals on my damned cell phone; the damned tower must have been knocked down in the landslide. Otherwise, I could have summoned any one of the men in the village. But you see there is no one here, no man, at least. Go, my son, help me in my time of need.

Lasnik looked up. The tears on his cheek dried up; his hooded eyes shone. He opened his mouth, tried to speak, but the words turned to dust and blew away. Moosa chewed on the ends of his moustache, biting his lips, exasperated.

Go, my boy, go now. Do you think I would have asked you to do this had my own sons been alive, eh? Aren't you like a son to me, young man?

A gust of breeze blew through the faded pink shalwar covering Lasnik's crooked legs. He shivered. Yet something warm penetrated his cold body, something comforting, his mother's breath when she blew a prayer over him on nights when his skin turned silver with the chill. Lasnik nodded his head, blabbering something about being *good son good boy dutiful boy Lasnik go Lasnik go fast Lasnik go Naushad house Lasnik bring Zarina Lasnik good boy Lasnik good son*. He struck his staff into the cobbled lane and made his way down, rushing, dragging his lame leg behind him as if it were the weighted end of a plough. It had not occurred to him or to Moosa that this was the first time in known memory that Lasnik had not stumbled over the words he nudged out of his mouth. It was the first time his speech had been smooth, unhindered, confident. But Moosa had not noticed this, for there was much that distracted him, things more important than the healing that love makes possible, words which are spoken with tenderness, words of belonging, of worthiness.

Moosa turned to go back into the courtyard, saddened less by Kulsoom's death, which was inevitable, considering the madness of her foolish act, and consumed more by the thought that he, Moosa Madad, Numberdar of Saudukh Das, had to beg a lame, witless boy wearing a woman's pink shalwar to do what his sons would have done without him even having to ask.

# Altar-Hik

## 21

Sometimes, Mahabakara told us, sometimes we feel that we have lost all that was precious to us. We try so hard to save all the things which make our world rich and beautiful: the trees, the water, the air we breathe, the soil upon which the seeds fall, to grow into trees in the Years of Plenty. We try to save our progeny from predators, but sometimes we fail, and instead of protecting our children, we place them in the path of danger, hiding them in places which appear to be havens of safety. And sometimes, when we believe that we have lost all that gave us reason to live, when we think that we have failed in our duty to shield our young from the hunter's intent, we are able to find ways to retrieve that which we thought we had lost.

Long ago, in the Old Times, before the Baltar Tree of the Boiber Valley began to wither, splintering apart, leaving its heart naked and unprotected from the merciless wind, my great-grandmother, the most beautiful markhor known on this side of the Black Mountains — tall, her horns curling upwards to a height of half a keslik, a tapered black beard lying against her red coat, her eyes round, shining like sunlight on the snow — gave birth to three exquisite kids. These she loved more than life itself. She named the first one Shurujano Paalo, the second was called Mamujano Paalo, and the third, the naughtiest of them all, was named Phacuno Paalo. One day, the mother went in search of food, to graze in the valley below the Towering Spire. As always, in order to make sure her children stayed out of harm's way,

238

she would hide them in the home she had built inside the fissure that split the black rock and gave her enough space to raise her young until they, too, could roam the peaks, exploring the ridges and spurs and crags of their homeland. She had fashioned a door out of the wood of the deodar tree. Each day, she would tell her children to lock the door from the inside, warning them not to open the door for anyone but her. That was how it was, and each day, once she had grazed on the tender shoots of grass growing on the side of the mountain where the sun spread its warmth with unbounded generosity, the mother would return to the place where her children were safe, waiting, hungry. She would feed them, clean them, nuzzle their necks, untangling their soft coats with her tongue, tickling their bellies with a soft scratch of her magnificent horns.

One day, while she frolicked with her kids, a son of Bhura Reechlo, the biggest bear that was, watched from the crest of the Towering Spire. This huge creature, the colour of walnut bark, waited until the mother had left for the grazing ground. He had not eaten for many days, his favourite meal of Turshoon evading him, even as he tried hard to hunt the small marmots which were so delicious yet so hard to catch. He was just too big and, now, too old to run after the scampering creatures who would disappear into their warrens before one could say, I Cry We Cry for the Yalmik Sky.

Now, he stood before the door to the house where the three kids waited for their mother to return. Calling out softly, in the voice of a female, he asked the kids to open the door. The elder of the three kids, Shurajano Paalo, refused to open the door, saying this doesn't seem like our mother – it is too soon for her to return. The bear called again, more plaintive, whining: Please open the door, dear children, it is your mother. At this, the second kid, Mamujano Paalo, said: It is not our mother. She does not have such a thin voice. The bear cleared his throat and spoke again, this time with greater authority. The third kid, Phacuno Paalo, was convinced that it was truly their mother and rushed to open the door. Once the bear was inside the house, he made

239

a meal of the three kids, burped, rubbed his fat belly and returned to his perch on the crest of the mountain.

When the mother of the three kids came home, she found the door to her house ajar. She called out to her kids. There was no answer. Frantic, she ran up the spur and called for them again and again, terrified that they had left the house on their own and were lost, or had fallen to their deaths in a ravine. She called and called, but there was no answer, only the sound of the wind blowing from the far peaks. She knew she could not return home without finding her kids, so she continued to climb the rocky spur, resting on a ridge, then making her way across the saddle to the far peak. Here she could see a large bear resting. From a distance he looked like a huge boulder, but she saw him breathe; she could see with her sharp, round eyes the hairs of his whiskers quiver as he exhaled deep breaths. Clearly, he was asleep, and bears only sleep once they have eaten their fill. She knew then that her kids had been taken by the bear. Screaming in fury, horrified that it may already be too late, she rushed up the crest, her hooves flying over the rocks and scree, carrying her to where the bear lay, curled, asleep, dreaming of his next meal. Without stopping, she lowered her magnificent horns and rammed them into the bear's belly, cutting it open with one deft shake of her head. By the time the indolent bear had opened his eyes, the three kids had tumbled out, skipping and prancing, bleating with delight, nudging their mother's teats, hungry. And alive.

# Chapter Twenty-One

The light from the window had shifted in the time it took Sabiha to write Nasser's name and cell phone number on the edge of the crumpled piece of paper now rolled up into a tight cylinder. There had been no nib on the pencil Lasnik had shoved through the hole in the wire mesh. Sabiha had peeled away the wood from the lead, biting down on the pencil to soften the wood. It was worn down to the last inch of its life. She had scrawled the name and number with the tiny bit of lead held tenuously in its slim shaft. Now she would wait for Lasnik to return and take her missive to Nasser. She trusted that boy, strange as he was. She knew he would not betray her. This was most important, for she could not endure yet another betrayal.

Sabiha watched the light as it moved across the uneven surface of the floor like a winged being gliding, gently stirring the air with the motion of its outstretched, feathered arms. She turned back to the window and arched her neck towards the gate. Getting the note to Nasser was her only chance to correct what had gone so terribly wrong. Surely, the young man who had professed his love for her, who had told her that he was sick with longing for her, who had whispered his devotion to her during stolen moments in the science lab, pretending to explain a chemistry experiment, writing a formula which was really a love poem, scrawling hearts and undying promises on the edge of her lab book, surely he would come for her, to ask for her hand, ending this terrible anguish of her incarceration, her degradation. She would wait for Nasser, she would wait for this deep chasm between her father and herself to be filled with love and trust and faith and all the things that had been promised to daughters, to wives, to a cherished beloved. She would wait for Nasser, counting the minutes, watching the gate. It didn't matter to Sabiha that there was a procession of crises that had come through that gate. It didn't matter to her that her father was preoccupied with things of more immediate import. All she wanted was Nasser to come to rectify this unintended mistake. Where was this man, the cause of so much heartache? Had he wondered why she had not come to school? Had he thought about her, missed her? Had he asked her friends about her, wondering what could be the cause of her absence? Would he come now that she had found a way to call him to her rescue?

Sabiha pursed her lips as the tears came flooding to her eyes. She strained her neck to watch the gate, almost toppling over the sacks she stood upon. There was no one about in her father's home, just a strange silence and a sadness which hung like a layer of smoke over the horizon at dusk. Sabiha stared at the gate, willing it to open, praying for Lasnik to reappear. That strange boy smelling of something pungent and stale at the same time seemed to be the only person she could trust. But where was he, where was Lasnik?

The fever that came over Lasnik suddenly frightened Sakina. He seemed to be seeing terrible things. He had returned from Moosa Madad's house limping, pale, whimpering like a wounded pup. Sakina had seen him once before like this, when the Periting had alighted upon him, that time when the rain had flooded the Chartoi, the water carrying away the summer's crop, leaving the village to measure each fistful of grain as if it was gold panned from the river. Lasnik had talked about the surging waters the night before the flood, through a haze of fever, mumbling in his sleep about hunger and death.

Now, Lasnik coughed and spluttered and brought up bile the colour of a goat's droppings. He vomited into the small, rusty tin Sakina had placed near him. She could feel the fever blazing. Restless, he flung off the miserable quilt she had thrown over him.

Lasnik opened his eyes and saw the largest Yatz of Zameen Andar standing before him, red eyes burning, his hair on fire, horns the size of lonely peaks spiralling upwards, snakes slithering across his hairy body, breasts bulging out of his ribs, his massive penis erect between legs the size of fallen pillars at Hele-Sehrun. He saw the Periting taunting him, hissing at him, telling him he wasn't man enough to wear proper trousers, that he wasn't man enough for anything because the tender flesh in his groin which burned when he saw Zainab and her budding breasts, that tender flesh was only good enough to be eaten as a single morsel between bites of his scrawny, useless limbs. They mocked him, threatened him with a gruesome death, now that he had failed the most beautiful Peri of all, the one with the golden crown on her head, the one who lived in that room in the Numberdar's house, the one who spoke to him and smiled at him with kindness held luminescent on the tip of the sun's tongue. He had failed her; now what awaited him? Where was his rope, English Madam's rope?

The distance between the little bridge cutting through the middle of Saudukh Das and the Numberdar's house was just over a mile. For a man who barely got around beyond his daily routine of waking up, washing, if at all, relieving himself, frequently, and religiously fetching a bottle or two of cough syrup from the local medical store, this distance was a fair way to go, especially as the reason for undertaking this journey had not been disclosed by the witless, dumb, lame boy sent with a missive for Naushad to come immediately to the Numberdar Saheb's house. The boy had spluttered nonsense about something terrible about to happen, or something calamitous that had already happened. Naushad had not been able to make sense of what Lasnik was saying, stuttering and mumbling, a string of saliva streaking down his chin. Naushad swallowed the coarse pancake his ancient mother had made, raw around the edges, soggy in the middle, a layer of walnut oil swimming across the mottled surface. Cursing his luck, a man not allowed to have a decent meal because his worthless wife had disappeared, probably consorting with that wayward woman Zarina, Naushad thrust his feet into his liver-coloured shoes and staggered up the incline to the only house sitting atop the summit of the hill overlooking the Winter River.

By the time Naushad stumbled across the gate into Moosa Madad's courtyard, he was winded, struggling to breathe, unsteady on his feet, which hurt from the pointed V of his coveted shoes. Moosa emerged from the room in the orchard. Wiping the sweat from his face, Naushad greeted Moosa, stepped towards him and offered a grimy hand. Moosa grunted, not meeting the man's bleary eyes, mucus settled into the corners like pustules. The two men stood in the courtyard for a moment. There were no words spoken. Then Moosa asked Naushad to follow him to the verandah. Naushad stood before the takht as Moosa pulled down the sheet from Kulsoom's face. For a moment Naushad stood still, staring at the yellow face, now bloated, a crimson bruise running from her eye to her jaw. Her lips were colourless; a cut coursed along the side of her mouth to her ear. Fine gravel clung to the raw wound. One eye was swollen shut, the other half-open, its gaze empty. Naushad could see the black river pebble of her cornea. There was no light in her pupils. He could see the sand and crushed mica clinging to her lashes as if they were her tears. He could see the small hole in her right nostril where she had once worn a gold nose-pin, sold to buy medicine when the eldest girl had contracted measles and almost died. He could see the place where her ears had once been pierced, sealed shut after the earrings had been sold to pay off a debt incurred when Naushad bought a motorbike and crashed it the same day, crumpling it against the side of a mountain.

Naushad let out a roar. He bellowed, shouting Kulsoom's name over and over again: *What have you done, what have you done?*

Moosa shook his head and stood alongside the raving man, hands folded across his girth, as if this was a normal thing that happened with the regularity of a birth or a marriage. Death was, after all, a marker of life itself, signifying the end of what we know on earth, the beginning of what is to be in heaven. Or hell.

True, Moosa had not seen a death as horrifying as this one, but it was known that women would die a ghastly death if they broke the rules of the Periting. So it was not a surprise for Moosa, just a terrible inconvenience, for now he had to arrange this woman's burial while there were more urgent things on his mind: taming his unyielding daughter and figuring out what to do with the wounded stranger dying inside the baiypash. On top of all his problems, he had to calm down this mad man, fevered with shock. Moosa would ask him to inform the imam and to fetch the cot from the mosque, knowing in his heart that this useless man would find even this last obligation towards his wife more than he was prepared to undertake. Useless, lazy, good-for-nothing Naushad. A dead-beat father and a lousy husband. But Moosa must ask him, for that was what tradition required. Once a woman was married and had left her childhood home, then, at the end of her life, her funeral bier was to be lifted by her husband or her sons. But

Naushad had no sons, and that seemed to be the greater sorrow for this pathetic, snivelling wastrel, a sorrow deeper than the death of his wife and unborn child. A son, perhaps? Could that child who died inside her belly have been a boy? Moosa asked himself, rubbing the palm of his hand against the bristle on his chin.

A son, the absence of a son was like a wound which never heals.

Lasnik knew there was something he had to do, but the sickness had made his head heavy, and the bile in his gullet made his tongue bitter. He had seen many things while asleep, many shapes that hovered before his eyes, darting from edge to edge of his vision.

Lasnik got up, waving his arms about, upsetting the rusted old tin can sitting beside him. His mother was startled; he pulled her near and whispered into her ear: *They will d-d-die. T-t-they will be f-f-found in the C-c-c-circle of Death.*

Sakina did not know what to make of it. She did not want to ask him who he was talking about, for often he only saw strange images of unknown form and face, and she would interpret them to the best of her ability, her imagining fed by fear and longing. She longed for the embrace of the man whose fragrance she could still smell on the shawl he had left hanging behind the door. She longed to hear him tell her that she and their son would survive that winter, without much food stocked in their tiny store, without fuel to keep them warm, without his comforting presence. Her every movement was weighed down with the knowledge that this man would never walk through the door and greet her and his only child, Lasnik, this man-boy who stank of urine and whose breath carried the acidic smell of ammonia and an empty gut. She knew that the boy's father would never return, that she, alone, would have to make sense of the things the boy saw and said. She knew this, and each day, each moment, she grew older with that realisation.

Zarina stood in the middle of the wooden bridge. Sakina called out again.

Sister, sister, please. Listen to me, sister. Wait for me, please.

Sakina gasped for breath, exhausted from her vigil at her son's side. After listening to Lasnik's puzzling pronouncement, she had made her way as fast as she could from her house to the bridge, looking for Zarina.

Sister, I need your help. It's my boy, Lasnik. He's very sick, keeps having visions. Burning with fever. Vomited all afternoon long. Very sick, he is. Lasnik. My boy, my son.

Sakina broke down, hunching over, both hands on her knees. Zarina held Sakina as she sobbed. She rubbed the distraught woman's back and steadied her.

Come, Sakina Bibi, I'll come with you. I have some medicine left in my bag. Let's see if it will help the boy. Come.

Zarina took Sakina's hand and led her back down the bridge. A strident shout ruptured the air.

You – wretched woman, Zarina! What have you done? What have you done, despicable woman?

The two women froze. Zarina turned around to face Naushad. He bounded onto the bridge with sudden alacrity and shook his finger at Zarina.

You. You are the one. You are the one who led her to her death. You are the one who I hold responsible for her death. You, wretched woman. Wait till your husband gets back from wherever he is, that fool. Does he know that he is married to a murderer?

Naushad lurched towards Zarina, punching the air. Zarina stepped back; Sakina stumbled. Naushad grabbed Zarina's handbag and pulled it. Zarina twisted the bag out of his hands and shouted:

What are you doing, man? Have you lost your mind? How dare you touch me? Get away from me. Accusing me of terrible things. You don't know what you are saying half the time.

I wouldn't touch you even if you were the last woman alive, you hear me? As for accusing you of terrible things, you tell me, then, eh? Tell me who murdered my wife. Eh? Tell me who sent her to the Chartoi. Eh? Tell me who pushed her over that cliff. You think the Periting did it? Eh? Do you? Do you? You did it, Zarina. You are responsible for the death of my wife, Zarina. Go, go and have a look for yourself. She is lying there, my wife, lying there, dead, in Moosa Madad's house. Go, go and see what you have done.

Sakina fell against the wooden barrier on the side of the bridge. Jade water surged beneath the bridge. A whirlpool circled between several large rocks. Zarina rushed past Naushad. Naushad spat, then made his way across the bridge, his liver-coloured shoes tapping rhythmically against the wooden planks.

The light from the small window had shifted now. Within an hour or so, four men had brought a woman's dead body into her father's courtyard, her father had sent Lasnik off to summon the dead woman's husband, the woman's mad husband had screamed and shouted, threatening to settle accounts with the person responsible for his wife's death. And Lasnik had disappeared.

Sabiha turned to face the drying flank of the goat her father had killed in the summer; it was a young animal, not yet ready to die, but there was no choice, her father had said. It had fallen from the cliff near the Doorway of Chartoi, landing on its back, something that rarely happened, the goat being the progeny of the sturdy markhor. This young animal might have lost its footing on a slippery rock, falling several hundred feet below the pasture where the four streams met. It had broken its neck, and was already dead when the young man who herded Moosa's livestock for a small compensation during the summer months found it. Moosa had slaughtered it nevertheless, passing a sharpened butcher's knife across its neck, purifying it of its beating blood, cleansing it for the platter of a believer.

She turned back to the window and stretched her neck towards the gate. Moosa stood by the cemented platform, holding the partridge in his cupped hands. He shouted for Khadijah, then Fatimah. Fatimah ambled through the orchard, rushing as fast as her full form allowed her. She stopped at the wall. Sabiha could see her mother's haunted eyes. Moosa roared. Sabiha saw the vein in his forehead swell up like a surging water channel. He held out his cupped hands and showed Fatimah the partridge. The bird did not move. Its neck flagged to the side, broken.

Zarina burst through the gate, her eyes wild, hair dishevelled, shawl trailing behind her.

Saheb, what has happened? What has happened, Saheb? Is she . . .?

Moosa turned around, the dead partridge held in his outstretched hands.

She is dead, Moosa said. He had tears in his eyes, and his lips shook as he spoke, choking on the words.

Zarina gasped. She put her hand to her mouth and moaned. Moosa stood beside her, the dead bird's feathers lifting in the slight breeze. Fatimah shook her head and took Zarina's arm, walking with her towards the verandah.

Leave him. He has lost his mind, sister. All he thinks of is his bird and that man inside. Come, she is here, your friend, Kulsoom.

Sabiha watched her mother turn away from Moosa as he gazed at the dead partridge with sorrow deep in his dark, troubled eyes. Then she stepped down from her perch, clutching a roll of crumpled paper in her hand.

A slight breeze stirred the blue sheet covering Kulsoom. Low waves rippled over the battered body. Khadijah sat beside the takht, one arm across her face, her head slumped against the rough wall behind her. Slowly, as if shifting a layer of top soil to cover seeds just planted, Fatimah uncovered Kulsoom's face. Zarina fell forward, weeping, calling to her friend, Kulsoom, *What have you done, what have you done?*

Moosa watched the three women in the verandah. Picking up the spade leaning against the wall separating the courtyard from the orchard, he walked towards the leafless trees, struck the dark soil and began to dig a small grave, the first of at least two that needed to be dug before the sun sank below the horizon.

A great force will shake the mountains and the river will stop flowing; its waters will lie still as if the river's soul had died. The snow will come late this year. The animals that pastured in the Nullah of Chartoi will need to be brought down early; a leopard who lived in the snow will be prowling around the Chartoi. This leopard will be hungry, no one will be safe any more, the snow has not fallen in its home this year, it will be forced to seek its prey lower down. This time, it will make Saudukh Das its hunting ground.

That was what Lasnik had said before the mountain had cracked and crumbled, a low groan emerging from the belly of the earth as the massive outcrop crashed into the river, damming it for a length of twenty-one kilometres, washing away the road, drowning the villages, the animals, the trees, the orchards, the fields. The leopard had survived; it watched from the ridge across the river.

Sakina said all this to Zarina without looking at her. Rarely meeting the gaze of even the women of the village, Sakina seemed to always scan the horizon for something she waited for. Only when Zarina had fished out two white tablets from her handbag and placed them in her palm did Sakina look at this kind woman's face. Sakina thanked her for helping her son endure the ordeal that visited him every time the Periting foretold calamitous events as they unfolded around the unsuspecting residents of Saudukh Das.

When she is buried, dear sister, when our sister is buried, will you come and see my boy? You know how much he cares for you, always talking about the magic in your hands, how you have healed his many injuries, how you do not laugh at him, how you speak up for him when others tease him. You must come, dear sister.

Zarina heard Sakina through a haze. She was not thinking about Lasnik and another bout of his frequent maladies. There was a greater calamity weighing her down. She asked Sakina for a bar of soap, a vial of camphor, some cotton wool, a box of incense sticks and several lengths of white muslin. Zarina would have to bathe Kulsoom's body and prepare it for the burial. There were no women in Kulsoom's family to undertake this task, other than Injeer Bibi, her doddering mother-in-law, incapable of doing anything except worshipping her son and occasionally changing the dirty, urine-soaked cloth tied around the youngest child's groin.

Sakina wrapped the goods inside six lengths of thin white muslin and handed the package to Zarina. She placed one hand over Zarina's and told her that she would not accept payment for these, that Naushad would not have the money in any case, so let it be something from her side. After all, Kulsoom was like a sister to us, and she suffered so much in her lifetime. We could do nothing to stop the anguish of her existence, let us give her a decent burial.

The sun was slipping behind the high peaks now, its rays oblique, falling against the fields and the orchards at an angle that cast stretched shadows over the dark soil. Zarina pulled her shawl over her head, wiping her face with one end. She must hurry back to the Numberdar's house. Soon the men would assemble to carry Kulsoom on her last journey over the bridge and through the narrow lanes of Saudukh Das, a village bathed in the magical light of the golden hour, the hour of respite, and, sometimes, the hour of regret.

Moosa peered at the plastic bag suspended from Hassan's hand. A tube of ointment, a roll of cotton wool and a bottle of spirit lay jumbled amongst a few blister packs of analgesic tablets.

I was able to get these, Saheb. That's all they had in the dispensary. There were quite a few injured who needed treatment after the landslide, Saheb, so this is all that was left. I tried to hurry back as fast as I could, the road being blocked for miles, Saheb.

Good. Allah knows I waited long enough for you to return. And so much has happened during your absence, you know. Now, go inside and wait for me. I have to go to the imam before sunset. I have to ask for the wooden cot to carry the dead body, you see.

Hassan looked up at Moosa. His mouth hung open. Had the wounded man died? Surely it was too late for the medicines then? What was the Numberdar saying?

Am I too late, Saheb? Has he died? The – the – stranger, the wounded man? Hassan stammered, the medicines in the blue plastic bag hanging like unheeded counsel.

Who? The wounded man? Oh no, my son. He is still alive, at least, the last time I checked, he was still breathing, with some difficulty, you know. No, no, the cot is for that wretched

Kulsoom, that loafer Naushad's wife. She was found dead, probably hurled herself off the cliff at Chartoi, you see. Could be the work of the Periting, if you ask me. Nobody believes this any more, young man, but I'm telling you, she should never have gone up there, you know. Now she's dead, just like that, Moosa snapped his forefinger against his thumb.

Hassan stared at Moosa. He had nothing to say. It was good that he had returned in time to save the wounded man. It was too late to save that woman Kulsoom, daring to climb to the Doorway of Chartoi dressed in red. Everyone in the village had talked about it, and he had known that things would not end well for that woman. He'd known it when he'd seen her the day he had gone with Noor to bring the firewood back for the long winter ahead, bringing down the wounded man instead.

Moosa patted Hassan on the shoulder. It was a relief to see this young man stand before him. It was as if all his troubles suddenly disappeared. Another man in his household, another soul who would look after these useless women in his absence: one spectre in constant mourning, one insubordinate mother of one wayward daughter, one beautiful young woman, soon to be the mother of his son, and one cadaver, soon to be buried. Once that was done, things would fall into place.

Once this nightmare was over, he would pursue the matter of his daughter's marriage. Hassan would make an excellent son-in-law: sturdy, willing, reliable. Look at how the young boy climbed over that huge pile of rocks, half a mountain, just to get medicines for that bloody man. Moosa took a deep breath, adjusted his woollen cap on top of his large head and watched Hassan walk into the baiypash where the bleeding man lay. How long will he be in my home? How long will I be responsible for him? It is said in the Holy Book that we must look after a stranger for three days and nights. Has it been that long? *It has been enjoined that indeed Allah provides for*

*His creation and rewards those who are hospitable towards their guests, looking after them in times of need, in times of hunger and want. Surely, Allah will increase our provision if we welcome strangers and give them succour. Surely, He will redeem us and reward us on Resurrection Day.*

Moosa sighed, slung his shawl over his shoulder, swung the gate shut and trudged down the steep path towards the mosque. He had waited long enough for Naushad to bring the cot that would carry the body for burial. He should have known that useless man would not be capable of even this small task. After all, what did he do for his wife in her lifetime that he should now do in her death?

# Altar-Altó

## 22.

The evening had begun to settle over the high peaks, shrouding the Temple Spire, shadows moving across the slopes and spurs. Bhura Reechlo gathered us around him. He said he had one more story to tell.

Tell us, we said. We gathered around him and waited, our mothers shielding us from the growing chill. Bhura Reechlo had a smile on his face when he began, clearing his throat and chuckling softly, a sound like a bird warbling in springtime.

This is a story which teaches us no lesson, no lesson at all, children. It is just a story and must be treated as such. It is a story told by an old creature, a beast who has lived out his life watching his own kind suffer, and survive, and suffer again. It is a story of how we, Spirit-Beings of Zameen Upar, have wanted to live in harmony with those of Zameen Par, how we considered them to be a part of the world we inhabited, without difference, without conflict, without hatred and malice. This is how it used to be, before we were hunted down mercilessly, the possibility of our disappearance becoming more and more real with every mangled corpse of our kind found on the hillsides and the meadows, deep inside the forests and along the banks of the Sherdarya, the Lion River. This is a story of longing and loss. Hear it, and heed only the sadness in the tale, for there is no lesson here, my children, except the lesson of regret and repentance.

Long ago, before Yakh-Sherlim was forced to leave her hunting ground, the snow no longer falling on the black rocks, a bear, just like me, brown and burly, prepared for the coming winter. As those of you who belong to my tribe know, it is common for our kind to seek out a plant called ajali, which we find growing amongst the wild grass. Just before winter sets in, we seek to eat this plant, which puts us in a state of torpor, helping us to sleep away the harshness of the Frozen Time when nothing but hunger grows. After about six mintiks, when the spring arrives with its blossoms and buds and birdsong, we awake and go in search of sustenance amongst the plants and berries and forage for nuts fallen from the trees.

One such spring, a strange thing grew out of the thawing land. A bear, an ancestor of mine, hungry, had been scratching the dark soil, still wet with melted snow, and had smelt something unknown to him. It was the stench of rotting flesh. The bear dug deep into the earth, throwing out clods of moist soil. Soon, before him lay the exposed knee of a human, the clothing torn to reveal a wound where a wild animal had tried to disinter the body. The bear, curious, but also afraid, continued to dig, seeking to understand this strange thing that grew out of the land which had hitherto only produced succulent grasses and satisfying berries. Clod after clod, the thing emerged out of the earth. It was a young woman, beautiful, her throat cut across the life-vessel which had bled onto her fair bosom. The bear, unable to believe that such a thing of beauty could be dead, brought the body of that young girl home. He fell in love with that beautiful face, her delicate hands, stiff and coated in dark soil. He dragged her to his den where he had spent the last six mintiks asleep. Once inside, he propped up the woman's body, making her lean against the wall of his cave. Then he brought her a spindle and some wool from the Dzho and growled meu-meu-meu, encouraging her to spin. That way, the bear thought, she would have something to do while he foraged for nuts and fruit, ensuring that both of them had enough to eat. And when winter came, she would have spun enough yarn from the wool to knit herself a coat with which to keep herself warm, naked as she was from head to dainty feet, her clothes having rotted in her shallow grave.

*Every day the bear would bring fruit and nuts and berries and lay these before the young woman's inert body. After a week had passed, and the offerings began to rot, and so did the flesh on the woman's bones, the bear had no choice but to eat her up. He did so, then roamed the slopes in despair, regretting having found her, having fallen in love with her.*

*We looked at Bhura Reechlo in disbelief. Why would one of the Spirit-Beings want to bring a human into his home? Did he not know that those of Zameen Upar and those of Zameen Par were not fated to live with each other; each constantly vigilant, constantly suspicious of the other?*

*Bhura Reechlo smiled, that soft, gentle smile that would lift his black mouth into a crescent. This was before the time of the Cut Path and the Travelling Wheel, he said. It was before we came to know our place, before the lessons that we learnt the hard way.*

# Chapter Twenty-Two

He stirred, mumbling, saliva bubbling in the thin crack of his mouth. Hassan stared at him, watching foam form on the edge of the man's dark lips. He was in the baiypash with the wounded man and one of Moosa's wives, hovering around the door leading into a small room in the corner. The woman was barely visible in that dark place; she seemed to press herself into the wall as if she was a part of it and not a living thing at all.

Hassan peered into the porous gauze of light falling from the sky, making out the woman's bulky form. She was the Numberdar's second wife, Fatimah, mother to the most beautiful girl in all the valleys beneath the sky, Sabiha. He had seen Sabiha just a moment ago, framed in the high window looking out towards the courtyard. She had called to him as Moosa swung the gate shut behind him. She had asked Hassan to telephone the number scrawled in the margin of a rolled-up piece of paper, to ask Nasser, the man who would answer, to come immediately to meet her father.

Hassan unrolled the cylinder of crinkled paper one more time. His sweat had seeped into the cracks where the note had been crumpled, bleeding the ink curled into a crude heart. He could not make out the words; they were just lines and loops he had never learnt to decipher. She had said he must call this man, *but do not tell my father: it is a matter of life and death*. He could read the number for a cellular phone; that much he had learnt to do, for who could not operate a cell phone now that the tower had been erected to catch and send signals from one end of the world to the other?

The wounded man gurgled, choking on his saliva. Hassan crushed the note in his hand and stuffed it into his pocket. In the corner near the storeroom, Hassan heard Fatimah mumbling her daughter's name, leaning towards the door to the storeroom, as if kissing the heavy wood, as if it was an entrance to a shrine: *Sabiha, Sabiha, my dearest daughter, what will he do to you?*

Hassan got up. Why was Sabiha in that room where families kept supplies for the long months of winter and odds and ends they did not need every day? Why was that beautiful girl in that small, suffocating room? Many discomfiting thoughts crowded Hassan's head. He walked out of the baiypash towards the orchard, one hand clutched around the note crammed into his pocket. Who was Nasser? Who was this man she wanted him to call?

He would need to think about this. Should he do this beautiful girl's bidding, even if it meant that his chances of marrying her would be diminished by the sheer act of being in contact with her without her father's consent? Who was Nasser? What was this note with the hearts and flowers etched onto its borders?

Walking through the verandah, Hassan stopped at the low wall bordering the courtyard. He could see the empty cage at the corner of the gate. What had happened to the surviving partridge? He had not seen it inside the baiypash, but then it was dark in that room where the stranger lay, where Fatimah sat as if mourning someone's death. The girl had said it was a matter of life and death, that Hassan must not speak to her father of the missive he held in his pocket. Should he tell the Numberdar, to whom he had committed his devotion and loyalty, hoping to win his favour? Should he keep this beautiful girl's secret, hoping to win hers?

Near the new room in the orchard, Zarina lifted the corner of a shawl strung across a rope stretched between two trees. Hassan could see the body of the dead woman shrouded in white. He turned away. Nothing was right. He would have to do something to make things better, better for Moosa Madad, father of the girl he loved. For without his approval, he had little chance of winning her hand. He would do the right thing. He would make things right. Sabiha, the one and only woman he would ever love, Sabiha, the name which pulsed in his eyes with the morning's light, Sabiha . . .

He would call that number and ask Nasser to come. It was the right thing to do, for in summoning the man who seemed to have won her heart, he would be doing what she had asked him to do, and in that deed lay the seed for a garden of possibility.


Dusk fell without declaration, like a name forgotten but which remains on the edge of memory, there and not there.

There were not many who gathered at the Numberdar's house that evening, waiting for Kulsoom's body to be carried out on the small wooden cot provided by the imam. Naushad wept. Several men comforted him, patting his back, whispering words of commiseration. He was inconsolable, blabbering about who was going to look after the daughters, who would look after his old mother, who would look after him? Moosa looked at him, weary-eyed, irritated with the spectacle of remorse displayed by a man who looked like a pile of discarded scrap set aside at the junk-dealer's shop.

Noor had come, to Moosa's great relief. He was finally back from his task of helping to clear the road. Tomorrow, for sure, the road would open and the wounded man would be taken to the nearest hospital. These past few days had been difficult, and it would be good to see the last of that stranger, even if it was propitious to receive a guest to whom one offered the

260

best one had, the most one was capable of providing. What was it the imam had said in his sermon the other day, immediately after the mountain had collapsed, destroying the houses in the surrounding villages, rendering the people homeless, without shelter for the night? Moosa remembered the words of *Surat adh-Dhariyat* well. He recited them under his breath:

*Has the story reached you of the honoured guests of Abraham? Behold, they entered his presence and said: 'Peace!' He said: 'Peace!' and thought: 'They seem unusual people.' Then he turned quickly to his household, brought out a roasted fattened calf and placed it before them. He said: 'Will you not eat?'*

Yes, this man was unusual indeed, without a name, an address, a scrap of paper that would reveal his identity. Yet, it was endemic upon a good Muslim that a guest, even a total stranger, be taken care of for at least a day and a night, at most for three days, after which hospitality would depend upon the charity and generosity of the host. Beyond that, the imam had said, it was not permissible for a Muslim to stay so long with his brother that he makes him sinful, for by prolonging his stay till nothing is left to offer him, surely the host may be forced to commit a sin for which he will, verily, repent.

Moosa shuddered. The evening was settling on the slopes, moving swiftly towards the plateau where Moosa's house stood, solitary, solid, a beacon on dark nights. It had been four days and three nights. Four days since the man had been brought into his home, since the first partridge had died mysteriously, since his daughter had shown herself to be insubordinate to her father's will, since Mariam had seen this wretched woman whose body now lay wrapped in a shroud, five layers of white cotton binding broken bones, waiting to be interred in the cold ground. It was time that all things that were necessary for the smooth running of his household, of the community, be restored; time for the man lying in his baiypash, breathing like a mare about to foal, to leave of his own accord; time for his daughter to tell him who wrote her that brazen poem, for that insolent person who dared transgress the order of things around here to be dealt with in a manner appropriate. And it was time for the battered corpse of the unfortunate woman to be laid to rest.

Moosa turned to Noor and signalled to him to get the others ready to lift the cot. Noor turned to Hassan, Hassan turned to Naushad. Moosa was the fourth man to lift the cot up onto his shoulder. Four men, four corners of the cot. Four days. A fourth night awaited. Moosa breathed long and deep, and stepped into the lane.

It was a slow procession, passing like a reluctant covenant through lanes cloaked in the day's last light. The sky was mottled with puffs of billowing clouds, grazed here and there by the sun's dying rays. Dappled strokes of vermilion swept across the haze rising over the river; a breath of cerulean blue hovered over the water, calming the flow, slowing the journey from peak to estuary. Between these layers, songs of remorse floated, drifting towards the island where Kulsoom's body was found, splayed against gravel and scree.

The four men were joined by four others, taking turns to carry Kulsoom on her last journey. A dozen more followed these men, children joining the funeral procession as if it was a game to be played, their laughter golden against the grey of dusk. Before the procession arrived at the graveyard upon the far slope of the hill, most of the men of Saudukh Das had come out of their homes, performing the obligatory ablution so that they may offer special prayers led by the imam in the open ground outside the mosque. Four times they raised their hands in prayer, praising the Almighty in unison:

*Allah o Akbar, Allah is the Greatest*
*I witness that there is no God but Allah*
*And Mohammad is his messenger*
*Allah o Akbar, Allah is the Greatest*
*Give your mercy to Mohammad and his progeny*
*Allah o Akbar, Allah is the Greatest*
*Forgive all Muslim men and women*
*Allah o Akbar, Allah is the Greatest*
*O Allah! This is your servant and the*
*Daughter of your servants coming to you*
*And you are the Best to whom one might go*
*O Allah! We know nothing of her except goodness*
*Please forgive us and forgive her and*
*Give her the best Place before You,*
*Replace her among her household with your Mercy,*
*O the most Merciful of the Merciful*

Kulsoom's body was laid on its side, a clod of hardened mud placed beneath her neck. Naushad staggered out of the grave, his hands crusted with soil. The talqin, someone said. Will you not recite the talqin? Naushad stared at the assembled crowd and spat a gob of dust-coloured phlegm onto the heap of soil piled up beside the grave. He wiped his forehead and mouth with his elbow, then mumbled something about it getting dark; the grave had to be sealed. The talqin can be recited once the grave is filled with soil, Naushad said.

You must recite it, brother, for you were closest to her, her husband, a man said.

You must recite it in her ear, brother, for her soul still hovers above her mortal remains, and it longs to be united with the Creator, another man said.

Recite the talqin, brother. She must testify that there is no God but Allah and that Mohammad is His Messenger.

Several men spoke at once. Naushad stared, bleary-eyed, at nothing. It was getting dark; the men were silhouetted against the last light. He shook his head, then picked up a handful of soil and threw it into the grave.

You must recite the talqin in her ear, brother. She must hear you, the first man said.

Yes, you must place your hand on her shoulder and lean down to her ear, then recite the testimony. Otherwise, how will she hear you?

Naushad bent down to the heap of soil and picked up another handful. He clenched the soil in his cupped hand for a moment, then looked into the eyes of the men who advised him of his duty towards his wife. He spoke in a trance.

She is dead. Don't you see that? She cannot hear me. If she had heard me, if she had ever listened to me, she wouldn't be dead, soon to be buried under this bloody pile of dirt, you understand?

Naushad flung the dirt into the grave and picked up a third handful. Rubbing the earth between his fingers, he looked from man to man and shook his head. He grimaced as he spoke to them:

What did you know of the trouble I had with her, eh? What do you know of her evil ways? She doesn't even deserve this burial, I'm telling you. What business did she have to climb to the Chartoi, in the shadow of the Doorway? Eh? Can you explain that to me? You think a woman like her, a woman who tempted the Periting, a woman like this, should be given a chance to testify? Why, if we knew that she had flung herself off that cliff, then she should not even be given a decent burial, for there is no mercy for those who take their own lives, didn't you know that? There is no forgiveness for her, my friends. She is condemned to the Fires of Hell, where she will, for the rest of eternity, throw herself off that mountain over and over again. But if you think the Periting, enraged at her wayward ways, pushed her over the cliff, then recite the talqin, my friends, recite it yourself.

Naushad turned towards the grave and threw the third handful of dirt onto Kulsoom's shrouded remains. Then he brushed his hands against the crumpled shawl he had wound around himself and walked away.

# Altar-Iskí

## 23.

Once, in the Times of Growth, there was an abundance of wild roses that grew in thickets at the edge of the forest. One such bush of wild roses had in its prized possession a beautiful white pearl. One day that pearl fell out of its grasp and rolled away into the forest where a bird found it. Eyeing the shiny pearl, the bird hopped up to it and picked it up in her delicate beak. The bush of wild roses asked the bird to return the pearl to her, but the bird, blinded by the shining pearl, shook its head and flew away to a distance. The bush of wild roses asked the thorns growing on its stems to prick the little bird so that it would return the pearl. But the thorn told the wild rose that it was tired of pricking and pricking, and that it would not prick the little bird. The bush of wild roses then turned to a fire smouldering nearby and asked it to burn the thorn so that it would prick the little bird who would not return the shining pearl. The fire, tired of burning, said it would not burn the thorn. The bush of wild roses then turned to the water in the stream flowing by to douse the fire because it would not burn the thorn that would not prick the little bird who would not return the shining pearl. The water said it was tired of dousing and dousing, so the bush of wild roses turned to the ox grazing in the Maidan and asked him to drink up the water because the water would not douse the fire that would not burn the thorn that would not prick the little bird who would not return the shining pearl. But the ox said he was tired of drinking, so the bush of wild roses turned to the man *in the field and asked him to kill the ox, but the man said he was tired of killing. The bush of wild roses asked the rat to chew up the man's leather boots, and the rat said he was tired of chewing. The bush of wild roses asked the cat to eat the rat, and the cat, said it was tired of eating. The bush of wild roses turned to the women who were winnowing sheep's wool to chase the cat, but the women said they were tired of chasing. The bush of wild roses asked the Wind of the Long Night to blow the wool away. Just then the Wind came forcefully down from the Hundred Mountains and blew the wool away. When the women saw the wool blowing away, they took their winnowing sticks and rushed to chase the cat. The cat was drinking the milk on the stove. The women beat the cat. A burning branch fell out of the stove, setting the house on fire. The rat ran from the fire and hid in the man's leather boot. The man wore the boot, the rat bit the man, the man whipped the ox, the ox jumped into the stream, the water spilled over and doused the fire, the fire died before it could burn the thorn, the thorn remembered to prick the bird, but the bird had flown away when the Wind of the Long Night had begun to blow from the Hundred Mountains. The hut was burnt down, the ox drowned, the man beat his wife, the cat ran away, the rat died of hunger, and the bird, she was never seen again in the Boiber Valley. And the bush of wild roses never saw her pearl again. To this day, the bush of wild roses still mourns the loss of the shining pearl. To this day, the wild roses listen to the sound of the howling wind and remember that sometimes it is best to lose something you think you love rather than to lose love itself.*

# Chapter Twenty-Three

The evening folded itself around the valley now. Somewhere, far away, the sound of a boy calling out to a lost animal floated long and forlorn on the still air. Zarina bathed and changed and assured her children that she would be back soon, worrying that her frequent absences from home would loosen the tie which bound them to her. She was distraught, unable to get out of her mind's eye the image of Kulsoom's bruised body and ravaged face. Zarina had wept her grief while bathing her dead friend. Not wishing to hurt Kulsoom's body more than it already was, Zarina had asked Mariam for a pair of scissors and cut the crimson shirt down the side, peeling it away from Kulsoom's body as if it was another skin. The shirt was torn at the shoulder, as if someone, something, had pulled Kulsoom before she had plunged headlong onto the forbidden island which held at its centre the Place of Assembly for the Yatz. Fatimah had poured warm water over Kulsoom's body, and Zarina soaped the grazed and scraped skin, caressing the taut belly where a child had breathed just some hours ago. Zarina had wept, her tears flowing freely, only Fatimah watching her, Mariam confined to her room. Zarina could hear young Mariam sob, muffled, choking sounds emerging from the little room with the fluttering yellow-gold curtains. As soon as Kulsoom's body was bathed and draped, Mariam was to be sent away to her sister's house in the next village; Moosa did not wish this terrible death to cast a portentous shadow over the prospective birth of his son. Soon, Zarina hoped in the depth of her heart, Mariam would become a mother, and perhaps Moosa would have the son he longed for, perhaps then some semblance of peace would settle over this lonely house at the top of the hill, looking over the Plain of a Hundred Sorrows.

That was what Kulsoom had wished for, a son. And that wish was not to be granted, if Zarina could understand the scribbling in the margin of the creased piece of paper tucked into Kulsoom's brassiere. It was the ultrasound Kulsoom had shown to Zarina when they had washed clothes at the river, just a day or two ago. There was a mark made in the margin of the small image of a shadowed embryo: the mark for a female child, a circle with a cross beneath it. Zarina had seen this when Kulsoom had showed her the image. She had understood it, but could not have imagined that Kulsoom would take the step that she did, resulting in her gruesome death. Kulsoom was carrying another girl, her fifth daughter. Kulsoom had unburdened herself of this unbearable reality.

Zarina picked up the parcel packed with bread and stew for Kulsoom's girls, slung her bag onto her shoulder and, kissing her children on their heads, bidding their Api farewell, she left. Sakina had implored her to come as soon as Kulsoom's body was taken for the burial. She said Lasnik was delirious, talking with words she could not understand. He had a raging fever and shivered even while buried beneath three heavy quilts. Sakina had been tearful when she had left Zarina with Kulsoom's body in Moosa Madad's orchard. But she was not mourning for the dead woman; she was grieving for her dead husband, without whom it was hard to face this strange condition that afflicted her son from time to time. She feared that Lasnik may succumb to the illness that ravaged him again and again. Then how was she to face the coming months of hunger on her own?

Zarina had just a few tablets for fever left. These would have to do; her bag was now empty of medicine. Whatever

Hassan had brought would be for the man in Moosa's baiypash. What a ruinous time it was, what misfortune had befallen them. And all this with Ibrahim so far away, no news of him for so many days, and winter settling all around the valley.

By the time the helicopter landed in the valley below the massive, snow-laden peaks, the sky had lit up with a million stars. High above them flashes of lightning cut through the dark night. Thunder rolled over the distant slopes. A team of medics stood on the perimeter of the helipad, a stretcher and a gurney parked neatly on the tarmac, side by side. Zaki was brought out of the helicopter and placed on the gurney. The medics rushed Zaki into the field hospital while Ibrahim tried to stand up on his own, peering at the men who had come to receive them at the base camp. He shook hands with the men, unmindful of the bleeding blisters, and stroked Malika as she stood, her tail stretched into a straight line, looking in the direction of the enclosure where a dozen German Shepherds gathered to stare at her, the globes of their golden eyes glowing. Ibrahim smiled despite the exhaustion, despite the strain of almost losing his life, almost losing his friend, Zaki. Then he pointed towards the barking dogs and shouted at them, raising his voice above the whirring of the rotor blades: Here! Here she is! Malika, the Queen of Wolves. She can teach you a thing or two about rescuing hapless soldiers like us from the grips of an avalanche. Are you ready for her, boys?

The rotor blades quietened down now. Somewhere in the distance, a cloud burst with winter's rain. And somewhere, far away, two other dogs sought shelter with men who knew that their own survival was in caring for all the creatures that lived on the same soil and breathed the same air. For what were we without one another?

★　★　★

Night had fallen, shrouding the little lanes and narrow alley-ways in deep shadow. In the distance a clutch of men walked back to their homes from the far slope where Kulsoom had been buried. Moosa walked at the front, the imam of the mosque and Noor alongside him. The men were quiet, an occasional cough rupturing the silence. The glow from the imam's cigarette lit Moosa's face. He frowned; his mouth was stretched tight against his teeth. The imam spoke about the need to pray for the salvation of the dead woman's soul, as much as for the deliverance of Naushad's mind and heart from the grip of evil forces that had clearly seized him, tearing him away from believers. It could even be that the Periting had cursed both Naushad and his wife, and look what devastation that has brought, the imam said. Noor looked at the imam briefly, then asked him if he truly believed in the Periting and the Yatz, being a man of the Book, a man of Allah. The imam shook his head, clicking his tongue, dismissing the supercilious question, waving his hands from the sky to the ground as if to say that all these things existed, they were part of the Creation of Allah. It was Allah who sent these beings to torture humans, or to set them on the right path.

Look, look at the way in which both of them were being punished, one with such a brutal life, the other with such a brutal death.

Moosa heard nothing of the imam's deep reflection on sin and sanity, on the sacred and the wicked, life and death, for in his head the only words that made sense right now were the ones Hassan had spoken to him as soon as the grave was sealed, the last handfuls of soil falling like rain upon the mound of freshly turned earth.

Hassan walked several paces behind Moosa, alone. In his hand he held a cell phone. He stared at the small, square screen, scratched in places, misty in others. He dialled the

271

number scrawled onto the tattered piece of paper he had shown to Moosa Madad a short while ago. There was a crackling hiss, then nothing, a hollowness, nothing. He dialled again, and again. Only silence. Hassan stopped walking. He turned back towards the slope of the mountain, now plunged in darkness, the crest purple against the silver of the sky. Without a word to Moosa, Hassan ran back to the top of the ridge where Kulsoom's grave lay sutured, palm prints sealing the soil. Breathing hard, Hassan stopped, his heart thudding against his chest. He held his hand high, peering at the bars on the screen that indicated the strength of the cellular signal. There was one bar only. Hassan climbed further up the slope. Here there were fewer, older graves, eroded, the collapsed frames of carved wood from another time strewn over ditches where burnished bones shone in the moonlight. Hassan held up his hand again. There were two bars, then three. Hassan brought the phone down to his chest and redialled the number. There was a long silence, then the buzz of a phone ringing.

Hello?

Hello. Hassan choked. His heart pounded in his ears. He was sweating now. A rivulet of cold sweat dripped from his forehead into his eye.

Yes? Who is calling? May I know who is calling?

The man's voice was even, smooth. An educated man. Hassan swallowed hard. Against the black shadow of the mountains, he was so small, so insignificant. This man, this man with a voice so refined, an air so superior, was the man she loved. Sabiha, the golden-eyed one. This was the man she had asked for. This was the one who had drawn the pictures of hearts and flowers on the piece of paper carrying marks he could not decipher, words that carried meaning not meant for him. This was the man to whom he had to deliver her missive.

I have a message for you.

A message?

Yes, from Sabiha.

Who? Sorry, your voice is breaking up, brother. May I know who is calling?

Hassan raised his hand above his head, walking up the slope. The bars slid up and down the side of the screen.

She asks you to come to see her father, the Numberdar.

Who is asking for me? Can you speak a bit louder, brother?

Hassan walked backwards, higher and higher up the incline. His hand was tired, he was tired. His heart was tired. Tears burned his eyes. He could barely speak the final words of the missive she had asked him to deliver.

Sabiha. She says you must come, tonight, to see her father. It is a matter of life and death.

Hassan brought the phone down to his chin. The tears flowed now. He had not wept like this since his baby sister had died. But this time the agony was deeper, much deeper, for whom could he tell of his suffering?

The air inside Sakina's room was stale, rancid, the pungent scent of burnt juniper rising from the hearth. Lasnik lay in the dark. Sakina lit a match and held it to the open mouth of a dented lantern, the glass globe around its flame cracked and dark with soot. The room was cold. The fire in the hearth had gone out; the air was laden with smoke, grey ash spilt out onto the floor. There were not many things inside the room: a few pots, an odd tray, a mirror held against a windowsill. In the wavering glow of the lantern's flame, Zarina saw the pallor of Lasnik's face. He stared at something above him, mumbling words, phrases, a low, muffled keening. Zarina bent down and felt his forehead for fever. Lasnik's arm shot out from under the heavy coverings. He held her hand down, pressing it against his cheek. Zarina sat beside Lasnik. He continued to stare at something on the stepped ceiling of the room. Then, without warning, he turned to look at Zarina with eyes that burned. He spoke in the voice of a lettered person, neither male nor female, but clear and distinct, each word formed completely, each thought, complete. He spoke without a break, not breathing between words, not turning his gaze away from Zarina:

*I will bind the thing that torments me for I will bind the Yatz of Zameen Andar I will bind the forces that keep me awake at night I will bind the bats and the birds I will bind the boulders and the bulls I will bind the burning juniper I will bind the upper pastures I will bind the chilghoza trees I will bind the green banners of the Peris I will bind the heat of the hearth I will bind the soot of the fire I will bind the leaves the grass the creatures living there for I am Lasnik son of Lance Naik Rahim Jan Hero of the Black Mountains I will bind these with the coil of the snake I will bind these with the Rope of Modernity.*

Zarina listened, her eyes wide. Lasnik had never spoken like this. It was not a voice she recognised. His cheek was hot; when she released her hand from his grip, her fingers were moist, clammy. Zarina got up and fumbled for the few tablets she had kept in the zipped pocket of her handbag. Giving two of them to Sakina, she said he must swallow these with a glass of water. Zarina cast a cautious glance at Lasnik. He was still looking at her. Now his eyes were as they always were: glazed, dull, unseeing. She turned to go.

Zarina stumbled out of Sakina's home and made her way towards the bridge. On the way she would deliver the food Api had prepared for Naushad and his family. Other neighbours were sure to provide a meal, at least for the next three days of mourning. Moosa's wives would have come, offering to help with the girls, frail little creatures, undeserving of such deep anguish.

She did not know how she would keep herself from screaming

at Naushad, screaming her grief, her anger, at what he had compelled his wife to do. She knew that Kulsoom had neither slipped from the precipice, nor been pushed by the Periting, that she had flung herself off, despair dragging her up to that terrible place from where so many women had looked upon the vast expanse of their valleys and had chosen, despite the infinite beauty, despite the children left behind, despite the birdsong and the lush meadows, the gurgling brooks and the scented orchards, chosen to end their lives at that very point where Kulsoom's battered body had been found.

Moosa slid open the bolt on the door to the storeroom. For a moment he faltered; his hand shook. Taking out a lock from his pocket, he slid the bolt back and hooked the lock into place. He clicked it shut, tugging at the lock to make sure it was secure. Moosa walked across the baiypash and sat near the wounded man. He watched Noor draw out a few strips of analgesic tablets from the plastic bag and put them aside, next to a small roll of cotton wool and wad of gauze. Noor asked Moosa if Zarina would come soon. Moosa shrugged his shoulders. He did not look at Noor.

Next to Noor, leaning against a wooden pillar, Hassan stared at the stranger's inert face. Had he brought the medicines too late to save this man's life? Was it too late to stop Nasser from coming here to claim Sabiha? Had he done the right thing, calling that man and asking him to come to the Numberdar's house?

There was a knock against the metal gate. Moosa looked up at Hassan. Hassan looked away, a sick feeling in the pit of his stomach rising into his gullet. He walked out of the baiypash towards the gate. A shadow drifted past the window high up in the wall. It was too late now to undo what he had done.

★ ★ ★

Zarina hurried over the bridge. She must do what she could for that man in Moosa Madad's house. Then she must return to her children. She was tired now, tired of always worrying about others, of always doing for others. There was so much that she could not repair. There was always something that was beyond her ability to make better. And there was no one to whom she herself could turn for comfort.

Sometimes it was too much to bear, the burden of caring for a family alone, waiting, constantly watching the far road for signs of dust being whipped up by a military jeep, bringing her husband home.

Ibrahim fell into a stupor while his hands and feet were immersed in a warm bath medicated with an antiseptic preparation. Blood-filled blisters had appeared on his toes, his nose had lost sensation, while his hands throbbed with pain, the wound bleeding, now that blood coursed unhindered by the freezing temperature of the post he had left behind. The post that had been buried on that awful night of devastation. The last post in a war without purpose and without end.

Now Ibrahim dreamt of his journey home. He saw himself in the jeep, Malika sitting behind him, guarding his most precious gift for Zarina. Surely, she must be waiting for him! Surely, his children would be watching the gate, waiting for sight of the jeep that would bring their father home. Surely, this nightmare was over and the journey home would be smooth and uneventful, for what could compare with the catastrophe they had survived?

*Hands and feet bandaged and bound, his toes and fingers treated for lacerations and frostbite, Ibrahim sat in the front seat of the jeep next to the driver. The jeep swung past a rocky protrusion, and Ibrahim could see Rustam and Sohrab peering at him from behind the grey mass. Ibrahim waved to them — the dogs leapt up and disappeared into* the sky, revealing behind them the form of a black horse with a man astride it. The horse was taller than any other creature Ibrahim had seen — taller than the height of a Baltar Tree. The man riding the horse carried a sword and a shield in his hands, and held these up in the air as Ibrahim drove past him. Beside the horse was a snow leopard, a bear and a wolf with golden eyes. These creatures were massive too; Ibrahim craned his neck to meet their gaze. They looked upon Ibrahim as if he was their progeny, as if he was their own. Suddenly, the sky turned black and dark clouds burst with rain, pelting the jeep with drops the size of a sheep's head. The driver turned to Ibrahim and expressed his concern that the journey between the military camp and the closest town would take longer than expected. Swirling rain veiled the road ahead; landslides blocked their passage, leaving narrow, treacherous tracks for men and beasts to climb across. It was not possible to proceed further, the driver told Ibrahim. We will have to wait till the morning, sir. I will see if there is some place where we can spend the night, sir. It's all right, brother, I am fine in the jeep. I have the dog with me, my friend, and you know there will be no place which will allow me take the dog inside. I can't leave her outside, brother, not this one; she is as dear to me as my own children. The driver turned around and looked at the grey-gold dog sitting on its haunches behind Haveldar Ibrahim Ali. The man smiled. He noticed a small plant wrapped in a woollen cap placed on the seat next to the dog. Peering at the slender branches and the bird-like buds of the plant, the driver shook his head and looked at Ibrahim. Sia-chen, sir. You are coming from Sia-chen. And you are bringing Sia-chen with you, sir. And this golden dog, is she from the great mountains too? Ibrahim nodded his head and smiled back at the driver, a silver amulet around his neck glinting in the light of the stars. He was Zaki, Mohammad Zaki, his friend, his companion, his brother.

# Altar-Wálti

## 24.

*They say the world will come to an end when a daughter conspires against her father, for that is a bond which is sacred, and nothing should sever that rope which ties a daughter to her father. But, our elders tell us, there was a time when a daughter, a princess, resolved to rid the kingdom of her cruel father, a man descended from the Yatz, a man who terrorised his subjects on the night of the full moon, for that is when he expected a newborn baby to be sacrificed for him to devour, limb by delicate limb.*

*At last, the Periting of Zameen Upar grew tired of his tyranny, his capricious tastes crowned by his propensity for cannibalism, a taste that grew accidentally. It is said that one day his cook brought him a mutton broth, the likes of which he had never tasted. After much inquiry as to the nature of the sustenance upon which the sheep had grazed, it was learnt that the woman who had reared the baby lamb had suckled it at her own breast, after losing her child born on the same day as the lamb. The King, merciless and greedy to satiate his unassuaged hunger, ordered that little babies who had suckled at their mothers' breasts be killed on the night of a full moon. In this manner, much to the horror of his subjects, every little child was sacrificed to his unending desire for human flesh.*

*After hundreds of such moonlit nights, dark for the hearts of the mothers whose children were brutally taken away from them, a young man, handsome and healthy, able to shoot an arrow from one ridge to another peak, snaring his prey from side to side, came upon the cruel king's beautiful daughter. The two young people immediately fell in love, and the princess wished to ask the handsome stranger to stay with her, in her father's palace. The young man confessed that he intended to do just that, for he was the son of a Peri and had heard of a cruel king who subjected his people to the worst terror of all. He agreed to marry the princess if she would kill her father. This, the princess refused, horrified that this handsome man should expect her to kill her own father. However, deeply in love with him, she said she would assist him to find the soul of her father so that he could destroy it. The princess used all kinds of ploys to convince her father to reveal the whereabouts of his soul, and after refusing food for many days, becoming weak and pale, she was able to get her father to tell her that his soul was of snow, that it would perish only by fire.*

*So it was that the people of the kingdom were asked by the princess and her consort to gather the branches of the juniper and fir trees, to fashion these into torches, and to light them, holding them aloft as they marched to the castle. As this procession of peasants proceeded towards the castle, the king began to feel more and more uncomfortable, gasping for air, screaming that the air was too hot for him to breathe. Agitated beyond consolation, the king mounted his steed and prodded him to jump across the castle walls. The horse jumped and landed in a pit cleverly constructed by the young man. As soon as the king found himself at the bottom of the pit, the peasants threw burning torches into the pit and destroyed the cruel king, leaving the kingdom in the hands of the beautiful princess and her handsome husband, a just and humane ruler who forbade the killing of any more babies. Instead, he pronounced that once a year, just before winter, every man would make an offering of a sheep to the king, who would feast along with his people, singing and dancing, swinging lit branches of the juniper tree above their heads, remembering that the evil ruler had been defeated by their ancestors, long, long ago.*

# Chapter Twenty-Four

Nasser was a tall man who looked taller with a head of thick, curly hair framing his chiselled face, the cleft in his chin clearly discernible even in the flickering light of the fire in the hearth. He was lean, slightly stooped, the doorways in the houses of Saudukh Das not high enough to allow him to pass through without bending his slim frame. Now, he lowered his head in the presence of Moosa Madad, the Numberdar of the village, the father of the girl to whom he had written a love poem, a careless, meaningless poem scribbled on a page from his science lab inventory. Next to Moosa stood Noor, discreet, eyes dark, a tidy moustache fixed above the curve of his mouth. Hassan took his place near the pillar in the alcove. The glow of orange flames in the hearth mixed with the sharp white glare of an emergency light and cast hard-edged shadows on the floor. Nasser removed his shoes at the door, shook hands with the men and followed them into the baiypash.

The fire crackled, hissed and spluttered. Moosa prodded the burning logs with a stick. He turned to Hassan. His voice was low, almost inaudible.

We need more wood, young man. You need to bring some kindling in from the verandah.

Hassan nodded and walked to the door. He did not look at Nasser. He could not look at this man, dressed as he was in the apparel of a city-dweller, a wide-collared shirt, smart jacket with many pockets, and trousers fitted over his pole-like legs.

His presence in this house was unbearable. But Hassan had done what the girl had asked him to do. He had done what Moosa had asked him to do. He had done the right thing.

Moosa sighed as he lowered himself onto the floor, near the hearth, facing Nasser. He passed his hand over his face, licked his lips and, folding his hands, one into the other, dropped them onto his lap.

The wounded man's uneven breathing was the only sound in the baiypash, and then Moosa's broken, beaten voice, speaking after a long silence.

You are new in this village, aren't you?

Nasser looked up. The beam from the lamp struck his glasses. There was a small burst of light at the edge of the frame. His eyes were gentle, large, hazel, fringed with dark lashes swooping upwards. He nodded, smiling at Moosa.

Yes, Saheb, I moved here just a month ago. Shortly after the new session at school started.

The school, yes, that cursed school. That's where all this trouble started, you see. That damned school.

Nasser stopped smiling. His forehead creased, the curls falling over his brow moving in a slight breeze from the door as Hassan came through, carrying an armful of firewood.

So, what do you do at the school, young man? Moosa's voice was strong now. He pulled out a cigarette and matchbox from his front pocket. For a while he rattled the matchbox between his forefinger and thumb, then, shaking his head, he struck a match and raised it to the cigarette held between his thick lips. Moosa inhaled, squeezing his eyes into slits. Nasser spoke, telling him of his transfer to this village from the large town where the river was being dammed, of his desire to study at the university in down-country, of his work as a laboratory assistant at the girl's school. Moosa opened his eyes. The smoke from his cigarette curled out of his mouth.

Lab-otry assistant, eh? Is that right, young man? Who do you assist? The young girls in the class? Eh?

Moosa stared at Nasser, his eyes squinting in the smoke. Noor looked up, surprised to see the Numberdar smoking after he had sworn never to do so, after the burnt bodies of his sons had been buried with full military honours, sons who were martyred not in war but because of a careless flick of a burning cigarette in the compound where the military vehicles were parked.

Hassan turned from the hearth and shot a glance at Moosa, his mouth dry. He had done the right thing. But what was Moosa doing? The tone of the Numberdar's voice was harsh, menacing.

I assist them with the experiments, with measuring the chemicals and making sure they pour the right liquids into the right beakers. Sometimes accidents happen, Saheb, terrible accidents. These can harm the girls, the students. So, I have to make sure that nothing wrong happens, that nothing goes wrong.

Moosa pursed his lips, sucking on the cigarette. He inhaled long and deep. Blowing out the smoke through the opening at the side of his compressed mouth, he sneered at Nasser, taunting him with the hand that held the cigarette.

So, you are the one who ensures that nothing goes wrong, eh? Is that right, young man? You make sure that accidents don't happen, isn't it?

Moosa flicked the ash from his cigarette onto the floor. The ash settled in front of Nasser's feet. Noor got up. He brought an empty saucer and placed it in front of Moosa. Hassan stayed by the hearth, his back to the other men. He stuck a log into the hearth, watching the coals crumble and scatter at the heart of the fire.

Yes, Saheb, I have to ensure that the girls follow the safety regulations and that they wear the aprons and also the masks and sometimes it is necessary also to wear the goggles to protect their eyes.

Yes, I'm sure all that is really necessary, especially when it comes to girls with golden eyes, eh?

Nasser looked at Moosa. He frowned. He tried to say something, but the words stuck to the roof his mouth.

Tell me, you assist girls with golden eyes, isn't it? Girls with golden hair. With golden eyes, isn't it?

Moosa said these things slowly, savouring the agitation playing on the young man's face. It was time for Moosa to seek retribution for the anguish he had suffered these many painful hours.

Nasser didn't speak. Noor shifted on his haunches, then put the medicines and cotton wool back into the plastic bag. He got up, signalling to Hassan to join him outside. Something unpleasant was happening here, something he could not understand. He knew of Nasser, recently employed at the school, a fine young man, educated, keen to help others learn. But what was this about girls with golden eyes and golden hair?

Noor tapped Hassan on the shoulder and asked him to get up. Moosa continued pulling on his cigarette. The door opened and closed, leaving just him and Nasser in the baiypash.

Is that what you do, young man? Is that what your parents taught you to do? Is that what you learnt in your uni-vusties? Eh? Tell me, young man.

I'm not sure what you mean, Saheb. I don't know what you are talking about, Saheb. Nasser stammered, eyes wide, face pale. Beams of light travelled across the curve of his spectacles. Nasser looked towards the door. Where had the other men gone? Where was Sabiha?

Moosa stood up. He flung the cigarette towards the hearth. The muscles in his neck stiffened. He called out to Hassan. Nasser got up. His long arms hung by his sides. Hassan returned to the baiypash and stood before Moosa. He had done the right thing; it was what he had been asked to do. What must he do now?

Where is that wretched piece of paper, young man? That piece of rubbish this man dared to write to my daughter, the daughter of the Numberdar of Saudukh Das. Let me have it. Give it to me.

Hassan pulled out the creased piece of paper from his pocket. His hands were trembling. Moosa snatched the piece of paper from Hassan's hand. Stepping towards Nasser, he waved it in his face. Nasser stepped back. Moosa bellowed, the tendons in his neck taut, blood gorged crimson in his face.

This. This is what you do, eh? This. This is what you write to girls with golden eyes. This is how you assist them, is it? Golden eyes, you bloody man. You dare to look at my daughter's eyes, you bloody, filthy bastard.

Moosa threw the crumpled paper at Nasser's face. Hassan winced. Nasser stepped back. He was almost at the edge of the platform where the wounded man lay. Moosa stepped forward. He spoke through clenched teeth. Droplets of spit flew out of his mouth, spraying Nasser's glasses.

What do you have to say for yourself, eh? What poor excuse do you have for such disgusting behaviour, eh? Do you even know what you have done, bloody lab-otry assistant?

Nasser swallowed, removed his glasses and wiped them against the front of his shirt. He hung his head and stared at Moosa's large feet. His voice shook.

Saheb, I did not mean any harm by this innocent little missive. It was just, just—

Just what, young man? Moosa stood a foot away from Nasser, leaving the young man no place to move. Just a stupid joke? Is that what you want to say? What did you think you were doing when you dared to write to my daughter, eh? Are you her *doodh-bhai*? Eh? Have you drunk milk at the same breast as my daughter? Tell me, tell me, young man, lab-otry assistant Saheb, just what did you think you were doing, writing this filthy rubbish, eh?

Saheb, I did not mean to offend anyone, Saheb, I did not mean to upset you—

Moosa lunged at Nasser with his open palm, striking him against the jaw. Nasser's head hit the wooden pillar. His glasses flew out of his hand. He clutched his head and moaned.

Moosa raged. Offend me? Upset me? You think this is something that causes mere offence? Eh? This, you filthy son of a whore, is far worse than a mere offence. It is an insult to my honour, do you hear?

Nasser squinted in the light of the emergency lamp, struggling to focus without his glasses. Hassan saw the glasses, lying close to Moosa's feet. He did not pick them up.

Saheb, I did not intend to hurt your sense of honour. I had every intention to seek your permission to marry your daughter. It is not as if I was—

Moosa struck Nasser again. Nasser reeled, then regained his balance.

So why is it that even before you sent your parents to seek her hand, you decided to go ahead and make arrangements to see my daughter, every morning and every night? That's what your stinking letter says, isn't it? Eh?

Nasser rubbed his jaw. There was a cut on the side of his lip. Blood trickled slowly down his chin. Hassan looked away.

Speak up, lab-otry assistant. Explain yourself to me.

Saheb, your daughter is an intelligent young woman. She would understand that I did not mean that we should meet every morning and every night. It is just a way of composing a poem, Saheb. Nothing more than that. Anyone who has read a poem knows that a lot of words are just there, just to give shape and form to your intent. Any educated person knows that, Saheb.

There was a moment of silence that lay across the baiypash like news of an incurable illness. Hassan stared at Moosa's feet. Nasser passed his hand over the bleeding cut, wiping it. Moosa took a step back, then another. He stopped at the hearth, folded his arms against his chest and looked at Nasser's spectacles lying on the floor. Without raising his eyes, Moosa spoke, the words raw and bitter.

You men from the cities, you come here and think that you have done us village folk a favour, bringing new ways of doing things. You think that with your education and your Western clothes, you are better than us. You think that we will not know what a poem is, or what the words you write to our daughters mean. You think that girls whose brothers are no longer there to protect them, that these girls are easy prey. Well, let me tell you something, young man, let me tell you that even if Sabiha's brothers are buried six feet deep, even if the ghee that I buried the days they were born will never be unearthed for their weddings that will never take place, now that they are gone, martyred, killed in the line of duty, it doesn't mean that my daughter is easy prey, that the old fool who is her father will not protect her from the likes of you, you understand me?

Nasser nodded his head, then shook it from side to side. He stepped towards Moosa Madad, holding his hands out in submission.

Saheb, like I said, I intended no harm, and I wish to marry your daughter, when she is of a suitable age, once she has finished school. She can even go to college once I start my MSc in university. She has a sharp mind, your daughter, and it would be a shame to take her out of school and not let her realise her worth.

Worth! Are you going to tell me about my own daughter's worth? What nonsense is this? Are you in your right mind, young man? Don't you know that at fifteen years of age a girl should either be married, or else buried? That is the tradition of our people around here, you understand me? You think that by getting an education you know better than us? You know my daughter's worth more than her own father would? All you do when you go to your uni-vusties is acquire horns, but only after your ears have been cut off. Have you not heard a single word I have said? My daughter is no longer going to school. She will be married to the first man I find for her, a man who knows the traditions around here, a man who respects these values. Like this young man, this Hassan.

Moosa jerked his head towards Hassan. Hassan couldn't raise his eyes to meet Moosa's. His ears burned, a fine sweat spread itself beneath his budding moustache, and his heart pounded in his ears. Hassan licked his lips with a tongue heavier than a slaughtered lamb.

For your information, lab-otry assistant Saheb, I have already sent word to this young man's family to prepare for the betrothal. I will prepare her dowry, and by the time the snows melt, the girl will be wed to him, this man, this sturdy fellow, capable of lifting an ox and carrying it across the Maidan to the Chartoi. That's the kind of man my daughter will marry, not some disrespectful, arrogant stranger who doesn't know how things are done around here.

Nasser clasped his hands together and hung his head. He spoke in a low murmur.

Saheb, I beg you, let her study. Don't punish her on account of what you felt was an outrage on my part. I can only ask you for your forgiveness, Saheb, but it is not the fault of your daughter. Let her study, and let her make up her own mind. Times have changed, Saheb.

Times have changed, have they? You, born yesterday, have come to tell me this, eh? And you're giving me lessons on what to do with my daughter, eh? Who do you think you are, lab-otry assistant Saheb? You're nothing but that sparrow who tried to kick the mountain and toppled over its own twig-like legs. That's what you are, you hear me? A bloody, useless, no-good sparrow, twittering away, flitting from here and there, bringing disrepute to the homes of honourable people. You are nothing more, you hear?

Moosa's voice shook as he spoke. The vein in the middle of his forehead swelled. He stepped towards Nasser, snarling.

I spit on your uni-vusty and on your learning. I spit on the parents who could not teach you the ways of our ancestors. One rotten sheep like you will spoil the whole flock your parents have bred, you understand? Don't you dare tell me what to do with my daughter, you hear me? In the old days our elders would say it is prudent to give one's daughter to an enemy, then slaughter her husband. I should do the same to you, but now there is no question of giving you my daughter's hand. Now get out, get out of my house, and disappear from here. Don't ever show your face in this village. I will speak to the headmaster at the blasted school. He can find a replacement for you. I'm sure there are many lab-otry assistants beneath every boulder in these valleys. Ones who know how to respect their elders, how to uphold traditions. Ones who know not to defile the honour of an honourable family. Bloody son of a whoring sparrow.

Moosa spat on the floor and wiped his mouth with his sleeve. The light from the emergency lamp began to flicker. Hassan walked across to where it hung from a peg on the far wall. He tapped it. The lamp flickered once or twice, then the light faded, leaving the room pulsing in the muted glow of the hearth.

Hassan walked back towards the centre of the room, skirting around Nasser's spectacles lying on the floor as if the frames held something malignant. He avoided Nasser's bewildered gaze. Moosa watched Hassan stepping past Nasser's glasses. Bending down, Moosa picked up the spectacles and tossed them towards Nasser, indicating an end to the conversation. The glasses landed near Nasser's feet; a lens fell out of the frame.

Here. Put them on. You are as blind as a bat, it seems, without your glasses. I don't want you to lose your way home once you leave this house. I want to make sure you find your way out of this village where I command what happens, you understand? I want you to go as far away as possible, you hear me, Mr Lab-otry Assistant, blind as a bloody bat, Moosa said.

Saheb, you call me a bat, you tell me I am a sparrow, you insult me, you insult my mother, now dead and cold in her grave, sacrificing her everything so that I could receive an education and get out of the small village where I was born and where I was destined to die had she not ensured that I could go to school and become something. Perhaps you do not see you are the bat who sleeps on his back and extends his legs upwards, pretending to hold up the heavens. Things are changing, Saheb. The Chinese are building the road, the government is building the dam, we need more educated people in our villages, we cannot fight against these changes and be like the fox who fell into the river and shouted at the villagers, telling them the whole universe was drowning with him. We have to adapt to these changes, Saheb, otherwise we will all drown in the ocean of ignorance.

Moosa glared at Nasser, breathing hard. His nostrils quivered. He moved forward, pushing Hassan to the side and thundered, his voice shaking.

You dare to call me a bat? You dare to call Moosa Madad, the Numberdar of Saudukh Das, a lousy bat? You expect me to let my daughter make her own choices? So that she can run away with you? Defiling the honour of this family? Bringing shame upon this house for ever? You dare to call me a bloody bat? You bloody son of a whore, no-good piece of rubbish, I'll kill you for that, you hear me?

Moosa swung back to the hearth and grabbed a thick, smouldering log. Hassan froze. Nasser stepped back, shifting towards the alcove where the stranger lay. Moosa swung at Nasser, wielding the burning log like a heavy club. The younger man staggered, tripping on the edge of the platform, falling on his knees. Moosa struck Nasser with the log. Sparks flew into the air; burning splinters fell here and there, and embers rolled into the far corner of the room. Nasser fell backwards, toppling over the wounded man. Moosa swung the burning log with both hands and raised it above his head. He brought it down with the full force of his strength. Nasser jerked his body aside. A deep moan rose from the platform. Hassan rushed forward. Nasser lay still, legs splayed out, one hand stretched over the stranger's face. Blood surged from between his fingers. Hassan reached for Nasser's arm and pulled him up. Nasser lurched forward. He was trembling. He wiped his bloody hand against the front of his shirt, shaking, and pushed against the platform, trying to raise himself. Hassan stared at the stranger lying in the dark alcove. Blood seeped out of a deep gash on the man's forehead. His skull had been smashed on one side, bone crushed like an eggshell. The man was dead. This, the outrage of a distraught, dishonoured man, he could not survive.

# Altar-Číndi

## 25.

*When morning carved its path across the gulleys and slopes, fingers of light caressing the summits and the saddles, curling along the curved lips of twisting tracks, gliding across the meadows, hovering over the silver miasma blanketing the Winter River, Tish-Hagur nudged the young one and steadied him on his tiny hooves, legs slender, bones still tender. He was hungry, and nuzzled at her underbelly as if he had not been fed for many nights and days. He was always hungry, always seeking the comfort of his mother's devotion, the fullness of her swollen teats. Tish-Hagur rubbed her nose against his, smelling the warm scent buried in his fur. She nudged him again, her nose against his belly, careful not to hurt him with her half-moon horns, perfect indentations cut at perfect intervals, adding to her beauty already celebrated far and wide. Tish-Hagur walked before the young one, stepping over moss and fern, mindful of the mirrored water reflecting the Yalmik Sky from hollows worn into the ancient rocks of her home. She walked from the forest to the far peak, the little one following her, falling behind, curious to smell the fragrance of wild roses as they opened their buds to the golden light that fell upon them now, stirring life inside even the hardest shell.*

*From the furthest peak Tish-Hagur could see them: a man, tall, white teeth gleaming in the sunlight, a thick, dark moustache brooding over fleshy lips. She saw the young one: small, thin, laughing, a tooth missing in his bud-like mouth. She saw them, and she saw that the man carried on his back a weapon with which he could take her life and that of her young one. But she did not flee, she did not coax her young one to run away, to hide. She did not flee, for she knew that with this man would unfold the story of the people of the Plain of a Hundred Sorrows. She had to let him take that shot, as much as he would have to let his son, Asghar, and the one older than him, Akbar, at home with his sickly mother, grow up, become men and perish in a fire set off recklessly by someone who feared being killed by a bullet fired by another man just like him, fearful, just like him, the dread in the hearts of these men the same, the desire to live the same.*

*Tish-Hagur knew that she could not alter the path of that bullet, that things must unfold as Nihibur had written them, that grief must carve its path into the hearts of these men just as the morning had carved its way through the valley cradled by the furrowed fingers of the Black Mountains.*

# Chapter Twenty-Five

Dark clouds blocked the light of the moon, casting immense, drifting shadows over the meadows and terraces locking Saudukh Das between mountain and river. Rain was expected any moment. Noor, uneasy, restless, crossed the bridge without noticing that the water had risen; somewhere, the snows had melted under the morning sun. Noor did not see the branches of the mulberry tree reeling in the cold gusts of wind stirring up the water beneath the bridge. He kept his unseeing gaze on the rough planks of the wooden bridge, a sudden spray of ice water splashing through the missing slats. Something was wrong. He had not seen Moosa so agitated. He had not seen the Numberdar smoke for many years now. Everyone in Saudukh Das knew that Moosa Madad had given up smoking when he buried his sons, declaring he would never go anywhere near the very thing that had set off the fire which had consumed his boys. They had said it was a cigarette butt flicked carelessly in the carpark of the military garrison which had set the petrol tank of a jeep on fire, leading to the explosion that had killed his sons and twenty-seven others. Moosa had sworn never to smoke again, declaring his resolve over and over again at council meetings, in the local bazaar, in the homes of friends and neighbours who remembered the story of his sons' sacrifice as well as they would remember the names of their own children.

Yet this evening he had sucked on a cigarette, taunting, berating young Nasser, exhaling indignation before flicking the cigarette butt into the corner of the room.

Noor made his way to Naushad's house. The women of Saudukh Das, forbidden from joining the funeral procession, had gathered here, bringing food and comfort to the little girls, still uncertain about what had happened to their mother. Many of the women were neighbours; some had come from the edge of the village. Most had known Kulsoom, the long-suffering Kulsoom, unable to break free of her negligent, brutal husband. Some said death had ended her suffering; others blamed Naushad for making Kulsoom take that fateful journey, for who didn't know what happens to women who dare to venture past the Doorway of Chartoi?

It was late now. Zarina met Noor on her way out of the small, cold, ill-lit room where Naushad sat, staring at the silent hearth. His mother beat her head and tore at her hair, cursing her fate, the fate of her son who was now burdened with raising this brood of daughters on his own. How could she, an old woman with failing eyesight, a constant pain in her chest, one leg in the grave, help him with this task, bathing the girls, dressing them, feeding them, sending them to school, then getting them married? How could the poor man, ill and weak with grief, possibly see to providing for these miserable girls? How could that selfish woman turn away from her responsibility as a mother, a wife, a daughter-in-law, leaving the family to fend for itself?

Zarina turned away from the airless room, searching the crowd of women for Fatimah and Khadijah. Noor met the three women at the door. He could see Naushad staring at nothing, his mouth working, no words coming, hands clutching at something in the air, the gestures of a madman. Noor turned away and stood near the women as they slipped on their foot-wear, preparing themselves for the walk up the incline to Moosa Madad's home. He offered to walk with them, protecting them from the dark and unknown, unexpected peril.

★　★　★

The sky was overcast. Shortly it started drizzling, heavy drops pelting the dusty path. Rain came down hard; thunder rolled beyond the meadows and slopes of the mountain. A sudden, jagged streak of lightning cut across the low clouds and pierced the sodden soil of the fields, lighting up, briefly, the desolate evening.

At the bridge, Noor asked Zarina if she knew a young man called Nasser. Perhaps. No. She did not know him. She was distracted, in a hurry. The man in Moosa Madad's house needed to be bandaged; she hoped Hassan had brought some supplies. And then she had to get home to her children. It had been a long day, a sorrowful day.

The rain came down fast and heavy. Noor unwrapped his shawl and held it over the three women to shield them from the stinging downpour. The wind picked up, tossing dried stalks of threshed corn into the frigid air. The women pressed forward, folding their heads into their shawls, braving the tempest. Noor stood tall, holding his shawl up like an awning. The four of them made their way to Moosa Madad's house, rain cascading down and the wind howling, the path ahead shadowed under a purple sky.

Blood from the man's injuries had congealed at the cusp of his shoulder and arm, forming a seal between his shirt and the mattress upon which he had lain. Moosa lifted the stranger's body with difficulty. Breathless, he grunted and gestured to Hassan. Hassan separated the dead man's shirt from the mattress, pulling apart the dark fabric drenched now in fresh blood, warm, smelling of hot metal. Moosa coughed; his eyes smarted. Smoke rose from the hearth, filling the room. He must remember to open the skylight and to get more firewood. A man worth his salt never let the fire out in the hearth, not when winter had descended with a fury that seemed like God's retribution for everything that had gone wrong here.

There was no time now to stoke the fire, nor to open the skylight.

Moosa held the dead man's body over the gaping mouth of the ribbed mulberry-twine basket. Hassan gripped the basket with both hands. Tenderly, Moosa lowered the man's body into the basket, folding his legs like the limbs of a young willow. He tossed aside the quilt that had covered the man and grabbed the bloodied sheet. This he draped over the man's body. Hassan lowered himself on his haunches, put his arms through the shoulder braces, and heaved the basket onto his back. Moosa secured the ends of the sheet around Hassan's girth. They left the baiypash and walked in the direction of the mountain, towards the Doorway of Chartoi, obscured now in the falling rain.

Rain fell without mercy. Khadijah clutched her chest and gasped for air. She asked to rest before the steep ascent leading to the plateau where Moosa's grandfather had built a simple stone and wooden hut many years ago. The three women and Noor took shelter beneath an ancient walnut tree. Here, the path curved around an abutting field. The rain continued to fall. The mountains, the Doorway of Chartoi, the trees, the silent fields, all disappeared in the vapour rising from the earth.

Outside Moosa's house, Noor took off his soaking cap and pounded on the metal gate. There was no answer. Noor shouted for Moosa. Again, no answer, just the sound of the rain beating on the gravel in the lane. Trudging to the gate, her shawl drenched and heavy, Fatimah shouted for Moosa. There was no answer. Fatimah called again. She called for Mariam, for Moosa. No one came. Fatimah pounded on the gate, beating her fists against the metal.

Sister, I believe that your husband was to send young Mariam to her sister's home in the next village. I remember he said he didn't want her to be here when Kulsoom was to be taken for the burial. Perhaps there is no one at home, Zarina said.

Surely Hassan is still here. I left him here when that young man Nasser came, Noor said.

Nasser? Who is Nasser? Fatimah asked.

Zarina glanced at Noor. Khadijah, swaying, sank down to the ground. Zarina put her arms around Khadijah and propped her up, holding her close to herself. The older woman was tired after the journey. It had been a long day for her, for all of them.

Nasser is a guest of the Numberdar, sister. I left the three men here when I went to check on Naushad, Noor said.

But who is he, brother? Who is this man, Nasser? We have not had a guest called Nasser before, I would have remembered. It was the name of my beloved brother, may Allah forgive his transgressions, Fatimah said.

Noor looked away. He cleared his throat and called out to Hassan. There was no answer. All of a sudden, Khadijah swooned and fell against the gate. It swung open.

A hot meal of mutton stew with fresh roti filled Ibrahim's belly as much as it dissipated his hunger for something familiar and comforting. Two nursing assistants had bandaged his feet and hands, applied a salve to his burnt nose and cheeks, massaged his limbs and dressed him in a pair of loose-fitting pyjamas. They sponged him with warm water, then washed his hair, promising him a cut and a shave in the morning, once he was rested, once the barber shop with the photograph of the Indian filmstar Shah Rukh Khan plastered onto its wall opened for business. Now it was time to rest, to consider the

Grace and Munificence of the Almighty for having brought him and his two companions down to safety. The officer in charge of the hospital agreed that Ibrahim could indeed travel to his village in the morning. After all, if he could survive the avalanche, what were a few blisters and burns?

Ibrahim enquired after Zaki; how was he doing, will he be okay? He had to get home, that young man, he had a wedding to arrange! The officer assured Ibrahim that Zaki was resting, that he would need several days before he could travel down to the south. They still had to determine how much damage may have been done to Zaki's extremities, and felt that it was a miracle that he had survived as long as he did beneath the weight of the broken glacier. A miracle, indeed. Ibrahim nodded, suddenly very tired. His eyes were glazed over when the crew chief came to see him, joking and laughing at the size of Ibrahim's swollen toes, fat and ruddy like new-born moles. Ibrahim laughed too, remembering other fantastic creatures, more magnificent than anything he had known, wondering at the things he had seen in his dream; or was it a dream, was this a dream, after the nightmare through which he had lived and died and lived again?

Thick, acrid smoke billowed from the small window set high in the wall of the storeroom. Fatimah pushed past Khadijah's wilted form and rushed into the courtyard, clutching her heart. The lantern in the verandah cast a circle of golden light, skimming the courtyard with a nimbus of pulsing waves. Fatimah fell onto the takht, breathing hard.

Sabiha, my child, what has he done to you? Open the door, Noor, open the door. Where is Moosa? Where is Hassan? And who is Nasser, Noor? Who is this man you talk of?

Fatimah moaned. She tore the veil from her head and stuffed a corner into her mouth. Noor pulled aside the bolt and pushed open the door to the baiypash. The room was dark. Ash shivered over a few throbbing embers. Black fumes rose from kindling burning in the corner. The acrid smoke choked Noor and Zarina. Both of them rushed towards the burning wood. Khadijah wheezed, her skeletal frame heaving. She cried out to Noor and pointed to the storeroom, coughing through the muzzle of her veil. Thick black smoke snaked its way beneath the door of the storeroom. Fatimah threw herself at the door. She tried to slide open the bolt. It refused to budge. Fatimah screamed, pulling at the lock.

Sabiha, Sabiha, my daughter, my child, what has he done to you?

Lightning tore at the sky, slicing through the tumbling viscera of thick clouds. A streak of white flashed through the room. The walls shifted, crashing into each other. Zarina looked up at the skylight. Thunder boomed, a thousand cannons roaring in receding waves. A shaft of faint, spectral light floated onto the lock. Zarina followed the wavering beam to the door of the baiypash. Moosa stood before the hearth, pointing a torch at the bolt locking the door to the storeroom. His shawl, drenched with rain water, covered his face. Only his eyes were visible in the cocoon he had woven around his head. He shifted the beam of light to the corner of the room. A stray flame licked at the broken limbs of the dissipated kindling. Twigs twisted into splintered fingers swept across the floor in the draft of thick fumes filling the room. Crackling leaves hissed like living things, curling into themselves, gyrating on the rolled camber of their coffins. Beside the detritus of the burning wood, cradled in a blanket of ashen velvet, frayed laces wavering in the blaze lit by the fate etched into the palm of Moosa's hand, the dead man's shoes sat side by side, the tired tongue of one wilted over the scuffed leather of the other.

★  ★  ★

The faint pattering of rain on the bush of wild roses outside the hospital ward's window brought respite to Ibrahim in gentle waves, soothing his aching bones, warming his limbs, bringing life back to his frostbitten toes, healing the raw flesh where his hands had been blistered, cut open, lacerated against the black rock of the mountain. Tomorrow, at daybreak, military transport would take him to the main town, and from there it would be a matter of some hours before he would be able to see the Temple Spire piercing the sky sheltering his village. He knew that road by heart; he knew every bend, every incline, every dangerous descent. He knew the narrow indents where village boys fried fish caught from the river, wrapping it in scraps of old newspaper for a small price, enough to buy a packet of biscuits from the small wooden shack built into an abandoned shaft. He could smell the fragrance of freshly cut lucerne; he could distinguish the narrow, wooden bridges spanning the Winter River, counting each one until he came to the one he would cross, turning left on the opposite bank, the jeep lurching up a steep, rough slope, boulders piled up on the side of the track, protecting man and beast from plunging into the white water of the glacial rivulet rushing from the Chartoi. When the jeep reached the top of that incline, near the small wooden mosque with the ancient carving of a man on horseback, holding a shield and a sword in his hands, he would ask the driver to stay for a moment. He would get out and stretch his legs, letting Malika stretch hers, letting her sniff the tendrils of diaphanous ferns unfurling against the black rock, letting her admire the gathering of wild flowers growing out of fissures in the dark surface where moisture ran down in indiscernible trickles from sources secreted in the towering mountain. He would light a cigarette, perhaps, or drink from the gushing stream, gulping the cool, clear water, washing off the dust of the journey and refreshing himself before removing his shoes at the doorstep of the mosque. He would bow in submission to the Almighty, the One God, and offer his thanks for bringing him back safely to the place he longed to be, amongst the stately poplars, the shade of the generous walnut trees, the shadow of the Black Mountains, always present, the only things constant in a constantly changing world. And he would gaze at the Doorway looming above him, carved into a cliff formed in some long-forgotten time before humans came to inhabit this place, before a mountain had broken in half and collapsed, leaving a granite face as smooth as a child's slate, waiting to be marked by time, by wind and water, the elements carving a doorway in a series of three perpendicular fractures cleft into the plane, the throbbing heart of a quest to understand that which was unseen, therefore incomprehensible.

Ibrahim closed his eyes and took a deep breath, savouring the scent of the dark, loamy earth outside the window where the rain lashed against the glass and the thorns of the wild roses scratched the smooth surface of the pane. Soon, he would be home.

The air was suffocating in that small room where the fire burned with abandon, casting shadows of cavorting creatures, winged beasts, scrambling across the uneven walls. Sakina cradled Lasnik's head in her lap, stroking his face with fingers thin and trembling with foreboding. She had lit the hearth with all the kindling she could find. Smoke curled up to the skylight; rain pelted against the window. Sakina wept, shaking her head, passing her hand over her son's burning forehead. He was still alive, still conscious, speaking strange words, staring at something in the dark, something Sakina could not see. But she could hear his words, strange incantations, speaking through the reed of his neck, the flute of the Periting, the vessel of their desire, the locus of their dominion. Sakina repeated an incantation to herself, whispering the words and blowing their power over her son's burning body:

> *In the fire will all things be cleansed*
> *for in the fire will all things heal*
> *for in the fire is the beginning and*
> *also the end*

★

Get away from that door, bloody woman, Moosa shouted. He strode across the baiypash and swept Fatimah onto the floor with one powerful cuff against her jaw. Noor moved towards her, breaking her fall. Fatimah keeled over, dropped onto her knees, tumbling forwards, humped like a capsized boat. Zarina screamed, then threw herself upon Fatimah as Moosa began to punch her, kicking her in her rump.

It is because of you, filthy woman. It is because you never kept that girl on a tight tether that this has happened, this terrible thing, this thing which will haunt me for the rest of my days and nights.

Moosa howled, pummelling Fatimah with his fists, striking at her with the torch. Fatimah screamed in pain; Khadijah cried, pleading with Moosa to stop, it was enough, the girl was still inside, the smoke from the fire will choke her, please stop, the girl will die inside, please stop this, Moosa, please stop this. Zarina held Fatimah's head in her arms, protecting it from the blows of a man driven mad by something that had happened while the three women were mourning the death of a luckless sister.

Stepping forward, Noor threw his arm out and held Moosa's hand above his head, loosening the Numberdar's grip on the torch. The torch fell onto the hard ground and rolled without purpose on its cylindrical form. Its anaemic light flickered, then snuffed out. Moosa gasped, shock falling out of his mouth in a yelp. Noor held Moosa's arm steady and asked him for the key to the lock. Moosa stared at Noor, words insensible on the edge of his tongue. Fatimah stopped wailing, Khadijah stopped pleading, Zarina held her breath and watched the two men in the faint light falling from the skylight. Noor dropped Moosa's arm. Moosa staggered towards the wall, steadying himself, and reached into the side pocket of his waistcoat. He brought out a ring with several keys bunched together along its curved clasp. His hands shook as he separated one key from the rest. This one he held up to Noor. He spoke in gasps, the smoke choking him as much as the shock of Noor's insolence stuck in his throat like a fish hook. He threw the cluster of keys at Noor.

Here. Open that door. It doesn't matter any more. The girl can be let out. I have made sure. I have made sure. There will never be another reason to lock her up again.

Fatimah looked up from the floor. She moaned, struggling to get up. She wailed, pulling her hair, tearing at her shirt.

What have you done, Moosa? What have you done? For Allah's sake, tell me what have you done?

Moosa spat into the corner, kicking the burnt kindling aside, scattering ash and the debris of unforeseen ruin across the floor. He raged, the tendons on his neck pulsing.

I have told him that if he was to ever come near my daughter, this wanton girl you produced, I would break his legs, I would gouge out his eyes, I would slash his neck. I told him that, woman, I told him that he would never live to see another day if he even looked at this girl. And if he still insisted, I would make sure the girl doesn't live either, do you hear me, Fatimah?

Fatimah exploded, fury erupting from deep inside her. She

said she was drowning, that if she spoke, the water would come rushing into her mouth, but if she kept silent, she would die bursting of rage. How could Moosa talk about taking the life of his own daughter? How could he even think like this? What had she done to deserve his wrath?

What has she done? You're asking me this? What has she done? Moosa shook Fatimah's shoulders, spluttering over the words, unable to stop the chaos of his mind from inciting him to strangle his wife. He pushed Fatimah against the door, shoving Noor aside as he struggled to fit one key after another into the lock, failing again and again. I'll tell you what she's done, Moosa said, his voice low, menacing. She has caused me to kill a man tonight, in this house, in this very house. She has caused me to commit murder tonight, do you understand? Moosa moved his hands to Fatimah's neck and pressed down on the dip above her clavicle. Fatimah gasped. Noor dropped the keys and tore Moosa's hands away from Fatimah. He stood between Moosa and his wife, clutching Moosa's hands together, then pulled him away from the door. Moosa protested; how could Noor behave in this manner? Did he not know that Moosa Madad was the Numberdar of Saudukh Das?

I cannot apologise to you, Saheb, for there is no time for these things right now. I need to know what has happened here this evening, Saheb. Where is Hassan? What has happened to the man Hassan and I brought into your home, placing him in your care? And where is that young man, Nasser, who came to visit you this evening? Saheb, you need to tell me these things.

Moosa glared at Noor. He struggled to free his hands from Noor's grip. Noor held on, shifting his feet to steady himself, knocking against Khadijah hunched over the floor, sweeping her hands across the burnt leaves and scorched wood, searching for the keys, repeating over and over again the names of Akbar

Ali and Asghar Ali. Zarina stepped away from the men. She walked to the far end of the baiypash where a lumpy quilt lay draped over a blood-soaked mattress. Throwing aside the quilt, she stared at the place where the wounded man had lain. She screamed, pulling back from the alcove. There was nothing there now, just a stained sheet and wad of crumpled paper, splattered with fresh blood.

Death comes unannounced, even if it is expected. There is never a specific moment when one can say that death is about to visit, that Aakhir is here, among us, ready to take the one marked for the journey. Sometimes we think that we can cheat death, deceiving it, pleading with it to come another day, when we are ready, more accepting that one who is deeply loved must go on a journey from which there is no return.

We are never ready. There is never an opportune time for death. And yet, there is sometimes a chance that we can lift the marked one from the path that death intends to take, charting out the journey with silent steps, swooping down while people shut their eyes in prayer, holding still their hearts. That is what Noor Hussein did, wielding the axe propped up against the wall and breaking open the lock.

The storeroom was drowning in dense waves of smoke. Sabiha was slumped against the bags of grain, Lasnik's orange nylon rope coiled around her neck like a snake. Beside her was the carcass of the slaughtered lamb that had hung from the hook in the roof. The nylon rope was strung from the hook, one end knotted, the other fashioned into a clumsy noose. Sabiha lay on her side, curled up against two tin trunks, one on top of the other. The rope swung from the hook, slack, swaying in the grey haze. Noor felt for a pulse; there was a faint, uneven tapping, barely perceptible.

Moosa lifted his daughter in his arms. He cradled her head

beneath his heart. The gold of her hair, scattered like a sheaf of wheat trodden by the autumn wind, spread across his chest. Moosa wept; he did not look up from the floor. Raising his head, he asked Noor to open the door to the baiypash. He would take his daughter to the nearest hospital, thirty kilometres away, on the other side of the lake that had formed when the mountain collapsed, the day his partridge had died, the day Kulsoom had been seen near the Chartoi, the day a wounded man had been brought into his house, the day he had locked up his daughter, punishing her for the offence of loving and being loved. Moosa asked Noor to stay with the women. It would take him the whole night to walk across the wreckage of the landslide to find help for his daughter so that she may live, so that he may find a reason to carry on living.

Moosa stepped into the courtyard. The moon shone its silver light on his daughter's face. He would walk the whole night, he would walk as many nights as it would take to bring his daughter back so that the moon may shine, the sun spread its light over this frozen land, where nothing grew now, except an abundance of wild roses.

# Acknowledgements

*An Abundance of Wild Roses* emerged from a fertile landscape peopled by characters who may as well have been telling this story in their own words, instead of mine. The fact that there are several stories intertwined together, much like the branches of an old creeping vine, merits mention of the many nurturers of the garden where this novel was sown and seeded. The encouragement provided by the Society of Authors, London, through the award of the Roger Deakin Endowment for the cultivation of the idea was fundamental to the sprouting of the novel. Without the financial support provided by the grant, and without the belief of the Society of Authors in my ability to honour Roger Deakin through my deep love of nature and all within it, I could not have travelled to these remote regions to live amongst the people whose story I have tried to tell.

My foray into even further outposts in northern and western Pakistan was made possible with the assistance of the Pakistan Army through the intercession of Lt General Asim Bajwa who organised my trips to the warfronts of Siachen, Miran Shah and Mir Ali. Major General Syed Najam ul Hassan Shah provided me details of rescue operations in the world's highest battlefield, Siachen. Brigadier Faisal Sharif, Commandant Army Canine Centre between 2013 and 2019, allowed me to befriend the most amazing dogs trained for rescue operations and for detecting IEDs. They are, truly, unsung heroes, as are their handlers. Brigadier Tahir Mahmood, a writer and poet, was instrumental in connecting me to the officers I have named above; now retired, he remains a good friend and well-wisher. The pilots of the helicopter which flew me to Siachen were Lt Colonel Faisal and Lt Colonel Mohammad Naveed Tariq. At the point where we were to land at 19,000 feet, these two men handed me an oxygen tank and asked me to fill my lungs and to step carefully into the deep piles of snow which threatened to consume me if I hyperventilated in lieu of the paucity of oxygen at that high altitude. At the base, on the largest non-polar glacier on earth, I was entertained by the Section Commander and his soldiers, who had prepared a tea fit for a queen – crisp samosas in a barren field of snow and piping hot tea served in ceramic cups! The protocol officer from the FCNA who accompanied me to this unearthly, frozen place was Major Shumaila, mother of two, companion and guide. There is no woman other than Major Shumaila who braved below freezing temperatures at the highest non-polar glaciers in the world draped in a military-khaki sari and matching boots gifted by my friend Jane O'Reilly, to whom I owe the debt of friendship and conviction in my writing and in my understanding of the female experience in patriarchy. I owe the same debt to Ritu Menon, my editor at Women Unlimited, New Delhi. To Ritu, I also owe the debt of finding nourishment in a land where her elders had lived before the rupture of Partition tore us apart and broke the continuum of the history that connects us like an umbilical cord carrying sustenance from a mother to a child.

At the Headquarters of the Northern Light Infantry 14 at Goma, Lt Colonel Ali looked after me and allowed me to visit the men recuperating in the camp hospital as well as the barber shop where a poster of the Indian film star Shah Rukh Khan was garlanded with plastic roses, befitting a screen god. Colonel Ali also allowed me to mingle with the beautiful

German Shepherd dogs who waited to spring into action for a rescue operation in case of a landslide or avalanche. These extraordinary animals provided me with the inspiration for Malika, the wolf-dog, in the novel. The stories of such rescues were related to me by Lt Colonel Nauman Ahmed Sayal, Army Aviation, Flight Commander, Karakorum Flight, Gilgit. Now retired, Colonel Nauman rescues homeless kittens and shares prescriptions for homeopathic medicine with me over a cup of tea on a rainy afternoon.

Amongst the officers of the civil services of Pakistan, I would like to thank Sibtain Ahmed, then Principal Secretary to the Chief Minister, Gilgit Baltistan, who served as Deputy Commissioner in Chilas when I was undertaking my doctoral research on forced migration and the disarticulation of culture as a result of development-induced displacement. Sibtain saved my life by moving me out of Chilas at the time a religious edict was pronounced against me by a conservative cleric wishing to cleanse the area of 'undesirables'. The fatwah called for my death; shortly before I was removed from the area, seventeen pilgrims returning home to Baltistan were burnt to death by the same cleric, perhaps as a warning to me. I pay tribute to the ones who lost their lives in this, and other, equally brutal, killings of people based on their identity. If possible, I would place wild roses on every grave of every person killed in the name of misplaced faith.

In the settlements of Gakuch and Gupis, I would like to remember the hospitality and generosity of Moosa Madad, for whom I have named the Numberdar of the story, and Noor Hussein, for whom I have named a young man of noble virtues and a well-groomed moustache. I shall never forget the young Lady Health Worker, Zarina, who explained to me her understanding of why young women in this region take their own lives just when life is about to begin. Drawing a window in the air with her hands, she said that by sending young girls to school, their elders create a window through which these girls can see the world. But then, Zarina said, drawing a door in the air, the elders do not create a door through which their daughters can pass and be part of that world. With the palms of her hands, she slammed the imaginary door shut and rubbed her hands against her shirt. I can never forget this image, nor her words.

Amongst my friends, I thank Shahida Khoro, *née* Daultana, for allowing me the quiet of her home while finalising the last draft of the novel. The constant supply of fruit, banana bread and cold milk, was instrumental in finishing the editing before the deadline, and for this I thank Shahida's housekeeper, Fatimah, of the ready smile and immense heart.

At Canongate, I cannot find adequate words for the people who believed in my humble submission. Ellah Wakatama for her constant confidence in the story and the style, Rali Chorbadzhiyska for her diligent overseeing of the entire process from draft to print, Gabrielle Chant for the final fine-tooth-combing of the draft, her scrupulous scrutiny of the plot line and chronology of separate stories which eventually run into the same river, and Leila Cruickshank for the words of compassion and encouragement when I experienced harrowing violence at the hands of law enforcement for writing a piece reporting on the operations to arrest the former Prime Minister of Pakistan, Imran Khan. I am grateful for her friendship and patience during a deeply traumatic period.

This novel is dedicated to my mother, Khadijah Marsina Ebrahim, born in Cape Town, educated at the London School of Economics, lived in Pakistan, and died in Skardu, northern Pakistan, after devoting the last twenty years of her life to saving the lives of women and children in remote villages such as the one I created for my story. Her life and work were not in vain, for in every Plain of Sorrow, a woman helps other women to defy death each time they give birth to another child, another reason to hope.